# A WASHINGTON STORY

"AND SO, from court to court throughout the towns and villages of all the diocese, scurried special accusers, inquisitors, notaries, jurors, judges, constables, dragging to trial and torture human beings of both sexes and burning them in great numbers. Scarcely any of those who were accused escaped punishment. Nor were there spared even the leading men in the city. . . . So far, at length, did the madness of the furious populace and of the courts go in this thirst for blood and booty that there was scarcely anybody who was not smirched by some suspicion of this crime. . . . Meanwhile notaries, copyists, and innkeepers grew rich. The executioner rode a blooded horse, and went clad in gold and silver. . . ."

—*Canon Linden, 1589*

# A
# WASHINGTON
# STORY

*by*

*Jay Deiss*

*Duell, Sloan and Pearce*
New York

*For the steadfast*

*Part One*

# 1.

THE morning was sultry, humid, and had about it none of the starched freshness of another day. Spring had come and gone. The cherry blossoms around the Tidal Basin had withered; the magnolia flowers in the White House grounds had flaked leaf by leaf to earth; the roses at Dumbarton Oaks had shriveled from the mounting heat. Only the odor of honeysuckle, clinging to the old bricks of Georgetown, remained—torporous and sweet.

Faith had a dull headache, felt melancholy, and the weather was corollary to her mood. Even the heaping bowlful of cornflakes and fresh raspberries Donnie brought from the kitchen evoked no interest.

"You look right sick this mornin', Miz Vance," Donnie said. "Pale as a ghost!"

"I'm not!" she said. "I didn't sleep well, that's all. It's the mugginess in the air. God knows why anyone ever built a capital city here!" She paused, idly turned over a spoonful of raspberries. Her voice was low-pitched, pleasing, but now resonant with a kind of pensive sorrow. "And I had a bad dream. . . ."

3

Thatcher was still sleeping off the effects of his drinking bout last night, and Jeanie had streaked away in the usual last-possible-moment rush for the pottie, so there was nothing to distract her recollection of the dream.

The scene was dark and foggy, but whether day or night she could not tell. She was running down the Mall, pursued by creatures she could neither see nor hear. Her lungs seemed about to burst. She thought: If only, if *only* I can reach the Washington Monument, surely I'll be safe! When she appeared about to reach the shaft, and was ready to shout with relief, it wavered like an object under water and turned into a giant hooded figure with gloating red eyes, a monstrous Klansman. Then suddenly arms seized her, began to choke.

She had started awake, sweating and freezing alternately, so full of fear that her shoulders felt tight and her throat paralyzed. She discovered that Thatcher had his arms about her and was fumbling for her breasts. Some time during the night he had recovered from his stupor, contrary to his usual custom, and had crept from the living-room sofa into bed with her. In revulsion, she pushed him away. They had not slept together in more than a month, and he no longer expressed desire for her except under alcoholic stimulation. But the alcohol was self-defeating; it made him fuzzy and ineffectual.

The vivid image of their first night together had never left her—the first night of their marriage. It had been a dismal failure. For all Thatcher's boasted experience he had not seemed to understand any needs beyond his own. She was left gasping, her body trembling like a sleek silver fish upon a barren rock—victim of an unexpected, too rapid, ebbing tide. Though afterwards their physical relationship had improved, Thatcher remained erratic, and she knew instinctively that neither of them was ever really satisfied.

4

In his drunkenness he continued to paw her crudely, and her body shrank from his touch. She was thankful for even the slight defense of her nightgown, and retreated from him to the other side of the bed. He mumbled, "Goddam you!"— but she continued to repulse him. His hands twitched with a futile gesture. His breath was acrid with an odor like burnt caramel, and made her ill. Nevertheless, she did not leave the bed, and, after he became quiet, she finally went back to sleep.

Now she found herself hoping he would sleep until she had left for work. That way she would be spared listening to the usual abject apologies, the sincere regret and self-flagellation, as well as further exhaustion of her own reserves of pity for him. He would, of course, despite his humility, continue to blame her for working, blame her for leaving Jeanie to the care of a nurse and a playschool, and continue to entertain the suspicion that she was having an affair with Mr. Cunningham, her Chief. She had been able to find no logic with which to meet the involved convolutions of Thatcher's reasoning. His refusal to accept facts had time and time again left her frantic. Now she was soul-sick with weariness at the impasse they had reached. Living with Thatcher had frazzled her nerves far more than doing without him during the war years. The old joy at being with him had changed to a constriction about her heart . . . a sense of tragic foreboding.

She noticed that she was still playing absently with the raspberries, had not taken a single bite. She put down her spoon, and thought: Can't eat—what's the matter with me?

In her moodiness, and under her thick lashes, her eyes appeared very dark—though in certain lights they were opalescent, a deep glowing color like sunlight-luster on a ripe plum. The color of her eyes seemed all the more remark-

5

able because it was so unexpected in a blonde. The eyelids were half closed, which was characteristic of her when she was thinking. Her brows were strongly marked, almost heavy, and imperfectly arched, so that they gave the impression of a broken brushstroke at the ends. When she responded to people, her eyes opened wide and took on a glowing warmth. Sometimes they sparkled from a sort of inner stimulation, as though she tapped private sources of amusement or vitality. People often talked to her for the delight of watching this animation in her eyes.

At first glance, her face seemed harmoniously regular and graceful, marked by high cheekbones and soft curves. But on analysis, taken separately, her nose was bold and a touch irregular, her mouth was wide and the lips full and strong. Her face conveyed a feeling of marked femininity plus strength. During office hours she appeared crisp and businesslike, though never distant or cold; but when she was relaxed, there appeared in her a hint of lushness, an unrealized passion, a potential for abandon.

She tanned, a beautiful shiny-bronze which matched her buckwheat-colored hair. She loved to stretch out in the sun, lazily soaking the hot rays into her small-boned shapely body. She kept her hair brushed back, smooth and shoulder-length, tied usually with a black ribbon around her head. Men were prone to look at her now, at twenty-six, more often than when she was younger. Since she knew that she was not conventionally beautiful, she admitted candidly to herself this pleased her. It had been, in fact, Thatcher's open and often expressed admiration which had given her such a feeling of security and pleasure in the beginning of their relationship.

After Jeanie's birth she had filled out, and the last angu-

larity of youth had given way to a fully proportioned female-
ness which was becoming to her. As her attractiveness to
other men increased, Thatcher's jealousy increased. Without fail, he became aggressively rude to any male who paid
her a compliment.

One night, when they were dancing on the Shoreham terrace, in an atmosphere of colored lights and Riviera um-
brella-tables, he had started a fight. The evening had turned
from romance to nightmare, and she still found it necessary
to shudder in embarrassment at its recollection.

For this increasing attention from others, Thatcher had
found a way to take revenge. While she was nursing Jeanie
he teased her about her breasts. He had made her acutely
self-conscious—though she had never confessed her feeling
to him or to anyone else. He called her, with an ironic laugh,
"My little sweater girl,"—and she had imagined her figure as
distorted and obvious. In those moments she hated Thatcher,
and secretly—oh, so secretly!—resented Jeanie and the long
months of nursing. But the resentment itself was a catharsis,
and through it she loved Jeanie that much more. Often,
though the period of her fullness was long since passed, she
would unconsciously attempt to tighten the shoulder straps
of her brassière.

She did it now, as though she felt discomfort under the
v-necked cotton blouse she had especially selected for its
looseness. She hitched up the strap with a quick movement
which revealed the dexterity and competence of her hand—
a hand rather larger and more strongly veined than usual for
one of her body type. It was, in fact, a hand which seemed
gifted with its own special facility, almost its own intelligence, it appeared so quick and efficient. It revealed its con-
ditioning, years of work with typewriter and stenographer's

7

pencil, though in its essential grace it might have belonged to either factory worker or pianist. Yet it was also a hand which, stroking a child's head, would soothe and reassure.

Donnie came in again, and Faith opened her eyes wide. She sighed at the return to immediate reality.

Donnie set scrambled eggs and a pot of coffee on the table. "Had trouble with Jeanie this mornin'," she said with quiet detachment. "Those fancy dresses her daddy give her— stamped her foot and said she *wouldn't* wear overalls to playschool! Had a turrible time changin' her mind!"

"How did you change it . . . ?" An evanescent tenderness and amusement played in Faith's eyes at Donnie's stories of her daughter's frequent naughtiness.

"Tol' her if she wore fancy dresses to school, she'd have to wear overalls to parties. That got her, plenty quick!" Donnie put her hands on her hips and smiled. "That chile is some pussycat!"

Donnie, born and bred in Washington, was plump and fifty, pecan brown, solemn-eyed, shrewd, intelligent. She rarely laughed, because, she said, she had found life no laughing matter—but she often smiled. She had two passionate regrets: she had received only a grammar-school education, and she could not carry a tune. Once she had also regretted not having any children, but over the years she had changed her mind. ("Things is too tough for colored folks," she said.)

Faith appreciated the excellent working relationship between Donnie and four-year-old Jeanie. Often Donnie could handle her successfully when no one else could—and Faith attributed this to Jeanie's intuitive awareness of the strain between herself and Thatcher. Children often understood many things which they could not put into words. In this fashion Donnie was for Jeanie a mother-image more secure than her

8

own mother, Faith sometimes thought regretfully as she caught herself feeling resentful of Donnie's relationship to the child. But Donnie had not pre-empted—it was Faith who had relinquished. And Faith knew this, no matter how carefully she covered it up with rationalizations about the complexity of her own life.

As for Donnie and Thatcher—between them was mutual distaste. Repeatedly Thatcher had urged that Donnie be fired, but Faith refused. "Jeanie loves Donnie," she said, "—and Donnie loves Jeanie. I won't do it!" And then she wondered if the primary reason Thatcher wanted to get rid of Donnie was because he could not bear the dilution of his daughter's love—and not, as he said in his Virginia accent, "Donnie is such a goddam uppity nigger!"

Jeanie danced back to the breakfast table, followed by her black Cocker puppy, Licky, a recent present from Thatcher. She began to stuff raspberries and cornflakes into her mouth. "Poor daddy!" she said between bites, "—missing raspberries again. *Yummy* ones!"

"He doesn't feel well," Faith said.

Jeanie was a live number, Faith thought, so marvelously free and unrepressed—the way a little girl ought to be. Too, she was really lovely to look at: light brown curls and infinite blue eyes. But Thatcher kept putting notions into her head— notions of propriety, grownup manners, witches and devils, angels and a marshmallowy heaven. He wanted to make a little lady out of her, the kind which once graced nineteenth-century drawing rooms. He was not content with a boisterous, natural, growing child.

What kind of foundations were they building? Faith asked herself unhappily. Someday a real shock was coming when Jeanie witnessed with her own eyes the kind of scene which had occurred last night. . . .

9

Faith had worked overtime, as was so often required of her. Sometimes, as last night when Mr. Cunningham had been busy for hours with the Secretary because of a crisis in Argentina, she did not get home until very late. On such occasions, Thatcher was either bitter or savagely abusive, venting the suspicions he continually harbored. As a result, she hated to work overtime, and became almost panicky when she came home late.

She had opened the door of their small colonial house in Georgetown and let herself carefully into the foyer. She was greeted by a rasping snore, and immediately she understood. Thatcher, drunk again, would be sprawled akimbo on the living-room sofa. He was in a glare of light, sleeping heavily.

Oh, God! she thought. He can be so nice when he wants to be—why does he have to end up like this night after night? She felt suddenly weary and defeated. Then she derived, unexpectedly, a certain comfort from the situation: at least she did not have to face him tonight, did not have to re-explain her lateness, feeling defensive and apologetic in response to his surly skepticism.

She looked at him. One arm was outstretched loosely toward the bottle of Haig & Haig on the coffee table. The bottle was empty. He had torn open the collar of his white shirt and disarranged his pastel-striped summer tie. But even now, in this drunken sleep, he was graceful, handsome. Even now, she was aware that her infatuation was not wholly over.

The fair, wavy hair was mussed as though her own hand had playfully ruffled it with a loving stroke. The brows and longish lashes were dark, and the line of his nose was thin and gently aquiline. Patrician was the word he used to describe his own face, but now it looked simply like a face in dissolution. On analysis, the mouth expressed a surprising

10

voluptuousness, and the angle of her vision seemed to give the lips an almost feminine cupid's bow. She realized suddenly that his mouth was weak, querulous, his poorest feature. It was his eyes, she remembered, which she had first loved: an unsullied cobalt blue, with a thousand teasing highlights. Such was the vitality of his eyes when she first knew him. Many mornings now they were different—bleary and blood-shot with liquor, sullen with disgust at himself and her.

Months had passed after his discharge from the Navy, when the war was over, before she permitted herself to accept the obvious, mocking truth: she had become nursemaid to an alcoholic. When she tried to slow him up or stop him, he retaliated—obstinate and openly filled with hatred. But once he was hitting the bottle, he clutched at her saving presence as he might have clutched at his mother's. That was when he demanded absolute attention, absolute devotion. Apparently he wished to absorb her wholly, leaving no room even for their child. That was when, too, the brooding jealousy of his wartime letters was again given expression. He seemed terrified that he might lose her; yet, in his ambivalence, determined to provoke her into unfaithfulness or separation.

This was the pattern when she was with him. When she was absent, he drank with the purpose of achieving insensibility as quickly as possible, so that often she came home from night work at the office and found him in a drunken sleep. Once or twice he had roused himself in a kind of sodden despair, and once or twice he had erupted into violence.

She had learned to leave him alone when he was quiet, so she walked restlessly around the room, switching off all the lights but the floor lamp by the grand piano. There, softly illuminated, was a small marble bust of Mozart, a present from Thatcher. It was one of his few gifts not clothing, per-

11

fume, or jewelry. He had lugged it all the way from London, a surprise memento of his first long leave. He knew she would like it because Mozart, at that time, was her favorite composer (since then, she had switched her first allegiance to Beethoven). The marble was, actually, an Austrian piece which had somehow found its way to England, and Thatcher had bought it on one of his perennial antique-shop hunts for dueling pistols, which he collected with enthusiasm.

Directed by some obscure impulse, she picked up the bust and studied it in the light. It was beautifully carved, and represented, she thought, the finest side of Thatcher. It reflected his love of quality. It symbolized the best moments—the delight of concerts, unburdened laughter, warm hands clasped together, the teasing kisses. And more than this, it represented a potential for what might have been: a continuing rapport, a deepening happiness. So, for what had been lost, and for what never had been gained, she was moved by nostalgia and sadness.

Possessed by this mood, and still holding the bust, she heard Thatcher stir. She turned toward him. He was struggling up from the sofa like a felled boxer intending to rush his opponent. He stood on his feet, hunched and swaying.

"So you're finally home!" he exploded.

"Yes," she said.

He took a step in her direction. "Nice quiet evening . . . !" he muttered, "but reverse English on eight ball. . . . Lonely husband waits for gallavantin' wife! You an' me—!" He took another step.

"Thatcher!" she cried, "—if you touch me, I'll hit you with this!" She lifted the bust above her head, her body taut, pulsating.

He fell back before her threat, collapsing again on the sofa. In his drunkenness, he leered. "If you don't leave that bastard Cunningham, by God I know a way to make you quit! I'll fix you . . . !"

Almost with the words, which faded into an indistinguishable mumble, his head wobbled and he passed out once more.

Suddenly she was limp, her arms and legs feeling unjoined in their sockets. And there was a heaviness to her body which made her fear she had lost all control over it, as though she had suffered a stroke. She wondered if Donnie had heard them again, and felt shame. She set the bust down on the piano with so little care that it made an echoing thump, and after a moment summoned the effort to drag herself upstairs to bed.

Now on this steamy morning she saw the breakfast table, but it lacked a third dimension, it lacked reality. She was too absorbed with the dichotomy in her life. But abruptly she became conscious that she was being stared at from behind, and she trembled with a close, uncomfortable feeling. She could not resist turning.

It was Thatcher.

He looked wretched. His eyes, shadowed by pouches, were so inflamed that they burned. He had not shaved, and his reddish beard made him seem haggard, dissembled. He was wrapped carelessly in a paisley silk dressing robe he had bought at Finchley's in New York during their honeymoon almost six years before. He had worn it then with a John Barrymore air, consciously attempting to impress her.

"Good morning," Faith said, holding her voice steady to conceal the pity which almost wavered into it, and which she dared not show.

He acknowledged her greeting with a curt nod, and sat down at the table in an aggressive manner completely at

13

variance with his usual contrition. As he drew in his chair, the legs scraped with an unpleasant rasp.

"Donnie—orange juice!" he called impatiently toward the kitchen. "About a gallon of it!"

"Yes, Mr. Vance," Donnie's muffled voice returned.

As he waited, he turned nervously the gold signet ring (family crest) on his left little finger, and Faith could see that his nails were freshly bitten to the quick. His hands had a tremor.

"Oh, Daddy—we've got raspberries!" Jeanie cried. "I told Donnie to save you some . . . !" She dug into the scrambled eggs.

"Thanks, sweetheart," he said, and managed a slight, twisted smile. "I'm glad *someone* around here thinks of me!"

"Now, Thatcher!" Faith said.

"It's true, isn't it?" he said with bitterness. "After last night, have you got the nerve to deny it?"

What's come over him? she thought. The overtones in his voice made clear that this morning there would be no apology, no confession of having transgressed nor any pleading for forgiveness. He did not wear the look of a man preparing for self-abasement as an antidote for guilt. On the contrary, his familiar arrogance seemed exaggerated, as though he had experienced a great personal triumph. He actually smirked with satisfaction as he lit one of his Virginia Rounds, the only brand of cigarette he would smoke. He sat silent, inhaled deeply, and blew smoke through his nose. As he watched Faith, his eyes began to glitter.

She was puzzled by his manner, instinctively disturbed, almost frightened. In some subtle fashion he was different inwardly. His attitude toward himself seemed to have changed. She decided to ignore this new tack.

"Hurry, Jeanie," she said obliquely, "—it's time for the

14

school station wagon. They'll be honking in a minute. You should be on the front steps now."

Jeanie crammed in the last mouthful of eggs, gulped the remaining milk in her glass, and darted off. "I'm gonna fingerpaint today," she sang over her shoulder, "—fishes an' whales an' lobsters!"

"Wait—!" Thatcher called, "you didn't kiss your daddy goodby!"

Dutifully Jeanie returned and kissed them both. With Faith she fused momentarily. "Oh Mommie!" she said, "—you smell as good as petunias!" Then she was gone, and the sparkle gone with her.

"I see you've dressed your daughter like a hodcarrier, as usual," Thatcher said to Faith.

Faith looked directly at him. "I won't go over that again, Thatcher. Crinolines and lace are not appropriate for fingerpaints. And as long as she's my daughter, I'm going to dress her sensibly for school, at least!"

"Better make the most of it," he said darkly, "—while you can!"

Neither spoke again during the remainder of breakfast. So weighted was their silence that the sluggish morning air seemed to undulate between them.

When she had finished, and was leaving the room, he roused himself and shouted after her, "My *best* regards to your gentleman friend Mr. Cunningham . . . !"

"I'll quit my job," she flung back, "—when you make enough money to support us . . . and don't drink it up!"

Running upstairs, she realized that she was crying—hot tears of anger and frustration.

15

# 2.

SHE sank down behind the largest of the three mahogany-finished desks in the outer office, and sniffed at the odor of furniture polish. The night cleaning crew had come and gone again, mysteriously, and yesterday's disorder had been transformed as though the seven dwarfs had been at work. The battleship-linoleum on the floor glistened with the multiple circles made by the waxing machine; and the wastebaskets, pregnant yesterday with litter, had returned to their virginal emptiness.

The room, like the whole building, was hushed, because work did not begin officially for another half-hour. Faith was usually first to arrive. She wondered sometimes if this efficiency sprang from devotion to duty, or whether it represented a mode of escape from Thatcher's breakfast complaints. Normally she took advantage of the quiet to straighten out the cluttered mess of papers on Mr. Cunningham's desk, check her own "Do Today" file, and skim through the Washington and New York dailies. But this morning she was burdened by an exceptional inertia, and it seemed to her she could not drive herself to begin work. Normally, too, she hummed aloud during this half-hour's interlude, but this morning she was mute. The encounter with Thatcher had left her nervous and distracted.

The outer office would be all hers today. Evelyn was on vacation and Maria was sick—just, of course, when a new crisis had arisen and Mr. Cunningham needed them most. Their absence was one of the reasons she had been forced to work so late last night—though in any event Mr. Cunningham would have wanted her. He depended on her so. Possibly she would have to work late again tonight. She shuddered in dread at the thought of another scene with Thatcher. She decided to ask Mr. Cunningham to requisition emergency help, just as soon as he came in.

Automatically she ran one hand across the immaculate surface of her desk, testing to see if the cleaners had left a speck of dust. Then she paralleled the large green blotter with the edge of the desk, and checked the order of the in-and-out baskets, the fountain pen and holder, the glass container of paper clips and rubber bands. Everything—in contrast to her room at home—was neat, in place.

She was proud of the desk, ordinarily. It was executive in size, not stenographic, and she rated the desk's prestige—for she was more executive-assistant than secretary. But this morning she experienced little pleasure in the desk. She felt, instead, immobile, exhausted. She longed, for a moment, to become an anonymous clerk in an enormous file room somewhere: then Mr. Cunningham could no longer make demands and Thatcher could no longer make accusations. But, she considered ruefully, becoming a file clerk would not solve the problem of being more often with Jeanie. . . .

Absently her glance roamed over the Mercator projections of North and South America which lined the wall expanse of the old-fashioned high-ceiling room. She was glad she did not work in the Department's European Division, where they were actively planning war. She could not, she thought, have stomached such a job. Though she had never seen a bomb dropped, she had had enough of war. Enough was enough, and she did not care for the results. All Wash-

17

ington seemed insecure and unhappy these days. The few remaining New Dealers were like uncomfortable houseguests who knew they had overstayed their invitations; the European emigrés talked uneasily of continuing revolution; and those in power were both wary of the future and afraid of change. Well, what did all of it have to do with her? Simply this: there was nothing in the atmosphere of the external situation to help her stabilize her personal life, as once—in the days of F.D.R.—there had been. She found herself daily building walls—insulating her office life from the larger life of official Government policy, insulating her personal life from her office life. And all these different lives were so enormously complex . . . ! She took up the *New York Times* and tried to read the foreign news; but to concentrate was impossible.

She sighed, and lit a cigarette, the first this morning. She held it between the red-lacquered tips of two fingers, as though an amateur at smoking—a habit which invariably annoyed Thatcher, who smoked as he did everything else: with a flourish. Actually, departmental regulations frowned on smoking—but Mr. Cunningham (in this as in so many other things) broke the rules by overlooking the habits of his staff.

Intent on the cigarette smoke, Faith did not move, but remained at the desk trying to organize her thoughts. Her number one job, she told herself, was to put Thatcher completely out of her mind. The continual bickering was a serious drain on her energy, and she had discovered that the only way to get through a day's work was to lose herself in practical, immediate tasks. But she was suffering acutely from the parting shot she had fired at Thatcher this morning. Perhaps she was suffering more from it than Thatcher, she thought with an element of self-pity. But she could neither justify nor excuse

18

herself in any way. She felt guilty, and she was sorry. This morning she had hit below the belt as cruelly as Thatcher. It occurred to her that she might phone him an apology; but she was afraid he might hang up before the proper words were formed.

Thatcher was so damned sensitive about his job—and how well she knew that hypersensitivity! Night after night he had unburdened himself about the state of affairs at the advertising agency where he worked. Somebody was always doing him dirt, he said. He had not advanced any in prestige or position since the war, and his salary had advanced but slightly—a serious matter in view of the inflation. On the other hand, during the war she had been upgraded from one higher salary to another—so that now, relatively, her income was much more important to them than before. Thatcher had disappointed her by greeting each promotion sourly.

At the last one, only a couple of months ago, he had remarked with a tart pucker to his mouth, "Reckon you're going to be the first lady President if you keep on politicking!"

And, parallel to every promotion, he had insisted with increasing vehemence that her money was not needed, that he could support them adequately—including upkeep of the house, the car, the maid, and Jeanie's private school. Yet, with the kind of inconsistency so characteristic of him, he had ceased contributing very much to their common account, and spent his money in whatever ways seemed most pleasant to himself. This meant that Faith spent everything, saved nothing, had no extra funds for all the little things she liked to buy and do. She cut her budget for new clothes, began to make over old things, reduced beauty-parlor trips to the minimum, and rarely bought the books and phonograph records she longed for. When she asked Thatcher for money,

19

he listened to her stonily, shrugged his shoulders, and said, "Next month."

So this was another conflict between them she had been unable to solve, and her mind went back more and more to the clear cut decision she had once formed: she could not live with Thatcher any longer.

But whatever the ultimate outcome of their relationship, she knew that tonight she must apologize to Thatcher for what she had said. Having reached this conclusion, she felt better. She could turn now to the day's routine, and work with a zest almost equal to her potential. There was so much to do: shortly phones would buzz, appointments would need to be arranged, conferences called, urgent mail answered, research done—anything and everything that Mr. Cunningham wanted.

Well, she had to shake out of it! The day was about to begin. She sought the compact in her purse, and checked on her appearance. Lipstick smeared again, she marveled. That happened each time she applied make-up when Thatcher had upset her, when she went through the motions like an automaton. Her hand must have trembled, because the line of her mouth was spoiled: she had curved up the corners as though trying to force a smile. She smiled now, pensively; the white even row of upper teeth appeared, and her wide mouth took on its full sensual richness.

She was re-applying lipstick when she heard footsteps echoing in the marble-tiled corridor outside. Diplomatic callers were rare at this hour of the morning. She glanced wonderingly at the swinging shutters in the center of the doorway. It was too early to expect Mr. Cunningham after late work last night. Also, the footsteps lacked his sprightliness; or, rather, she thought in self-correction, his former sprightliness . . . for, as he put it, he had lost his illusions and found nothing to take their place. And certainly the footsteps were not Henry's, because he never made any noise when he came to fill the inkwells.

The footsteps grew louder, nearer. The man was heavy and wore metal clips on his heels. The sound stopped as a pair of legs, in baggy seersucker trousers, appeared below the shutters—and at the top, a portion of a soiled white panama hat. The man hesitated, then pushed open the shutters with a barely audible swish.

He stopped just inside the door, and looked at Faith with a slight frown. He was bulky, but more fat than muscle. His face was fleshy and sagging. Innumerable varicose veins gave his cheeks a high color.

"Can you tell me, ma'am, th' whereabouts of Miz Faith Robles Vance?" he said, in a thick Southern accent.

She put down the lipstick. "I'm Mrs. Vance," she said. Was it her imagination, she wondered, or did he actually lay greater stress on the *Robles* when he spoke her name? Or maybe it was the slurring effect of his accent?

"That's just dandy!" he said, taking off the panama hat. He began to mop his sweaty forehead with a rumpled handkerchief. From his forehead, the handkerchief went to the top of his head, where he dabbled at the bald spot in the center of thin neutral hair.

"Some fun!" he went on, "—playin' hide an' seek on a mornin' like this. That flatfoot downstairs had me chasin' around lookin' for you all over th' place. Devil of a note!"

"Oh," she said. He puzzled her. His stare had seemed so intent because his eyes were small, she reasoned. She was curious as to his mission, but oddly uncomfortable in his gaze. She sensed that he himself felt uncomfortable when he looked at her. Had he formed some preliminary picture of

21

her in his mind and was surprised now because she did not seem to fit? She recalled the deference in his voice when he first spoke to her: *ma'am*, he had said. She had caught at once the key—the Southerner addressing a lady.

"I got something for you, Miz Vance," he said.

From his tone she knew that the deference had run out. Once, when she was a little girl, a big boy had sounded like that when he dropped something crawly into her trusting hand.

"Yes?" she said.

He removed from an inner coat pocket a slip of folded pink paper, letter size. He flopped it open and held it out for her to take.

"What's this?" she said.

"Cain't you read!" he said, almost abusively.

With a mechanical gesture she accepted the pink paper. Mechanically her eyes recorded the seal of an official document, the original signature of the Speaker of the House of Representatives.

"I don't understand," she said.

'It's a subpena, sister. Don't tell me you don't know what a subpena is!"

So she had slipped from ma'am to sister, she thought irrelevantly; he spoke with the ingrained authority of a policeman. He must surely consider her a criminal.

"You are commanded," he went on, as though to make certain she understood, "—to appear day after tomorrow morning before the Committee, at eleven o'clock. They got some questions to ask you. See?"

"There must be a mistake!" she cried. "The wrong person—!"

"Naw—they don't make mistakes." He set the misshapen

22

panama on the back of his head and started for the shuttered doorway.

"But why *me?*" she called after him, bewildered, incredulous. "What have they subpenaed *me* for?"

He shook his head. "I reckon you know that better'n anybody else except *them*—so why you askin'?"

The shutters continued swinging gently for a moment after he passed through. Except for the pink paper in her hands, she might easily have been dreaming. But she could feel the paper, hear it crinkle—so it was real. In any event, she told herself calmly, there was nothing to get excited about. Somewhere along the line of the vast, creaking Government machinery somebody must have made a mistake. Identity, probably. There was only one thing to do: wait for Mr. Cunningham. He would straighten out everything in a jiffy.

Relieved and confident, she glanced at the clock. It was exactly nine.

Then she noticed that her pulse had accelerated, but only a trifle.

# 3.

FOR the first time in her career, she became a clock-watcher. Gradually the hours stretched out longer and longer, and she grew more and more impatient. Mr. Cunningham did not come to the office, nor did he telephone until noon. He would be tied up with the Secretary indefinitely, he said, and she was to wait until he returned. She did not tell him so, but she would have waited—regardless. She was holding the pink paper in her hand, memorized now after the tenth reading.

Contrary to the usual pattern, the rush of business she had expected did not materialize. It was as though Mr. Cunningham's absence was sensed throughout the Department, and his office was left to its own devices. There were few calls, no telegrams, no harassed messengers, no excited conversations in Spanish, no arrivals of slick obsequious attachés from trade delegations or embassies. Ordinarily Faith would have been delighted at such a breather. Today she automatically took care of correspondence, caught up on filing, smoked twice her regular number of cigarettes, and tried to concentrate on some data relative to the important tin mines in La Paz where the misery of the workers had caused so much trouble. But even this, to her astonishment, could not hold her attention.

She took a late lunch, as usual, with a casual girl-friend who was a translator and with whom she liked to talk Spanish. She arranged with old Henry to eat his sandwiches in the office and listen for the telephones (Negroes were not permitted to eat in the main cafeteria). Old Henry was a dignified, gray-haired man who had an excellent knowledge of several Romance languages. She often lent him Spanish books from her father's library—since Washington was a Jimcrow town, Henry had trouble at the public libraries. He worked in the Department's messenger room, and could do little favors now and again to show Faith his appreciation. He had to be content with knowledge he could not use: *Más vale saber que haber* was the proverb he often quoted to her with a little smile.

When she came back from lunch, Henry said, "Mr. Cunningham got a call from the Personnel office. I told 'em where he was."

"Oh!" Faith said, "—I should have warned you: he didn't want to be disturbed!"

"They insisted," Henry said solemnly. "Claimed it was imperative to find him."

Such alacrity on the part of Personnel was unheard of. "Good heavens," Faith said, "—what's got into them? Something must have happened."

Henry left, a doleful expression on his face. Personnel was an ogre: the lower your classification, the more liable you were to be eaten. Faith made a note to check with Mr. Cunningham to be sure they'd found him, and dismissed the matter.

But thinking of Personnel made her think of the wonderful way Mr. Cunningham had treated her. Occasionally she found herself wondering if she cared more for Mr. Cunningham's praise than she did for Thatcher's approval. Was she peculiar, abnormal in this? Shouldn't she be more concerned with pleasing her husband than pleasing anyone else in the world? Yet she could not stifle the joy which leaped in her each time Mr. Cunningham said casually, "A swell job, Faith—a swell job!"

Simply thinking of Mr. Cunningham—without Thatcher Thatcher Thatcher interwoven—made her glow. Long since, she had acknowledged unblushingly to herself that she was guilty of hero-worship. Perhaps, otherwise, she would never have clung so obstinately to this one job, or to any job. She had worked for Mr. Cunningham since the very beginning of her Government service, through consolidations, transfers, reorganizations. Where he went, she went, too. His failures were her failures, his triumphs her triumphs. She followed closely his interpretation of events, and his philosophy . . .

that is, until recently. Since then, a shadow, sometimes even a big black cloud, had fallen between them. "Faith—" Mr. Cunningham remarked once with impatience, "—you still appraise the world in terms of the simple dialectics of the Spanish War: fascists versus democrats. Things are much more complicated now. This is a cagey game we're playing!" Much too cagey, she thought, and wondered if he believed himself, or if the fine new title and handsome office they'd given him had made him more reluctant to raise a dissenting voice in the formation of policy.

Duval C. Cunningham was tweedy and pipe-smoking where many of his present colleagues dressed like Wall Streeters and preferred English cigarettes; the "striped-pants boys with spats," they were derisively called in other departments. He was also old-fashioned Scotch Presbyterian, whereas many of his colleagues either openly or covertly had strong Roman leanings—a matter which bore a subtle weight, and which he had several times discussed with Faith in uneasy confidence. "Religion ought not to be injected into politics," he complained, "—but it is, and I don't know exactly how to meet it." "About all you can do is saw wood and say nothing," she answered, laughing, "—and maybe they'll forget you're a dangerous Calvinist!" He shook his head. "I'm not so sure—and I'm not so sure that I ought to keep my mouth shut about some of the things that go on. . . ." Afterward, when she thought about the conversation, she regretted that she hadn't encouraged him to fight. Why hadn't she? Maybe, she thought, she didn't want to jeopardize her own job, either. She felt ashamed of herself.

Mr. Cunningham was an expert in his field. Originally, he had been an economist whose specialty was foreign trade, and whose subspecialty was Latin-American commerce. Aroused by the New Deal, he had given up his university chair and accepted the call to Washington. When his path crossed Faith's for the first time, he had become a key-man in the Office of Inter-American Affairs, and his star was rising with unusual brilliance. When the functions of his office were transferred to the Department, he transferred too, and Faith was carried along. He was a hard worker, idealistic, and honest, and his qualities had usually been recognized by the men at the top. But of late, Faith had seen both the bounce and the devotion gradually ooze out of him.

They had taken a shine to each other, he later remarked, during her first interview. A mutual friend at the Pan-American Union had sent her to him. Though she was shaky on typing and shorthand, and vague on policy, she spoke Spanish fluently—and he hired her on the spot. Later on they did things about Civil Service.

After two years at Bennington, her mother's health had so deteriorated that Faith refused to return to college, and decided to get a Washington job instead (with secret reluctance, and equally secret resentment toward her mother). The minute she was ushered into Mr. Cunningham's office, she felt easy and comfortable, as though she had dropped in to chat with a well-liked professor at college. He leaned back in his swivel chair, his pipe locked in his teeth, and clasped his hands behind his crew-cropped head. He murmured questions at her through the clenched teeth, and in a few moments she found herself doing all the talking. She told him about her courses in economics and sociology, but she left out Renaissance Art and Spanish Poetry—they didn't seem appropriate to a Government office (she had planned to teach Spanish literature after graduation). The matter of language she took for granted. When she had finished, he relaxed forward in the swivel chair, scratched the back of his neck, and said, "You'll do very nicely!" And when she

27

was leaving the office, he called after her, "*Salud!*" She turned and looked at him a moment, delighted and smiling. "*Salud!*" she said. From then on, they had a perfect understanding. She began, as he put it, as an office girl, and became his right hand man. She protested this as male chauvinism, but he laughed at her and revealed her first efficiency rating. It was "Excellent." After that, it was always "Excellent."

She put down the "Do Today" file, which she had been fingering unconsciously, and glanced at the clock. Almost six —and no Mr. Cunningham! What had happened to the afternoon? It was too bad, because he would not be able to do much about the pink paper after office hours. Nevertheless, she would talk to him tonight, so that arrangements could be made first thing in the morning. There was a whole day's grace. She could at least be thankful for that.

She fidgeted, and wondered what to do with herself if he did not come in for an hour or two. That would mean another telephone call of explanation to Thatcher. Perhaps she should tell Mr. Cunningham flatly that she could not work overtime any more.

Outside, a car backfired and she jumped. She was glad she had made Thatcher stop calling for her: she was afraid he might insult Mr. Cunningham someday. How nervous I am! she thought. How silly! It's nothing, this business. Either a mix-up, or some sort of meaningless routine. They're putting everybody through the mill these days. A Red under every bed . . . somebody should make up an old maid joke. . . .

She got up from her desk and went to the floor length window. She noted with unease that a storm was gathering. The Washington Monument was an impressive golden needle in a late sunray which broke through the clouds like a searchlight. Once she had seen the Monument struck by lightning.

A puff of warm moisture-laden air whiffed through the window, and the venetian blinds stirred. A strange, brassy light was developing, like a landscape seen through the thick glass of an old bottle. Looking across the White House lawn, she speculated on whether the people hurrying along under the ancient elms of the Ellipse would make shelter before the storm broke. She could hear faintly the trolleys clanging on Pennsylvania Avenue, the motormen harassed by jammed-in passengers and the rush of homeward traffic. Suddenly she felt lonely, intangibly depressed. Home . . . everyone else but her, going home. She wanted to be with Jeanie.

In the remote distance, thunder percussed. The wind began to rise with tropic violence. A man's straw sailor rolled along the sidewalk and into the street, to be crushed by a hurrying Army limousine with three stars on the license plate. The wind increased, surged down the Mall, driving before it black cumulus clouds like huddled sheep. Lightning flickered. She could see in her mind the waves rising on the Potomac, hear the yawping wind.

Perhaps this was the source of her unease, of her latent fear. It went back six years, to a sailboat party on the river. And just such a sudden, violent squall. After the boat went over, she managed somehow to come up from the turbid depths of the river, somehow to cling to the mast. She reached out and pulled to the mast the boy who was her date. There was a frantic animal thankfulness in his eyes. Later they were rescued by a harbor police launch. Hauled dripping into the launch, Thatcher had clutched her hand and begun to sob.

Over the Mall the clouds burst open and rain deluged. Unable to control her apprehension, she reflexed away from the window. At this moment, she heard Mr. Cunningham's office door slam. Her emotions and memories were so tangled that she took a full minute to remember the immediate problem before her, the pink paper. Her impulse was to rush at once to Mr. Cunningham, but something held her back.

Apparently this was one of the times when he did not want intrusions: otherwise he would have come in through the outer office to make some jocular remark. She waited with short-breathed expectation for his buzzer; even when he would see no one else, he sent for her. He would be sitting down, shuffling his papers, examining the notes she had left him. Then, the buzzer. But the buzzer did not sound.

She waited a while longer, yet nothing happened. She was left no choice but to take the initiative. She rapped, and opened his door slowly. He had not heard.

He was sitting at his big desk, as she had visualized, but his back was toward her. He was staring out the floor-to-ceiling window. The aqueous sky was dissolving into dusk, and the twilight was diminished by the heavy maroon velvet drapes which hung at the window. The cavernous old office seemed unusually gloomy, in no way relieved by the large bright-colored Covarubbias picture-maps of Central and South America which had seemed so attractive when they were framed and hung upon the walls.

The rug muffled her steps as she approached. "Mr. Cunningham—" she said hesitantly.

He whirled around to her with the surprise he would have shown had she popped a paper bag. She noticed that he appeared worn and drawn, much older than the short haircut gave him the right to appear. There were circles under his eyes, and the lids were somewhat puffy.

"What is it?" he said. She had never known him to be so brusque.

"I—I want to talk to you about a personal matter—"

One thing she never did was bring her personal life to the office; that is, for discussion with others. Though she knew the details of the other girls' affairs, and all their joys and sorrows, and though Mr. Cunningham often told her about his boys and sometimes his quarrels with his wife—Faith, in turn, never talked about her private life. But the pink paper, though personal, was public, too. She had not realized that she would feel any hesitation at telling him about it.

"Shoot—" he said.

"I waited for you all day," she said, irrelevantly.

"So?" he answered.

He was not helping her at all. He seemed unfriendly, almost angry, for some reason. He picked up a pipe and sucked at it erratically, making a whistling sound. She was stung by his attitude, and nearly decided to leave him alone. But the anticipation of eleven o'clock day-after-tomorrow drove her on.

Finally she burst out with it. "I've been subpenaed—!" She was unable to finish, unable to fill in the details, because she was paralyzed by his face.

He was gazing at her as a complete stranger. She had the awful sensation which once had possessed her on a psychology class visit to a mental hospital's schizophrenic ward—the sensation of two worlds. Now Mr. Cunningham was in one world and she in the other, and there was no possible means of finding a bridge. She knew this clearly before he opened his mouth, before he said a word. Something had happened to him, something dreadful. Or was it . . . something which had happened to her . . . ?

At last he spoke. "I know," he said wearily. "I got a phone call about it, from the head of Personnel. They don't take the matter lightly—"

She stumbled on with what she had to say, determined to

31

get through with it. "I was going to ask you to arrange—or have the Department arrange—to call off the hearing. I'm sure there's some sort of mistake . . . there's nothing the Committee could possibly want *me* for!"

"My dear Faith," he said, sounding almost like himself, "—you ought to know better than that. And you know very well there's nothing I can do—!"

She was astounded. "You mean, you won't even *try?*"

He averted his eyes from her face, and his shoulders drooped a little. He seemed so tired that he was barely able to speak. "Anything I might do for you would be of no significance. The Department itself is powerless to influence the Committee. Moreover, the Department is alarmed that one of its employees should be subpenaed by the Committee. Appropriations for the Departmental budget are pending, and this sort of thing can easily have a negative effect. You know the trend of the times. The Department feels now that the most important thing is to protect its reputation, in the light of probable Congressional attacks based on your hearing."

Fury was seeping into her in minute trickles, swelling gradually into a stream. "You are saying that the Department doesn't care, really, whether I'm innocent or guilty— all it cares about is avoiding a smear! For its budget, its dollars, its jobs!"

The shaft had struck him. He swung back to her, with a pleading expression in his eyes. "See here, Faith, I'm not telling you how I feel, I'm telling you how the Department feels. I'm not the Department's top policy maker: I wish I were! Things would be different! All I can do is carry out orders. I have no recourse. . . ."

"*That,*" she commented bitterly, "has been said before, and it rings no different here!"

"One thing more: be sure, please, to sign a leave slip covering the amount of time you spend at the hearing—just in the event of a Departmental investigation. . . ." His tones were now so low she could hardly hear him. "Incidentally, the office phone is tapped."

"I see. They suspect you, too!"

He nodded, and rubbed the back of his neck. "Faith, the best advice I can give you, personally, is this: unless the Committee clears you explicitly . . . resign!"

She looked at him, her throat swelling with stubborn anger. "*I will not!*"

As she ran from his office, he cried, "Faith—Faith, I'm sorry!"

She paused long enough to reply, "—*Salud!*"

She slammed the door, and stood trembling. Thank God, she thought, neither of the other girls was there. If they had overheard, she could not have faced them.

With no hesitation she grabbed the phone on her desk and dialed the operator. In an agitated voice she said, "White House, please—!"

The line crackled with static from now far-distant lightning.


# 4.


THE rain had ended some time ago, and the glistening asphalt of Connecticut Avenue was beginning to steam faintly. The broad surface changed color periodically with the varying red, amber, and green of traffic lights —an effect like surrealistic moons upon a motionless sea. Into the wake of each moon led the wavery, opaque tracks of automobiles which had sailed through time and space and left this record of their passing. Then with mathematical rigidity a lighted trolley, empty of passengers, floated down its own fixed path toward the vanishing point in perspective.

There were sounds—the insect-like whirr of the automobile tires, the raucous clang-clang of the trolley—but Faith did not hear them. Sight was necessary to her progress, and unconsciously she was aware of the Avenue and its appearance; but even the sudden, violent honking of a taxi did not move her to awareness of its danger. For at this moment the threat of bodily injury seemed to her trivial.

The danger passed, and she crossed the street to the right-hand side. She had decided to walk home, and this was the course she always followed to windowshop the fashionable small establishments. Like the reflex actions of an animal which has thoroughly learned a maze, her feet were taking her where they had been trained to go. She exercised no volition: she was not sure that all this was not part of a protracted dream. It seemed almost as though she were viewing the whole experience impersonally, like a foreign-language film, in a language she did not understand, and without captions. To reassure herself of reality, she stopped under a street lamp and opened the black patent-leather bag swung over one shoulder by a long strap. Yes, there was the pink paper, exactly where she had put it. She looked at it disbelievingly; she had felt sure it would vanish.

A sharp pang of unease struck her; momentarily she confused the pain with hunger. But she knew she could not permit herself the luxury of a wrong diagnosis. The pain was fear. She was afraid to show the pink paper to Thatcher. What would he say? She shivered. Here was the new element in her life: fear of Thatcher. In spite of all the conflicts in their marriage, overt and hidden, she had never believed that she would be afraid to face him on any issue. In this reaction, she was totally unlike herself, she thought. What had she to be afraid of?

Nothing. The answer was, emphatically, nothing at all!

Her first passionate anger, at the office, had given way to scorn. The scorn was in proportion to the great respect she had held for Mr. Cunningham over the years, and she could find no phrasing adequate to express her contempt. She had never dreamed that he would knuckle under in such a situation. A few years back, when the House had denied salaries to three Government employees for their views, he had been one of Washington's most vocal critics. It was, he said, a bill of attainder—and prohibited under the Constitution. Shortly thereafter, in a special message to the Congress, President Roosevelt had said the same thing. Mr. Cunningham had been very pleased with himself and the President. "F.D.R. was absolutely right in attacking!" he commented to Faith. "You can't win *any* victory without a battle!"

So now, she thought, Duval Cunningham had joined the ranks of summer soldiers.

Her instant reaction had been to go above and beyond Mr. Cunningham—straight to the top. It was useless, she knew from experience, to waste time with endless petty bureaucrats. Utterly useless, aside from the time factor which pressed her. The hours between now and the hearing were so few! Never before had she conceived of a physics of time: that hours, minutes, seconds could be compressed to seem like decimal fractions of themselves. Or, conversely, they could be exaggerated by the laws of refraction which applied to a concave mirror. The time since she had talked to the White House struck her as more interminable than all the hours she had waited for Mr. Cunningham.

It seemed impossible to wait until tomorrow morning for her appointment at the White House—but the knowledge of the appointment was itself a great comfort. She knew there was at least one man in Washington who could and would help her, a man whose advice was sought and pondered by Presidents and Kings.

She felt inclined to laugh at herself. Why, she had reacted to Mr. Cunningham's renege (there were stronger words to describe his action, but she would not use them) as somberly as if she had been condemned to some Nazi concentration camp. Sometimes Thatcher accused her of having no sense of humor because she did not laugh at the same things he did. Well, this pink paper business would turn out to be one thing she could laugh at! Maybe Thatcher would laugh too —after it was all over.

In much better spirits, she paused before Jean Matou's brightly lighted window and admired a lovely negligee. There were also some sheer suntan nylons she liked and made a mental note to buy tomorrow. And black underthings trimmed with delicately beautiful handmade French lace— too expensive, no doubt, but the sort of thing Thatcher used to buy her and said were most flattering to the graceful lines of her hips. She wasn't so bad looking, after all, she thought gratifyingly. In New York, during the last week of their honeymoon, Thatcher had outfitted her completely at Bergdorf's —despite her protests because she knew he could not afford such extravagances. Maybe she should buy these things in the window for herself—dress up as a surprise for Thatcher. Maybe a little lace would help restore the old mood between them.

She wandered on, up Connecticut Avenue, noting that the asphalt was nearly dry by now, idly pausing here and there to inspect a fine piece of antique plate or a cluster of orchids in a florist's window. But through all her impressions, memories of Thatcher floated like disembodied wisps of things past: snatches of conversation and the way he called her *Ducky* the first time (chosen, he said, because of her yellow hair and dark eyes) . . . his charm when he told Uncle Remus stories in a soft, warm dialect . . . the reassuring strength of his arm as together they watched the moon rise at Water Gate concerts . . . his critical approval of the Chippendales in her Georgetown house (they were her mother's antiques, and had been equally admired by her father) . . . the dashing way he demonstrated his ability to fence (an art also practiced by her father) . . . the long moonlit country rides in the open Packard convertible, fluorescent yellow in the night. He had been so gay, so good for her! And she had been so very much alone, so very shy!

She had come, now, to Dupont Circle, and she cut directly across it under the ancient, spreading trees. In the exact center was a marble fountain, carved water-maidens supporting a shallow bowl. The whole effect was like a huge, unusual goblet, and the water spilled over with the delicious tinkle of champagne. She paused, and looked again at the fountain. This was where they had stood one morning in the early hours before dawn, and he had kissed her for the first time. To recall this was to recall a joy that was also pain.

It had been a whirlwind day, the kind she had sometimes lived in fantasy, but never experienced. It had been complete in every way, except at the end they had avoided sexual fulfilment—she because she was afraid, he because (as he explained afterward) he was afraid he might lose her. Later she considered that he had said something with an unconscious double meaning; but at the time she had accepted his attitude at face value. Indeed, years passed before she discovered it was his code to sleep with any woman except the one he loved. He demanded, compulsively, that his own wife "be pure" when he married her. But all this was yet unwritten on the scroll of their relationship, and in the beginning each was struck with wonder at the beauty of the other.

She was celebrating her twenty-first birthday, drenched in memories of her parents. Earlier she had accepted an invitation to visit her former college roommate, Mary Margaret Haswell, in Baltimore—but at the last minute she canceled the plan. She felt, curiously, a sense of treason at abandoning the Georgetown house: it had been the scene of so many never-to-be-lived-again delightful birthdays . . . birthdays transformed into real fiestas by her father, whose Spanish enthusiasms had been the perfect counterbalance to her reserved New England mother. Her sensations, always, had been of security and happiness: she knew that she was loved.

So she resolved to stay at home, play records from her father's flamenco collection, re-read favorite passages in Unamuno, and look over the scrapbooks and photograph albums of her childhood. She would use the day, in a sense, for taking stock. She felt very old, in despair that thus far she had accomplished nothing in life. What she wanted, she knew now, was to have some fun; but the soul-washing of this day prevented it. Years after, she could laugh at the image of herself as a tragedienne; but at the time, she was so lonely that the loneliness was real, a tangible ache.

It was the weather which defeated her. The end of April was too lovely to stay indoors. She looked out at the sunlight through the new leaves of the tree canopy over the street, and sighed. Through an open window she smelled the air in all its springtime sweetness, and she thought of the apple blossoms and budding pink azaleas in the Virginia countryside. She surrendered, and put on her riding clothes.

That was where she had met Thatcher. Their trails merged unexpectedly in a grove of flowering dogwood, and suddenly each was riding alongside the other. In her romantic mood the impression of a classic centaur struck her. Broad-shouldered, flat-bellied, handsome and correct in a checked tweed riding jacket, he sat very straight on the English saddle and managed the horse with a kind of effortless arrogance. She tallied three points: he wore no hat, and the sunlight played teasingly through his fair, wavy hair; his calves strained within his boots, tense and purposeful like the legs of a polo player; and his sorrel horse was blooded, wholly submissive to him. He was almost overwhelmingly graceful and self-composed. Later she became aware of his face.

Her horse whinnied, and a squirrel dashed madly into a hollow tree.

The young man smiled at her. The smile was ingratiating, intimate, so personal in texture that she had the feeling he would explain—very naturally—that he had been waiting for her a hundred years in this wood, that she had broken a spell which had been cast over his life. (She knew now that she had failed to break the spell.)

She returned his smile. The horses' hoofs beat a rhythm on the leafed-over forest path.

"May I ride along with you?" he said. His tone was formal, but easy and friendly.

She liked the way he lazed the horse's bridle through his fingers, liked the way he seemed to belong to the horse. "Yes —certainly," she said.

"My name is Thatcher Vance," he said. It was then that she became fascinated by his eyes—an almost pure cobalt blue, sparkling with vitality like sunlight on deep-sea water. His nose was rather thin, his mouth generous but slightly mocking—a combination which conveyed the same self-conscious superiority, the same arrogance as his posture. But the odd part was, the arrogance was not offensive, but pleasing.

She had hardly introduced herself before they came to an old hand-hewn rail fence on the edge of a meadow. He spurred his horse and took the fence in a clean jump. She followed, but with less assurance. His eyes laughed, and she responded at once to his triumphant zest. "You ride as if you grew up on a horse—" she heard herself saying. But she was thinking: he rides exactly like my father. . . .

"I did, more or less," she heard him say. And almost before she realized what was happening, they were exchanging confidences dating back to childhood.

She revealed that she had lived in Washington most of her life, that both her parents were dead—her mother, for a year; her father, since she was twelve.

Thatcher's face expressed surprise. "From your name, Robles—" he hesitated over the pronunciation, "I thought perhaps you were a foreigner." He smiled, and added, "A Senorita, si—?"

For her, this was an old problem: no one ever spelled or pronounced *Robles* quite right on the first try. And it was true that sometimes she wished desperately that her name was Smith or Jones or Green; but regularly she chided herself for the wish because of her loyalty to her father. A name did not have to be Anglo-Saxon to be American! This time weariness tinged her voice as she explained.

"My father," she said with slow emphasis, "was once an attaché in the Spanish diplomatic service. He was stationed in Washington. That accounts for *Robles*. My mother was from New England, a Prentiss. That accounts for *Faith*. Do you see?"

"I see!"

"And oh yes—one thing more: along about 1685 a Prentiss was tried for witchcraft. So watch out!"

"I shall," he said gravely. "But I'd better warn you—I've got Brer Rabbit's left hind foot!"

He had no further difficulty with her name.

He hailed from Tidewater Virginia, of the landed gentry, and had been fatherless since he was a small boy. He had gone to the University of Virginia, and he spoke nostalgically of his undergraduate life and his fraternity.

"It was a terrible wrench, leaving college and having to earn a living," he said. "Such a dull business, earning a living!"

"Do you work for the Government?" she asked.

"Oh, no!" he answered with a touch of scorn, "—thank God no! I'm in an advertising agency."

She flushed. "I work for the Government—"

He laughed pleasantly. "I'll forgive you," he said, "so long as you're not one of the crackpot New Deal professors."

She worked for one, and he was not a crackpot, she thought with indignation; but she shrugged it off. What was the value of a controversy with Thatcher Vance? He was too nice to talk to, too nice to be with.

They rode along for a while in silence. The sunlight flickered through the new leaves and mottled the earth like a gigantic leopard skin. She almost forgot her companion . . . until, suddenly, her horse shied.

"Look out!" she heard Thatcher cry, and simultaneously his arm overlay hers, gripping the reins, and they were touching thigh to thigh. "It was a snake," he said, after he had quieted her horse. "You weren't watching—you might have been thrown."

She breathed hard. "Oh—thanks!" she said. He smiled at

41

her again in that so personal, so ingratiating manner, and she realized that her heart was thumping mightily for another reason quite different from her fright.

After that, the wonderful dream continued. They had cokes in a musty crossroads store, and idled among primroses on the banks of a swift-flowing brook. Then she found herself having dinner with him in a back-country inn that looked like a picture in one of her storybooks—an English inn along the river Dee. Somehow, after rushing home to change clothes, they wound up dancing at the Congressional Club, drinking champagne and meeting his smartly dressed, sophisticated friends. He seemed to know everybody, and everybody seemed to know him. From their faces it was easy to judge how much he was liked—especially by the women he spoke to. And even on this first evening she saw the moody antagonism in his eyes when she received attention from other men.

But now these reactions had become self-destroying in their magnification beyond the bounds of reason. They had got beyond control. How could she have known that the water in the goblet fountain would turn bitter, that the memory of the first kiss would taste of ashes?

The fountain repelled her. She felt hot, and her body was sticky. The rainstorm, instead of cooling, had only succeeded in making steam. She returned to full awareness of the present.

Nearby crickets persistently signaled mates. A slight drip-drip still continued from rain-wet leaves. The cacophony of traffic noises around the Circle had not diminished. A sailor in whites strolled past, and gave her the eye. She wondered languidly what would happen if she should respond. She was not yet that miserable, she told herself. The sailor was followed by two young men, walking fondly arm in arm. Too late for the sailor, a prostitute appeared from the shadows, over-rouged and flashy in a big summer hat.

Faith sighed, and with flagging steps went on across the Circle. She navigated the street with care, and ducked into a drugstore. It was a delight to escape from the humidity. She sat gratefully on a stool next to the air-conditioning outlet. She breathed deep satisfying breaths, and felt suddenly that she had not breathed since she caught the first glimpse of the man in the soiled panama.

She glanced about curiously. No, it was impossible that he should appear in a place like this. It was too shining, too sanitary, too wholesome! Nevertheless, when she noticed a white panama, slightly soiled, on a hook in the rear, involuntarily she started.

"Limeade," she said in a low voice when the waiter approached. She drank it hurriedly and departed.

She turned into Q Street. At the bronze buffalo bridge, she held back. She was almost home. The earlier mood of ebullience, of near-swagger, had wholly passed. If Thatcher were at home, she would have to face him. It was possible he could read in her face that she was in trouble. The fear of him would not go away. The real question was: dare she tell him the truth? She saw that emotionally she was back to the exact point where she had started.

She found herself disorganized, unsure of what to do next. At the thought of another scene with Thatcher—this scene over the pink paper to end all scenes—she felt sick. There was a spastic stabbing somewhere in her body. Was it nausea, or a constriction about her heart?

The limeade had been so sour. She wondered if it might come up.

Thatcher was waiting for her in the living room, agitatedly

smoking a cigarette, and drinking straight scotch from an Old-Fashioned glass. He was dressed in a white linen dinner jacket, with black bow tie and maroon boutonniere. He looked almost as handsome as of old.

"Where in *hell* have you been?" he said, glowering. "I've phoned all over creation for you! Don't tell me you've forgotten Elaine's party as usual . . . !"

She blushed, and ran upstairs to change—humming with a gaiety which astonished both herself and him.

# 5.

ELAINE MONCRIEFF BEVERLY had effected, in her own way, a subtle influence on the history of the United States. This was a fact tacitly recognized in Washington; but the fact had never appeared in print, and probably never would. It was her pleasure to bring personages together who had matters of mutual interest to discuss —but who might not have met less openly without stirring up a murmur or possibly a cyclone of suspicion. Faith was well aware of Mrs. Beverly's proclivities, for Thatcher had retailed many an anecdote which secretly Faith considered shocking—but always, for harmony's sake, refrained from saying so.

Despite the relief with which she had greeted Thatcher's announcement of Mrs. Beverly's party, actually there was no one spot in Washington Faith would have more preferred to avoid—on this evening of all evenings. It was probable that someone from the Department would be present—and certainly not a someone with whom she would feel any congeniality whatever. She was filled with foreboding lest someone from the Department, in the know, might let slip word of the pink paper. It was not hard to visualize Thatcher's recoil from such a public scandal.

Thatcher was part of the younger set cultivated by Mrs. Beverly to keep her soirées light and gay. There was a whole younger crowd which revolved primarily about the British, French, Spanish, and certain Latin-American embassies, the State and Navy Departments, the Air Force, and to a lesser extent the Army. Sprinkled in were a few people from the Hill, and also emigrés from the old governments of Eastern Europe. Mrs. Beverly was given to remarking that, since the war, her parties weren't as gay as they used to be—thanks to the wretched Reds who had changed the personnel of so many embassies!

Mrs. Beverly herself was anything but young, and Faith often marveled at how she managed to stand the pace of her life. She drank heavily, and was reputed to have done so ever since the suicide of her only son, twenty years before. Immediately thereafter she had been divorced from her husband. She was wealthy in her own right, and continued to live in the grand manner of the twenties—keeping the details of her past a mystery. She had entered actively into Washington society when her brother had become, for a time, a Cabinet member and doors everywhere were opened to her.

It occurred to Faith tonight that, often as she had been to Elaine Beverly's house, she had never really known the woman. Certainly she was invited only because of Thatcher —and she suspected that she was disdained, just barely tolerated as his wife. Thatcher himself had shown some sensitiveness to this condition, on occasion, when he had urged

Faith to exert herself more at the parties. "You can at least try to act interested in my friends," he said once in irritation, "—*try* to seem as charming as you used to!" She had sniffed and said, "I don't know how to be anything but myself."

This evening, in the car, driving out Massachusetts Avenue to Mrs. Beverly's house, she sat silent beside Thatcher until they had almost arrived. Suddenly she said, "Thatcher, why are you so fond of Elaine Beverly? She's old enough to be your mother. . . ."

"That's why I like her," he said sharply, "—she's fragile and aristocratic looking, exactly like Mother!"

Faith had not anticipated such edginess in him, and she wondered if an explosion of some sort was impending. She recalled that he had been jumpy for several days, and everything he said was lacerating.

Mrs. Beverly's house was touted as an exact copy of Marie Antoinette's *Petit Trianon,* and was so described by drivers of sightseeing buses. It had spacious gardens barred from the street by a high wrought-iron fence and hedge, through which passersby could catch glimpses of the activity within. As Faith and Thatcher approached the house, it was evident that the party—a buffet supper—was already in full swing. The sky had cleared, and the night conveyed a tropic sensuousness.

"We're late!" Thatcher said reproachfully. "Elaine will be furious. She's leaving for Maine tomorrow."

"You could have come without me," Faith said.

"I wish I had! But I've done it so many times already there's a rumor we're getting divorced!"

"Sticks and stones—"

"People think you're running around!" he said bitterly.

They lapsed into silence, and climbed the stone steps of the house. A butler admitted them.

"Good evening, Judson," Thatcher said.

"Mrs. Beverly was asking if I'd heard from you, Mr. Vance," the butler said. "I told her, not a word."

In the garden they were greeted at once by Elaine Beverly. "Oh, my dears!" she said, "—I was terrified that you weren't coming! This is the last little gathering till fall, you know."

"Faith had a headache," Thatcher said, "—but fortunately she recovered."

Faith smiled as sweetly as she knew how. "I couldn't spoil Thatcher's evening," she said.

"I have some new people I want you to meet," Mrs. Beverly said, "—but first, mint juleps! I'm sure you're parched, after this dreadful day."

"I'm dying of thirst—" Thatcher said.

Covertly Faith glanced around. In the crowd of twenty-five or thirty people she recognized many familiar faces, and she nodded and smiled to those who noticed her. No one was there from the Department. In her jubilance she felt almost friendly toward Mrs. Beverly—and for a moment the old woman seemed less brittle than Faith had ever seen her. Certainly Elaine Beverly's face was a relief map of her life, ridged and furrowed by dissipation. Her blue-white hair was carefully coiffed in the latest fashion. The faded eyes had been adroitly brightened with mascara, the thin lips had been broadened with rouge and bore a pleasant smile. The narrow, aristocratic nose was curiously like Thatcher's, and, had it been a little longer, would have given her a horsey appearance. But as she was, she would have photographed not too badly on a first night at the opera, or shown up well before newsreel lights at a White House reception. Her face never really cracked except on rare occasions: sometimes,

47

when she was drunk and had only a few cronies about, she would go to her magnificent grand piano and sing in a husky voice which still bore traces of its former contralto beauty. There was one recurrent song:

> *My senses fail,*
> *A burning fire devours me—*
> *None but the lonely heart*
> *Can know my sadness.*

On these occasions, Faith was always sorry, deep in her heart, for Elaine Beverly.

She realized that she was accepting automatically a silver julep mug, heavily frosted and blooming with mint. "Faith, darling," Mrs. Beverly was saying, "—you're very fetching tonight in that frothy little white cotton thing you have on. But you're looking a little disturbed too, about something— even a little pale under that lovely suntan of yours! You brood about Thatcher too much! There's someone here I want you to meet—someone really charming, a really flashing Latin! Thatcher will kill me when he sees this man!"

Faith allowed herself to be steered away, and in a moment Mrs. Beverly was introducing her to a dark, smooth-featured young man whom she called Senor Jose Quiepo de Mola. Quickly Faith discovered that his English was almost non-existent, and obviously she was expected to entertain him for the evening in Spanish. It was a neat trick, and Elaine Beverly had immediately disappeared.

Ordinarily Faith tended to be smilingly blank around the people at these parties. There never seemed to be anything to talk about because she had never been able to identify herself fully enough with their world. Their amours and gossip did not particularly interest her, their political conceptions left her bewildered, and their fabricated small talk was completely beyond her capacity. They all sounded to Faith like the white Russian count who wrote a chit-chat column for Cissy Patterson's society page. To complicate matters still further, she was under strict instructions from Thatcher never to admit that she worked in the Government as a glorified secretary. (She recognized his humiliation that his wife worked at all—but she could not understand why working as a secretary seemed to compound the humiliation.)

But with a Spaniard she had a special interest; she was, to begin with, *simpatico*. She had at her command much of Spanish folklore, the best of Spanish literature, and a passionate interest in the current events of Spain. This was her heritage from her father.

She was about to burst into excited questions of Senor Mola, when abruptly she checked herself. "You have just come from Spain?" she said slowly in English.

"I have," he said in a very heavy accent. "I am at Embassy. I was personal aide El Caudillo himself!" His voice was lacquered with pride.

"Oh!" She drew away from him slightly, because she did not want him by any accident to touch her. There was very little about El Caudillo she did not know. Nor had she forgotten the Embassy, and the last time she was there.

It was the farewell reception before the Embassy was turned over to the fascists, for Franco's regime had been recognized by the United States Government. Prying eyes had watched from behind curtains at the windows of Mussolini's Embassy across the street. She had walked sadly upon the uncut lawn and into a hallway littered with trunks and packing boxes. An old lady in a black lace mantilla sat in an anteroom fanning herself and crying. And in the patio, the

Ambassador, a scholarly man with a dark Vandyke beard, opened a bottle of the oldest and finest sherry, and pouring it, said, "To Spain!"

Now, to Senor Mola the expression in her eyes must have proved disturbing. He stood awkwardly for a moment, and said, "You will pardon me, please, Senora?" He left, pretending that his julep mug was empty.

She returned to her smiling blankness, obvious in her isolation, and temporarily forgotten by the hostess. She tried to fortify herself for the next episode: she seemed to be, she recalled, especially attractive to Hungarian Barons—but with them, she could at least talk horses. At these parties of Elaine's she seemed to attract a stream of men, none of whom ever stayed with her very long. Perhaps, she thought, if she were essentially less shy she might have adjusted herself easily to them—letting them flow over the surface of her consciousness but never penetrating. But alas, she was not Dresden china!

She had an opportunity to observe Thatcher, engaged in animated conversation with an exquisite English girl of her acquaintance, Constance Coningsby. Connie's dress was an orchid summer frock which bore all the earmarks of a Paris design. She had a typical British complexion, clear, almost ruddy. Though she was rather stiff, she seemed to enjoy immensely whatever Thatcher had to say. Several times she sipped her julep and laughed. Thatcher laughed, too, and his eyes were glowing with the light of calculated conquest. It had been a long time since Faith had seen Thatcher's blue eyes gleam with such engaging intimacy. Looking at him now, it was so patent that she had failed to make him happy; possibly, she thought, no woman ever could—but certainly Faith Robles had failed. She felt no inclination to try to place the blame: the failure had been a matter of circumstance, temperament, and a whole complex of imponderables that neither one nor the other had known of.

It was a long while before she had come to understand that he had idealized her into an impossible image of perfection, and that he would exact standards of her he could demand from no one else—and especially of himself. When their engagement was announced, Mrs. Beverly had looked at her over the thin bridge of her nose and almost snorted, "Thatcher is a wolf, my dear! You would do well to harbor no illusions!" Faith had dismissed these words because she sensed, obscurely, that for some reason Elaine Beverly disapproved of their marriage—perhaps because age was always jealous of youth, or perhaps because Mrs. Beverly transferred to Thatcher the dual affection once felt separately for son and husband. Faith now wished that she might simply dissolve, leaving Thatcher to his English companion . . . or to Elaine Beverly.

How long these thoughts occupied her, she had no conception. Her impressions were of a chiaroscuro of moving figures among foliage—a kind of montage effect of colored lights, white-coated Negro waiters, and swishy dresses . . . all accompanied by a standard cocktail hum. Shortly food would be served, and she would have to settle somewhere with someone. She glanced about with anxious distaste. It was then that Mrs. Beverly caught sight of her again, and sailed to her rescue with a man in tow.

Dear Elaine, Faith thought—so eager to keep me from being a wallflower, so eager to keep Thatcher free and unencumbered! She wears herself out!

The man in tow was on the borderline between youth and middle age, pink of face, and beginning to go bald. In his early twenties he had definitely been handsome, but now he was tending to paunch, and his hands—clutching two julep mugs—were white and soft. Despite his linen dinner jacket, his appearance was not so suave as Faith had come to expect of Mrs. Beverly's guests. In his walk and manner he betrayed a trace of uncertainty, and Faith guessed that this was the first time he had been graced by Mrs. Beverly's hospitality.

His name was James Grayson.

"I'm sure you know who *he* is," Mrs. Beverly chatted on, after the introduction. "Everybody in Washington knows, and someday everybody in the country will know. Just mark my words—you'll see!" She was gone again, with a little pardon-me-I-must-run nod, and he was stranded.

His name meant nothing to Faith, and she wondered if she could conceal her ignorance, avoid the threatening *faux pas.* "May I help?" she said, offering to take one of the juleps from his hand, since she had finished her own drink and set the mug aside.

"Oh thanks," he said with relief, then added apologetically, '—I was getting it for somebody, I don't know who. All these foreign names and titles mix me up. But of course they're a mighty fine bunch of people!" he finished heartily.

His eyes were searching her face, and she knew without being told that he liked her looks. Liked them in the way so many men had appraised her solely as a lovely piece of flesh. Whatever else there was about her, they never saw; and she resented and hated them for it. Grayson was of this species.

"Hey," he burbled, "your name sure sounds familiar!"

She said wryly: "I have a nice old American name, don't you think?"

"You sure do—and I have to admit you look one hunnerd percent!" The words slurred, he grinned, and his eyes missed focus.

She recognized, belatedly, that he was drunk, but carrying

his liquor like an old hand at the game. She wanted to get away from this man, now, before it was too late and something embarrassing happened. He was sure to paw her, sure to suggest a walk down a garden path. She decided to try to ease him into general conversation, and then escape. She sought for the vaguest question she could think of which would not betray her.

"Do you expect to stay in Washington long?" she said.

He grinned again, a grin that slid from one side of his mouth to the other. "I sure do!" he said. "And continuing as general counsel of that famous you-know-which Committee of the House!"

She knew which, instantly, and the earth shook. She would have gasped if she could have found breath. She knew that the blood had receded from her face in one great rush. A single thought began to pound in her head: she had to get Thatcher away from here before his path crossed Grayson's!

"Will you excuse me?" she said without preliminaries; "I want to run in and check my make-up—it's so dark here in the garden!" So lame, so innocuous, so obvious! she thought. But she had to escape at once.

"Maybe we could eat together?" he said, his voice now smooth and confident.

He sensed his advantage, she thought, and would press it. His face informed her plainly that he would offer to be her friend. Already she was retreating, in a panic.

"I'm promised!"

"But I'll see you again!" he called after her, triumphant.

She fled in horror to Thatcher. She clutched at his arm, distracting him from Connie. He turned to her with marked irritation.

"What is it?" he said, reacting to her face.

"Thatcher, I'm ill!" she said. "I want to go home, *now!*"

"We'll take you upstairs and call a doctor," he said. "What's the matter?"

"No!" she said, tense and almost crying, "—I'm going home! Please take me!"

He gave her a laconic, resentful look. "All right," he said.

# 6.

As usual on the mornings when he was not incapacitated by a hangover, Thatcher dropped her off in front of the main entrance to the Department. He had said practically nothing during the ride downtown, and practically nothing during breakfast. Indeed, he had been extraordinarily taciturn since the moment last night, when, safely in the car, she had offered an explanation for her illness.

"Faith—" he said as he started the engine with a jab at the starter, "what *is* the matter with you?"

"I don't know," she said. "I'm . . . I'm just overwrought, I guess. I shouldn't have come to the party. I've got . . . the curse. And a splitting headache."

"Huh!" he snorted. "You females!"

She was surprised that he had not offered more resistance, and was grateful for this favor. In an effort to make up for the disappointment she was sure he felt, she rubbed her head against his shoulder, and said softly, "—I'm sorry, truly!"

"Oh, forget it," he said.

This morning she had dressed carefully, concealing the agitation she still felt over the Jim Grayson episode. She was almost feverishly eager to wind up the matter of the pink paper, and could hardly wait to get to her appointment. Nevertheless, she allowed everything to proceed according to established pattern, and only when the car and Thatcher were safely out of sight did she turn away from the Department and walk rapidly down Pennsylvania Avenue. By noon, she thought, the whole affair would have become ancient history—to be happily forgotten.

The morning was exceptionally bright, and she responded with cheer to the weather. It was a great relief after yesterday's mugginess, and she disregarded the foretaste of furnace heat conveyed by the sun's rays. The trees and the Avenue, the people and cars were sharply limned on the retina of her mind.

By the time she was admitted to the East Wing of the White House, she was feeling calm and confident. From her smooth make-up and composed expression there was no evidence of the emotional turmoil she had experienced. The entrance guards had deferred to her as a pretty young woman in a yellow chambray dress; the poker-faced Secret Service man had almost permitted himself to smile; and inside, a dignified old colored gentleman said to her respectfully, "This way, please ma'am."

She enjoyed being invested with part of the power and prestige of someone else's name—for simply to call on this man was to establish a measure of importance. As she walked down the long, thickly carpeted corridor, she considered her good luck in knowing Brigadier General Melvin Thompson, and almost purred with a sense of well-being.

Melvin Thompson was a member of the inner circle of White House advisers. For uncounted years he had been a Congressman, and was canny with the knowledge of many people and events recorded in the filing system of his own memory. It had been his policy to stay out of the spotlight: he was prop man, prompter, director, playwright—but never the actor. It was easier and more satisfactory to have others speak the lines. His general's rank had been conferred merely to accent his authority with the military; he could not distinguish one end of a gun from the other. But he could call the directors of every major corporation and banking house in America by their first names.

The shrewd, professional fixer was not, however, the Melvin Thompson Faith knew—though she was aware of his existence. The Melvin Thompson she knew was medium-sized, jovial, kindly-eyed . . . a man of paternal appearance, but unmarried . . . a man of substance, but always sharing. With Faith (whom he called "Chickie" for the same dark-eyes-yellow-hair reason that governed Thatcher's choice of nickname), he was given to homilies like "Great aches from little toecorns grow"—and, when she was older, "Mothers are the invention of necessity." Later on she guessed that his homilies were quite different when the boys got together in one of those famous smoke-filled hotel rooms. On every birthday until her marriage she received an expensive present from him.

She had rarely seen him, however, since her mother's death. Occasionally she ran into him at an official gathering of some sort, and he would slip his arm around her and whisper as intimately as though he were her father: "I hope our Chickie is very happy these days?" Indeed, for a long time she had regarded him much as a favored uncle—after, that is, she had gotten over the jealousy which swept her (as defender of her father's memory) when he first payed court to her mother.

Hannah Prentiss, her mother, was a strong personality—a woman who had never been successfully conquered by the

Puritan repressions. Had she been conquered, she would never, in the first place, have married a Spaniard . . . nor in the second, a dashing, zesty man like Luis Carlos Robles. A year or two after her husband's death, she began to take pleasure in Melvin Thompson's company, though he was totally unlike the man she had married. It was not until afteryears that Faith began to understand the implications of the relationship—and by then she begrudged her mother nothing. She was able to understand, also, that the friendship with Melvin Thompson in no way diminished the love Hannah Prentiss had borne her father. But why the two had never married was one of the questions she was at a loss to answer. Both, perhaps, preferred things the way they were. . . .

He had rearranged his schedule so that she might have an appointment during the morning, and he had not asked why she wanted to see him. He had made it clear that, whatever the reason, he was always available to her. When she reached the door of his office, she was still radiating satisfaction at the thought of having a friend so powerfully placed, a man who understood every intricacy of Washington and the Congress, a man who held a hundred strings on the fingers of his own two hands.

He greeted her with a kiss on the forehead. "Chickie, dear," he said, beaming, "what's been keeping you away from me? Don't you know it hurts the vanity of an old codger like me to think he's forgotten . . . ?"

She seated herself comfortably in the big leather chair in front of his desk, and glanced around the room. "I've never seen this office before, Melvin," she said. "You've certainly got a collection of pin-ups!"

On the walls of the simply furnished office were framed

autographed camera portraits of two Presidents, three Secretaries of State, the British and French Ambassadors, two
Balkan kings, the President of the Senate, and the Speaker
of the House, along with a scattering of lesser dignitaries.

"Well," he said modestly, "I've done a few favors in my
time."

She smiled. "All this, and steampipes, too!" She glanced at
the high ceiling, where steampipes were exposed, angular
and unaesthetic.

"Yep," he said, "—and in wintertime the dern things drip:
one thing I haven't been able to fix!"

They laughed together.

"Melvin," she said casually, "I need your help—unimportant little me. I've been subpenaed by the House Investigating Committee."

He sat up straight in his chair and slapped his desk with
the flat of his palm. "You *what!*" he cried.

"I said . . ."

"Good God—*you!*" He sat back in his chair again, and
locked his hands over his slight round belly. "—*You*, of all
people! What *have* you been doing?"

"It's ridiculous, isn't it?" she said, smiling. "I think they've
made some mistake . . . of identity, perhaps, or something.
Will you have it called off for me, tell them they've made a
mistake?"

She paused, waiting. He did not answer, but merely stared
at her. Finally she said, timidly, "The hearing is set for tomorrow morning at eleven, so there isn't much time."

"Well-l-l," he said, "you've certainly come up with a jaw-
breaker!"

"I know," she said, with humble deference. "I didn't think
it was much of anything, until I discovered the Department
is absolutely on its ear about this business. I think they're

silly, but they're taking it hard—all jittery about appropriations and such."

"They have a right to be!" he said, with a sharpness which surprised her.

"I expected them to be concerned about an employee's welfare, but they weren't!" She sounded caustic, now, and her voice was tinged with the anger evoked by Mr. Cunningham.

He shook his head. "This business, Chickie, is bigger than an individual. And the welfare of the Department is more important than the welfare of one person. They can't be too careful!"

She was beginning to feel cornered. "But Melvin, the Department's welfare ultimately depends on the welfare of its employees. How can an agency operate if its people are scared out of their wits?"

"Possibly . . . possibly," he said; "but I don't think we ought to debate philosophy of government. Your problem is the immediate thing—and I might as well be frank in the beginning." He cleared his throat, formally. "Now I know what you're going to say, and believe me, Chickie, it hurts like the mischief to be so blunt with you, but it would be highly unwise for the White House to get involved in this affair! If there's nothing wrong with your record, you'll come out all right—"

She stiffened. "Wrong? What do you mean: *wrong?*"

"Well-l-l," he shrugged and waved one hand, "you know. Some mighty nice folks haven't been too astute when it came to bucking Government policy. Got themselves involved in fronts, and such like. Of course, everybody has a right to his own opinion, but why shout from the housetops? These are times when a little close-mouthed horsesense goes a long way. . . ." He looked at her narrowly. "Of course, *I* don't know what you've been up to, but *they* must, or they wouldn't be hauling you in. But I'm sure, in your case, there's nothing to worry about. You just sit tight, Chickie, and you'll come through okay. . . ."

"Listen, Melvin," she cried, "—doesn't the White House know what that Committee has been up to . . . the smearings, and all the rest!"

"Oh, sure, sure," he said, rocking slightly in his swivel chair, "—we know. But it's highly improper for the Executive Branch to interfere with the Legislative. Besides, every time we've tried it lately we've got our fingers burnt. Actually, we're powerless when it comes to that Committee. All aside from the fact, of course, that there's nothing wrong with the *objectives* of the Committee. I'll grant you they've been a little careless in their methods, sometimes—but maybe, when you total the whole score, they've done more good than bad. I guess, basically, they're doing a worthy work."

"*Melvin!*" she groaned.

He shrugged his shoulders again. "Well, Chickie dear, that's all I can tell you. But you'll come out all right. Just don't worry!"

"One question, Melvin," she said, getting up and realizing she was dizzy on her feet, "—one question: do you believe that the daughter of Hannah Prentiss could *possibly* be un-American?"

He flushed, and hesitated. "Well-l-l," he said slowly, "—most people believe where there's smoke there's fire. I'm not saying I subscribe to the theory, but it's too bad, Chickie, that it had to be you!"

With a stunned gesture she clutched her bag, burbled goodby, and retreated—leaving Melvin Thompson aston-

60

ished at her abruptness. She was dying, she thought, for a drink of pure, cool water.

# 7.

THE sky was burnished, and the noon sun ricocheted infra-red off the sidewalks. It was one of those breathless noons, indigenous to Washington, when all life moves with an effort, and green leaves hang tarnished and drooping from the heat.

The sizzling heat penetrated the soles of Faith's sandals, while she stood aimlessly staring down Pennsylvania Avenue. The experience with Melvin Thompson had not left her angry, nor even particularly hurt. She was too dazed for any emotion.

It was only three minutes' walk from the White House steps to the cannon-flanked portals of the Department, but Faith did not turn toward her office. The deep shadows cast by the foliage in Lafayette Park looked inviting, and she found herself wandering along the curved walks. She bent and drank from a bubbling fountain; the water was lukewarm, savorless. She wrinkled her nose in distaste.

Automatically she chose a bench and sat down. Pigeons strutted jerkily around her, waiting to be fed. Some ruffled their feathers and cooed. There were few strollers, due to the heat, and the pigeons' majestic self-possession was rarely disturbed. Ostensibly Faith was watching the pigeons; actually, she saw nothing. Her eyes were open, but no visual images registered. She neither thought nor felt: she was in a state of shock. For the time being, she was wholly unable to assess the condition of her affairs.

Gradually, however, she became aware that she had sat on this bench before. A dim memory kept pushing up into her consciousness. Then she realized she had chosen the very spot where the young Norwegian officer had kissed her.

It was summertime, as now. She was helping out as a hostess at the USO in the old Belasco Theatre, opposite Lafayette Park. A young soldier, in a foreign uniform she did not recognize, approached her and asked her to dance. He was as blonde as Thatcher, but wholly different in all other characteristics. Somehow, she was never sure just how, she had subsequently found herself sitting on this bench.

Very conveniently, there had been a moon, and the equestrian statue of Andrew Jackson doffing his hat toward the White House made a gallant silhouette. There was, in spite of Andrew Jackson, a European atmosphere to the park, with its bronzes of Lafayette, Von Steuben, and Kosciusko. Faith almost felt that she was somewhere in Europe, meeting secretly to discuss Resistance plans. So she was hardly astonished when the officer informed her he was leaving by plane next day on a secret mission. She guessed that he worked with the underground.

He was a lieutenant, and his name was Eric. He would not tell her his whole name, because, he said, he had already revealed more than he ought. He spoke American English, not English English like the Europeans who had been educated at Oxford or Cambridge. He learned the language, and got his education, he told her, in the Norwegian merchant marine. And he looked it.

Even in his uniform he looked steel-springed, resilient. He walked as he danced, with a slight roll of the body like a man making certain of solid deck underfoot—his land sea-legs, he called them. His hands were impressive: large, big-knuckled, tough. And he had a little squint to his eyes when he smiled—a squint which may have been only a protection against glare at sea, but which nevertheless gave him a quixotic expression of humor and playfulness.

After the kiss, what had happened had seemed inevitable. And perhaps it was. Thatcher had faded away from her consciousness as though he had never existed, had never warped her life. She took Eric home with her, though how she had invited him, she could not recall. Only later did she realize how badly she had wanted him, how badly she had needed him.

She had been so alive, in every sense, that night with Eric! Even its memory still held the power to stimulate. She could still feel, still acknowledge sensation. She was not dead, she was not old! Life! She was alive! She knew what it felt like to be—fully—a woman. She could know again! Gradually the vagueness was passing from her. She was again able to think of herself as a human being in context—a personality.

"Shoo!" she cried to the pigeons. Startled, they took to the air with a batting of wings. She derived a singular pleasure from the beauty of their flight. Her dark eyes glowed.

She must, she thought, find some way to act on her immediate problem—the pink paper. Suddenly a new solution came to her, and she marveled that she had not discovered it sooner. Perhaps the reason for her slowness, she told herself, was in her individualistic way of thinking. Her first concern, after the bewildering subpena, had been to think of how this *one* or that *one* might help her. But what one person might be afraid to do, a group would not fear. In unity was strength. She was unsure, now, of the origins of that phrase: maybe Benjamin Franklin said it, or maybe Abe Stone. . . .

The Union of course was the answer.

But there was another side to this coin. It would be hard to estimate whether Thatcher would be more abusive over the pink paper, or over the Union's handling the matter. She hesitated now—but was there really any choice? Where else might she turn for defense?

That she had ever joined the Union at all was quite accidental, though at college she had acquired a theoretical grounding in what unions were all about. It happened that when she was working for the Spanish Loyalists, she met a young fellow named Tommy Burkett. He had a wide grin and crinkly eyes she found appealing. He was freshly out of Yale, so they had many acquaintances in common. He was an architect, and he wanted to clear the slums and build decent houses everywhere. He was also greatly concerned about Spain, and about unions. She saw him frequently at Spanish gatherings. And after them he often asked her to come with him for a cup of coffee or a beer. These sessions were rarely personal—there were too many other things to talk about. One night, nevertheless, she realized she had developed a real school-girl crush on him, and found herself patterning her activities on his. She never missed a meeting, she always stayed till the end, she volunteered to serve on any committee of which Tommy was the chairman. So, after a time, when he asked her why she didn't join the Union, she couldn't think of the feeblest excuse. She would have joined an Arbor Day committee if Tommy had approved. He took her around to headquarters, introduced her to Abe Stone, and she applied for membership that very afternoon. But shortly thereafter, Tommy was transferred to the West Coast regional office of his agency—and, aside from a few desultory letters, she never heard from him again. She was sorry, because he was so very, very nice . . . and wished sometimes she had told him so.

Though she seldom went to Union meetings, she had not dropped out. She paid her dues regularly, now and then asked other people to join, and on rare occasions offered her house for money-raising affairs. The Union, in truth, became a matter of principle with her in two ways: she saw that if she believed in unions theoretically, she ought to support *a* union in actuality. And, basically more important, she refused to back down in the face of Thatcher's constant attacks on the Union. She felt he was trying to cow her, deny her the right to her own opinions, and reduce her to the classic female subservient role.

He had said nothing on the subject until—perhaps emboldened by an officer's uniform—his first long leave home during the war. On this leave (never to be forgotten because Jeanie was conceived) he was expansive with the story of how his ship had rescued a handful of Nazi U-boat men, including the captain and the first mate.

"Since my German is pretty good, naturally I was picked to interrogate the krauts," he said at table. "Before we landed, I got to know those fellows. Hell's bells—they're no different from us! Especially the educated ones. You know how I've always admired the Germans!"

Softly, Faith replied, "But Thatcher, they're fascists!"

"That rot!" he exclaimed. "I've heard all that rot! War is just a game, and the other side is the enemy. They shoot you, you shoot them! Now I'm shooting at some of the very people I used to drink with at the German embassy. . . ." He had absorbed too many cocktails, and was more oratorical than usual.

"But Thatcher—" she said in a strained voice, "they *are* different from us: they're *fascists!*"

He shrugged it off. "They're different from us in one way, yes: they're more efficient at making war. Their officers, like ours, are gentlemen, good fellows on a party—if you know what I mean. What have the Nazis done that's so terrible? Disciplined the labor unions, cleaned out the Jews, attacked the Reds—well, all that's nothing to hold against 'em. Now, is it—I ask you!"

She said quickly, "Look, Thatcher: I'm a member of a union—am I so dreadful? Would you want me 'disciplined' on account of it . . . ?"

She knew the blood had drained out of her face.

He stared at her in disgust. "You're completely nuts to associate with that riffraff! By God, when the war's over, and I'm home, you're going to resign—or else!"

"We'll talk about that later," she said in a rigidly controlled voice. "You've forgotten that I was a member when we were married—and then it didn't seem to pollute you!"

"You held out on me—you didn't tell me! Christ, I would have been embarrassed if I'd known! Imagine, a Red—"

"I didn't make a point of it," she interrupted in defense, "because I wasn't very interested or very active."

"I know your kind," he said thickly. "Good Godamighty— what are we fighting this war for, anyhow? The union carpetbaggers and the Reds . . . !"

She stiffened. "The President says—"

"Don't dish me out a lot of stuff from *him!* He's a Red himself!"

For the first time she noticed her hand was shaking so violently that she had spilled coffee on the tablecloth. She pushed away with a sudden gesture and ran out of the dining room. When Thatcher came to her, she was huddled on the sofa, crying.

"I'm sorry, Ducky," he said, "I wasn't attacking *you*. I'm sorry!" He stroked the soft downy hair on the back of her neck.

She was struck by the polite, insincere tone of his voice. She knew now that something irrevocable had happened in that moment. Perhaps it was because she had experienced one of her sharpest disappointments in Thatcher, or perhaps it was because he had attacked the great father-image who had meant so much to her. She could not say for sure. But something drained out of her feeling, and she resolved to defend her right to make her own judgments.

This was not the last of such arguments with Thatcher, by any means. But a subtle change took place in their character. While Thatcher came to repeat the same refrain of opposition, in varied forms, increasingly she refused to debate or even to listen. Her unwillingness to quarrel, Thatcher interpreted in a different manner: "What the devil's the matter with you?" he cried. "You're mighty high-hat—you won't listen to what *I* have to say: just act like I'm a nincompoop or something! I've got as much right to a point of view as you have!"

Of course, he did have. But rarely could they find a common area of agreement, even for a quarrel.

So, considering now the matter of the pink paper and the Union *versus* Thatcher, there really was no choice. Unresponsive to the relentless heat, she jumped up from the park bench and began to walk briskly. The pigeons whirled upward again.

"Oh, the *hell* with Thatcher!" she muttered between her teeth.

She was sure she had found a champion at last.

# 8.

UNION HEADQUARTERS was a ram-
shackle old mansion on a side street. Once before it had been
Union Headquarters, for during the Civil War it had shel-
tered Abraham Lincoln's chief-of-staff. As Faith, climbing
the stone steps, read this fact on a neat bronze plaque, she
wondered if Lincoln had ever pulled himself up by the
wrought-iron banister, had ever entered in fatigue and dis-
couragement and come away buoyed by fresh hope for the
people's cause.

She could remember, when she was eight or nine, how her
father and mother had taken her to Ford's Theatre and told
the story of the shot fired by John Wilkes Booth. "You are
an American, Faith child," her father said; "you must learn
about all these things." Then they crossed the street to see
the room where Lincoln died. She had gazed at the bed
where gradually his life had ebbed away, and tears came
into her eyes. The striped wallpaper in that room she could
visualize to this very day . . . the striped wallpaper, a print
of Rosa Bonheur's *Horse Fair,* and her father's rever-
ence. . . .

She shook aside these thoughts and hurried into the dim,
cool recesses of the brick building—a sudden welcome relief
from the copper glare of the sun. For a moment her eyes had
difficulty adjusting, and then she recognized the receptionist:

Thelma Hill, a chic, good-looking Negro girl who had worked as a junior statistician in an office adjoining Faith's before the war.

"Why Thelma!" Faith exclaimed, "—what on earth are you doing here?"

Thelma laughed a low, tremolo laugh. "They got me, pal!"

"I don't understand," Faith said, genuinely puzzled.

"It's simple," Thelma said. "First they re-classified me from a Professional rating to a Clerical; then they abolished the job. Then I tried to transfer to another agency. No soap. No jobs. Now I'm here. My first day, and you're the last customer I expected. Don't tell me—" She paused and looked narrowly at Faith. "Surely not *you!*"

Faith found herself blushing. "I want to see Abe Stone. It's—it's a private matter."

"Oh," Thelma murmured, "—I'll tell him." She disappeared through a rear door.

While she waited, Faith could hear the robot-like thump-thump of a nearby mimeograph machine and the jazzy rhythm of typewriters. Stencils and leaflets, she thought, leaflets and stencils: education for your own welfare. There were Union leaflets scattered on a handy table, and thumbtacked on a bulletin board several petitions to be signed. Dutifully she unscrewed her fountain pen, read the petitions with care, and signed her name boldly to each. She sighed. She knew that sooner or later photostat copies would reside snugly in half a dozen secret files. But she felt no sense of fright, only a slight astonishment that so much time and tax-money and personnel would be expended in keeping track of such exercises of Constitutional rights. . . .

Thelma returned as Faith was replacing her fountain pen in her purse. "All right," Thelma said, jerking her head backward over her shoulder, "—he says come right in."

Secretly, Faith had always been much impressed by Abe Stone, even a little in awe of him. She felt a vague respect for anyone who had been able to resist the almost overwhelming drive for money and social standing—and she awarded this respect to professors, talented New Deal administrators, some clergymen, certain artists and writers, and labor leaders of the new type.

Stone was bent over a bare metal desk, working on a stack of papers. He looked up and smiled slowly. About forty, he was not large, but he gave an impression of massiveness, of solidity, which was immensely reassuring. His features seemed carelessly molded, and he was not in any way handsome; but the artlessness was in itself artful, was his strength, his power. A few pits in his neck and cheeks made him look rough hewn—a fit subject, Faith thought, for a Jo Davidson sculpture. Though he represented a white collar union, he would have appeared more at home in blue denim. How much was her evaluation of him colored, she wondered, by her knowledge of his origin in a Pennsylvania steel town . . . ?

"What cooks, Faith?" he said.

Her rhapsody was shattered by his directness. "I've been subpenaed."

"You too?" he interrupted. "My God, what a dragnet!" He sucked in his lips, rubbed his cheek with his right hand as if he were speculating on the need to shave. He had stubby, powerful hands. "I wouldn't expect them to go after you."

"I don't understand it."

"You don't?" he said in some surprise. "Well, perhaps not —you," he conceded. "I mean, it *is* hard to understand why they would pick on you. After all, you're hardly a key labor leader, you haven't made speeches about civil rights, you haven't defended minorities, you haven't publicly attacked

70

the foreign policy, you haven't—hell, what *have* you done, anyway?"

"Nothing," she said humbly.

"That's bad," he said, laughing, "—if you had done something we could sure enough fight for you!"

"I'm sorry," she said with real sadness, "I can't plead guilty to anything."

"Even so," he went on, "they're planning to hit you on something, or they wouldn't have summoned you. Maybe you're a Red?"

She glanced up in amazement, to see if he was kidding her. But he was dead serious, and the question required an answer. "I suppose," she said, "—it all depends on your definition." She was thinking of Thatcher's point of view.

"And my definition you expect to be different from theirs?"

"Naturally." He himself, she knew, was constantly under fire.

"Well, that's pretty intangible, so we'll dismiss it. The question is: what's to be done next?"

"Yes," she said anxiously, "—that's it." She glanced at the clock. The time was almost one-thirty. In a worried voice she said, "The hearing's set for eleven tomorrow."

"My God, why didn't you say so in the first place!" His calmness momentarily disappeared. "Are they going to let you have counsel? Is it an open hearing, or a closed, secret, one . . . ?"

"I don't know," she said, flustered. "I hadn't thought about such things. All I'd thought about was getting the whole business called off!"

It was Stone's turn to look at her in amazement. "To do that you'd need an *in* with one of the industrial or organizational backers of the Committee—and they're plenty shadowy, believe me, plenty far in the background. You never

71

heard much of Thyssen, Siemens, and Krupp in the early days of Hitler, did you? They were there all right, but carefully hidden. Hell, *you* know how things work around this town! *You* know how the average Congressman's mind is made up on an issue! But why am I making a speech? Oh, because I didn't expect you to be so naive! You shocked me for a minute. The thing now is to defend you. . . ."

He paused, and lapsed into inner consideration.

She waited patiently while he thought, waited for his words as though he were to deliver the final judgment on her doom. Her heart was not fluttering. She felt a strong optimism that something good would come out of what he was about to say. It *had* to: he was that kind of man. She tapped a cigarette and lit it. Surprising, she thought as she smoked the cigarette, how actively alive she was beginning to feel. The jolt provided by the pink paper must have done something to her nerve endings.

Musingly, he began to talk. "I don't for the life of me see how they think they can get away with attacking people like you. Hell, you're as American as Pollyanna—no insult intended! When they go after you, they're going after everybody—and everybody ought to see it that way. If you're not safe, who is? Everybody has said or done something at least once in his life that the Committee—by *their* standards— could object to. They start with Government workers, and they go on and on. Labor leaders, writers, artists, teachers, scientists, the works! Next they'll be hauling in small businessmen: anybody who refuses to join the Chamber of Commerce or NAM will be suspect. Oh, boy, what a shakedown— I could almost enjoy that!" He rubbed his hands, then shook his head. "No, I wouldn't—for by then we'll have *fascismo* pure and simple. And brother, that's not for me!" He paused as though contemplating the prospect. "Now, to get back on the beam. Since you're so solid, you need a defense equally solid—"

She interrupted with laughter. "My mother was, for a while, a Daughter of the American Revolution. Do you think I could get them to issue a statement?"

He laughed too. "Not *that* solid, please! What I meant was: you need a lawyer from a reputable, conservative firm to defend you. The tactics in your case should be very simple— you're more American than the Committee itself. By the very act of attacking you, they themselves become un-American— though I hate to be guilty of using the term as loosely as they do, and nobody has yet defined it legally. Maybe in your case we can get a definition, something clear cut, a point of departure for future arguments."

"So already I'm a case?" Faith said. "And I'll go down in history as *The American vs. The un-Americans?*" But she knew she was deceiving herself by the light touch: inwardly she trembled. She did not want to be a case for the history books. The thought frightened her; it had too many ominous implications—courtrooms; black-robed judges, thrill-seeking audiences, puzzled juries. Oh no! She did not want to be a case. That sort of thing was for heroes or martyrs—not for her!

"Look," she said earnestly, "I want to get out of this business the quickest, easiest way. I haven't much money, but I'll use every cent. Don't you see: all I want is to be left alone!"

He assessed her gravely. "Yes, of course. That's what we all want—but leaving alone doesn't serve the Committee's purposes. You haven't any choice: you fight or you're flattened."

"I don't want to be flattened!"

"But you're going to need help—a great deal of help. There is a lawyer here who sometimes lends us a hand in critical emergencies. His firm is the oldest, most conservative in town. He himself is a junior partner—a young fellow, with brains, influence, and political savvy. The trouble is that lately he's gotten tired—defeatist. He thinks the country now is like Germany in '33: labor divided, repressive legislation, warscares, redscares, witchhunts, the progressives on the run. . . . He doesn't understand clearly that as things grow worse, more and more people will rouse themselves—that our tradition is different from Germany's."

"Oh, no—don't send me to him!" Faith cried. "I need somebody to lean on. Really and truly, I'm scared!"

Stone shook his head, and examined her face thoroughly once again. "It may be," he said pensively, "—you can lean on each other. That way, it could become a joint victory."

She hesitated. "Very well," she said, finally. "If you think this procedure is wisest."

She sighed. It wasn't what she had wanted. Not at all.

# 9.

THE law offices of *Sterling, Hardy, Hutchinson & McKee* were located in the heart of Washington's little Wall Street, the block on 15th below H Street. Unlike the stone and concrete desert of Wall Street, trees still managed to struggle for life—and now, in mid-afternoon, cast shade oases for which pedestrians were duly grateful.

Faith stood in one such shadow, her yellow dress a bright spot of color, clutching a slip of paper in her hand. On the paper was written the address she was seeking (for she had been afraid to trust her memory), the name of the firm, and another name: Dane Chandler.

She did not know exactly what had passed between Abe Stone and Chandler, for their phone conversation had been private—but Chandler at length had agreed to see her. Faith herself was filled with an intense reluctance and doubt. If Chandler was insecure within himself, uncertain of what he believed, she did not want him. As for his position, his prestige, she was dubious of its value: what good had been her pull at the White House?

After the exhilaration of the talk with Stone, she had tobogganed into a new depression. She felt more alone, more lost than before. The impersonal hands of her watch kept moving second by second toward her fateful Armageddon, and with every passing minute she seemed less well prepared than before to face it. What would Chandler say to her? Something like, "Too bad, Too late, How sad!" Even after Stone's build-up of Chandler, such an outcome was entirely possible.

She crumpled the paper and threw it into the gutter, stifling an impulse not to see Chandler at all, but to run away . . . somewhere, anywhere, disappear into the city and never again be seen. The impulse was infantile, and she knew it. Nevertheless, she could not dissipate the feeling that she was sleepwalking when she entered the lobby and checked the directory for the suite number. She quickly found it: the penthouse.

Except for the air-conditioning units, she was further depressed by the office furnishings of *Sterling, Hardy, Hutchinson & McKee:* they were pretentious in the best of taste. She had plenty of opportunity for observation, because Mr. Chandler was busy, the ice-bound secretary said, and

75

would she be good enough to wait? She waited on a handsome leather sofa decorated with brass-headed upholsterer's pins. The scheme of the suite was leather and brass: the lamps were early-American brass fixtures, and the library—glimpsed through an open door—was paneled and padded with leather. Century-old lithographs of English jurists, black-robed and white-wigged, adorned the walls. The whole place had an intangible atmosphere of expensive cigars and gold watch chains, Faith thought. Big money was about; but not, of course, left lying crassly for people to see. But you knew it—were assaulted with it—the moment you opened the door.

In the reception room was a large and impressive grandfather clock—not an antique, to be sure, but an excellent reproduction of an early American piece. Normally the ticking of such a clock would have lulled Faith into a painless acceptance of passing time, even, perhaps, have made her drowsy. But now with each swing of the pendulum she became more frantic. This delay was Dane Chandler's method of expressing his resistance to taking her case, she thought. He was probably thinking of her now as an unmitigated irritant and was wishing to God she'd go away.

When, twenty minutes later, a masculine voice burred out of the intercom on the secretary's desk, saying that Mrs. Vance might come in now, she felt that hours had passed—and was, in consequence, defensive and belligerent.

"This way, please," the secretary said so frigidly that Faith suspected awareness of her mission.

He was sitting behind what seemed to her a vast expanse of leather-inlaid desk. At the slightest sign of hostility on his part she might have bolted, so skittish had she become. But he did not wait for her to enter the room; he got up—a lanky, athletic-looking young man in a white linen suit—and came to her in a smiling manner she would never forget.

"How do you do, Mrs. Vance?" he said, and took her hand. "I hear you're in trouble?" His tones were cordial, well-modulated, but slightly flat—hinting, she thought fleetingly, of Middle Western origins.

She responded with a wry smile, unexpectedly at ease after the flutterings which had possessed her as she waited. "Yes," she said, "by now I've reached the point where I admit I'm in trouble. At first I thought the matter was of little or no importance—a slight mix-up, and after a telephone call or two everything would be straightened out. Now I find myself consulting a lawyer!"

He laughed. "You sound as if you were being forced to delve into black magic. Lawyers aren't *that* bad!"

"I don't know," she said. "There's an impression abroad that lawyers, bankers, and personnel directors all fit into the same demonology!"

He laughed again. "I can see that I'm starting under a handicap."

"Yes," she said, lifting the imperfectly arched eyebrows, "—you are!"

He led her automatically to a comfortable chair behind his desk and indicated by a nod that she was to take it. As she settled herself, she felt still better, for she abhorred consultations across wide, forbidding desks—consultations in which one became the suppliant and the person behind the desk became an inaccessible, inhuman figure who could be touched neither by logic nor emotion. This way, she knew that she had a chance of reaching him, of talking to him on an equal level. They would be simply two human beings discussing her human problem, and the cold approach of the legal technicality would subtly become impossible.

77

He offered her a cigarette from a silver box on his desk, and snapped flame from a silver lighter. As she sucked the flame to the cigarette's tip, she noticed his hand. It was strong, long-fingered, and rather knobby about the knuckles, as though formed—at least in part—by physical labor. She looked up quickly into his eyes, and there passed between them a communion of mutual sympathy. Each knew there was something intangible about the other to be especially liked, perhaps admired. He extinguished the flame, and the moment between them passed. But it had been a moment of the utmost intenseness.

"Do you have the subpena with you?" he said, getting bluntly to the point. "Abe Stone gave me a broad outline of your case. But I'd like to see the subpena."

*Case*—there was that word again, and she had visions of some irreplaceable part of herself being crushed between the heavy dun covers of a law book . . . and for long years after, gathering dust on forgotten library shelves. The word put her teeth on edge.

"Do you have the subpena?" she heard him repeating; she was not conscious that she had failed to reply.

"Yes," she said hastily, and extracted the pink paper from a chaotic mixture of handkerchief, lipstick, compact, driver's license, and coin purse. "Here it is!" She handed it to him with repugnance, as though it had an evil smell. Actually, it was perfumed with a sediment of powder which had escaped from the compact.

He sniffed at the document, and permitted his broad mouth a slight, mercurial smile. "Well, this is certainly something new," he said. "One would expect a whiff of good red herring!"

It was her turn to laugh. She did, and felt increasingly reassured. She took a drag on her cigarette, and watched his face while he read.

He was in his early thirties, and she had a fanciful impression of a touch of Tom Sawyer in him. A small-town boy, perhaps—educated, polished, grown-up. There was something about him utterly unlike the typical big-firm bright young lawyers she usually met at Thatcher's parties. Ordinarily those lawyers exuded (like so many of the Department's key men, with their cultivated accents) the atmosphere of expensive Eastern prep schools. They were always so conscious of being upper class, she thought, so conscious of superiority of dress and manners—or, euphemistically, of intelligence. They formed a clique on a certain stratum, from which other lawyers were excluded: especially Jews, and the impossible outlanders from the West. In the firm of *Sterling, Hardy, Hutchinson & McKee* she unconsciously had expected that kind of junior partner—and part of her present shock and happy reconciliation was due to Dane Chandler's difference from her pre-formed image.

She found herself liking keenly his broad, lean face with its reflective gray eyes, neat nose, and quizzical half-smile. He had straight chestnut brown hair, parted on the left and carefully brushed backward at an angle from his forehead. But what intrigued her and inexplicably softened her toward him was a swash of freckles across his nose and cheekbones, dimly spattered, true, but visible enough to recreate a hint of the face in youth. Though he was mature, she thought, he would always look young. There was a certain piquancy to the thought.

Her eyes strayed momentarily from Chandler for a glance around his office—for somehow it had not seemed so formal, so forbidding as the reception room. It, too, was lush, expensively furnished and carpeted; but there were two significant differences which she noted at once.

The first difference was in the bookshelves. In addition to rows of monotonously bound law volumes, there were the colorful jackets of current books on politics and economics, and also a sprinkling of novels—most of which she recognized as dealing with serious themes. So, clearly, he had broad interests beyond the law. She did not know exactly why, but she considered such interests reassuring.

The other difference was one which seemed to have a special, personal meaning. Neatly framed on the walls were a half-dozen lithographs of courtroom scenes—but not, like the outer office, glorifying English jurists dead and gone. The lithographs were, instead, Daumiers—savage satires on advocates and judges. Some of the lithographs she knew well, and it pleased her to see them here. The nearest one showed a prisoner in the docket, gagged and held by judicial functionaries—while the judge admonishes: *You have the floor. You are free. Speak up!*

She related the Daumiers to her own Goyas, and wondered if Dane Chandler would like her collection. Intuitively, she guessed that he would—and became suffused with warmth at this identity of taste and outlook.

Her reaction now was diametrically opposite to the chill which had fallen upon her when she had first shown Thatcher the Goyas . . . By one hand she had led him into the small room which served as her father's study and library, and from a wide drawer in the bookshelves removed a portfolio. The etchings were from the series called "Ravages of War" and they had been her father's prize possession. She displayed them lovingly.

"Brrr—" Thatcher had said, "they're too grim!"

80

"You don't like them," she said. "It's war I don't like. These, I think, are magnificent. During the civil war in Spain I induced Mother to sell some of them and give the proceeds to the Loyalists. I would have sold them all, I think, if the Loyalists had held on any longer. My father was a Republican, and I'm sure he would have wanted me to. It hurt to part with them. . . ."

"I collect hunting prints," Thatcher said.

She had returned the portfolio to the drawer with an oddly helpless gesture and a feeling of blankness which she could never forget.

Looking now at the Daumiers, she glowed with *sensibilité* . . . and gradually returned her attention to Dane Chandler and the pink paper.

In his white linens he seemed well groomed in an unostentatious way—and made her abruptly aware of her own appearance. After the trying hours she had gone through, she must by now look like a mop, she thought with annoyance. Almost desperately she wished she had paused for a check-up —for at least fresh lipstick and straightening the ribbon in her hair. She wondered, too, if her brassière was tight enough. There could be no excuse for looking like a Hearst cartoon of a radical!

Chandler's voice, with the odd flat note, brought her away from her imaginary mirror. "I wish I could tell you your case is unique, Mrs. Vance," he was saying, "but unfortunately it isn't. Unlike some others, you even have a few things to be thankful for. Take one example: you weren't served a subpena directing your appearance *forthwith*—luckily, you were given a specific time."

She cocked her head slightly. "I don't understand—"

"As a matter of legal fact," he said, "a *forthwith* subpena

81

merely means appear within a reasonable time. But Committee agents have slipped into the habit of using such subpenas more or less as warrants of arrest. If you happened not to know your rights, you might be hauled off immediately to a hearing without the slightest chance of preparation. Of course, it's a clear violation of the Constitution—"

She frowned, incredulous. "You mean, *I* could have been dragged out of bed in the middle of the night?"

He glanced at her as though visualizing such a scene, and his eyes flecked at a thought which obviously had nothing to do with law. "Yes—it's true, if an agent should choose such a time. With you, I think there would be a different story—but many people panic at the sight of an official seal, and do whatever they're told. Committee agents have also been seizing documents—when actually documents can *never* be seized by subpena."

"I haven't any documents."

"Not even any love letters tied with a pink ribbon?" he said, with the flickering smile. "The ribbon would be enough to incriminate you!"

She shook her head no, solemnly. Save Thatcher's love letters? Good heavens, she had burnt them every time. They were not letters to save in a casket, scented by a sachet . . . not love letters at all!

Perhaps he saw the cloudiness in her eyes, for he said, "I didn't mean to frighten you. The agents aren't likely to rough you up—even though that has been done. Rude and peremptory, that's about the limit now. . . ."

"Listen," she said, "—tell me quickly What Every Young Girl Should Know About the Gestapo!"

He was amused by her irony, but the amusement quickly passed, and the contemplative expression returned to his eyes. "I think we had better get on with the next steps. First, we'll call the Committee's general counsel, Jim Grayson. He can clear up certain points."

"Yes," she said grimly, "—I've heard of him!"

He buzzed his secretary through the intercom: "Get Jim Grayson for me, please, wherever he is. If they say he's in conference, insist on talking to him. It's urgent."

He turned to Faith in explanation. "Sometimes Grayson is a hard character to catch. Does most of his work, it seems, in the bars around Capitol Hill. Usually he won't respond to a page call unless he happens to feel like it. Says people bother him too much with their problems. I told him once he had no right to complain: he was a servant of the people. 'Yeah, sure,' he said, 'but the lousy sonsabitches keep gettin' in my hair!'"

They laughed together, and she found their harmony pleasant; indeed, it was almost as if they were having cocktails alone somewhere, chatting, unfettered by the creeping imminence of tomorrow. How nice it would be, she thought, to talk to this man freely. He continued mysteriously to stimulate her, to give her a tingling, sharply alive sensation. She supposed that somewhere in her body glands were shooting jets of life-juice into her blood stream, and she was responding at a high pitch. Momentarily she felt unafraid of the Committee, or any of its works. She was impregnable, astonishingly secure. And now, far from being reluctant for Dane Chandler to become her counsel, she felt almost indecently eager for him to commit himself as her champion. She yearned for him, suddenly, as a tower of strength. . . .

Echoes of the laughter still reverberated in the far corners of her mind when he changed pace without warning. "Do you know, Mrs. Vance," he said soberly, "—exactly what you're up against?"

Instantly her security seemed less certain. There was an overtone of caution, of warning in his voice which intuition told her was alarming. "I don't know," she said in a somber key, "—all this sort of business is new and strange to me. I must admit I'm afraid."

"You've never been to one of the Committee's public hearings?"

"No—I've read about them in the papers."

"Then you don't know, actually, what takes place—or anything about the Congressmen on the Committee?"

"Oh, vaguely, a little. About what the average disinterested person would know."

He grinned slightly. "Well, from now on you're no longer a disinterested bystander in the way your Congress works. You are, in fact, Exhibit A. Why do you suppose they subpenaed you?"

She looked at him with wide, troubled eyes. "I haven't the faintest notion!"

"Well, I'll tell you something," he said. "They're not really concerned with the truth of whether you're subversive. Not concerned with facts, nor with justice—but with proving a thesis. The thesis, reduced to its baldest terms, is very simple: the country is being undermined by Reds. A Red, according to them, is likely to be any person or group outside big business and its satellite organizations. They actually want to whip up nationwide hysteria—and, completely mad as it seems, they are hankering after war. So where does Faith Vance fit in? Obviously, she must be a Red or she wouldn't have been subpenaed. And if she isn't a Red, they'll say she is, and that's just as good or better than the truth, because most people will believe it. Hitler had no corner on the technique of the blatant lie. It's being used very successfully in Washington, D. C. So, now, how can Faith Vance defend herself . . . ?"

She was staring at him in dismay. "Oh my God!" she cried, "—what happens if I refuse to go, or refuse to talk?"

"You're cited for contempt. And if upheld by a court, you're fined or sent to prison, or both."

She quivered. "Is there no way?"

"None," he said, "none whatever, this close to the hearing. If we had a week, there are all kinds of pressures we might bring to bear. But there must always be a *quid pro quo* in the pressures—you scratch my back and I'll scratch yours. People on the Hill rarely do something for nothing. There ought to be a division of government called *Favors, Unlimited*. If you had powerful relatives in banking or industry, that would be the biggest help—"

"I have no relatives at all." The words were barely audible.

"Your husband?"

She shook her head. She would not put into words what she might say about Thatcher's people.

Chandler, noticing that her hands were clenched in her lap, offered her another cigarette. She took it absently, her mind still on Thatcher. Here she was, deeply involved in what was probably the greatest crisis of her life (at last she had accepted the genuine seriousness of her situation), and her husband was not yet informed. And here she sat, in an attorney's office, not knowing which way to turn next, floundering and bewildered—wondering if the man would become her counsel, wondering what the arrangement might be, wondering where money would come from, wondering how Thatcher would react at the inevitable revelation. Good Lord in heaven! Why wasn't she weeping and wringing her hands? She was caught in a complicated net not of her own weaving—and yet the net continued to seem unreal. She needed to pinch herself and wake up. The sleek, suntanned skin of her forehead creased with anxiety.

"Listen," she said with a touch of wildness, "if I can't get out of this crazy subpena, tell me what to do at the hearing!"

He paused, clasped his hands in a way which reminded her of a childhood rhyme: *here is the church, here is the steeple. . . .* He nipped thoughtfully the two fingers which comprised the steeple, then suddenly disassembled the whole gesture.

"Above all," he said, "—you must not let them push you around, or put in the record improper conclusions drawn from inference. You'll find them sly at that—and also sly at using the technique of guilt by association. They have, in effect, turned topsy-turvy the basic underlying principle of Anglo-Saxon jurisprudence: they assume you are guilty until proved innocent. And they try to turn your evidence against yourself. You must, before the hearing is concluded, insist on the right to make a statement in your own behalf. You will probably be forced to challenge them."

"I?" she said, "*I* challenge a Congressional Committee? Oh, I could never do that!" Her heart was wavering like her voice. The thought lodged somewhere in the pit of her stomach, clutched her in a momentary spasm. "I'm afraid by the time it's over I'll be squeaking no louder than a mouse!"

"Suppose you were a mouse," Chandler said, "and you knew there were large and dangerous cats lurking around. What would you do?"

She smiled wanly. "Run away!"

He shook his head. "No—there are no openings in the room where you're caught. What then?"

"Oh!" she cringed, "I don't know!"

"If you felt differently," he said, "and didn't mind becoming a *cause célèbre,* an interesting test case could be developed by challenging the Committee's legal authority to exist.

In a case called *Cobbledick v. United States* it has been settled that the validity of a broad subpena may be challenged by simply refusing to obey it. . . ."

"Oh, no!" she said; "I'm not the person for that! You'd need a crusader . . . a martyr, maybe. Somebody much steadier and braver than I—I'd never have the nerve."

Smiling, he said, "All right, Mrs. Vance, you're absolved. We'll see what happens tomorrow before deciding to make a Dred Scott out of you. You have certain rights, which you must not forget—no matter how they load their questions."

As she listened, a clenched fist took hold of her bowels, and it was not the clenched fist of Communism.

# 10.

AN HOUR later, the briefing was completed. She had filled an ashtray with cigarette butts, but Dane Chandler had not smoked at all. Now he leaned back in his chair, selected a cigarette for himself, and said, "Any questions?"

"Not now," she said, "I have to think first." Her eyes, half-closed, were hidden by the long lashes.

Her mind was whirring like the springs in a complex mechanical toy. She had, among other facts, told him about her job, the negative attitude of the Department, Melvin Thompson's failure to back her—and also outlined her college background and her interest in the Spanish Loyalists. He listened quietly in these periods, and seemed to fit all the pieces together like a picture puzzle as she talked. There was only one significant omission: she hardly mentioned her husband at all. If Chandler noticed it, he said nothing.

As he surveyed her speculatively through his cigarette smoke, a veil of melancholy seemed to slip over him. The mercurial smile had ceased to display itself, and the clear gray eyes had clouded with a mood like late November. The easy, relaxed quality which had characterized him seemed to disappear, and a tenseness took its place. He turned slightly. His eyes focused on an undefined point outside the window, where afternoon shadows angled grotesquely across rooftops, and heatwaves distorted objects like imperfectly blown glass.

"I wonder," he said in a soft voice, and his tones were no longer flat, "I wonder what I would do in your place? I often wonder what I would do if I were thrown smack into the middle of the firing line. . . . It's so easy to advise, so damned hard to act!"

In a sudden revelation like the writing upon the wall of Balthazar's palace, she understood what was troubling him. He was afraid of himself. He had progressive intellectual convictions, but he was afraid he lacked backbone to sustain them. Everything in his life mitigated against his beliefs: his business associates, most of his friends and, above all, the way he made his living. He was burdened day in and day out by this duality in his life—and he was afraid of what he might do if put to the test. She noticed now faint shadows under his eyes, faint contracted lines of worry in his face, which she had not seen at first. There was a subtle suggestion of recurrent sleeplessness, of a brooding unhappiness. Oddly, she felt that their roles had been momentarily reversed, and she pitied him—wishing also that she might help him if she could. There had been a hint, but only a hint, that he was considering a possible offensive: the hypothetical case which would challenge the Committee's legal right to exist. And her response to that had let him down. She felt ashamed. She had been put to the test already and she had failed. There was no reason, now, why he should not bid her good-day when she walked out the door, and become no further involved in her affairs. She had offered him nothing, and could expect nothing. And if such were the course of events, she could not blame him: she could blame only herself, the weakness in herself which she had earlier condemned in him. She was wretched, utterly wretched in a way which had no counterpart since the night of her father's death.

On impulse, she said, "How do you happen to know Abe Stone? He told me you'd handled several union cases." She recognized that in her mind Abe Stone was the counterpoint of Chandler and herself. Or, said another way, she thought, on the slide-rule of life Stone marked the maximum point where Chandler would like to be. And Faith Vance? A cipher, she told herself bitterly: hardly more than a double cipher!

"Yes," Chandler answered with a muted sigh, "I took on several cases at Abe's request." He paused, then added rather hastily, "Entirely on a personal basis, of course! The firm has never been involved in any way."

"I can imagine!" Faith said, her lips touched by a smile. She wanted to ask what the senior partners thought of these personal activities, but refrained. Dismissed them, surely, as eccentricities—the sort of little aberrations which could be forgiven in a brilliant young lawyer who had made a great deal of money for the firm.

"As for Abe—" she heard Chandler saying, "I've known Abe for years. First met him in Pittsburgh, when I was there on corporation business involving union contracts. We were on opposite sides of the fence, but we hit it off at once. We sensed something in each other that we mutually respected, I guess. Ever since, I've used Abe as a sort of father confessor. I see him fairly frequently, and we talk things over. He keeps me on the beam—" Chandler laughed wryly, "—most of the time."

He turned and idly rubbed the leather inlay of his desk, as if to polish it. It was a gesture of uncertainty. He broke off abruptly. He was being buzzed on the interoffice phone.

His secretary's voice echoed, precise and deferential. "Mr. Chandler, I've finally located Mr. Grayson. He's on the line."

"Oh," said Chandler as he picked up the phone, "I'd almost forgotten."

"Hello! Hello!" a voice barked at the other end, so that the earpiece vibrated tinnily.

"Hello Grayson," Chandler said, "you've subpenaed a client of mine for tomorrow morning: Mrs. Vance. I want to know—oh, oh yes, I see—"

The voice at the other end continued to vibrate, but unintelligibly. It was no matter anyway, because a geyser of relief poured through Faith. He had said: *a client of mine.* He had not failed her! She was no longer isolated, no longer separated and helpless. There was a person, and an organization, she could rely on. The release of anxiety became a physical sensation. She wanted to laugh aloud, cry for joy. It was Christmas morning again, and there was proof that she had not been overlooked. Suddenly she could not think of him any more as Mr. Chandler. He was not Dane, either. He was my attorney, my counsel. She began to trill in her mind little phrases: *On advice of my counsel . . . You will hear from my attorney. . . .* Oh, my God—what a relief!

She returned to the phone conversation. "Frankly, that's

90

just what I anticipated," Chandler was saying. "And you know what I think about it! You can expect me to give my client the fullest protection!" He slammed down the receiver. "Insolent bastard!"

He drummed his fingers on the desk in an irritated tat-a-tat, the only nervous gesture she had seen him use. From this, in view of his former restraint, she could guess at the turbulence in him, the genuine violence of his emotion.

"They're not yielding an inch," he said to her in a hard voice, and she was astonished by the cold gray marble look of his eyes. "Your hearing is to be closed—secret as a Star Chamber. And one of the most damnable things about it is that they can say anything they please about you later, and you have no recourse whatever! The gentlemen are privileged—as you certainly know—and nobody can sue them for libel. Furthermore—" He paused and looked at her steadily. "Furthermore, you *won't* be permitted to have counsel. You'll have to go it alone."

Her elation collapsed; but she clung stubbornly to a new feeling which seemed to her of the utmost importance. "No—" she said, "no, I won't be wholly alone. I have the knowledge that you and Abe are behind me. You don't know how much that helps!"

# 11.

THE windows were wide open, and the early evening seemed no cooler than the day. The sheer white organdy curtains hung inert; the only movement was the flutter of moth wings outside the screen. Faith, suddenly rebellious at convention, had refused to draw the shades while undressing—in the forlorn hope that at least a little coolness might be wafted in.

The air was too hot and too sticky for clothing, and she sat before her mirrored dressing table in brassière and panties, removing cold cream from her face. An electric fan on the floor hummed like her thoughts; but the fan's humming was mechanically smooth and impersonal, while her thoughts were chaotic and vividly intimate.

Tonight she felt rebellious about everything. The sensation of fighting back from a corner had not left her. She had come home at her regular time, just as if she had spent the day at the office—trusting to luck that Thatcher had not tried to reach her during working hours. When he greeted her without a challenge, she was reassured. The deadline on telling him about the pink paper—and about Dane Chandler—was not yet. One thing above all else she did not want tonight: conversation with Thatcher. Thank God he was going out for an evening of poker—or so he said.

A whiff of Thatcher's cologne floated to her: *Aphrodisia for Men.* Her lips tightened with a slight ironic smile, and she remembered her thoughts twenty-four hours ago in front of Jean Matou's window. The lacey French aphrodisiacs had been forgotten completely, in competition with a more compelling pursuit: survival. Curiously, she felt no need of Thatcher now, no need whatever. It was almost as if she had never known him, and her body had been shorn both of past desires and future passion. She was struck with a sudden skepticism of instinct, wondering if she would ever want him again.

She finished the cold cream, and, now without make-up, looked at herself critically in the mirror. It had been years since she had indulged in a narcissistic orgy, examining her whole body and wondering how she would appear when she was older. There seemed little perceptible change, except that the shadows in her eyes were deeper. The smooth face, the high cheekbones, the dark eyebrows like a broken brush-stroke, the wide rich mouth all were essentially unchanged. No, only the sharpest observer would find much difference in her face—though she knew, within, that the face now belonged to an adult and not to an adolescent.

But the changes in her body, she thought, would be obvious to anyone who had known her in the past. She stripped off her brassière with a gesture of indignation. Sweater girl, indeed! How unfair of Thatcher! When he talked like that, he revealed more than his attitude toward his wife: he revealed also his contempt for all women! With her left hand she weighed tentatively her right breast: she was fully a woman now, as she should be—but she was not slack. The nipple pointed upward and she did not need to wear a bra unless she chose. Dane Chandler had been conscious of her body; she had seen it in his eyes—and his response had not been, like Thatcher's, mockingly unfavorable.

She smoothed back her shoulder-length hair, tawny

blonde, in an unconscious stroking movement, as though she wished to soothe and reassure herself. She needed reassurance, she thought, not only because of the ominous threat implicit in the pink paper—but because any woman who is being wasted needs reassurance. There was something intrinsically damaging in the knowledge that Thatcher had made no effort to touch her in a month—however relieved she might be that he had left her alone. Was it worthwhile for a woman to try to keep up her appearance, when her husband had made plain that he no longer loved her? That quick appraising glance of Chandler's—oh, so slight and quick!—had been so very reassuring. She had to admit that was part of the reason she felt so secure in his hands.

The sharp initial clack of Thatcher's electric razor sounded, then gave way to a steady, offensive buzzing entirely different from the soothing hum of the electric fan. She recalled that charming scene in *Victoria Regina*, where the naive young Queen is enchanted by the Prince Consort's shaving . . . imagine a re-take with one of these zzzzzuzzing mechanical things of Thatcher's! She had laughed aloud at the Queen; but had she not sat this very afternoon and gazed at Dane Chandler with such a look as Victoria had given the Prince Consort? She came near blushing, now, at the thought. Something had happened to her in Chandler's presence—something which had left one part of her floating dreamily ever since.

What kind of a wife would a man like Dane Chandler pick? The question nettled, then left a vacancy, an ache. She would take good care never to meet his wife, if she could help it. How unbearable to discover that he too had made a mistake in marriage! Better never to know!

There had been an ebb and flow between them . . . a harmony . . . a common pulse beat. She was swept by a mysterious loneliness; tears formed, seeped slowly from her eyes.

The electric shaver stopped. Thatcher came into the room in shorts and T-shirt, the shaver in his hand. Obliquely he looked at her.

"What are you crying about?" he said.

"I don't know."

He said nothing, but without warning bent and kissed her on the back of the neck with unusual tenderness.

She dried the tears with kleenex and went on undressing.

In the shower, she was able to relax to a degree. Her skin pinked and refreshed, she slipped on a thin white nightgown and began to pick up the clothes which she had thrown helter-skelter. She had learned to force this routine, because Thatcher made almost a fetish of neatness—and tomorrow morning, with the hearing before her, would be no morning to invite a quarrel over sloppy habits. After a stringent day at the office, it had always seemed such a relief to be able to toss your stockings and underthings wherever you damned pleased! But no more. . . .

The picking-up accomplished, she went into Jeanie's room for a goodnight look. The child was sleeping peacefully. She had a sweet, faintly milky odor, like a little baby. Faith stroked the brown ringlets for a moment, kissed the damp brow. Sighing, she returned to her own big four-poster bed with its white muslin canopy.

She had told Thatcher she had a headache, was retiring early. Actually, she was emotionally exhausted. Until she lay flat on the bed she had not realized the pink paper incident was proving such a strain. She resolved to sleep, and with stubborn persistence kept her eyes closed, and counted. The nightgown constricted her and the sheets were hot to the flesh. To relax, she imagined the unreeling of an endless hose —and then laughed at herself for having chosen a Freudian symbol. Her dreams lately had been so full of symbols: Thatcher assaulting her with a knife or a dueling pistol—but she was not terrified. And sometimes at night, half-waking, half-sleeping, she had created fantasies in which she met the Norwegian lieutenant again. She tried that now, but the pink paper intruded.

She had to get her thoughts away from the subpena and its absurdity. Her fear of telling Thatcher about it was convincing proof to her that the time had come for some new, decisive action on their relationship . . . perhaps another effort at separation. Perhaps this time it would succeed.

The evening of the first try had been almost a duplicate of last night at Mrs. Beverly's, but in winter—shortly after a session with a psychiatrist. Having made a decision to leave Thatcher, she had been unable to put the decision into effect, unable even to force herself to broach the subject to him. Opportunities arose, but she kept thinking: maybe things will take care of themselves, maybe things between us will improve! The moment finally came with a quarrel about so trivial a thing as her evening wrap.

Starting home in the car, he had said, "Faith, why don't you jar loose with some of your Government dough and buy a new fur coat? That moth-eaten polecat you wear makes me feel embarrassed!"

He was more than half drunk, and she told herself she ought not to give way. But her nerves were too frazzled. "Oh Jesus!" she said. "Who do you think finally paid for the car you're driving? I'll trade you the car for a new fur coat!"

It was true. The flashy yellow Packard had taken two years of careful saving, two years of denial on Faith's part. He had

96

left the convertible with her very cavalierly when he went into the Navy. As it turned out, he always needed cash for something and never sent the payments. By now the canary yellow had faded to a dreary buff, the fenders were dented and scratched, the chromium had rusted, and the top leaked the bitter winter wind of the night.

"Oh, Christ!" he said. "Always throwing your superiority up to me! I've got a bellyful!"

In the alternating brightness from the streetlights they passed, she could see that Thatcher's mouth was set grimly, that his lower jaw protruded like a child's in a tantrum. When he stopped for traffic signals, he slammed on the brakes so that the tires skidded; and, starting up again, he deliberately ground the gears as though he wanted to destroy them.

"Thatcher," she said quietly, "—we don't get along any more. I think we ought to get a divorce. I'm going to leave you."

He exploded. "You're crazy!" he cried. "You're absolutely out of your wits! I don't understand how you can even *think* such a thing, let alone *say* it! You've got to take it back!" His voice sounded frightened, so much so that his emotion seemed incredible to her.

"You're just talking!" she parried with intenseness. "You know you're not in love with me any more—haven't been for a long time. As for me, I just feel numb. You don't stir me to any emotion except wanting to be left alone! I'm fed up, too! Fed up with drinking, fed up with Mrs. Beverly and her parasites, fed up with your sly criticism which always makes me seem inferior—and particularly inferior to your mother! I want a divorce!"

He did not answer, but gunned the car as though anxious

97

to get home. When they reached their house, however, he did not stop, but drove on at a reckless speed.

"Thatcher!" she said in alarm, "—where are you going?"

"Riding," he said. "We're going riding until you change your mind!"

He reached out with a shaking hand and switched on the radio, turning up the volume very loud. The music was a Viennese waltz: *Two Hearts Beat in Three-Quarter Time*. For the moment, she did not challenge him, but sank back bewildered and exhausted on the faded red leather seat. It would be useless to appeal to him in this mood, until the peak of his violence had passed—useless, and perhaps dangerous. She could see now that she had wounded his pride more deeply than she could possibly have guessed; had, in truth, delivered such a blow at his self-esteem—so delicately, delicately balanced—that he might never do, now, what she wished. She sensed at once that he interpreted her rejection of him solely in sexual terms—oh, if only she were not so direct! If only she might have been adroit enough to have been cast off by Thatcher! Then he might have been tractable enough, even vastly relieved, at the end of their relationship. Oh, how she had muddled!

Thinking these thoughts, she was not clearly aware of the direction Thatcher was taking. With a shock she recognized landmarks which told her they were heading out of town on the Baltimore pike, the main route of heavy trucks, and likely to be dangerous from patches of ice. She glanced at the speedometer: the needle was pushing toward sixty, climbing slowly, fraction by fraction, sixty and beyond. Ahead, the car's lights were ineffectual against a swirling gloomy precipitation which threatened to become sleet. She began to long anxiously for the shrill whistle of a police patrol. She looked at Thatcher again, hunched over the wheel, peering with smouldering eyes into the darkness. She recoiled from him, for the first time distinctly afraid.

"Thatcher! Are you trying to wreck the car!"

He shrugged. "I don't give a goddam!"

The speedometer continued to climb. They were doing seventy now. A truck, a stretch of unseen ice, and—she shuddered.

"*Please*, Thatcher, stop!"

"Not until you take back what you said!"

He passed a truck lumbering along like a dinosaur. The car swayed and the tires hummed a deadly warning. It was after midnight, and all police had mysteriously vanished. The car righted and held the road. But if there had been ice. . . .

She realized suddenly that not only was she Thatcher's prisoner, he was a prisoner of himself. He could not help, in a sense, what he was doing now: it was the only way he knew to frame his defense. He possessed no power of analysis, but only reflex. He meant what he said. He would drive until the gas gave out or they were wrecked. No, he would wreck them before he was forced to stop. His urge toward self-destruction was now inflamed beyond the bounds of all reason. He would drag her along, destroy them both, leaving Jeanie— with his mother.

The speedometer needle quivered at eighty.

"Thatcher!" she screamed, "—stop, I say! Stop this! I won't divorce you! We'll try to work it out . . . but for God's sake stop!"

Instantly he took his foot off the accelerater, and the car gradually slowed. He turned off into a by-road and stopped. Then he took her in his arms and kissed her passionately.

But her lips were chilled with fear, and she could not respond. She pushed him away, her teeth chattering. "Oh,

Thatcher," she cried; "—what a dreadful thing you've done!"

He reacted instantly. "Have I?" he said; "—what have *you* done! And you'll pay for it someday, too, by Christ!"

At these memories she was tossing now, a million miles from sleep. She almost envied Thatcher, out somewhere dissolving his most repressive self in alcohol and oblivion. Food, she exclaimed to herself; food, that was what she needed! A glass of milk, a cracker, a couple of aspirins!

She switched on the bed lamp, and the first object she saw was the clock. Only eleven! Exactly twelve hours from this instant, she thought, I'll be standing before— Her heart quickened, and her gown clung to her body with sweat.

Her eyes strayed, became fixed on Thatcher's photograph in a leather frame beside the clock. Thatcher, at the age of fifteen, decked out in the snappy uniform of his military school. She had asked him, soon after they were married, for the photograph of himself he liked best—and this was the one he had chosen. He looked very handsome in the uniform, very erect and arrogant. He had assumed the dramatic self-confidence of a general with thousands of robots to command. This was Thatcher, then, as he visualized himself at his best—Thatcher at the very peak of his life: age fifteen.

But something about the Thatcher of the photograph suited very well the Thatcher of the last few days. She puzzled a moment, and knew: he was staring at her with the same mockingly triumphant smile.

At this recognition, she felt a strong subjective shock, which became fear cumulative almost to terror. She huddled on the bed, and for a long time she sobbed over the mess that had been made of her life.

# 12.

YESTERDAY morning's pretense of going to the office was not again necessary, as Thatcher—very restless and apparently more saturated than usual—was still sleeping when she left the house. Nevertheless, she left at her usual time, that Thatcher might not wake and find her at home. She caught a cab and directed it straight to Capitol Hill, feeling thankful that she did not have to face Mr. Cunningham; he had become so repugnant to her.

In an effort to make a good impression on the members of the Committee, she had chosen one of her most attractive outfits: a pearl gray shantung dress with a rainbow sash, red sandals, a short string of oversize red wooden beads, and a red straw bag . . . altogether, she thought, a vogueish ensemble—but not too much so. She was satisfied with her appearance, satisfied that she looked like any one of hundreds of thousands of middle-class American women—except, of course, she was different. She was one distinct and unique personality: Faith Robles Vance.

She had time to kill, and she decided to spend it like any average sightseer. The day was overcast and murky, so that the marble buildings, lacking sharp delineation of line and shadow, gave the impression of great masses of stone . . . cold, even vaguely forbidding. She stood in front of the long flights of steps leading up to the colonnaded Supreme Court building and studied the inscription on the pediment: *Equal Justice Under Law.* That was what Dane Chandler believed in, she thought; perhaps someday, a better day, he would become a Justice of the Supreme Court. Who knew? Stranger things had happened. While she thought this over, she paused and smoked a cigarette by one of the majestic fountains. She had almost finished the cigarette before she noticed the slight tremor in her hand. Was it caused by thoughts of Chandler, she wondered, or by the imminence of the hearing?

She rambled on past the Neptune bronzes, and up the many steps to the Library of Congress; she had decided to inspect once again the Declaration of Independence. She recalled her father's pride when she had memorized it at school, and how he loved for her to recite it, with gestures. What an enthusiastic American he had become! The parchment was enshrined as always in the polished bronze cabinet, protected by yellow glass and an armed guard standing at attention. These words, she thought, and the Gettysburg address, were the greatest in the English language.

*We hold these truths to be self-evident: that all men are created equal; that they are endowed by their Creator with inherent and unalienable rights; that among these are life, liberty, and the pursuit of happiness. . . .*

She glanced compulsively at her watch; not yet time, but almost. She would ease along toward the old House Office Building: it would never do to be late. As she left the shrine, she had the sensation that the guard was watching her. How silly to think this! Of course he watched everyone, and most of all—probably—pretty girls.

Precisely on the dot of eleven, she entered the anteroom of the Committee's hearing chamber. A dark-haired, pimply-faced girl (some Congressman's relative, Faith thought) was seated at a small desk, typing in desultory fashion. Oh, my, Faith thought, *she* wouldn't last fifteen minutes at Mr. Cunningham's office!

"I'm Faith Vance," she announced.

The girl checked a sheet of paper. "Uh-huh," she said without looking up, "—just sit anywhere. They'll get to you directly." She went on typing as though she had not been disturbed.

Faith chose one end of a long, straight-backed bench, uncushioned and badly scuffed from years of service. As she sat down, she became aware that her chest felt tight and her stomach queasy. She was reacting as if she actually had something to be afraid of. Apparently just being under suspicion was enough to create a sense of guilt for a non-existent crime. . . . She waited.

She stared at the fifteen-foot double doors to the hearing room, closed tight and muffling the occasional shouts which she could hear from the other side. She watched particularly the big brass doorknobs, decorated with intricate, rococo designs copied from European palaces. When the doorknobs turned, she told herself, her time would be at hand. . . .

A half hour later the knobs turned, the doors opened, and Faith tensed in readiness. Three angry, red-faced men came out, accompanied by a guard. The doors slammed shut, and the men went away muttering. The expression on the guard's face was one of amused scorn.

"Who were those men?" Faith hesitantly asked the girl at the typewriter.

"Labor leaders," the girl said in a bored, languid voice. "Yesterday one was cited for perjury, one for contempt. Maybe the third one will be let go."

"Why were they cited?"

"One talked too much, one wouldn't talk, and I don't know about the third one. Maybe he testified against the others."

"Oh!"

The typewriter clacked on in haphazard fashion. Faith waited.

"It's getting hot in here," Faith said.

"Is it?" the girl replied. "It's air-conditioned."

"Oh," Faith said.

After a while, one of the brass doorknobs turned, and Jim Grayson came out of the hearing room, carrying a sheaf of papers. Faith recognized him at once, in a burst of loathing, but he did not appear to notice her.

He threw the papers down on the typist's desk, and said curtly, "Take care of these!"

Then he turned toward Faith, and momentarily his placid face betrayed astonishment. "Why, it's you!" he said, as though he had expected her to be someone else. He sauntered over to her. "Well, this *is* a pleasant surprise!"

"Yes, it's odd, isn't it?" she said, noticing his fingers again. They seemed even more white and puffy than when they had held the mint julep.

"The Committee is adjourning for lunch now," Grayson said. "You wouldn't care to join me?"

"I—I have . . . ," she weighed the possibilities, "I really must. . . ." She knew that she couldn't face eating with this man even if it meant that she might somehow—"I'm sorry," she said, "I usually skip lunch in this awfully hot weather. I'm really not hungry." She could smell liquor on his breath.

"Well, you needn't wait here," he said, and added sharply, "but be sure to be back by two o'clock."

He returned to the hearing room, and slammed the big door behind him.

104

Dazed, Faith got up and smoothed her skirt. Two o'clock! Apparently they had no conception of schedules, and considered everyone they called as completely at their service! Perhaps she had better phone Dane Chandler now, instead of waiting until after the hearing, as he had instructed. No, there was no use. What could she say? Merely that the thing was dragging. He would expect that. She had troubled him enough already; she would wait until it was all over.

Nevertheless, the thought of talking to Chandler consoled her, and she forgot part of her irritation as she escaped from the anteroom into the long sepulchral corridor.

The lunch hour passed quickly. She had fish and chips at a little hole-in-the-wall restaurant, and though the sweltering day was abominable for greasy food, she scarcely knew what she was eating. Lunch finished, she wandered over to the Capitol building, continuing her sightseeing tour. The House had not been convoked, but the Senate was in session, having met, as usual, at noon. She slipped into the gallery and listened for a few minutes. The Senators were debating military appropriations, but all the arguments seemed to be in favor. Depressed, Faith decided that she had heard enough.

She returned to the House Office Building, and was puzzled at the complete hush which had come over the marble hallways. Other than the guard at the entrance, there seemed to be no life about; the atmosphere was tomblike. She walked as silently as she could, afraid of making noise. Something about the place seemed in association with another part of her life. Then she got the connection: there was, in spite of the marble, a curious court-house smell here—a blend of odors . . . soggy cigars in brass spitoons, disinfectants in public toilets, must bred from sunlessness. These were the odors which had offended her when she went with Thatcher to the old court-house in Tappahannock for their marriage license. . . .

She discovered that she was lost. She had forgotten the number of the hearing room, and her instinct for direction failed her. She strayed into a corridor which seemed to lead in the right direction, and came to a door which appeared to be the right one. She opened the door, and was amazed to find an enormous room filled with long rows of desks, at which girls were busily at work on card index files. Along the sides of the room were scores of file cabinets, no doubt filled with similar cards. She shut the door quickly: she knew where she was, without being told. How ironic, she thought, that the Committee would leave such a room unguarded! She fled down the corridor, now heedless of noise, and opened another door. It was the anteroom with the listless dark-haired typist.

She sat down, panting, on the hard wooden bench. The girl took no notice of her. Faith glanced at her watch. Exactly two o'clock. She waited, expectant.

Shortly Jim Grayson breezed in, nodded to her, and disappeared behind the great double doors. She speculated on whether the Congressmen had arrived early, or used another entrance. She knew they were there, because the muffled sounds had begun again.

Time passed. Grayson drifted in and out with papers, nodding on each occasion. As he opened or shut the doors, the volume of sound would rise or fall. She was too confused to catch the words.

She sat in a kind of stupor, not thinking. Now and then she smoked a cigarette, and once she burned her fingers when she failed to notice how short the cigarette had become. She began to long for the typist to say something to her, something that would indicate a glimmer of feminine sympathy between them. But the girl said nothing. Evidently people who were subpenaed were beyond the pale of humankind. . . .

Jim Grayson reappeared, and said casually with a smirk, "By the by, turns out I knew your husband in the Navy. Only man I ever saw who could manage to smuggle liquor aboard every trip! I tried it, but I got the brig. Oh, well, Thatcher Vance helped me over the driest spots. How did you happen to marry such a thirsty fellow, anyway . . . ?"

Faith looked at him, dumb. How could she answer for him a question which she could not answer for herself? It would take all afternoon to explain; and probably she could convince no one but herself.

Grayson waited for an answer, but receiving none, said, "Oh well—I'm a thirsty fellow too!" He ambled to the door opening into the corridor, and paused. "Don't be mad at us," he called back in a kidding tone, "—we'll get to you sooner or later. Have fun!" Then he was gone.

Her mind played with his words about Thatcher. She had so much hoped that Thatcher would settle down after he came out of the Navy, and her disappointment had been proportionate to her hope. She had known readjustment would be trying for him—it was hard to catch the swing of civilian life. Every leave he had gotten drunk, and stayed that way—plastered. But each time he apologized before he left—apologized so contritely and sincerely. On leave, he seemed to want to keep her in evening dress, as though his marriage was only part of a glorious shore party. Though she had gotten little satisfaction out of his visits, all this was easy to forgive in a man who was cooped up on a ship at sea through a long, long war.

But liquor smuggled on board, drinking with a crony like Grayson! Her heart leaped with fright. How well, actually, did Thatcher know Grayson? Did Thatcher ever see him any more? Thatcher had never mentioned him, never once. Thank God Grayson had not, at Mrs. Beverly's party, realized she was Thatcher's wife! Or had he—and concealed it?

But now, now—would Jim Grayson go to Thatcher with the whole horrible tale of the pink paper?

She could feel sweat forming under her arms, across her back; she could feel the tension between her shoulder blades, within her breast. She got up and took a step forward, as though about to run away. She glanced covertly at the girl typist.

The girl looked up. "Well?" she said.

"Nothing," Faith said; "I was merely straightening my dress." She sat down again, her heart thumping at a fearful rate, her lips swollen and sticky. "Water—" she said helplessly.

"There's a cooler in that closet," the girl said, indicating with her head. "Get yourself a drink."

Faith drank, gulping papercupful after cupful. When she finished, she gasped, "Oh my!" and returned to the bench.

She realized that she was physically and nervously exhausted. She was sure she would begin to scream if the waiting went on much longer. Her watch said five o'clock.

Gradually the earlier torpor returned to her.

She was about to go to sleep when the bronze knobs turned and the great double doors opened. A tall raw-boned man with bushy pepper-gray hair appeared, and stood motionless. In a flash of fright she recognized him from Dane Chandler's description: P. J. Garrison, the Committee's chief investigator. He was a renegade radical, and was noted for his castigations of his former friends.

"Faith Robles Vance?" he said. His manner was severe and cold.

108

"Yes," she breathed.

"Come in," he said softly. "It's your turn now."

Automatically she hitched up her brassière strap, and followed him.

# 13.

THE hearing room opened before her, grandiose and impressive. She was reminded of a Hollywood set, designed for a scene in *The Great Waltz*. The room was flanked by rows of Ionic columns on either side, and dominated by a giant crystal chandelier. Surely the Emperor Franz Josef would appear at any moment, in medals and full panoply, accompanied by a flourish of trumpets.

Newsreel cameras and a battery of kleig lights were placed strategically toward the center, and farther forward was a large press table with scattered microphones. Obviously careful attention had been given to publicity—when wanted. But the very absence now of press and audience was ominous in its implications. Faith knew that the hearing would be more perfunctory, less restrained. The Committee members would act and talk as they pleased, and who might gainsay them?

A uniformed guard was stationed inside the door, and Faith caught a whiff of spearmint gum as she passed. At the far end of the room, five Congressmen sat behind a massive semi-circular desk mounted on a dais, like archangels on Judgment Day. At a table on a lower level sat two stenographers. Uncounted rows of folding chairs were empty. Through the center aisle of these chairs Faith walked, following Garrison.

"Stand there," Garrison said, and indicated a spot which might have been the hub of the semi-circular desk.

She stood stiffly at attention, clutching her red straw purse, while Garrison took his place near the stenographers. Of the five Congressmen, she recognized only three—and she would have been sure of them, from Chandler's descriptions, even without the printed name plates on the desk before each man.

The Chairman, Howard Skinner, sat in the center. He was a wizened man, too small for the big desk. He had a heavily lined face, with sagging pouches under his eyes, and a shock of white hair. He fondled the gavel lovingly.

On the Chairman's right sat Chauncey Daiken, a Southern Democrat, the unacknowledged leader of the Committee, its real power and dominant personality. He was so much a type as to be a caricature of himself: square-jawed, leather-lunged, cigar-chewing. His tousled straight blonde hair fell uncurbed over his forehead; his eyes roamed restlessly around the room and finally focused on Faith's body. She colored, and looked beyond him.

On the Chairman's left sat Modie Vincent, a young man, a liberal Democrat. He had very dark hair clipped short, so that it looked like a soft animal pelt, and bright black eyes. His face was thin and sallow, and his chin tapered to a point. He was not unlike a young college instructor; involuntarily Faith was reminded of Mr. Cunningham. He played with a yellow pencil, turning it end to end and running it slowly through the thumb and forefingers of his right hand. His expression was impassive, inscrutable.

The other two Congressmen, Republicans, Faith thought,

110

looked roughly like down-at-heel smalltown businessmen who couldn't meet a payroll, and so had turned to politics to make a living. They were probably expert orators on private enterprise. Middle-aged, they seemed tired out.

Suddenly Chairman Skinner banged the gavel as though quieting a large and disorderly audience. "We sit today as a Subcommittee," he intoned in a sonorous voice. "Administer the oath!"

Garrison shoved a gilt-edged Bible across his table, and motioned Faith to put her hand on it. She did so, and Garrison said, in a rapid falsetto: "Doyousweartotellthetruthand nothingbutthetruthsohelpyouGod?"

"I do," Faith said, trembling.

"What is your name?" Chairman Skinner said.

Surprised, Faith answered in a clear voice, "Faith Robles Vance."

"Mrs. or Miss?"

"Mrs.," she said, still more surprised.

"You are employed by the Federal Government as an administrative assistant, in the Executive Branch?"

"Yes."

"How long—?"

"Eight years. I started as a stenographer."

"You have gathered a great deal of information about the Government in this time?"

"Why, I—of course, anyone would have to."

Chairman Skinner looked at her sternly. "But you have also been interested in foreign governments!"

"Hold it just a minute, Mr. Chairman," Daiken interrupted, "—we can pursue that line a little later. Right now I want to find out a few salient facts about this young woman." His voice had a Southern softness, a cadence which sounded anything but harsh or dangerous.

111

"Why certainly, Congressman," Chairman Skinner said. "The witness is yours."

Chauncey Daiken clamped hard on his cigar, so that it tilted at a thirty-degree angle. The stenographers hurriedly turned to fresh pages, as though they knew what was coming. The two nondescript Congressmen slumped more markedly in their chairs, and one of them leaned forward and put his head in his hands. Modie Vincent remained impassive.

"Young woman," Daiken said, his eyes narrowing, "—are you an atheist?"

"Why, I—" Faith paused, remembering Dane Chandler's warning. This question was intended to set a precedent, Chandler had said. *By law* (and she could remember his exact words, even in her present excitement) *the Committee is empowered to inquire into only those matters pertinent to the investigation. Under the Constitution, any man may believe anything he chooses about religion—there is no standard American belief or non-belief. Such a question cannot possibly be pertinent to Americanism. If you answer this one, yes or no, they'll follow through with others which can destroy you—though you're guilty of nothing!*

"Quit stalling!" Daiken said. "Go on—answer!"

She felt faint, and something inside her seemed to be swelling as though it would burst. "I—I—don't consider that question pertinent," she finally managed to say. "Religion is a private matter. I—"

"You defy the Committee?" Daiken shouted.

The shout frightened her. She was about to give in, answer Daiken's question, when Chandler's quiet words came back to her: *You must not let them pillory you, browbeat you. They will if they can. Only you can stop them, by standing up to them.*

112

"I don't defy the Committee," she said in a low voice. "I'm trying to cooperate with you. I'll be glad to answer if you'll ask me proper questions."

Chairman Skinner rapped sharply with his gavel. "It's not your prerogative to admonish the Committee, Miss," he warned. "You answer the questions respectfully or you'll get in trouble!"

For a moment there was a lull, as though breath was being drawn for the next round. The stenographers waited, their pencils poised expectantly. Chauncey Daiken struck a match and re-lit his cigar.

"Have you—" he said calmly, puffing smoke, "—any Jewish blood in your veins?"

She was utterly astounded. "Why, not that I know of!" she said promptly.

"You're not *sure?*"

"How could anyone be sure?"

Daiken turned toward the Chairman. "She's not sure!" he said, and laughed. Then he leaned over and whispered in Skinner's ear, and the acoustics were such that Faith heard every word: "She's stacked like a Rachel, all right!"

She flushed, and for the first time her dark eyes smouldered hatred. She felt self-conscious as she had not since Thatcher first began to taunt her.

"Perhaps—" Daiken said with an intonation of elaborate courtesy, "perhaps you'll be good enough to tell us if you associate with Nigras?"

"What do you mean by *associate?*"

He knocked the ashes from his cigar into an ashtray. "I must point out, young lady, that it is not your business to ask us questions. It's *our* business to ask *you* questions. Do you associate, or have you ever associated, with Nigras?"

113

"Everyone in America associates with Negroes!"

"Mr. Chairman!" Daiken roared, "—this young woman is incorrigible! If this keeps up I'll be forced to move for a contempt citation!"

Chairman Skinner rapped with his gavel. "Answer the questions!" he said, frowning.

"I'll try one more," Daiken said. "Do you believe in free love?"

"That's ridiculous!" Faith said, coloring again. "Of course not!"

"Well," Daiken said, "we do seem to have gotten one thing definite out of this young woman!"

"I have a question," the Chairman said. "Do you, or do you not, believe in democracy?"

"Of course I believe in democracy," she said, almost crying. "I believe there ought to be a lot more of it!" She looked at their faces; they were eyeing her intently now. There flashed across her vision the cover of a comic book she had noticed in the restaurant at lunch. A fair-haired girl, stripped nearly naked, bound and gagged, was being tormented with sharp sticks by a band of evil-looking men. On the men's faces was deep sadistic satisfaction, and she had shuddered. It was only a comic book . . . but now she felt herself bound and gagged, tormented by the invisible sharp sticks of men's fantasy.

She noticed that Garrison, who seemed to frown perpetually, had scribbled a note and was passing it up to Chauncey Daiken. The Congressman chewed his cigar as he read it. To Faith he said brusquely: "Do you know a man named Abe Stone?"

"Yes," she said.

"Ah!" he said, and then, to the stenographers: "Make a special note of that! She knows Abe Stone!"

114

Daiken continued: "How often do radical groups meet at your house?"

"They don't!" she said, indignant at the way he had phrased the question. Was he referring to the times she had lent her house for Union parties? she wondered.

"That conflicts with information we have received from a reliable source!" Daiken said. "Don't forget you're under oath, and the penalties for perjury are severe!"

"The foreign thing is more important," Chairman Skinner said impatiently. "I want to know: Miss, did you or did you not work for Red Spain?"

Faith choked. "If you mean, did I work for the Loyalists against the Fascists, the answer is YES! What I did was little enough, but I'm proud of it!"

Daiken said: "So you admit a direct connection with a foreign power?"

"I admit no such thing! I also worked for Bundles for Britain—does that make me a British agent!"

"What were the names of the people who instructed you in the Spanish work?" Chairman Skinner said.

"That's a matter of public record," Faith said, blazing. "You can find them out by consulting newspapers of the time!"

Faith turned toward Modie Vincent, who had once made speeches in favor of aid to the Spanish Loyalists, and mutely appealed to him for help. He returned her glance with a flickering smile, but said nothing. Suddenly he busied himself with packing tobacco into a curved pipe and lighting it. He began to puff leisurely, emitting a cloud of smoke. The pipe seemed too large and too heavy for his narrow face.

"Miss," the Chairman said solemnly, "—I want to warn you now that I don't like your attitude. You have not shown a proper respect toward the elected representatives of the

115

people, in the way you have phrased your replies. You don't seem to realize you are appearing before an official instrument of the United States Congress!"

"Oh, I do, I do!" she said faintly; and while she was speaking, one of the unknown Congressmen—the one who had put his head in his hands—got up and wandered off as though he was thinking about something wholly unconnected with the hearing. He disappeared through a small door behind the dais.

"Well, now that we understand one another, we can come to the point!" Chauncey Daiken barked. "Are you a citizen of the United States?"

"Yes, of course."

"But your father's name was Rubles?"

"Yes, Robles." She corrected his pronunciation.

"Spaniard, huh?"

"He was born in Spain, yes. But he—"

Daiken pounced. "Have *you* got a birth certificate?"

"Why, no—" she said, bewildered.

"How can you prove you're a U. S. citizen, then?" He was triumphant.

"My mother told me where and when I was born!"

"Will she swear to it?"

"She's—she's dead." Suddenly a new fear stitched through Faith; but she did not know what she was afraid of.

"Ah!" Daiken said, and turned again to the stenographers. "Get that!" He paused and took the cigar out of his mouth. His eyes gleamed. "Are you a Commonist?"

"Why—" She was about to answer, when Chandler's flat but warning voice came back to her. *Political belief, whatever it may be, like religious belief, is an improper subject for investigation by the Committee. The Committee should be concerned exclusively with overt acts designed to overthrow*

116

*this government, and overt acts exclusively. To deny free-*
*dom of political belief is to establish thought control, and is*
*a true subversion of the Constitution. Don't let them bully*
*you!*

She caught her breath. "I object to the question as outside
the scope of the Committee! My personal beliefs should be
of no concern here! I want my objection entered in the record—!"

Daiken did not let her finish. "You refuse to answer the
question?" he snapped.

"I don't refuse!" Faith cried. "I object! And I claim my
privilege to object, for the record!"

"You have no privilege to object!" Chairman Skinner said.
"That's just a legal fiction spouted by a bunch of radical lawyers. It's my duty to warn you that you can be cited for contempt of this Committee, and that conviction may carry with
it a one thousand dollar fine and a year in prison! Do you
want to go to prison? Think twice before defying the Committee! Now answer the question!"

"Considering the spirit in which the question is asked, I
can't answer it," Faith said. Her heart was beating wildly
now, she felt stifled and dying, as though she could not
awake from the horror of a grotesque nightmare. Oh my
God! she thought—if only Dane were here to help me! She
noticed that again Garrison, frowning, was passing up a note
to Daiken.

Daiken read the note, and said stealthily, "If you aren't
a Red, how does it happen that we have a report, from an
authentic source, that you *brazenly* display on the piano
in your living room a bust of—Karl Marx!"

"It's a lie!" Faith cried, her voice shaking. "The bust is Mozart! Go and see for yourself . . . !" She was gasping for
breath, now.

117

"She denies it!" Daiken shouted. "In the face of the evidence—!"

Impelled by a blind force of resistance, a desire to strike back, Faith cried out: "I want to make a statement! I want to know who my accusers are! I want the right of cross-examination! I want counsel! I want to make a state—"

"Quiet!" the Chairman yelled, banging his gavel. "Quiet! It's entirely too late in the day to make a statement. We're all tired and hungry. You just write out something on a piece of paper, Miss, and maybe we'll put it in the record. In the meantime we'll take under advisement the matter of your contempt of this Committee. Hearing adjourned!"

"If I show contempt for this Committee, it's because the Committee has shown contempt for my American rights!" Faith cried.

But no one was listening.

The Chairman gave a final rap with the gavel, like a reflex action, and the four Congressmen got up in a body. With the frowning Garrison, the stenographers, and the guard, they walked out the small door—leaving Faith alone and trembling in the great room. The abrupt, contrasting quiet was heavy and oppressive. Suddenly she realized that Jim Grayson had not returned.

She groaned aloud, "Oh my God!" and collapsed into one of the folding chairs. She was ill, exhausted.

She had an impulse to feel herself, to look in a mirror, to be sure that this mangled creature was she. I feel like a bug, she thought, a bug which has been stepped on—but crushed, not killed. Slow death; that's it. A scrap from *Alice in Wonderland* flitted out of her childhood: *"I'll be judge, I'll be jury," said cunning old Fury; "I'll try the whole cause, and condemn you to death!"*

She laughed hysterically.

For the first time she noticed the clock high in the wall behind the empty dais. The hands said ten minutes past six. Quick, an inner voice whispered, call Dane Chandler!

Frantically she ran out of the hearing room, into the silent corridor, through the pillared entrance, down the flight of marble steps into the street. The outside air struck her like a blast from an overheated oven, and suddenly she began to sweat. The evening sky was molten.

She found, at length, a public phone booth in the little restaurant where she had lunched, and in the stuporous heat of the booth dialed Chandler's office—a number she had memorized. The line rang and rang, but there was no answer. The office was closed for the day.

The odor of fried fish assaulted her.

She darted out of the booth, and with nervous, self-obstructive haste, thumbed through the telephone directory. At last she found the C's. She ran her finger along the line of Chandlers, but failed to find what she was seeking. She went through them again.

No Dane Chandler was listed.

Her heart jetted, and for an instant she thought she was going to faint.

*Part Two*

# 1.

SHE struggled helplessly and the dream went on. She was bound hand and foot, and the Chairman was pounding with his gavel near her head. She uttered a sound that was half-moan, half-cry, and in the dream could hear herself. Gradually consciousness began to come back to her, and the pounding noise became louder.

Thatcher was beating her pillow with a newspaper.

In relief that the dream was not real, she gave a silly little laugh. The newspaper cudgel was the technique they had used for housebreaking Licky. Was Thatcher teasing? Then his words formed themselves into understandable sounds, and as their meaning penetrated, the laughter gurgled into silence.

Cold frenzy was in his voice; but there was also a marked element of fright, even panic. "For Christ's sake, Faith, wake up!" he was crying. "Wake up! Wake up!"

She summoned full consciousness at his alarm, defensively preparing herself for some ghastly emergency concerning Jeanie. Then Thatcher spread the newspaper in front of her face.

"Look at this!" he shouted.

There it all was, in its full horror and starkness, letters two inches high and black type: DAIKEN LISTS 39 REDS IN GOVERNMENT!

So now Thatcher knew, had gotten the full shock from picking up the paper at the breakfast table. She shivered, and glanced away from the paper to his face. It was a welter of conflicting emotions which were not as clear to her as his voice had been. She could understand the anger, the fear, even outright shame—but why the curious contrition that blended with his panic? Yet in the confusion of her own re-actions she had not time to analyze Thatcher's; she was too shattered inwardly, too defensive. She shrank back as though he had charged her with some loathsome crime, and she was guilty.

"Thatcher, I—I—"

"Listen!" he said coldly; "—last on the list, in alphabetical order: Faith Robles *Vance!*" He paused, then added in a fierce irrational burst, "Vance! You might have been careful whose name you involved!"

She tried to plead with him. "Thatcher, I'm *not* involved! It's an accident—a mistake! I'm sure it will be straightened out all right; it *has* to be! I haven't *done* anything!"

He stared at her and said nothing while she sat up in bed and shook the tawny hair back from her face. She knew that her dark eyes were dilated wide as she returned his stare without blinking. "I'm not guilty of anything," she said, in an effort to impress him again with her innocence. She longed suddenly for him to take her in his arms, caress and soothe her, assuring her that he believed in her and would fight for her.

"Thatcher, please—" she said, and her voice was filled with the longing.

"*Vance!*" he said again. The cobalt blue eyes which once

124

had smiled with invitations to dalliance now had a metallic quality. He stood before her, unbending, the newspaper clutched in his hand. He had the ramrod straightness of his picture in uniform at military school. She had never seen him so outraged, or so completely possessed by his own emotions. He seemed to be carrying on extensive conversations, all violent, within himself.

"How in the name of all that's holy," he said at last, "—do you expect me to explain this mess to people? I've got a date to play golf this morning with the boss and our biggest client: how in hell can I explain it to *them* . . . !"

"You don't have to explain it," she said slowly. "Ignore it! Nobody believes what Daiken says—and everybody knows the Committee's reputation!" In spite of herself, however, in spite of the bold words, she could not help her tones from sounding defensive.

He waved the newspaper helplessly and threw it onto the bed. "I don't know what in hell I'm going to say to all our friends."

Sudden anger swept her. "*Your* friends. I don't have to explain to mine!"

"You're a hundred per cent bitch who deserves all that's coming to you!" he said, and stalked out of the bedroom.

Faith, trembling, picked up the paper and read the news-story in detail. It made her feel physically sick. It was the same story she had read scores of times about others. In revulsion she dropped the paper.

She glanced out the window.

It was a lovely morning, a perfect day for outdoor play-time. A wispy breeze stirred the white organdy curtains, and sunshine spattered the trees like golden yellow paint from a prodigious brush. How could the earth seem so beautiful, she thought, to a person so bruised and black inside?

She was still gazing out the window when Thatcher reappeared in the doorway, and saw that she was crying.

"Faith," he said, "I'm sorry about all this. I truly am. It's just that I—"

Then he turned suddenly and left, as though about to say more than he intended to.

She was bewildered. There was contrition in his voice, but not understanding. He seemed to be apologizing for himself, without any awareness of her pain.

In their elmtree nest outside the window, baby robins chittered as their mother perched with a wiggling, juicy worm.

While Faith lingered over her breakfast coffee—which she liked to do on Saturday mornings—Jeanie sat on her lap and prattled. This was a social occasion regularly observed between them, a kind of catching-up on all that had happened during the preceding week. Faith hoped these sessions compensated a little for the blank afternoons when Jeanie came home from school and found no welcoming, reassuring mother.

"I love my teacher," Jeanie said in singsong; "an' I love Donnie, an' I love you, Faith." Then she paused, and added airily, "But of course I love my Daddy best of all!" she gave Faith a sidewise glance, as if waiting for the reaction.

"Yes, of course," Faith said, snuggling her gently. "Of course you do. And it's all right not to like your mommie sometimes when you feel like it, because you love her, too—and she loves you."

"Even when I'm bad?" Jeanie asked, with a touch of doubt.

"Even when you're naughty, I always love you," Faith said.

Jeanie sighed. "Sometimes you spank me an' forget to apologize."

"Oh, do I?" Faith laughed. "I'm sorry!"

Jeanie laughed too, and breathed contentment.

"Some pussycat," said Donnie, who had come in to clear the breakfast dishes.

Faith looked directly at her, wondering if she would comment on the newspaper headlines. Earlier, the tones of Thatcher's voice had reached the bedroom in abusive corrugations—and Faith knew that he was taking out his anger on Donnie. Often she wondered why Donnie did not leave them. But now Donnie made neither complaint of Thatcher's treatment nor mention of the headlines. She seemed as serene as ever; and in consequence, Faith felt a faint tremor of shame at the degree of her own agitation.

She hugged Jeanie, and, in a soothing rhythm (more for her own benefit than Jeanie's, she thought) began to sing an old favorite:

> "I went to the animal fair;
>     The birds and beasts were there.
> The big baboon,
>     By the light of the moon,
> Was combing his auburn hair. . . ."

The telephone rang. Faith broke off the song while Donnie answered.

"Yes, she's here," Donnie said.

"Who is it, Donnie?" Faith asked, inwardly astonished at the catch in her breath, the sudden sharp beat of her heart. Why should she be so afraid? It was absurd that a mere telephone call could induce such a reaction in her.

"It's Mis' Haswell callin' from Baltimore," Donnie said.

And Faith knew that she had betrayed herself to Donnie by the relief in her eyes.

"What's all the monkeybusiness?" said Mary Margaret's voice, clear and vibrant as it used to be at Bennington. "Faith, love, you're spread all over the Hearst press like a debutante who eloped with a jockey! For goodness' sake, give!"

"You know as much as I do," Faith said, a little testily. Sometimes she envied her ex-roommate's freewheeling unmarried freedom, and sometimes felt old, worried and tired by comparison.

Mary Margaret brushed over her words. "Love, they've printed that gorgeous picture of you they took back in the days when you were just a girl, visiting at my house. Bet enrollment in the Communist Party jumps over night, and you get tons of fan mail. 'Some Red!' Dad said when he looked at the paper; 'I always thought she ought to be in Hollywood!' "

"It's not funny," Faith said.

"I don't like the somber sound you give off," Mary Margaret said. "I'm coming right over and cheer you up!"

"Thanks, darling, but please don't. I've got enough on my hands without having to separate you and Thatcher today."

"Well, cheer up!" went on the bright voice. "Phone me once a day, and I'll tell you over and over what nonsense the whole business is! You know *that*—so don't act silly!"

"I won't."

"All right, *don't!* If they keep bothering you, I'll send the whole damn bunch a can of Rough on Rats!" She hung up.

Faith turned away from the phone with a sense of elation. Well, *some* people you could count on, anyway.

It was strange that Thatcher had always hated Mary Margaret so, she thought. The feud had begun at the wedding. Mary Margaret was her maid of honor.

She was an angular, intelligent, flat-breasted, belligerent feminist, an expert tennis player and organic chemist. Her fluffy bridesmaid dress hung awkwardly upon her, and somehow she seemed to have an excess of elbows. But she had a wonderful sense of humor, genuine laughter, and, on occasion, a sharp tongue. With Thatcher she was very polite, as though guarding herself against something—and with Faith she was all cool confidante and older sister.

In her presence, Thatcher never once unlimbered, never once acted his usual gay and charming self. He was, instead, extraordinarily stiff—even frigid—toward her.

"I expect, Miss Haswell," Thatcher said to her over drinks the first day she arrived at his mother's house, "—I expect you'll find conversation in Tidewater Virginia mighty dull. We don't know much about anything but horses and hounds."

"It all sounds interestingly inbred," she replied. "Maybe I can look up the local Juke and Kallikak families—" and would have gone on, except for Faith's warning eye.

Faith was so disturbed that on the night before the wedding she spoke to Thatcher about his attitude. "Thatcher, dear, I do wish you'd try to be a little nicer to Mary Margaret," she said tentatively. "She's very close to me—and a really swell person."

His face mottled slightly and he blurted, "What you see in her is beyond me!"

It was a personal insult. Blinded by tears of chagrin, Faith dropped the wedding present she was unwrapping. It was a Steuben glass vase, and it broke. Thatcher's face, as he picked up the pieces, was white and taut. Could it be, Faith wondered, that Thatcher was actually jealous of her old roommate? The tears had dried while she thought, and she noted, idly, an iridescent rainbow on her lashes. But she failed to feel the relief characteristic at the end of a storm.... . .

Good old Haswell!

The phone rang again. This time it was Abe Stone.

"You okay?" he said.

"Yes," she answered firmly.

"Good. I'll get the details later. Don't think this will be the end of it." He paused. "How did you like Chandler?"

The question shattered her poise; a moment passed before she could pull herself together.

"How did you like Chandler?" Stone repeated.

Short-breathed, she said, "Fine. Just fine!"

"He was friendly and gave you helpful advice?"

"Yes, very!"

"That's what I wanted to know. I understand you haven't reported the hearing to him yet. Get in touch with him on Monday. And keep on pitching. You'll be hearing from me again."

The conversation was over.

She could not believe that the question about Chandler had so unnerved her. She needed, she said to herself, to get a grip on herself. This business was doing things to the composure she was so proud of. She had reacted to his name like a schoolgirl caught drawing hearts on a blackboard. She was, she insisted, a grown woman who had no right to emotional frills.

But now she felt unaccountably gay.

"Jeanie, Jeanie—!" she called. "Time now for our Saturday shopping!" Her words had a lilting quality, and, for all their prosaic meaning, might have been transposed into song.

Her mood was now in harmony with the morning, and she and Jeanie and Licky romped along beneath the Ginkgo

130

trees, with their fan-shaped leaves, which lined the street where they were walking. She broke off a branch and gave it to Jeanie.

"Look, sweetie-pie, little Japanese fans for your dolls."

"Goody!" said Jeanie, and promptly switched Licky, who was pulling her on leash.

The old stone walls covered with English ivy, the white clapboard and red brick houses with their green shutters, even the cobbles of the Georgetown street, seemed this morning to have an extra-sensuous quality. Faith was extraordinarily aware of all tangible things, extraordinarily aware of the lights and shadows, sounds and smells of the day. She had the curious sensation of having just risen from a protracted illness in a hospital, and was now engaged in a going forth for the first time in many months. She seemed to be gifted with new eyes. The only explanation she could find for her irrational lightheartedness, she thought, was solely the sudden release from tension—the reassurance that she did not stand alone. Objectively, her situation had not changed; but somehow she felt better prepared to meet whatever might come.

The first stop on these Saturday shopping excursions was invariably the dime store, to buy Jeanie a little present. In place of a weekly allowance, which Jeanie was not yet quite old enough to handle, she was permitted to select any toy or picture book which cost no more than a quarter. Sometimes the selection consumed as much as half an hour, before Jeanie was fully satisfied with her choice, and Faith often filled the time by chatting with the salesgirl. They had become very friendly, and the salesgirl, through Jeanie, knew Faith's name. Faith, in turn, had learned that the girl had quit high school in her sophomore year to go to work. She was, like Thatcher, an emigré from Virginia, and almost as

131

flaxen as he; but unlike Thatcher, she hailed from the mountain backcountry and looked down on Tidewater aristocrats who had never learned to work with their hands. She was pretty in a simple, quiet way, and sometimes Faith secretly envied her freshness.

"Mornin', Mis' Vance," she said, and smiled at Jeanie.

"Mornin'," Jeanie said, accurately mimicking her accent —but somehow it was only funny and not offensive, the way she did it.

The two women laughed.

Just then Jeanie spotted a miniature bathinette, and began ecstatically to put the tiny rubber baby in and out. Licky became equally busy sniffing the floor.

"See by the paper, you're famous, Mis' Vance," the salesgirl said.

Caught by surprise, Faith felt herself blushing. Instantly she was on the defensive before a person who always, in the past, had proved friendly, but whom she did not really know. Suddenly she felt sullen and uncommunicative.

"You might put it that way," she answered roughly.

"Oh, I didn't mean no offense!" the girl said in embarrassed haste. "I only meant that—"

That what? Faith thought. *That what?*

The girl caught her look, and an expression almost of pity passed across her deep blue eyes. "I guess," she said, "some of you folks don't know how to take it—" She glanced about, evidently searching for the supervisor, and, not seeing him, went on in low tones: "Remember last year when all of us here was on strike? Remember what happened to *us?* Didn't you read in the paper how th' Company said we was Communist agitated, that we done it for th' Reds? Well, you know good an' well why we struck! What th' Company said was so funny we got to callin' each other Comradd! Now when I see

132

somebody plastered all over the paper, I always think what happened to us. That's what I meant. You see?"

"Oh!" Faith said, feeling a direct and personal sympathy which was, in a way, wholly outside all her previous experience. She was putting herself in this girl's shoes, partaking of someone's else life. Yet for all the differences between them, they now shared a common experience; and thus she was able to return that sympathy which only a moment before had been so willingly extended to her. She felt, in spite of all the newly frightening connotations of the word, comradeship with this girl.

"Thank you," she breathed; "—thank you so much!"

Then she paid for the bathinette, collected Jeanie and Licky, and, smiling, went on her way.

The smile stayed with her, inwardly and outwardly, for the better part of an hour.

She took Jeanie home, where her favorite friend from play-school, Billy Seagrave, was scheduled to visit. She kissed Jeanie, left hurried marketing instructions with Donnie, and dashed off to her appointment at a beauty salon. One of her few real luxuries was a periodic shampoo and hair-set by a professional, and she rationalized the cost by telling herself that she had to look nice at the office if she wanted to keep her job. The rationalization was necessary because she patronized Etienne's—one of the most expensive salons on Connecticut Avenue.

Swathed in the luxurious afterglow of the shampoo, she sat relaxing under an electric hair drier. The warm air was soothing, and she felt more nearly at peace than at any time since the ubiquitous pink paper was served upon her. The smile lingered on her lips, subdued and almost undersurface, yet nonetheless real. Several times her thoughts turned to

Thatcher, but she refused to let him intrude—she needed this little moment of peace, she told herself, to fortify her will for all the other hours of her life. She did not want to think of Thatcher, she did not want to think of trouble. It was enough now simply to be vegetable, animal, and mineral . . . to be at peace. Sometimes, in the nights, when sleeplessness drove her to consideration of how different her life might have been, she wanted to cry or scream and scream. But not now. Not now.

As she continued this emotional drowsing, the soft music from a radio in an adjoining booth gave way to the news. At first she was aware only that the newscaster's voice was pounding with the insistence of a noisy pump, until suddenly she caught her name. Her backbone stiffened with an abrupt movement and she sat upright.

Someone switched off the radio, and she heard the murmur of other voices in the booth. Now her senses were acutely alive, and she strained to hear.

The voices were female, in whispers. Two operators were talking.

"Sure, that's her," one said. "I don't know her first name, but it's her."

"She's got her nerve," the other one said.

"Don't look like a radical, that's a fact," the first one continued; "but you never can tell, these days. Why, I used to do one of the Embassy Russians, and didn't know for weeks that she was a Red! Hair was too fine, hard to set!"

"You wouldn't catch me working on a Red, if I could help it!"

"Oh, she's probably a spy all right. But she won't get nothing out of me! I'll bet she'd like to know what a British Embassy wife told me last week—but wild horses couldn't get it out of me, much less *her!*"

134

"They ought to run her out of the country! Let her go to Russia, if she likes it so much—probably where she come from, anyway!"

The voices trailed off.

In a few moments the operator, brisk and efficient-looking in her crisp white uniform, returned. "How is it, madam?" she said. "Almost dry? Are you comfortable?"

"I'm not comfortable," Faith said. "Please comb my hair and let me go."

Her heart was beating wildly, and the smile had vanished from her lips.

On the street, she wandered aimlessly, passing Jean Matou's usually magnetic window without seeing it. But her eye was caught by a newsstand. The headlines were there, bold and black, all variations on a single theme. She felt a fatalistic attraction for them, a masochistic urge to buy them all and read and re-read the terrifying news. She was about to do so, when the cover of the *New Republic* caught her attention: its lead article was an attack on the Committee.

She opened her purse, found a dime and a nickel, and was about to take up a copy of the magazine, when a new fear struck her. This was Washington. Even a child knew better than to buy publicly any publication which was leftish. She hesitated.

The fat old woman who kept the stand said in a loud voice, "*New Republic*, miss?"

From the sound of the voice the fear was crystallized. Faith dropped the coins back into her purse. "No thank you. Nothing, now. Nothing at all!"

She told herself what she had done was ridiculous, but she had to exercise conscious control to keep from running away from the stand. She was a fool, she thought. She should have bought some other paper and slipped the magazine under it. But that was an admission of secret guilt. She could not! It was her right to buy what she pleased; but the fear possessed her more strongly, conquered her. She shivered. She wanted peace; she wanted to be left alone. Entirely alone!

She imagined she heard footsteps behind her, but now she dared not turn around to look. Instead, she darted into a drugstore and sought a phone booth. With nervous fingers she dialed Dane Chandler's office, on the off-chance that he might be there. He was.

"I've got to see you!" she said desperately. "I can't wait until Monday! This business is doing something to me—I keep feeling, oh, horrible! Like things were chasing me!"

His voice twanged even flatter than she remembered, but the warmth had not gone out of it. "Why, of course," he said. "I was disappointed at not hearing from you after the Committee session. How about lunch, right away? I'll meet you at Hall's?"

"Wonderful!" she said. "Oh, wonderful!"

As she hung up, she thought: *disappointed,* he said. Was he really disappointed?

The thought gave her comfort, and she breathed more deeply.

Then she noticed that the man in the next booth was looking at her, and suddenly avoided her eyes.

She fled.

# 2.

THE cab sprinted along Constitution Avenue, dominated by massive Government buildings with columns and facades like Greek and Roman temples. For the first time Faith, looking distractedly out the cab window, was conscious of their overwhelming coldness. She thought with nervous irony: how essentially un-American *they* are. Then she laughed at her own temerity, and wished that the cab would cease creeping.

The cab turned right, crossed the Mall, and headed south toward the waterfront. In a moment the Greek and Roman colossi had given place to century-old slums. By one of those tricks of association the mind plays sometimes, she remembered the indignation Tommy Burkett had heaped upon the Capital's sprawling slums. Tommy Burkett, fresh from Yale and bursting with the idealism of an architect who wanted to build for the people. Tommy Burkett, with his wide grin and crinkly eyes.

For a moment Faith forgot the present in the past. How young, how unformed, how naive she had been in those days! Perhaps Tommy had so considered her, and that was why he had never responded fully to the rapt admiration she gave him. Perhaps he had even thought her dumb, fit only for the kind of social graces girls learned at finishing school. A girl like that would be no good for a man who wanted to pull down slums and build and build. . . .

She sighed. After Tommy Burkett, she had fallen in love with Thatcher.

This was her mood—one of temporary retreat from present fears—when the cab pulled up in front of Hall's restaurant. "My, how quickly we got here!" she said to the driver as she paid him.

The weight of indefinable sadness and loneliness which had settled upon her caused her to contract her brows into a slight frown, so that the broken-brushstroke angle was accentuated. Worry clouded the normal brightness of her eyes, and dissipated the youthful eagerness of her expression. Automatically she tugged at one brassière strap, and the gesture returned her to full awareness of the time and place. Oh, I *can't* see him like this, she thought. Then she added: oh, hell—this is business, not a date!

Firmly she walked toward the door of the old red brick house which concealed one of Washington's most famous restaurants.

Nevertheless, she hesitated. She could not tell exactly why she felt so indecisive, why her breath seemed a little stifled. As though one part of her sought to divert another part, she found herself noting idly the intensity of her purple-black shadow on the sidewalk . . . the sunlight-dappled water of the river, only a stone's throw away . . . the gently-heaving bulk of the Norfolk steamer at its pier.

Norfolk! Another steamer, coastwise, bound for New York. Aboard, Mr. and Mrs. Thatcher Vance, in the honeymoon suite, surrounded by baskets of fruit and flowers. . . . Now that marriage was all over but not done with: washed up, wasted, a complete flop. But there was no going back to re-live, to change or try to remake the failures that were now indelible in the history of their lives. Too late! Somehow, she felt physically wasted, depressed, disillusioned with her own life. These feelings, she realized, were not new to her. They had merely been brought to a head by the pressures generated in her current experiences. The pink paper, in some ways, seemed to her less a political document than a personal one. It had been, indirectly, a summons to assess her own life.

Faintly but distinctly she heard the *ding* of the river steamer's bell striking twice. Two bells: one o'clock. The sound brought back remembrance of night at sea, the star-pierced cup of heaven inverted above an endless black horizontal plate—like an abstract painting. Standing on the forward peak, they had watched the phosphorescent cleavage of the water, made love, and Thatcher had taught her about the ship's bells. Now the memory was more bitter for all its former sweetness.

She shook herself emotionally. Wool-gathering in midday! She had come here for help, but her mind turned instead to faded romance. She reproached herself, and, summoning her accustomed professional exterior, entered the doorway. She had come here as an accused Government employee, she told herself, not as a woman.

Dane Chandler was waiting for her in the courtyard garden, and for this she was grateful. Subtly, the place took the edge off the client-counsel approach she had resolved on only seconds before. As Chandler rose to greet her she was impressed again by his lanky bigness; when she saw the welcoming light in his calm, gray eyes, the quick, ingenuous smile, the faint swash of pleasing freckles, she felt almost undone. He was too much of a person; she could not, no matter how hard she tried, remain cold to him. She felt an abrupt, unreasoned anger at Abe Stone for having involved her with this man. All the same, she welcomed the electric feeling of her hand in his, the firm pressure he applied—though the touch of him accentuated a certain emptiness in her own life and increased her sadness.

"I'm so glad you didn't wait any longer to call," he said as they were seated at the table covered in a red-checkered cloth. "I expected to talk to you immediately after the hearing."

When she phoned him from the drugstore she had felt voluble, as though she had to pour out at once everything that had happened to her. Now she felt, oddly, there was nothing to pour out—that he would understand everything that had happened without being told. Yet now he thought that wilfully she had not called him.

"I called," she said, "but nobody answered at your office. The Committee delayed my hearing until the day was almost over."

"Then your hearing was only a formality. They didn't expect to extract much from you. Doubtless the press release including your name was already mimeographed before your hearing. They work that way."

"I remember, you warned me. But I think I half-doubted you."

He looked directly into her eyes for a moment, and she was aware again of that same intangible feeling which had passed between them when she first went to his office. "As a matter of fact," he said, "I called you at home last night—but you weren't there, and I didn't leave my name with the maid."

"I—I dragged my husband out to a movie," she said, conscious of her reluctance at mentioning Thatcher; "I had to do something to get my mind off the hearing." She paused, wondering why Chandler had not left his name with Donnie. There was only one explanation: he guessed that she had not

140

told her husband about the subpena—that she was afraid. He had read her fear from her words and actions in his office. He was more acute than she had credited him. If he had guessed at her unhappiness, what else might he be thinking . . . ?

"I have a confession," she said. "I tried to reach you at your home. But I couldn't find the number—"

He smiled. "No, I suppose not. We keep it unlisted."

Momentarily she had visions of an ultra-social-register wife who was very conscious of techniques at acquiring prestige, and this of course was one. A wife who would shepherd him, guard him, see that he met only the right people, and above all keep him from straying . . . She swallowed suddenly, aware of an obscure disappointment. Absorbed in these thoughts, at first she did not hear his next words clearly.

"I should have given you the number, Mrs. Vance," he was saying. "But you see, I live in a bachelor household with five other lawyers—and to protect the peace and quiet of us all, we keep the phone unlisted."

At the word *bachelor* she felt a mingled twist of joy and pain within her, even though, by his formal use of *Mrs. Vance*, he had kept his statement on a purely business level. Perhaps he too distrusted the instinctive rapport between them. Perhaps he too wished to tamp fires which thus far had only begun to glow. It was astonishing that two people could meet and look at one another, say so little, and yet have so much happen between them. But it was not a new thing: it had gone on since man's beginning. Only the exterior circumstances were new. . . .

She was looking away, over the garden wall, at the masts of sloops and sailboats limned against the deep blue sky.

"I think," he said suddenly, drumming his lean knobby

141

fingers on the red-checkered tablecloth, "we'd better place our order now . . . How about broiled lobster and a bottle of chablis?"

The white-coated Negro waiter hovered over them. Faith had told Chandler about the hearing in detail, and he questioned her sharply on a few points, particularly on the matter of the bust of Karl Marx, which had so bewildered her. They were served, now, a soupbowl in which swam shortcake in a sea of strawberries, topped by a huge swirl of whipped cream.

"I'm glad you selected this place," Faith said impetuously, looking around at other people, at the blooming geraniums and the trellised vines. "Such a lovely day to eat in a garden!"

"Do you come here often?" he asked.

"No, never," she replied with a touch of regret. "My husband hates the place. He hates seafood, and he says the painting of Adam and Eve in the barroom is gauche." Oddly, she found that she could mention Thatcher more easily now.

Dane Chandler laughed outright. "Well, it's a pretty famous painting, you know. Even figured in an investigation of Washington subversive activities—an investigation by the Texas Legislature. They wanted to smear F.D.R. and the New Deal. Claimed radical orgies went on here . . . with nude pictures, and all. Little behind the times, though: story goes this place was Grant's bawdy house."

Faith laughed too, the low ripple of musical laughter people found so appealing. "That disposes of the orgies. What about the radicals?"

Chandler's face lost its amusement. A brooding somberness came into his eyes, as though he listened in his mind to an invisible bugler who played *Taps* for a lost cause.

142

"Oh," he said with a restless movement of his hands, "I used to come here often before the war. I knew all about the radical meetings. I was an informal executive secretary for a little group of Senators, Congressmen and members of the Executive Branch who used to meet here more or less regularly and talk about national problems and how to get legislation passed. I can remember when George Norris came here and talked about cheap electric power for the farmers. I can remember the Little Flower when he warned us about fascism. I can remember the time Harry Hopkins came to tell us confidentially, straight from the President, that we'd never see a Federal budget under nine billion dollars again!" Chandler paused and laughed bitterly. "Now we spend many times that for arms alone—"

The brooding look had changed to a hard gray steeliness, and Faith remembered her early impression of Chandler's strength and maturity. He would be a tough adversary, she thought, no matter how unequal the battle. She felt a little shiver of delight that he was on her side.

"One thing—" she mused, "one thing about you I don't understand at all: how is it that you, in a firm like yours, should have the slightest interest in these matters . . . the slightest interest in handling a case like mine?"

To her surprise, he reddened, and the freckles appeared more markedly across his face. "That's sort of a long story," he said, "and to get it all straight, you'd have to start with a young fellow back in the Nineties who was a Populist—my dad. And you'd have to take into account a boyhood in Alton, Illinois, where once a mob murdered Elijah Lovejoy for defending his printing press and his right to say what he thought. You'd need to add the influence of a professor of philosophy—Forsyth Crawford—at Beloit College, where I went to school; and also the tradition of Brandeis when I was

143

at Harvard Law. But more than anything else you'd need to weigh the impact of the Great Depression, added to the experience of a year and several summers' work in a canning factory. So there you have it," he wound up, smiling, "—and it's hardly a biography for *Who's Who.*"

"It's the kind of biography that *ought* to be in *Who's Who,*" she said vehemently. "But I must tell you I had a feeling when I first saw you—a feeling that you didn't entirely belong to Sterling, Hardy, Hutchinson and McKee . . . or Harvard either, for that matter. I thought, maybe from something in your voice, that you were a Middle Westerner; maybe you grew up on the Mississippi River, in a Mark Twain sense—and weren't really adapted to the things which went on in those paneled offices. I realize now that it wasn't geography which lay behind the trouble in your eyes. . . ."

He flushed again. "You're psychic! Perhaps you don't know it, but Alton is on the Mississippi, a little way below Hannibal, Samuel Clemens' home town. He happens to be a hero of mine. He wrote something once, in *The Connecticut Yankee,* which Washington would do well to ponder these days. He said: '*You see my kind of loyalty was loyalty to one's country, not to its institutions or its office-holders. The country is the real thing, the substantial thing, the eternal thing; it is the thing to watch over, and care for, and be loyal to. . . .*'"

Chandler broke off, dropped his head and watched his fingers form into the church and steeple trick. "I'll admit to you," he said in a muted voice, "I'll admit I've derived more satisfaction from Abe's cases than from any others I've ever handled. They've challenged me, excited me, worked me up sometimes to a pitch of enthusiasm like Clarence Darrow at the Scopes trial. And sometimes I've thought—"

144

He paused so long that she put in a word to help him. "Yes?" she said softly.

When he lifted his head, there was anger in his face—anger, obviously, at himself. "Never mind! You have problems enough without hearing other people's. We have to prepare for a possible contempt citation, and we have to figure out what the devil the Committee's after by that oblique attack on your citizenship. *Are* you a Spanish citizen—*are* you an American citizen? I don't want to frighten you, but if there's any question of your citizenship, the difficulties they can make for you are almost endless. With the Committee, the question of perjury arises in addition to contempt. The Civil Service Commission will be interested. The Bureau of Immigration and Naturalization will have something to say. The FBI will cut in for a share of you. Each of these agencies has its own staff of investigators and secret agents to keep up with you. And last, but by no means least, your own Department may raise its own type of merry hell. You'll become a set of numbers in card-index files; your personality, even your most intimate personal life, will become subordinated to your case. I've seen it happen—and I don't want to see it happen to you!"

In a quick gesture he took her right hand in both his. "Please," he said, looking into her eyes, "—this is not to frighten you, but to inform you. You can't act intelligently if you don't understand the full potential of danger ahead— most of which will probably never come to pass. But you *must* know precisely the odds against you. Now I want you to tell me how it happens that you have no birth certificate? I want you to start with your father and mother and their marriage. . . ."

She felt her hand tremble in his. "All right," she said halt-

145

ingly, "I'll tell you as much as I know." She paused, as though organizing her thoughts. She made no effort to withdraw her hand from his, nor did he give any indication of releasing her.

"My mother," she said finally, in the reminiscent voice of one who repeats a story heard many times, "was Hannah Prentiss, the only child of a country doctor, Gorham Prentiss of Blue Hill, Maine. In this little village across the bay from Mt. Desert Island, she lived an uneventful but happy childhood. A cousin of hers, who spent summers at Bar Harbor, invited her to a party one weekend when an extra girl was needed as a partner for an attractive guest from Washington. The guest was a young attaché from the Spanish Embassy, and his name was Luis Carlos Robles. Somehow the improbable happened: they fell in love. Though the match was frowned on at the Embassy for many reasons, including the fact that Hannah Prentiss was a Protestant, they more or less eloped and got married in Boston. Carlos Robles had never taken his Catholicism very seriously, and now he gave it up altogether—practically speaking. This was a serious blow to his future in the diplomatic corps. Nevertheless, through powerful friends in Spain, he kept his post. My mother, aware of the official disapproval, avoided Embassy social life as much as possible. Actually my parents seem to have preferred this isolation because it intensified their dependence upon one another, and they were very much in love.

"The following summer, to be near Washington and yet avoid the heat, they took a cottage on Chesapeake Bay. The place was called Slade's Port, and it was not much more than a fishing pier, and a general store. That's where I was born, a month early. My father was in Washington, and nobody else was there but the maid—who acted, as it turned out, as a very efficient midwife."

Chandler broke in. "What about your birth certificate?"

"My father made a point of not registering me as a Spanish citizen, which aroused further ill will at the Embassy. I wasn't baptized, either—they never got around to it. I may have a birth certificate, but I don't know where to look for it. When I was only a few months old, my parents went to Spain. I can still remember, very vaguely, my Spanish grandparents. There was a big, white stone house with a red-tiled roof, a patio with bright flowers and caged birds. I remember strong sunlight, black angular shadows, and a lovely woman with many petticoats who held my hand while I peeked over into a fountain."

Chandler smiled. "Little-blonde-you must have seemed sensational in your grandparents' household."

"When I was five, we came back to America, where father became the Washington representative for an import firm, bought a colonial house in Georgetown, and settled down. He loved this country! He used to read American history by the hour, and taught me more than I ever learned at school. He decided to become an American citizen, and took out first papers. One day he had a heart attack—I was twelve then—and died." She stopped, but after a moment added in low tones, "Then, my mother, too. . . ."

"Well—" Chandler said, "we may have quite a search on our hands to prove that you are you. If your father had wanted you to be a Spanish citizen, it would have been necessary to arrange with the Embassy your registration as such. Otherwise, you were an American. We'll have to get the Spanish Embassy to check their records."

She looked at him and shook her head. "You won't find the

147

name of Robles very popular there. My father's province was Cáceres—one thing he had in common with Franco. My father, from the very beginning, was secretly a Republican. He hated the feudalism in Spain. After he left the Embassy, he became active against the monarchy, the hierarchy, and the Falangist fascist movement. Sometimes he received threats, and he would get very excited. I'm sure if he had lived he would have gone back to Spain to fight in the Civil War."

"Hmm-m," Chandler said. "What about your Prentiss relatives?"

"Gone, all gone. My mother had no brothers and sisters. The cousins are dead or scattered heaven knows where. And my great-aunt, the last survivor of the clan except me, withered away last year—so old and dried that the neighbors said it was hard to tell the difference of death in her. So you see."

"And your Spanish grandparents?"

"Dead, too."

"So it's your word against the United States Government. Somewhere, somehow, we have to find a scrap of paper—an official record, an affidavit, even an old letter, which tells the time and place of Faith Prentiss Robles' birth. We may not need it—but the hunt will have to begin. . . ."

She smiled at the way he put it. Even though the client relationship had been breached only once by his eyes, and once by his hands, he seemed ever so much less like a lawyer than he had in his office. For one thing, he had not, this time, talked law. For another, two people could not talk intimately about even a few details of their lives without becoming personal.

"Do you know Spanish?" she said with curiosity.

He shook his head that he did not.

"What you just said," she went on, "is an old Spanish proverb: *Las palabras vuelan, Los escritos quedan.*"

He looked at her strangely. All he did, however, was tink his knife against his wine glass, with uncharacteristic nervousness.

"Yes sir, here's your check, sir," said the waiter—though it was evident from Chandler's face that nothing was further from his thoughts.

As they got up to leave, a balding man who had sat near them finished his coffee and paid his bill. Idly Faith noted his face; it seemed remotely but tantalizingly familiar. When they left the garden, the man followed shortly.

Though she did not look back, she was sure she heard footsteps behind them. In the street, the glare of brick and pavement seemed to smite her, or perhaps she was giddy from the wine. She felt suddenly faint, weak in her legs and arms, as though she could neither run nor defend herself.

With a convulsive movement she turned toward Chandler and clutched at his sleeve. "Mr. Chandler—" she whispered, "oh, Dane, I'm afraid—!"

"You needn't be," he said.

# 3.

THATCHER was a devout Episcopalian, but an erratic churchgoer. Usually his Sunday morning hangovers interfered with exercise of his religious responsibilities —so that he preferred, all things considered, an occasional Evensong at the Cathedral for absolution and remission of sins. He preferred the Cathedral, too, for the pomp and beauty of its ceremonies and rites. He envied the acolytes, had several good friends among them, and not infrequently remarked that he wished he had lived in the Middle Ages —so that he might have been a priest.

Hence Faith was surprised, and yet not surprised, when Thatcher announced this Sunday morning he was going to church. There was an element of unease in the way he said it, and Faith wondered if he feared that she might offer to accompany him. Was he ashamed of being seen in public with her, merely because her name had appeared on one of Congressman Daiken's notorious lists? She decided to test him.

"Do you want me to come with you?" she asked.

He squirmed, ran his hand absently through his wavy blonde hair. "Well, of course you can if you want to," he said; "but I wasn't exactly *expecting* you to. I'm going because I feel the need of it."

She wondered if his conscience was hurting because of last night. They had gone to a small party at the Egyptian Legation, a very informal affair, and Thatcher had gotten more than ordinarily plastered. Normally at diplomatic parties Thatcher was more discreet—but with the Egyptians he did not seem to care. Or perhaps for some other reason he did not care. She had been embarrassed by his behavior, and discreetly had managed to lure him away before he passed out entirely. No one had commented on her listing, but she noticed that she was treated with extraordinary politeness— and Thatcher's friends more than ordinarily retained their distance.

About church she said to Thatcher: "Anyway, I can't go. Late yesterday I got an invitation to attend a meeting of all persons accused by Daiken, to consider possible action. Meeting's at the Statler, noon today."

150

"Good Lord!" he exclaimed, "—you're not going to get mixed up in a bunch like that, I hope!"

"I certainly am," she said firmly. "I'm going to use every possible means of fighting back!"

"Why don't you get a lawyer, some big shot?" he said. There was an edge to his voice.

She hesitated. "Maybe I will," she said.

Thatcher grimaced and went out of the room, biting the nails of his two right forefingers as he went. He had offered no other discussion of her problem; he seemed almost afraid to mention it.

Sighing, she lay back for a moment on the chaise-longue in the bedroom, thinking of the nervousness Thatcher had displayed of late. Superficially it appeared to parallel her own current uncertainties and fears. Her own discomforts, she thought, might be reflected in Thatcher; was it possible that he had known intuitively that she was in trouble, even before he read the list in the newspaper? His behavior had not been what she expected. True, he had displayed sharp anger at the newspaper list—but he had not rehashed all her activities that he had objected to over the years, berating her in the I-told-you-so voice she anticipated. And she had expected his anger to be more violent than sharp, much, much more abusive. Perhaps now that such a crisis as this had come in their lives, he was even more afraid of losing her than in the past. She knew that sometimes he longed to be free of her—as sometimes she longed to be free of him. The difference was one of dependency. Their needs of each other were entirely different. Thatcher longed to be free, but could not free himself. Unquestionably he depended on her, but also he hated her for his bondage. Of all the sources of friction between them, this was the one of which she was most aware.

The moment on the chaise-longue lengthened into minutes. She lit a cigarette, watched the smoke mingle with the sunlight in the room, remembering. . . .

Shortly before the harrowing ride with Thatcher on the Baltimore pike, she had thought of going to a psychiatrist. They had spent a miserable Christmas—quarrel after quarrel—and one way or another Jeanie had reacted to their tension, responding with tears and unruliness. If Jeanie cried again, or Thatcher argued again, Faith thought, she would go out of her mind. The situation had become unbearable. She first debated, then firmly resolved to see a doctor.

On the choice of doctor, she floundered a bit, but finally made an appointment with a man Mr. Cunningham had once highly praised. Despite her resolution, at the last moment she almost backed down. It seemed impossible to tell any living being the truth of relations between herself and Thatcher. But, with trepidation, she went.

She rang the bell and stepped into the waiting room. Nobody was there, and all her own movements were deadened by the thick carpet, the tapestry on the wall, the overstuffed furniture. A short time passed, and she heard a muffled, unseen door close. She assumed that a patient was leaving the doctor's office, privately, by another exit. Everything here was so discreet.

Then, without forewarning, the doctor appeared. He didn't look in the least as she had expected. He was utterly ungodlike, smiling and pleasant and casual, a little man with a wandering nose and neat hair gray at the temples. "Good heavens," she had murmured half-audibly, "what *did* I expect?"

Once in the inner office, she glanced at his diplomas on the wall—including one from George Washington University. So he's a local boy, she thought; he must know Washington

152

inside and out, mostly inside. She glanced at the leather couch, too, somewhat distastefully; but he did not ask her to lie on the couch. Instead, he offered her a comfortable chair and a cigarette, and said, "Well, Mrs. Vance, what's bothering you?"

"My husband, Dr. Norton," she said simply.

She talked for an hour. The talk was a catharsis, and at the end she felt immeasurably better. But she had told him, as it seemed to her, everything—and he had prescribed nothing.

"But what am I to do, Dr. Norton?" she cried in a tumult of anxiety. "What am I to *do?*"

The casualness was all gone from his face, and gravity had taken its place. "I can't tell you what to do," he said; "you must make your own decisions. But perhaps I can help clarify a few points for you, and intelligent decisions will seem more possible.

"First, let me say that I see many people here in Washington who are neurotic or have neurotic tendencies because of office pressures to which they can't adjust. The governmental hierarchy seems to produce great frustrations in many people. You know the reasons why as well as I do; but you would be surprised if you knew how many have mental breakdowns.

"Your husband, however, is a different type. The root of his problem goes back deep into his childhood experiences. Any significant change in his attitude would probably have to be made by psychoanalysis, and extensive therapy at that. Further, he would have to *want* to be helped, and even then the analysis might fail.

"You can reasonably expect, I think, that the impasse between you will not remain static. If you decide to remain married, and your husband does not seek help, you will have to content yourself with a far from adequate sexual life. You will have to accept the fact that your husband is immature in

153

many ways and bear with his emotional tantrums as best you can. You will, in fact, have to deal with him increasingly as if he were a child, and not a fully developed marital partner. You can estimate for yourself what your life will be like under these conditions.

"Now, as for your little girl. The strained atmosphere surrounding her is far from desirable for healthy growth and development. Unstable children very often come from homes where intense conflict—either open or unconscious—exists between the parents. Sometimes it's better for the child if the parents separate, though every child actually needs two parents. Nevertheless, when one parent is very sick emotionally—"

In that moment a new quietude came into Faith's heart, and in that moment she resolved to separate from Thatcher. She felt almost happy. She knew very well that Thatcher would never seek help: the nature of his illness was such that he could not. For herself she felt sorrow, but for Thatcher a deep pity.

Dr. Norton talked longer, but she did not tell him of the decision which seemed to have formed unaided within her. How to accomplish it was another matter—a most difficult one, as time and the Baltimore pike proved.

She had not, in ensuing months, relinquished the decision. She had merely postponed it. But as time passed, separation seemed more and more impossible of achievement, and she was less and less sure that it was desirable. The level of her own indecision seemed to rise as relations with Thatcher worsened. . . .

The cigarette burned her fingers, and she dropped it hurriedly into the ashtray by the chaise-longue. She looked at the two graceful suntanned legs half-revealed through her negligee, and sighed. The next problem was how to tell Thatcher about Dane Chandler, and his interest in her case. Every moment of delay, she thought, was increasing its explosive potential.

She was tieing a black ribbon around her aureate hair, still day-dreaming, when both her movement and reverie were interrupted by a timid knock. It was Donnie, wearing an apologetic expression. Her face said plainly that something was seriously wrong.

"Why Donnie!" Faith said, "—what's the matter? Are you sick?"

"I reckon I might as well tell you the truth, Miz Vance," Donnie said, " 'cause you'll find it out sooner or later. First I thought I could kinda keep it secret, jus' let it drop without no mention. But las' night I got to figgerin', and I knowed weren't no use. . . ."

"Donnie!" said Faith in alarm, "what on earth are you talking about!"

"It's about Billy Seagrave and Jeanie—"

"He didn't come to play yesterday, I know, but what's odd about that?" She said it as though, secretly, she *did* expect something to be odd about it. Her defensiveness came out in a note of slight hostility, as though Donnie were to blame.

"Well, Miz Seagrave, she telephoned—" Donnie said, hesitating. Seagrave was a potent name in Washington, even among domestics, because they heard their employers talking. The Seagraves were much sought after on a certain level; he was a top man in the Bureau of the Budget, which had a great deal to do with settling the amount of agency appropriations requested from the Congress. Every important official made a point of knowing Seagrave. Pursestrings were in-

155

volved. As for the Vances, the friendship lay chiefly between the children; nevertheless, the adult contacts were on a cordial basis.

"Yes?" Faith said, that strange, lumpy feeling returning inside.

"Well, Miz Seagrave, she said to give you a message: she said, 'In view of current uncertainties, it would perhaps be best if the children did not visit back and forth any more.'" Donnie lowered her eyes. In memorizing the words, she had also memorized the tone. The tone was frosty, even harsh.

Faith winced. Dear Donnie, trying to protect her from this hurt! Donnie, obviously suffering herself over it—suffering especially for Jeanie, Faith knew.

"You did right to tell me, Donnie," Faith said calmly. "You must always tell me when these things happen."

"Yes'm," Donnie said, and backed away.

Faith's outward calm did not ease her wretchedness. In an automatic manner she went on dressing, her thoughts whirling and chaotic. When she had finished, she called Jeanie in from her backyard play and gave her a big hug.

"Mommie's going out for a little while," she said. "Be a good girl while I'm gone."

Jeanie rubbed the sand off her nose, and looked up thoughtfully. "Faith," she said, "what does 'famous' mean? When they say your name on the radio, is that what 'famous' means?"

"Yes, dear," Faith said, "that's what famous means." She turned aside, so that Jeanie might not see the quick tears which welled in her eyes.

From beginning to end, the meeting at the Statler seemed to Faith like disjointed scenes from a play. In the first place, only she and the chairman, a professor of political science,

156

wise and owl-like in old-fashioned round horn-rimmed glasses, were on time. In the second place, the music from a string orchestra, playing Viennese melodies, kept wafting into the ultra-modern meeting room, confusing romance with reality.

One by one they straggled in, thirteen of the thirty-nine. The others either did not deign to come, or were afraid. They introduced themselves to the chairman as they came in, and he, in turn, introduced each around the circle. Soon Faith knew the names and position of everyone there. She was impressed by the chairman's reflective eyes and his atmosphere of being at home in the world.

They were a varied lot, and Faith was astonished by their diversity. One was an agricultural economist, a wizened man, who had spent his mature life keeping up with the problems of milk-marketing in the United States. Another, an energetic, handsome woman with a mop of flying yellow hair, was a school-building specialist and a leader in the progressive education movement for twenty years. Another, a quiet, heavy-set young man with thick glasses, was a nuclear physicist. A bulbous middle-aged man was a lawyer. A nervous, stringy young man was a ghost writer. A fat-faced, bland maiden-lady was a home-economist. A soft-spoken, soft-eyed young Negro girl was a public health lab technician. A pimply-faced boy with straw-colored hair was a messenger. An awkward, pale girl with a Nebraska twang was a stenographer. A nondescript man with bloodshot eyes and a whining voice was a statistical analyst. An oldish man with calm eyes and rugged features was a geologist; he wore a pince-nez on a black ribbon and listened while others chattered. And there was Faith.

"My God," Faith murmured, "where am I! Are these people Reds?" She had comic visions of such a crew overthrowing the Government. If there was an ounce of force or violence among them, it was not visible. The whole thing was obviously a mistake, a ghastly joke being played on feeble mortals by some boisterous god from Olympus. Presently, when the god had had his fun, the whole crowd of them would be whisked back to their desks in the wink of an eye, and their monotonous lives would go on exactly as before. And the memory of this experience would be taken from them, like the characters in *A Midsummer Night's Dream*, because the god would find their antics more humorous that way.

She laughed aloud, and suddenly felt embarrassed for having done so. The others stared at her. No levity was in their faces.

"I think we'd best come to order," the reflective chairman said, tapping his pencil on a notebook. "We all know why we've come. I called this meeting in an effort to explore the possibilities of joint action in our own defense. As things stand, we can easily be picked off one by one. We are helpless to defend our jobs, and, far more important, our reputations. We have been labeled in the public press without possibility of effective reply. Every one of us is bound to suffer. I wonder how many of us even had the 'opportunity'—if you want to call it that—of a Committee hearing before our names were given to the press? May I have a show of hands—?"

Faith glanced around. Only about half had been heard. She shuddered.

"So we have been smeared, by anonymous accusers, without the right of self-defense," the chairman went on in a level voice. "We have been treated as though the Constitution did not exist."

"Hear, hear!" someone cried.

"Possibly we ought to organize as a group, elect officers, and have continued meetings," the chairman said. "Possibly we ought to consider a joint defense, legal if necessary. Possibly we ought to begin by issuing a joint statement—"

"Mr. Chairman," the statistical analyst with the whiny voice cried, jumping to his feet, "I'm opposed to that! How do we know that everybody here *isn't* a Red? I won't sign my name side by side with Reds!"

The geologist with the bony face and the pince-nez on a black ribbon raised his hand for attention, and was recognized by the chairman. "Mr. Chairman," he said slowly, putting on his pince-nez with precision, "we ought to consider each step carefully before any decisions are made. We ought to analyze the effect of a joint statement, its advantages and disadvantages, before we take a negative position with regard to it. I think we may, however, accept the general premise that collective action is more likely to prove effective than individual action. Where the newspapers most certainly would print little, if any, of the individual statements we might make—surely collective action in a matter of this kind is so novel that they might print a joint statement in its entirety."

"Hear, hear!" cried a voice. Faith saw that it was the woman with the flying yellow hair who spoke.

The statistical analyst jumped up again. "You talk like a Red!" he shouted. "*Collective* action! That's the kind of talk that got you into this trouble! You condemn us with such talk!"

A babble of excited voices drowned his words, and this point was as far as the meeting ever got. The discussion raged back and forth, pro and con, with little clarity and no decision. Faith grew more and more frightened, shrinking inwardly. Such fools! she thought. Only two or three made sense. But she felt helpless to get up and say what she herself thought. She had neither the strength nor the boldness. She saw that others were frightened like herself: the pale stenographer, the boy-messenger, the Negro girl. What chance of defense did these lesser ones have? They would not have "connections" on tap, learned societies to make statements, brilliant lawyers to defend them. They were lost, lost . . . unless a common means of defense could be found, unless they had unions to come to their rescue.

"A number of us here are scientists," the heavy-set young nuclear physicist was saying in a thoughtful, carefully measured voice; "we ought to consider the effect of the Committee's witchhunts on freedom of thought, on freedom of scientific investigation, and make a statement—"

But he got no further. The man with the bloodshot eyes yelled, "You're a Red! You ought to be barred from the meeting! *I* think we ought to close our traps, dodge Commie fronts like the plague, and the Committee will leave us alone—"

Quietly Faith slipped out a side door. She was surfeited. She was almost gagging, and the bedlam still hammered against her eardrums.

Even the oven blast of the street, in contrast to the air-conditioned meeting room, was a welcome relief. The out-of-doors, the Sunday afternoon, seemed peculiarly normal. Couples in light summer clothes strolled by; taxis cruised aimlessly; a diplomatic limousine honked with impatience at a careless pedestrian; a boy and a girl, both in shorts and both beautifully bronzed, pedaled by on a tandem bicycle.

But for all the warmth of the street and its reassuring life, Faith could not shake off her sense of depression, her inner chill. Something dreadful had happened in that room, because something dreadful had happened to all the people in it.

Then a thought crossed her mind, which, a few days before, could never have occurred to her at all. What if, she asked with a tremor, what if one of the people in that room was an informer? What if one of the people in that room made it his business to report to the Committee all that had happened . . . ?

It did not matter, really.

What mattered was that she had been brought to the point where she was afraid even of those, who, like her, stood condemned.

# 4.

THE week began on a discordant note. Though Thatcher had mumbled specific instructions that he be awakened for an important production conference, no amount of shaking stirred him from a heavy-breathed slumber. Then Faith noticed the open bottle of sleeping pills in the bathroom cabinet, and understood the reason why.

It was unlike Thatcher, however, to take sleeping pills on top of liquor. He had come home from his golf game tanked, irascible at having been sent out to his club to play with a client, an automobile dealer whom he considered boorish. He constantly feared that this man would one day hit him up for membership. When Faith saw him, she marveled that the Packard had gotten home intact. It was obvious that Thatcher was much too drunk to drive out to Warrenton for the party they were to attend. And Faith was greatly relieved.

Thatcher, she guessed now, must have sobered up some time in the night, and, unable to sleep, have had recourse to the sleeping pills. She shook him once more, angrily, and gave up. She was sure that he would be furious with her for not rousing him. He would charge her with deliberate failure, and explanations would only compound his fury.

The day was lowering, overcast with soggy, heavy clouds. A mood of defeatism seemed to saturate the whole earth, and Faith was soaked in it like a sponge. Somehow, she thought, she had to counteract her reaction to yesterday's meeting. She resolved to see Abe Stone at once.

She was waiting for him at his office when he came in, before the clerical staff reported.

"Well," he said in surprise, smiling in his slow way, "what brings you here so early in the morning?"

Clasping her bag tightly, she said, "I wanted to tell you about a meeting, that's all."

"Okay," he said, and motioned her into his office. He sat her down beside his green steel desk.

"I can't help feeling upset by what's happened," she said. "Maybe I'll get used to it."

"Yes, you will. As a matter of fact, I'm very proud of you— and so is Chandler. . . ." He paused, studying the sudden light in her eyes. "Yes, I got the whole story of your hearing from him. He thinks you did a dignified job. He couldn't give you any higher praise."

Joy radiated through her. "I'm pleased," she said. "It's childish to feel so pleased, I know. But I can't help that, either."

He smoothed his freshly shaven cheeks, which had a slight bluish cast, with his stubby, powerful hand. "I suppose not." Smiling faintly, he sighed. "You're lucky to have captured

162

Chandler's imagination. I guess it's lucky for all of us—I've been afraid we might lose him."

Struck by a new apprehension, she said, "What do you mean?"

"Well, picture Chandler's situation for yourself," Stone said, rocking gently in his swivel chair. "Do you think it's easy for a young man with a bright future in a high-powered law firm to take on cases like these?"

She was glad he had generalized, avoiding the use of *yours*. The discussion would be easier if they could avoid injecting Faith Robles Vance as a person. After all, she was only one of many who had been caught in the vast and terrifying machinery of Governmental investigation.

"No," she said in a low voice, "—I'm sure it's not easy."

"No," said Stone, "it's not. Especially if, like Chandler, you're in line for a partnership in the firm, and you're considered the fair-haired lad."

"Yet he keeps on taking your cases—why?"

"Hell!" Stone said explosively, clenching both hands on his desk, "—consider the dirty work he has to do! A few odds and ends like trying to take tidelands oil away from the people of this country and give it to the big corporations! Like finagling millions in excess profits taxes away from the U. S. Treasury and back into corporation hands! Like smoothing over the Nazi cartel tie-ins of some of the biggest goddam corporations in this country! You think that kind of stuff makes an honest man sleep any better nights? You think that kind of work could ever make a man like Chandler happy? He takes your case to salve his conscience, to put it blunt. It's like he says—if he doesn't, he's a goner for all the rest of his life!"

"Oh!" she said.

"And you probably wonder how he gets away with these extracurricular activities? I'll tell you how: the partners think it's amusing, and—more important—a touch of liberalism won't hurt the general reputation of the firm. But, brother, let things get really tough! Then we'll see how long they'll put up with this liberal stuff. He will have to make a choice, as cold and calculating as ringing up the dollar sign on a cash register! It's my opinion, from little things Dane said of late, the partners are getting restive now. That's why I wasn't sure he'd take your case—and why I'm so relieved he did."

Faith was surprised by Abe Stone's implied irritation with Chandler. Such emotion, she thought, was a reflection of the insecurity and anxiety of Washington. The pressures that were applied day after day without surcease.

"Well—" Stone said, "this is getting us no place fast. You came here to tell me something. What was it?"

"Nothing," she replied so serenely that he could not help noting the sudden change in her attitude, "—nothing at all. What I was going to say is not important at all."

He gave her a cryptic look. "Okay, kid. But when you need me, I'll be here. Just holler."

Her serenity was undisturbed. "When you need *me*, I'll be there. Just call."

She left him stroking his face with the powerful, stubby fingers.

The moment she walked into her office, she knew that nothing in her professional life would ever be quite the same again. It seemed like centuries since she had waited impatiently to tell Mr. Cunningham about the pink paper—centuries since the storm on the Mall and the appearance of the subpena-server in the rumpled seersucker suit.

164

Glancing at Maria and Evelyn, the other girls in the office, she knew instantly that Faith Vance was as much a subject of malicious conversation as if she had produced an illegitimate child. Yet in Maria's face was a fleeting compassion.

Both girls were typing at top speed when Faith stepped through the swinging shutters of the door. Both stopped as by command.

"Oh, Faith, we've missed you!" Maria said.

"What does it feel like to be famous?" Evelyn said, mingling curiosity and scorn.

Maria was a short, plump little brownie from New Mexico, and she spoke the Spanish of the region. Once she had confided to Faith that she had Indian ancestry. She had come to the office through regular Civil Service channels. She was an excellent worker, and had been a boon to Faith on many projects. But Evelyn was their problem child. Though she had Civil Service rating, someone somewhere had pulled strings, and she had ended up in Mr. Cunningham's office. Though at best she was a mediocre typist, she had a stenographer's classification and salary. She often complained that Faith kept her from advancing by not recommending a higher efficiency rating to Mr. Cunningham. A small-town girl, she hated Washington. She managed to look poorly dressed no matter how much she spent for her clothes, and her shoes were always run over and her hair slightly frowsy. Evelyn lived in a rooming house, and her social life was almost non-existent, though sometimes she went to the movies on Saturday nights.

Neither belonged to the Union. Nor did Faith, as their supervisor, urge them to join.

"How does it feel to be famous?" Faith repeated as she put away her bag in her desk and tried to collect herself emotionally for work. "I'll tell you how it feels: infamous!"

They began typing again with as little notice of her as if she had just returned from a conference.

After she got her desk in order, she asked Maria with a nod of her head toward Mr. Cunningham's office, "Is *he* in?"

"Uh huh," Maria said, continuing with her typing, "—but nobody's seen anything of him. Acts like he's sulking in his tent. Seems more upset than you do."

"Oh," Faith said.

Gradually the morning wore away, under the abrasive of time and her impatience. Not once did Mr. Cunningham buzz for her, not once was there any indication of life in the inner office. He's got to face me sooner or later, Faith thought; why does he keep putting it off . . . ?

Old Henry, his sepia face thoughtful and melancholy, came to fill the inkwells and replenish the paper clips. "Mighty sorry to hear what happened, Mis' Vance," he said in an undertone. "Mighty sorry! Looks like they jus' go after the nice people."

"Thanks, Henry. Thanks very much," she said, wondering if she sounded abrupt and rude. But somehow she knew he would understand, no matter how she sounded.

The lunch hour arrived at last. "Anybody free?" she said to Evelyn and Maria. "I'm starved!"

Evelyn looked away hastily. "Not me. I've got a—a date."

"Er—me too," Maria said.

So, even though they work in the same room, they don't want it thought that *voluntarily* they associate with me, Faith thought in amazement. They're afraid for their jobs. How would *I* act if it were one of them . . . ? She realized that she was shaking inwardly. She wasn't sure, she didn't know, she couldn't even guess how she would act if it were one of them. It was easy, now, for her to say she'd stick by them.

166

But in these few days she'd learned so much! How could anyone know agony until he'd experienced his own . . . ? Really, they didn't mean to hurt her—she was sure of that. Or did they? Did—did Evelyn, especially?

She began to wonder wildly if it were Evelyn who had denounced her in revenge for petty gripes. Oh, no, it was impossible! "I'm not hungry, to tell the truth," she said, denying her statement of a moment before. But she wasn't hungry now, not now. They had made her sick in the pit of her stomach. Food suddenly was repulsive to her. "Maybe I'll run out for a sandwich later on," she said vaguely.

"I'll bring you one," Maria said. "What kind?"

"Anything," Faith said. "I've got a lot of work to do." The explanation sounded lame even in her own ears.

"G'by," Maria said as she went out with Evelyn. She seemed nervous and upset.

In the quiet of the office, Faith sat and meditated. The obsession grew that she must, somehow, find out who had denounced her. She was sitting still for the first time in days, without extraneous things to distract her. She became increasingly restless, longing for action, any kind of action. She went over the hearing again in her mind, endlessly repeating each question and her answers. *They* knew who had accused her, that was certain. They knew, but they would never tell. Then the face of Congressman Modie Vincent came to her. He was a liberal—if she could only get to him . . . ! If she could explain to him, individually, that a dreadful mistake had been made . . . if she could make him see how the Committee was destroying something incalculably precious inside her, something that had to do with her ideas about democracy, and justice, even America itself. . . .

Maybe Modie Vincent. . . .

Her spirit leaped, hope shone in her eyes. There was a way! Of course! Why, oh why, hadn't she thought of it sooner . . . !

Frantically she scrambled through the telephone book, looking for the number of the Mayflower Hotel.

# 5.

Faith glanced up as the bronze clock in the ornate lobby of the hotel dinged four times. The strokes, unlike the décor, were unobtrusive. She was aware, from past experience, that she was not expected to arrive on time —and she guessed that her punctuality, like everything else about her mission, might prove irritating to the person she had come to see. Nevertheless, she was resolved not to fail.

Quickly she examined everyone in the lobby, without seeing the expected face, then peered down the long promenade distinguished by its row of huge crystal chandeliers. No, he was not in sight. She sank back luxuriously against the cushions of an overstuffed sofa, and idly checked the rigging of the model *Mayflower* which dominated a large table in the center of the lobby. She could remember the first time she had seen it, brought here as a child by her father. He had wanted her to see exactly what the *Mayflower* looked like, and had been delighted when the vessel intrigued her. Since then she had seen it many, many times—but she never forgot its meaning.

She had always enjoyed the Mayflower Hotel as a kind of crossroads of Washington. At this moment in the lobby she could pick out three tall Texans in Stetson hats, leathery-faced, and drawly-voiced in the fragments of conversation she caught. A plushy businessman in a double-breasted blue suit self-consciously escorted a high-heeled blonde in flashy clothes. A svelte matron efficiently steered a governess and two small girls in straw sailor-hats through the lobby, the governess speaking rapidfire French to the girls all the while. An East Indian in a resplendent turban, surrounded by a mountain of hotel-stickered luggage, was moving majestically toward the desk. A somber faced priest was looking with disgust at a train schedule. And bellboys ran hither and yon like jerky, life-size marionettes.

She was, now, slightly ahead of the cocktail hour. Shortly the swarm of Navy, Army, and Air Force officers would begin, recreating the atmosphere of wartime. When Thatcher was in the Navy, he used to bring her here to show her off to his colleagues. Before that, while she was still in school, she had come with many dates for dancing. And she had come to debutante parties here, too—"black-and-white balls" they were called, meaning clothes, not races.

Suddenly she felt weary with the Mayflower. Same old thing, all these years, over and over. Maybe she had been in Washington too long. Maybe she should have quit her job long ago, and forced Thatcher to take that step he so often talked about but never consummated—a move to New York. Maybe in a different environment Thatcher would have proved more successful, been happier. And she would have been freed of the curse of Government . . . the curse, specifically, which had been visited upon her in these last few days.

She became restless again, anxious to complete this appointment. She was considering use of the house phone, when she realized he was standing over her.

"Buddy!" she cried, springing to her feet. "I missed you in the crowd—didn't recognize you. But no wonder—it's been eons since I last saw you!" At once she checked herself: she was greeting him with too much enthusiasm. This was the wrong way of accomplishing what she wanted to do. "Though, really," she went on in her most relaxed and winning voice, "—you've hardly changed at all."

"Anyhoo—" he said with a wry expression, "I haven't got a shiner."

He was referring to the incident, in the early days of Faith's marriage, and ancient history now, when Thatcher had taken a poke at him. They were dancing on the Shoreham terrace, and Buddy Brooks had cut in once too often for Thatcher's comfort. The upshot had been a brawl, and profuse apologies on Faith's part. She was ashamed of Thatcher, and concerned for Buddy—who had been one of her old standbys in the days when she went to school at Miss Madeira's. Buddy had always protested that he was in love with her—but she had never taken him seriously. In those days he was trim and sleek, darkly but conventionally handsome. He was still sleek, but too well fed.

She cringed at the thought of how Thatcher might react if he caught them together now. But she laughed lightly, as though the black eye, gone and forgotten, had been of no importance whatever. "You have a memory like an elephant!" she said.

He laughed with her. "For such things I have. Come along now, let's go have a drink. All right?"

"All right, indeed—I'm dying of thirst!"

The headwaiter kowtowed to him instantly, and picked a

choice table, half-hidden by palms, at the edge of a fountain which glowed like alabaster. It was a perfect rendezvous for the romance-minded; but to Faith it was off-key and irritating. In that setting, Buddy would certainly want to get personal. She looked at him shrewdly—perhaps not even yet had he given her up, at least in the sense of physical desire. Sure enough, they were hardly seated before his knee found hers and exerted a steady pressure. She did not withdraw, though she derived no sensation from his touch.

"Something cooling—a planter's punch, that's it," she said.

"The usual," he said to the waiter.

They made small talk while waiting for the drinks, and Faith speculated on the best way to approach her subject. Buddy's father was probably the single most powerful lobbyist in Washington, had been for many years, and Buddy was following him step by step. The Old Man, as Buddy called him, was not a "legislative representative" in the usual sense, but kept a private office and apartment at the Mayflower as a place of business. He did favors for various interests whose financial backing traced to a powerful Wall Street bank; and in a single day he might be involved with legislation concerning commodities as disparate as beef and real estate. Faith had seen his name in the paper (something which rarely happened) in connection with the drive against price controls after the war, and she knew that for years he had plugged steadily for lower income taxes in the upper brackets.

Once, before her marriage, she had sat at dinner in this very hotel with Buddy, his father, the Speaker of the House, and two Senators who were chairmen of important committees. She had listened with wonder to the conversation. Mr. Brooks, a leonine deep-voiced man, seemed to be explaining something to them, something completely over her head. "I told the Governor not to sign that bill," Mr. Brooks said,

"—but the damn fool signed it anyway! Said he was going to speak to the President about my 'interference.' Can you beat that—after all I've done for him!" One of the Senators had tightened his lips and said, "He's been getting off the reservation quite a bit, lately. Got labor on the brain. Don't think he can win without 'em." Mr. Brooks had scowled. "There's something else he can't win without—as he'll discover some fine morning!" "Never did like two-timers," the Speaker of the House chimed in, "—never did, and never will." Then they had all laughed about something, and had another round of drinks.

The planter's punch and Brooks' scotch and soda arrived. Faith sipped thankfully at her straw, and wondered why it took so much courage to ask a simple question.

"Buddy," she said abruptly, "do you remember with that elephant memory when you said one time: *If I can ever do you a favor, let me know?*"

"Sure," he said, a pleased look in his eyes, "you know darned well I'd do anything for you, Faith."

"Buddy," she said, holding her voice as steady as possible, "did you see my name on Daiken's list the other day?"

"What!" he cried. "My God—no!"

In reflex action, his knee pulled away from hers—and she trembled at its absence as she had not trembled at its presence. "Yes," she said, "—it's some kind of a mistake, and I'm trying to straighten it out. That's why I need you."

His face chilled. "Oh—I see!"

"I want to get to Modie Vincent. He'd never see me if I simply called him for an appointment. But I remembered you know practically every Congressman by his first name. Will you call him for me?" Her voice was shaking, and she hated herself for showing such emotion, but she could not

172

control it. "This is terribly important to me, Buddy—you can't imagine how important!"

"Of course I know Modie. But—"

"Listen, Buddy," she said frantically, "—you've got to do it. You've *got* to!" She was losing control, and was afraid that suddenly she might cry. She realized that she had come, in a few short hours, to stake a great deal on this interview. It seemed to her to open a way, it might solve everything for her. She laid her hand on his arm and utterly humbled herself. "Buddy—*please!*" she implored.

"Well," he grumbled, "I guess so. I'll call him now."

He excused himself, and reluctantly left the table. While he was gone, an orchestra began to play and couples took to the dance floor. Faith kept sipping at the straw, unaware that her drink was finished. Ages and ages seemed to pass. Her thoughts were inchoate, suspended.

Finally he returned. "I got him," he said. "Wants you to come down to the Hill right away. He's leaving town tomorrow."

"Wonderful!" she breathed in vast relief. Then she noticed the rigid line of Buddy's mouth. "Buddy—I haven't complicated things too much, have I?" There was concern for him in her voice. In the beginning it had not occurred to her that such an intercession would be embarrassing for anyone but her.

"Faith," he said, and the word was sharp, "I want you to understand clearly that all I did was make an appointment. I did *not* defend you."

Her lips tightened. "That was all I expected or wanted you to do," she said. "And for that, I am grateful."

He pushed back his chair, to indicate she ought to leave. She had the feeling that they had become complete strangers.

# 6.

SHE examined the name plates beside doors with dark heavy frames and old-fashioned transoms, until she found one with the sign: MODIE VINCENT (D). She debated momentarily whether to knock or walk in, and decided on the latter. The door was heavier to swing than she had expected.

The secretary, a middle-aged shapeless woman in a flower print dress, was eating an apple. She put down the apple and looked up inquiringly. She was obviously skilled at protecting the Congressman from unwanted intrusions.

"Yes?" the secretary said, with a demanding intonation.

"I'm Faith Vance." She wondered if she had spoken overloud as though to a deaf person.

The secretary took on all the characteristics of an iceberg. "One moment." She disappeared into the other of the two rooms allotted each Congressman.

This room, Faith noted in the secretary's absence, had a peculiar mustiness mingled with the odor of furniture polish. It was almost unbearably neat. The woman, Faith thought, was probably one of those indefatigable housekeepers, who, being unmarried, took out all her frustrations on the office. And she understood intuitively that Modie Vincent was probably the kind of man who would want an older woman to manage his affairs.

174

The shapeless secretary returned. "Go right in," she said, but there was no kindness in her voice.

Faith went in, closed the door behind her, and stood quietly waiting for the Congressman to put aside the copy of the *Encyclopedia Britannica* he was reading. The room was dim and shadowy from the overcast day, and he had found it necessary to turn toward the window. He was puffing slowly on the great curved pipe which seemed too large for his narrow jaw, and appeared unaware that anyone had entered.

Faith's heart palpitated uncomfortably, and she swallowed a time or two as she waited. Then she scraped her shoes, but without effect. Was he deliberately trying to destroy her composure, or was his concentration truly so great that he did not know of her presence? The office, she saw, was littered with newspapers and books; the bookcases overflowed and papers were stacked on the floor. The desk had heaps of letters piled on it. Here was a man, she thought, who could throw away nothing—and she wondered how he got his work done.

Finally she cleared her throat. "Mr. Congressman," she said.

He started, and swung around in his chair toward her. "Eh?" he said, "—how did you get in here?"

"Your secretary," Faith said, provoked.

"Oh, yes," he said, as though remembering, "you're Miss—?"

"*Mrs.* Vance. Mr. Brooks telephoned about me."

"Why certainly," he said, his face brightening, "I know now. You were called before the Committee the other day. Oh yes, I remember very well. The Spanish girl. Won't you sit down?" He waved toward a dilapidated leather sofa

175

which gave evidence of many years' use. A big, polished brass spittoon stood beside the sofa.

As she was being seated, Faith said politely, "Not Spanish. I'm an American."

He put a marker in the Encyclopedia and laid it on a bare portion of his desk. "Well, we won't argue, young lady. There's no need for that. What did you come to talk to me about?"

Once down on the sofa, it was difficult to breathe, difficult to collect her thoughts. She was sitting so low in relation to the desk that it seemed enormous; and Modie Vincent, with his sallow face, beady eyes, and cropped hair, loomed over her. He seemed to compel her attention.

"Why—I wanted to explain." Suddenly she felt confused, uncertain of how or what to explain.

He took the curved pipe out of his mouth with a slow gesture, and smiled. "You may confess to me. A confession is always best in the long run."

"Confess?" she said, bewildered. "I have nothing to confess! I wanted to explain that the Committee has done me an injustice, that the hearing was unfair. I thought that, of all the members of the Committee, you—"

He interrupted before she could get any further. "Now, young lady, I hope you understand that I always try to do right by people, that I always try to see every point of view. But evidence always carries so much greater weight than any protestation. I truthfully don't see what you expect to achieve." He spoke with great seriousness, as though he had wrestled with this and similar matters in his soul, and come to immutable conclusions.

Suddenly Faith understood that, from his point of view— and unlike some of the other Congressmen who obviously

176

were conscious of their roles—this man was in truth trying to do the right thing. But something had captured him, some fear, some single-purposed drive, which would accept no admissions of error on his part. More, he had launched on a crusade, and he saw in himself a knight bearing banners. He was no ordinary Congressman, but an intellectual, a seeker after absolute truth in a lying world, an idealist sincere in the manner of the Inquisition.

How could she make him understand? "Don't you see, Mr. Congressman, that my reputation has been ruined without giving me a chance to defend myself? That I've been defamed by anonymous accusers without right of cross-examination? Don't you see that my Constitutional rights, my *American* rights have been—"

"I'm afraid not," he said, shaking his head impatiently. "I've heard that kind of talk so many times, after having seen a dossier full of evidence! I was once a Socialist myself, and I understand why minority rights must be protected. But when it comes to Communists, that's quite a different matter!" He was becoming agitated.

"But—" she said.

"But nothing!" he cried. "You've been scorched in the Commie fires, and you can expect to pay the penalty! Look at their record! They've destroyed the socialist parties everywhere! They've exalted the masses into a new kind of religion! They've destroyed the fundamental freedoms! They're Godless! They must be scourged from the earth!" Now he was very excited, and had begun pounding his desk with his fist. "Yes, of course some innocents will be swept along with the guilty! That can't be helped. It's too bad you're among them! We can't be blamed if you're drowned when we turn hoses on the conflagration . . . !"

177

His eyes glittered, and Faith saw that he was no longer aware of her as a person. He was making a speech to an imaginary audience, rousing them, thrilling them.

Her shoulders slumped and her head bent. She was frightened and sickened by this man. Murmuring, "I must go," she gathered up her purse and hurried out of the room. Behind her the Congressman continued to rail and shout and the words echoed after her.

In a day or two, Faith thought with bitterness, she would find his speech in *The Congressional Record*—printed there for all posterity to read.

She stood on the flight of marble steps, confused by indecision, and gazed absently down the Mall. The clouds hung so thick and heavy that the top of the Washington Monument was obscured in mist. It was late afternoon, and already the trolleys were jamming with homeward bound Government workers.

This was an old part of Washington, and the sidestreets, with their redbrick two-story row houses and overarching trees, retained much of the atmosphere of ante-bellum times. Such was particularly true on a misty day, which hid ugly details and smudged sharp edges of the old buildings. Faith felt like wandering these streets aimlessly, wander till exhaustion. Wander down to the Anacostia flats, where the Bonus Army had camped, where the Union Army had once built watch-fires. Wander, in the mist and fog, down to the river. . . .

Behind her, footsteps sounded on the marble, and in a burst of apprehension she turned to see who made the footsteps. It was only a uniformed guard from the building, but for one panicky second she wondered if he might be coming after her. He drew abreast and paused, without giving her so much as a look. Her heart subsided in relief. Grimly she questioned whether she had become irrational. Then she ran with unnecessary haste for an empty cab.

"Fifteenth and H," she said to the driver. Then she realized that without thinking she had given Chandler's address. The implication startled her. In a sudden rush she decided to go to Thatcher's office before he quit for the day, and get it over with. She had to tell him who her lawyer was—she had to relieve at least a little of the pressure! Calmer now, she redirected the cab driver.

Thatcher had forbidden her to come to his office. Only the sense of urgency made her do it today. Thatcher's firm, though one of the largest Washington agencies, was not much by New York standards—and Thatcher was all too conscious of this fact. Further, his own role was so subordinate, so much that of a glorified flunky, that he could not bear to have his wife witness it.

She got off the elevator on the fourth floor of the office building and approached the pretty telephone operator-receptionist who had a desk and switchboard at one side of the small foyer. The girl did not recognize her.

"May I help you?" the girl said.

"Mr. Vance, please," Faith said. "Tell him his wife is here."

The girl lifted her eyebrows slightly. "Yes, certainly."

She flicked a small lever, and Faith could hear a buzzing down the hallway in Thatcher's office.

"He doesn't answer," the girl said.

"I'll just have a look," Faith said; "sometimes he doesn't answer when he's busy on an account." Before the girl could think of an objection, she was gone. Employees she passed in the hall paid no attention to her.

She came to a door with a frosted glass pane and the name, "Mr. Vance," neatly lettered in gilt. The door was partly open, and she could see that the office was empty. Thatcher hated this office, and it was one of his continual embarrassments. A cubby-hole, furnished with a battered wooden desk and leather-covered swivel chair, the office was not in accord with Thatcher's conception of an executive's sanctum. A more proper setting, he had remarked, would be a suite twenty-five or thirty stories up, furnished expensively and luxuriously as befitted a person of his background. Thatcher's office was in dramatic contrast with the scale of his social operations, too. It was not surprising that he chafed over his employment, and complained sometimes that the firm's president kept him around chiefly to entertain clients at various bars and country clubs.

Feeling an obscure disappointment and sense of loss, Faith went back to the foyer.

"Mrs. Vance," the receptionist called, "I checked and discovered that Mr. Vance left over half an hour ago. I doubt if he'll be back tonight. He didn't anticipate your coming?"

"No," Faith said gravely. "Thank you very much." She pressed the down-button for the elevator.

When she got home, she asked, after a warm welcome from Jeanie, whether Thatcher had come in. He had not. Nor did he show up by dinnertime. After holding dinner as long as she dared tax Donnie's patience, Faith prepared to eat alone.

Picking with disinterest at the jellied consommé, immersed in her thoughts, she did not hear him when he stepped softly behind her and kissed her on the back of the neck. She jumped and gasped from the surprise.

"Oh, Thatcher!" she cried. "What a start you gave me!"

"Sorry I'm so late," he apologized, sitting down immediately at the table. "You shouldn't have waited." He slipped his napkin into his lap and began rapidly to work on his soup.

She was aware that he had been drinking—but either not so much as usual, or else he was holding it better. Suddenly he stopped and tore open his shirt collar, in the gesture of an exasperated man exceptionally hot—though in fact the evening, because of the mist, was somewhat cooler than usual.

When he had finished the soup, Faith said in a mild, tentative manner, "I went by your office this afternoon. I had to go down to the Hill, and I wanted a ride home."

He glanced at her disapprovingly. A slight flush was in his cheeks. "Well—?"

"You weren't there, that's all."

He scowled. "I met a fellow for drinks."

She never pursued him like this, never questioned him, never tried to corner him. But something in his manner stirred her curiosity, set her to wondering why he had kissed her, why his behavior seemed so out of the ordinary and so strange. To resist asking a direct question seemed impossible, however much it might stir him up.

"Business appointment?" Her tone bore more of a query than the words.

For a moment he appeared possessed by an odd stupefaction. Then his eyes sharpened with anger. "Yeah, sure! Who else?" He deliberately stitched the question with a heavy irony.

"Oh, I don't know—" she said, some malicious little trouble-making devil taking possession of her.

"Go to hell!" he said, plunking his spoon on the table.

At this instant the telephone rang, and Donnie, walking unobtrusively as though wishing to pretend she had not heard their quarrel, answered the call. She kept her voice muted.

"The Vance residence," she said, and paused to listen. "Who may I say is calling, please?" She listened again. "Oh —well, just a moment, please."

Dubiously, hesitantly, she came into the dining room. "It's for you, Miz Vance, a gent'man who won't give his name."

As Faith got up from the table her heart tripped, in mingled pleasure and panic that the call might be from Dane Chandler. No—it could not be. Dane Chandler would give his name. But Abe Stone, calling on special business, might not. . . . Out of the corner of her eye, she saw the sour expression on Thatcher's face change to what was unmistakably a brooding anxiety.

She went to the phone. "What!" she cried. After a long pause she added in a half-sob, "I see. Yes, yes—I'll be there." She hung up blindly.

Returning to the table, she dropped with a heavy, lifeless movement into the chair. Her face was pallid, and her eyes were dark pools of horror.

Partially rising and reaching toward her, Thatcher exclaimed, "Why Faith—what's the matter?"

"That—" she said in the thin tones of the mortally wounded, "was what is called in other countries The Secret Police. They're after me."

Thatcher fell back into his chair. "My God!" he said. "My God—I never expected *this!*"

# 7.

THE last thought in Faith's mind that night, and the first thought next morning, was the curt telephone summons. In between was a fantasia of dreams like Doré illustrations, which left her exhausted and confused. She was chased by things, which, in daylight, seemed formless, and therefore all the more terrifying.

In the mirror, she was shocked at the appearance of her face. It bore marks of real suffering. Her eyes were dull and ringed by cadaverous circles. Her mouth was drawn, the lips compressed, and indicated a tendency to quiver. She brushed her hair carefully and cold-creamed her face, but she looked little better.

During the night, Thatcher had made some effort at reconciliation by stroking her body in an effort to soothe her. But she could not feel him, and had recoiled from his touch. There was a patent insincerity in his movements which was, in fact, infuriating to her. She could not remember ever having loathed him so much.

She dressed mechanically, selecting her black linen skirt and a fresh, full blouse. She wanted to look neat, respectable, not flamboyant. This was a rationalization of her desire to be as inconspicuous as possible, unobtrusive, smaller than a mouse. Perhaps they would overlook her, forget her, if she seemed sufficiently unimportant. If only she could become invisible!

They had given her so little time. Report at 10 A.M., the man on the telephone had said, and be prompt. If they knew anything about her at all, they should have known that she was always prompt, she thought. But apparently that was not the kind of personal characteristic they were interested in.

And another thing: come alone, the man said. You may not have witnesses or counsel. The phrase spun round and round in her head: you may not have witnesses or counsel you may not have witnesses or counsel you may *not* . . . *you may not.* . . .

Thatcher, for once, was up early and out of the house. He had very little to say. Evidently the sight of his wife was more unsettling to him than she had realized. Or perhaps he, too, like so many of the others, was afraid of contamination. At this thought, she felt like a leper. She was beginning to shrink from going out in public, from going to the office, from going anywhere.

This morning she took over from Donnie the routine of getting Jeanie off to school, and derived an enormous pleasure from being with the child. Jeanie, as though she sensed Faith's agitation, chose to be charming—an effort to compensate for her mother's unhappiness, Faith thought. Jeanie was delighted at having her mother dress her, and promised, as a reward, to paint a "raspberry fish for framing." As she prepared to dash for the station wagon, Faith called her back and kissed her on the damp temple half-concealed by the nestling brown curls.

Appalled by the abrupt emptiness of the house after Jeanie had gone, Faith turned at once to her own immediate concern. First she called her office, and explained that she would be delayed. Next, she called Dane Chandler. When she told him what had happened, he whistled.

"I've been expecting this," he said, "but hardly so soon. Once the various agencies start competing with one another over you, somebody is bound to get mauled. Now, here's a very important point: *don't sign anything*. Don't sign anything, under any circumstances. Even if they threaten. Got it?"

"Yes," she said dutifully, feeling, without any logical basis, a stirring of hope merely because she was talking to Chandler. "Yes, I've got it."

"Fine. Can you come by my office when they've finished with you?"

"Can I? Of course!"

As she hung up, she realized that she could breathe without hurting inside.

The morning sun was slowly dissipating the mist which clung so tenaciously to the earth. The street was steaming hot, and already dogs panted and little children ran nearly naked in wisps of playsuits. To Faith, used to the office at this time of day, the morning seemed abnormally quiet, ominously so. And the peace and calm which marked the exterior of the Federal building forebode the storm, she thought.

They had not told her to go to the great columned structure between Pennsylvania and Constitution Avenues, where the Chief had his offices, but to an annex on K Street. The great building had overflowed with Their activities, and They had swarmed into other buildings all around the Capital. There were so many of Them, and They were so very busy.

She was not aware, until she stood before the annex, that she thought of Them in such fashion. But They had become impersonal, an abstract force which, once set in motion, could never be stopped. In Their might and power They rolled on and on, an avalanche of inconceivable proportions, in which the individual became as dust. Though her conscious mind told her that she, Faith Vance, was caught in this avalanche, nevertheless she could not believe it. Such a disaster was like death, impossible to imagine.

Now she had to command herself to move, otherwise she might have stood rooted before Their annex forever. By moving, she might even escape the avalanche. She lifted one foot, and then the other, and, somewhat to her surprise, discovered that she was heading toward the doorway of the nondescript building which concealed Them from her frightened, staring eyes.

She was met by a uniformed, armed guard. "Yeah?" he said, "what is it?"

It was he who snapped her back into reality. "I'm scheduled to report to Room 5B," she said with a boldness she did not feel.

He retreated slightly and took up a phone from his desk. "Five B," he said. In a moment he went on. "This is O'Brien. You didn't gimme no mornin' schedule yet. Got a girl down here." He listened, then banged the receiver down in irritation.

"Your name Vance?" he asked.

"Yes," she said, almost in a whisper.

"Okay, okay!" He pressed a button, and another armed guard came out of a door on one side. "Take her to 5B," he said, jerking his head in Faith's direction.

She followed the second guard into a rickety elevator, and they ascended slowly to the fifth floor. Passing each floor, Faith could see long bays filled with clerical personnel and filing cabinets. And at each door was an armed guard.

The fifth floor was different. It was broken up by portable partitions into small offices—"consulting rooms," Faith thought with irony. One of these was marked with a large, black letter B. To this office the guard delivered her.

She was met by a bored, sandy-haired young man whose eyebrows and lashes were a light straw-color, as if bleached by the sun. She might easily have passed him on the street without notice. An equally bored stenographer was sitting with an open pad and a freshly sharpened pencil.

"Jus' take that chair," the young man said. His first words marked him as a Southerner, and she guessed Arkansas, though it was difficult to say for sure.

She remembered a remark once made by Mr. Cunningham about the South's being a prime breeding ground for policemen. The Southern colleges, he had said, were canvassed with especial care for white, Anglo-Saxon, anti-labor, middle-class students. Then they were offered training, jobs, badges, and glory. And such recruits flocked to the ranks. Recruits, like this one. Federal agents. For whatever purpose, a secret police.

As the sandy-haired young man turned toward his desk, she happened to see a bulge under his coat which revealed a shoulder holster. With a sharp intake of breath she wondered if they considered her so dangerous. She closed her eyes, then opened them again and tried to smile.

"Now, we've got a consid'able number of questions to ask you," he said, settling himself before a manila folder. "Answer *yes* or *no* as often as possible, the more so th' better, an' speak slow enough for th' stenographer to take down what you say. But first I wanta put you under oath. Remember there are tough penalties for perjury, jus' in case you get to feelin' like you wanta mix things up a bit. Make myself clear?"

"Yes . . . entirely clear."

"Here we go. What's your name?"

That was the beginning. The questions went on and on. Where did she work? How long? Name of immediate superior? When and where born? Parents' names? Married? Husband's name? Child's name? Maid's name? Address? All addresses for past five years? Schooling? Travel, where and when? Why?

She told the story straight, with as little display of agitation as possible. The questions were asked in a swift bored patter, and the answers listened to without facial expression. The stenographer transcribed like an automaton. Then without warning the context of the questions changed.

"Have you ever been fingerprinted?"

"Of course," she said, "all Government employees have been fingerprinted."

"Did you make remarks in opposition to bein' fingerprinted?"

"Why—I don't remember."

"Yes or no?" The soft Southern voice sounded surprisingly inflexible.

"I said—I don't remember!"

"Do you belong, or have you ever belonged, to an organization which advocates overthrow of the United States Government by force an' violence?"

"No! No—of course not!"

"Have you ever made remarks derogatory to the United States Government?"

She hesitated. "Not derogatory in the sense you mean. But I've criticized policies, certainly. That's my right."

The young man permitted himself a slight smile. The smile was not friendly, however, but cynical. "Have you ever made favorable remarks about the Union of Soviet Socialist Republics?"

188

She grew bewildered. "Why, at one time or another, about some things, and during the war—why, what a ridiculous question! I can say what I like about that country, this country, or any other country!"

The agent stared at her. "I did not ask you for an exposition of your views. I asked you a question to be answered, yes or no. Yes or no?"

"The question is impossible to answer!" she said, her voice shaking.

"Have you ever read the works of Karl Marx?"

"Part of them," she answered promptly, thinking of the bust of Mozart, "in college economics. Can't say that I understood them too clearly, though I got the drift."

"What newspapers do you read?"

"Any one I happen to pick up," she said, becoming angry.

"I asked for a specific list—" he said.

"Well, it's none of your business!" she burst out.

He paused, and nodded significantly at the stenographer, who wrote with exceptional speed. "I would like you to cooperate in this interview," the agent said. "It will look better in the record. I'll ask you another question. Was your father an American citizen?"

She swallowed. "No—but he intended to become an American citizen. He'd taken out his first papers when he died."

The agent smiled again, in an aloof way. "Did you enter this country at the age of five, with your parents, from Spain?"

"Yes," she said, then added rapidly, "—you clearly understand, I hope, that I was born in America?"

"You said that in answer to an earlier question," the agent replied, with about as much animation as a robot. "Did you

189

at any time receive payment for your activities in behalf of Loyalist Spain?"

She could feel the tendons in her neck tighten, and she was more racked by anger than by fear. What were They trying to do, she thought—label her as a foreign agent? There was some sort of Act, with all sorts of penalties, requiring foreign agents to register with the Justice Department, she knew; but she could not remember how long the Act had been in force, though she had heard it mentioned occasionally at the office. Good God! Surely They—

"Why do you delay?" the agent said. "Did you understand the question?"

"Of course I understood!" she said sharply. "Do you think I'm an idiot? And as for the answer: My activities for the Spanish Loyalists were entirely voluntary. Nor do I feel it necessary to apologize for them, or defend them!"

"That completes the list of questions," the agent said, almost as though Faith had not spoken at all. "Is there anything additional you'd like to say?"

She had the queer, disjointed feeling that he'd memorized his spiel like a door-to-door salesman, that he could rattle it off blindfolded, and that, actually, he'd heard nothing she had said. The stenographer had been hard at work, so everything was down in writing, and it didn't matter whether the agent heard or not. Nevertheless, she felt a powerful desire to beat against him with her fists, to *make* him hear, to make him understand that he was dealing with a human being. But she knew it was useless.

"Yes," she said, "I've got something to say!" She paused, to note whether her words had any effect on him. His face remained blank. But there was a reaction from the stenographer: she was quietly folding her notebook and getting ready to leave. So whatever was said, from now on, was doubly use-less. Notwithstanding, Faith resolved to have her say.

"I don't understand, in the first place," she went on, "why I have been called here. I don't understand the purpose of this investigation, or what you want with *me*. I've done noth-ing—so you're just wasting your time and the taxpayer's money. And I don't like a lot of the questions you asked! I think they were unfair and loaded! I think—"

"Okay, skip it!" the agent interrupted. "If that's all you've got on your chest, I'll jus' note in the record you made a protest. That's what we usually do. No point in taking up time and paper with the speech." He nodded to the stenog-rapher, and she made an additional notation. "The interview is closed. Come back here tomorrow at 10 A.M. to sign the transcript," he said.

"Thank you very much!" Faith said, stifling with anger. "But I won't come tomorrow! I won't sign anything unless I'm represented by counsel, and have an opportunity to ask some questions myself!"

"You'd better come," he said ominously, but his face showed a hint of dismay. "It won't be liked higher up if the transcript isn't signed."

"*I won't sign anything*," Faith said. "Now, may I go?"

She was afraid that in another moment she might fling his onyx marble fountain-pen desk set at him—and then there'd be the devil to pay. She had to get out, before she blew up into a million billion little pieces, and shattered the place from the force of her anger. The only thing that saved her was the incongruous thought: I'm quite a Senorita, after all! At that, she almost laughed, and her composure came flooding back.

When at last the guard appeared, the relieved agent dismissed her and turned to the stenographer. "Gee, kid, I'm bushed!" he said.

The reaction did not hit Faith until she was standing, free, in the steaming street once more. After the Congressional hearing, this thing seemed a farce, an anticlimax. She leaned against a lamp post and began to laugh. What pompous asses They were, what fools! What—what— She could not go on. Then suddenly she shuddered, and her body felt cold. Oh no! This was the real thing! She was underestimating Them, underestimating the meaning of this investigation. They only played marbles for keeps.

Inconceivable days, these, filled with inconceivable people and events. But true. Agonizingly true. Now her major job was to force herself to understand that a secret dossier was being assembled under the heading, "Faith Vance."

In the U. S. A.

Unnerved and trembling, she started for Dane Chandler's office. A single thought dominated her: where would she be without him?

# 8.

IT WAS now the quiet hour before dawn. Thatcher's thumping and bumping in the bathroom had waked her, and she lay listening, pretending to be asleep. He had not come home for dinner, and had sent no word. Exhausted by the day's events, she had gone to bed at nine o'clock, though she had considered waiting up for Thatcher.

She was anxious to talk to him. Lucky she hadn't waited, she thought now.

She lay in the four-poster with only a sheet and a thin nightgown covering her. This was more than enough in the breathless, humid night. All the windows were open full, and she could hear tree frogs and crickets with their patient, interminable chirping. A hound dog bayed, probably from somewhere in the Negro section, and a whippoorwill uttered its cry. Yes, Washington was, in spite of its European buildings, the American South. Then she heard a sound rare in the city, a sound which, for no explainable reason, filled her with nostalgia: a steam locomotive whistle. It was a sob, a wail—a melancholy comment of the machine on human destiny.

She had not been cheered by her visit with Dane Chandler. He had listened gravely to her account of the interrogation, and made a few notes. He had seemed pressed for time, harried, and only at the conclusion of their brief talk had favored her with the open but quixotic little smile she found so engaging. As she was leaving, she had mentioned her experience with Modie Vincent. Chandler's face had turned grave again. "I wish you had checked with me, first," he said. "I'd have advised you against seeing Vincent. Perhaps you've done yourself no harm, but you've done no good, either."

"Yes I have," she countered, "I've learned something. I've tightened my inner line of defense, so to speak."

"All right," Chandler said, "we'll count it a tactical victory."

Nevertheless, she felt down in the dumps at his reaction. She tried to conceal her emotion from him, and believed she had succeeded. Her depression was not one whit improved when, a few minutes later, her mind busy elsewhere, she bumped into Elaine Beverly leaving her bank.

"I thought you were in Maine," Faith said, not caring whether she sounded hostile.

"Down on business, my dear," Mrs. Beverly said. "And so glad to have run into you, too! I've read the papers. How is poor, darling Thatcher making out? I should think this publicity would simply crucify him . . . !"

"I don't know—he hasn't told me," Faith said with vexation. "He isn't the one under attack, you know!"

The thin lips puckered in the wrinkled face. "Now, my dear, don't take offense. You mustn't get cross and bitter! Going around angry will upset your digestion and spoil your looks—then what will Thatcher think of you? You come have lunch with me, and tell me how in heaven's name you got involved in this dreadful mess."

"No thanks," Faith said, backing away, "I'm—I'm in an awfully big hurry. Must get back to the office!" She knew very well what would happen once Elaine Beverly's tongue started wagging. Anything she said would be held against her. "No thanks!" she repeated, and turned and ran.

The afternoon at the office had been routine. Nothing out of the ordinary had happened. Mr. Cunningham had rushed off, Maria said, to New York on some United Nations business, to be gone for several days. And the bad taste left by Elaine had lingered.

It would be like Elaine to rope Thatcher in immediately; she certainly wouldn't rest until she got the details of what was going on. But now Faith didn't care. It didn't seem to matter, here in the quiet dawn, not matter in the least.

This browsing was interrupted when Thatcher plopped into bed. The springs creaked, and Thatcher said "Ah-h-h . . ." with a weary inflection. As usual, Faith could smell liquor; but he appeared to have perfect control of himself.

Faith turned on her side and half sat up in bed, wondering, as she did so, how two people could share a bed and yet have it seem so empty. "Thatcher—" she whispered. "Thatcher," she said more insistently, "I want to talk to you a minute. If you sleep late, I won't see you at breakfast, and—" She hesitated. Maybe this wasn't the time to tell him, after all. Maybe it would be better to phone him at his office.

"What is it?" he muttered, resentful at being disturbed. "Can't we talk some other time . . . ?"

From his impatience she knew she had chosen the correct moment to break the news; he would be so concerned with his physical want of sleep that he would not probe her with detailed questions.

"No—" she said, "it's important."

"About the quizzing they gave you?" He spoke with apathy, as though he had ceased having any interest in her affairs. He half opened his eyes.

She could see, in the semi-darkness, that he was on the verge of going back to sleep. "I've got a lawyer," she said. She wanted to shake Thatcher, make him listen, make him feel concerned about her.

"Oh," he yawned, "—is that all? It's about time, I'd say."

"The lawyer's name is Dane Chandler, and he's coming for dinner to talk about my case." She held her breath. She had decided on the strategy of throwing them together without further delay. By so doing, she might be able to deflect Thatcher's inevitable suspicions.

"Oh, all right," Thatcher said, yawning again. He inhaled deeply, preparatory to sleep, when an additional thought struck him. "How'd you land this fellow Chandler?"

She hesitated. "Through Abe Stone," she said with trepidation.

Lifting his head, Thatcher said, "Can't you leave that guy alone! Aren't you in trouble enough as it is? He's probably palmed off some shyster on you, and you'll be worse off than before! For Christ's sake, when will you learn some sense about those Reds!"

"He's not a shyster!" she cried with indignation; "he's with Sterling, Hardy, Hutchinson and McKee!"

"Oh-ho," Thatcher said, "so that firm is taking on your case, big-shot you. You must have a mighty important case, to rate that kind of talent. I don't know how you do it." He paused and stared at her through the slowly increasing light. "Reckon I'll look over this fellow Chandler pretty carefully tonight. Nice of him to be so interested in my wife. Sure as God made little green apples, I'll have a good look at him. . . ."

He turned on his side, his back toward her, and went at once to sleep.

At the end of the working day, she left the office promptly and hurried home by cab to dress for Chandler. To her surprise, Thatcher was already at home, pouring himself some bourbon from a decanter.

He pulled at his nose with an exaggerated gesture of elaborate thought. "Well-l-l—" he said; "you don't seem to have much trouble getting home on time when this fellow Chandler's involved."

"This happens to be a matter of great importance," she replied frigidly. But she could not help blushing.

The cool delight of the shower calmed her, did something to help still the turbulence which had distracted her all day long. She could not decide, no matter how honestly she considered the question, whether her restlessness was more occasioned by her case or by the futility of her marriage. It

196

was enough to admit to herself, now, that she was dressing for Chandler, for him alone, and not for the lawyer but the man.

Jeanie, who had been playing by herself in the back yard, wandered in and out with her puppy while Faith was dressing. "Mommie," she said, "I'm lonesome. There's nobody to play with." Her lips puckered.

Faith called her and, giving her a kiss, said, "We'll see about that. You go tell Donnie to start your bath, and you can use Mommie's big powderpuff afterwards. Would you like that?"

"Oh-h-h, lovely!" Jeanie cried, and ran off.

Around Faith's eyes was a swelling feeling. It was like a scrap she remembered from Vergil, ". . . lacrimae rerum." Before she slipped on her dinner dress, she finished bathing Jeanie and got her ready for supper and bed.

When Faith came downstairs, Thatcher glanced up.

He whirled the ice in his highball glass. "You look gorgeous, honey," he said. "Absolutely gorgeous. I'd forgotten you could look that way."

"Thatcher," she said in a mechanical voice, ignoring his comment, "I do wish you'd wait to mix drinks till guests come." It was a useless remark, she knew, but she had to say something.

"Oh, he'll get plenty, never fear. I'll see to *that!*"

"Please, Thatcher," she said pleadingly, "let's not quarrel!"

He let his mouth droop. "Were we?" he said, in pretended astonishment, inhaling smoke from his cigarette and blowing it out through his nostrils.

She *was* gorgeous. She could see it in Dane Chandler's eyes when he took her hand to bid her good evening. He had never seen her dressed in anything like this flimsy chartreuse

197

dinner frock, low cut for coolness, and smart in a restrained, sophisticated sort of way. The warmth of her suntanned skin was emphasized, the tawny hair became a richer gold, and her dark eyes lost their daytime plumcolor and became almost black. She was, she knew with pleasure, a striking woman. And her voice sounded mellow, deeper than usual, richer with a thousand little harmonies. Instinctively she knew that Thatcher was at once aware of these things, aware of Chandler's effect on her, and her reaction. "Good evening, Mrs. Vance," was all that Chandler had said. She was thankful for that, and thankful for the note of propriety and formality in his voice.

"We're so glad you could come, Mr. Chandler," she said.

Not once, in Thatcher's presence, did the sustained note of formality between them lapse or vary. Evidently Chandler had guessed about Thatcher Vance all he needed to know.

Thatcher, for his part, was the perfect host. He was like a spoiled child on good behavior, showing off. Everything he did was with his oldtime flourish. Consciously or unconsciously, Faith thought, he was exerting himself to show his superiority over Dane Chandler.

"How about a whiskeysour, Chandler?" Thatcher meant to be gracious, but a slightly patronizing tone crept into his voice. "I'm one up on you—I'll make yours double." He tilted the frosted cocktail shaker to pour Chandler's drink and overflowed the glass. It was evident that he was more than one up.

Chandler smiled pleasantly. "That's enough for a good start." He sipped at the drink with measured slowness, as though he intended to make it last for quite a while.

"See you're wearing the screaming eagle," Thatcher said,

198

nodding toward the veteran's discharge button in the lapel of his white linen coat. "What was your outfit?"

"I was attached to the Judge Advocate General's office."

"So you were a desk soldier!"

"Regretfully, yes. I wanted to run a machine gun. But they told me to obey orders and keep quiet. So I had no alternative."

"I saw plenty of action," Thatcher said, with the bravado of a small boy. "That's the Navy for you—always in the thick of it. Even the desk goldbraid has to go out and take a turn, now and then. Great institution, the Navy!"

"So the Navy says," Chandler remarked drily, his voice flatter than usual.

"Oh, don't get me wrong," Thatcher said, helping himself liberally to his cocktail, "—far be it from me to defend the Washington brass! I know what *they* did during the war . . . !" His face darkened into that jealous mood which had so often characterized it during his periods of leave, when he would catechize Faith as to her activities in his absence. "So you were in Washington all during the war?" he went on as though completing a thought in his own mind, and looking directly at Chandler.

"The entire time. The entire interminable time, I should say."

"Did you know my wife?" The question came with explosive abruptness.

Chandler returned Thatcher's look with impassive calm. "I'm sorry to say I did not. If it hadn't been for the activities of a certain disreputable Committee, I'm afraid I should never have had the opportunity of meeting her."

To Faith it seemed there was something calculated in Chandler's statement; nor was she prepared for the more

199

than obvious confusion which overwhelmed Thatcher. He fumbled with his glass, set it down awkwardly, and searched his jacket for cigarettes though a box full sat on the coffee table in front of him.

She had been tempted to laugh at Thatcher's boasting about the Navy. He had hated and despised it so. Actually, he had launched his Naval career as a lark; then, in disgust, had moved heaven and earth to get out of the Navy—but without success.

They had been married only six weeks, and relations with Thatcher were still an idyll. One Sunday afternoon they went for a walk—hoping for therapeutic effects from the brisk air and sunshine, hoping to overcome the effects of a party the night before. They were crossing the Connecticut Avenue Bridge over Rock Creek, high-arched and guarded by reclining stone lions, when they ran into a friend of Thatcher's.

"Heard the crazy news over the radio?" the friend shouted, though they were quite close. Without waiting for an answer, he went on shouting. "The Japs have bombed hell out of the U. S. fleet! Roosevelt has called a joint session of Congress and of course it's war!"

She could never forget her feeling of suffocation, like being again in the depths of the river. She clutched Thatcher's arm tightly, but he did not even look at her. The next morning he applied for a commission in the Navy.

When he reported this action, she asked, puzzled, "Why Navy? I thought you went to military school?"

"Oh yes," he said, "but the Navy appeals to higher type fellows. That is, as officers. You know what I mean: gentlemen."

He was very optimistic about his chances of becoming a lieutenant-commander. "I know exactly the right people," he said blithely. But to his surprise, and pain, when the commission came through it was only an ensign's rating. In a rage, he would have declined it had he dared. The final insult was his assignment to an Atlantic mine-sweeper.

And shortly after, the letters had begun—the letters which she had never saved, but burned or torn into tiny little bits. Their threatening tone bewildered her and made her miserable. He got the idea that she ought to have his mother, Julia, come to Washington to live with her. Because Faith declined with firmness, he took to brooding over her refusal. He hinted darkly at what he called "ulterior motives."

"I simply can't understand your reasons," he wrote. "Mother would be a great help to you when the baby's born. I don't like the thought of leaving a child with a darky, unsupervised. Of course there's nothing wrong with a real *mammy*, but I never have felt comfortable around Donnie. There's something persnickity about her. And another thing, Mother could be a companion for you in the evenings—that is, unless you're running around with people I don't know about. Living here on a ship day after day and thinking about you in Washington all alone with the brass gives me the jim-jams. I honestly can't understand your opposition to having Mother. . . ."

And, as the war dragged on and on, the theme ran like a *leitmotif* through his letters more and more frequently. "If I should come home," he wrote another time, "and find some bastard in your bed—I'd kill you both on the spot! You say Cunningham's married and has three kids. What does that prove? I wish you'd take a job under some older man—or a woman. I tell you I'd feel ever so much better about it. It's not that I don't trust you—I do. I trust you as much as I trust myself. . . ."

Poor Thatcher, she thought, who trusted her as much as

201

he trusted himself. The comparison stuck in her mind, like a grain of sand in an oyster—but it produced no pearl, just irritation. She guessed about Thatcher, and she was piqued—even, sometimes, violently, furiously angry. It sat ill that he should lecture her, and she would write him stinging letters in reply. Then she tore them up. After all, Thatcher was at war—lonely, even more lonely, in a sense, than she herself. It was hard to make judgments about the demands of the flesh.

She was brought back to the present by Thatcher's voice. He had found and lighted a cigarette, and made some small talk which had not registered with her. Clearly he had recovered his poise.

"By the way, Chandler," he was saying, "what was your rank?"

"Went in as a captain," Chandler replied, "and ended as a lieutenant-colonel. Pretty routine sort of advancement."

Thatcher pursed his lips. He had always looked sourly at those who outranked him. "Lucky you," he said. "Promotions came faster in the Army. That's where I made a mistake."

Faith was about to interrupt with some safe platitude, when dinner was announced.

They did not talk about her situation until after dinner, over coffee. Thatcher had remained polite, but increasingly distant, and Chandler had made no effort to penetrate the barriers thus erected. He did not seem to care what Thatcher thought, except that he was careful not to jeopardize his own relationship with Faith.

Faith realized with a shock that she had not, at any time, looked squarely at either of them. She had not dared. The easy, pleasant warmth remained behind Chandler's swash of freckles, as each time she had met him. The ingenuous

202

smile remained in evidence, as did the leanness of mind and body. She knew that her admiration for him was betrayed in her face.

Thatcher's handsome arrogance emphasized his childishness. The patrician set of his face seemed a foil for inner insecurity. And the undue concern with haberdashery—the over-meticulous tie, the over-exact set of the pocket handkerchief—made him seem obvious.

Thatcher put down his demi-tasse. "What I can't understand," he said with jarring emphasis, "is why such a hullabaloo should be made about my wife? She doesn't know any atomic secrets. Maybe she's been indiscreet at times, but—"

Dane Chandler glanced at him oddly. "Possibly there are all sorts of reasons, including the fact that the authorities must keep busy in order to justify their appropriations. Even where subversion doesn't exist, they tend to invent it. Surely, Mr. Vance, you've lived in Washington long enough to know this."

"I?" Thatcher said, getting up and beginning to pace one end of the room. "I? Why in the name of kingdom-come would I know anything about such matters? I never have paid the slightest attention to Government and I never intend to! Let 'em stew in their own damn juice, I say! Or let 'em—well, anyway, to hell with them. All of 'em! That's the way I feel about the stinking Government and all its works!" He had become very agitated, and was controlling his hands only with an effort.

Faith, astonished, made an attempt to soothe him. "Thatcher, dear," she said, "I'm sure Mr. Chandler didn't expect you to have any special knowledge of Government procedures. I don't think I remembered to tell him you're in industry. . . ." Then she turned apologetically to Chandler. "We've all been so overwrought—even Jeanie. . . ."

"Yes—" Thatcher said, bristling, "we certainly have!" Then he added stiffly, "If you'll pardon me, I must leave now. I have some work at my office. . . . Of course I'd like to hear the details of the case—"

When the door closed behind Thatcher, a curious silence settled over the living room, a silence of rapport which follows when a disturbing third personality has been removed from the presence of a congenial pair. Gladioli in tall vases and long-stemmed roses suddenly seemed refreshed. From outside the open floor-length windows, this morning's tree frogs and crickets were audible again. A car honked, and silence again absorbed the room.

"More coffee?" Faith said with an effort.

"No thanks," Chandler said, stirring himself. He leaned forward in his chair, and his hands made the now-familiar church-and-steeple gesture.

"Open the doors and see all the people," Faith remarked softly.

He smiled the wide, pleasant smile. "Yes," he said, "—by all means." He paused, cleared his throat in professional fashion. "The first point—"

"I'm listening," she said.

"The first point is that I have no information, absolutely none at all, on the birth certificate—thus far, that is. Of course it's too soon yet for anything final."

Disappointment filled her eyes, and she allowed the long lashes to hover over them.

"I haven't approached the Spanish Embassy—I'm saving it for last."

She sighed. "I haven't told you yet, but the Quiz Kids—" she interrupted herself with an ironic laugh, in which

Chandler joined, "—the Quiz Kids have been going after me hot and heavy."

"You mean—they've called you for another interrogation?"

"No, not that. But they're sleuthing me. I mean, they're calling on people I know, asking all sorts of silly questions. I learned today they'd called privately on the other girls in my office—wanted to know whether I was faithful to my husband!" She blushed, for the words had seemed especially difficult to say.

"Routine," Chandler said, easing her embarrassment, "—strictly routine. They'll check clear back to your college days, maybe beyond. Instructors, roommates, boy-friends if they can find them. In short, the works. After all, they have a lot of personnel. Why not use 'em?"

"Yes," she said with a worried expression, "they went to the White House to ask Melvin Thompson why I talked to him. That proves the office phone is tapped—they couldn't have found out any other way. He sent me a special delivery note."

"Apparently Thompson trusts the mails more than he does the telephones—even in the White House," Chandler said, permitting himself a wry smile.

"And our maid, Donnie," Faith said, "they've actually grilled Donnie!" She got up and pushed a button near one door, and in a moment Donnie appeared. "Please repeat what happened this morning, will you Donnie?" Faith asked.

"Well," Donnie said, wiping her hands on her apron, "this here man shows up an' flashes a badge, an' I thought, oh-oh trouble's a-comin'! Sure enough, he says he's a special agent, an' he wants to know if I ever see any radical-lookin' people come here. An' I say, 'What you mean, *radical-lookin'*?'

'You know,' says this fella, 'foreign, *un*-American lookin'.'
'Boss,' I say, 'cause I can tell he would like me to say Boss,
'—Boss, I reckon I don't rightly know: ain't nobody comes
here but *nice* people.' Well sirree, his face fell an' off he
went, draggin' his tail behind him!"

Chandler laughed, and Faith too could not help smiling.
The whole affair still seemed so fantastic that it was hardly
more real to her than a few disjointed kaleidoscopic scenes
from a detective thriller. It wasn't Faith, it couldn't be Faith,
*They* were after. It was, it must be, someone else by the same
name in a book. Chandler broke her reverie.

"Donnie," he said, "you should have been a lawyer."

Chortling, she returned to the kitchen.

"Speaking of law," Faith said impulsively, "the Daumiers
in your office have haunted me. I simply can't forget them!"
And then the impulse worked itself out in its full meaning.
"I have a collection of Goyas—my father's. I'd like to show
them to you." She understood, only after the words were
out, just what she was doing. It was the contrast again, the
contrast between Thatcher and Dane Chandler. It was the
resentment she had never forgotten when Thatcher had commented, *I collect hunting prints*. Then she had not recognized the resentment. She knew, now. Maybe the essential
disharmony between them had begun in that very phrase.

"Oh, yes," Chandler said with unassumed eagerness, "I'd
like to see them!"

She led Chandler as she had once led Thatcher into the
small paneled room, tiered with books, which had been her
father's study. She drew out the portfolio and explained,
as she had once explained to Thatcher, how she had sold
some of the etchings for the Loyalist cause in Spain.

Chandler said, "It must have hurt to part with them."

"It did hurt," she said. She tilted her head and looked up

206

into his wide-set gray eyes. He was standing close, so close that she was conscious of the little wrinkles in his skin and the bigness of his body. In his arms, she thought, she would seem so small. There passed between them the same electric identification which had occurred in their first look. It tingled, vibrant, charging the atmosphere like a physical force. Her lips and her eyes, she knew, were giving her away.

He hesitated, and the muscles of his whole body tensed. Then he turned sharply aside and remarked in a brusque, businesslike voice, "I have news for you, Mrs. Vance. Tomorrow we may learn about your accusers. I've arranged to secure your dossier." The words were spoken with a note of hoarseness, as if he had forced himself to talk.

"Thank you," she said quietly, slipping the Goyas back into the portfolio. But at that moment she did not care about her accusers. She had stood on the verge of something which might have changed the context of her entire life, in a way that anonymous accusers could never change it—and she had lost that something. She felt suddenly an overwhelming tiredness, a weariness more acute and penetrating than any she had ever experienced. She wondered how she could keep on with Thatcher, or, indeed, continue to live at all. . . .

She looked at Chandler again, a look of blame and hurt, and she imagined his face was taut with strain. Perhaps he was berating himself for having allowed such an impasse to arise.

They returned to the living room. As he passed the piano, Chandler stopped to examine the bust of Mozart. He took the bust in both hands and sat down meditatively on the piano stool.

"So this," he mused, "—is Wolfgang Amadeus Marx!"

He was still sitting there when Jeanie wandered down the stairs, nightgown rumpled, brown curls askew, blinkyeyed. "Mommie!" she said, clutching a fuzzy duckling, "I dreamed bad an'mal things chasing me!"

Chandler smiled at her, a smile of warmth and reassurance, and set the bust aside.

Then Jeanie did an extraordinary thing. She went straight to Chandler as to an old friend, and climbed up beside him.

Half in embarrassment and half in pleasure he cradled her against his arm.

# 9.

ROBERT CAHILL was an exceptional Senator, an exceptional man. He was fortunate in hailing from a State where "the interests" were relatively weak, and could be dealt with without compromising all of his basic beliefs. Compromise he did, and with full awareness. But he was fond of saying privately that if you added up all his deeds in the Senate, both good and bad, the good would outweigh the bad. "And that," he would conclude, "is a better record than 99.44% of the distinguished gentlemen in the Senate." As one result, he had been a Senator for twenty-seven years.

He was the sort of man, after all his experience in the Senate, who was neither surprised nor shocked by anything; he was impervious to any chicanery, to any nobility. In spite of the power of Big People, he maintained a lingering faith in Little People. He was one of the few Senators to whom access was as easy for a workingman as for a businessman. And he had managed somehow to retain the respect of all his fellow Senators, even those who feared or mocked him.

These facts were part of the briefing Dane Chandler gave Faith on their way to the Senate Office Building in the early afternoon. He had brought his own car, a Ford convertible, that they might talk without being overheard by a cabby—a precaution well known to be wise. For one brief happy moment, with the car's top down and her hair blowing in the wind, Faith had felt completely carefree—but the weight of this mission bore her down, and she could think only of the horror of having a dossier.

Last night, when Chandler had informed her of arrangements to see the dossier, she had been too numb to react to his words. It was hours later that she realized the unusual nature of the accomplishment. Securing a dossier from any agency with a special investigative force could be done only on the highest levels. And to secure a dossier from Them was a triumph. It might, or should, contain a compendium on the dossiers built up by other agencies—including, maybe, the records of the Congressional Investigating Committee itself.

"How did Senator Cahill do it?" was the first question she had asked Dane Chandler this afternoon.

Chandler wrinkled his forehead, and Faith noticed the way he squinted in the glaring sunlight. "Well, the Senator was pretty mysterious about it," he said. "But it's obvious he has information of his own on somebody—somebody important. A few telephone calls and presto!"

"Can't the whole thing be called off by the Senator just as easily?" Faith asked, but without any hope.

"Ah!" Chandler answered, "that's a horse of another color —red."

Now Faith was beginning to feel almost afraid to learn the contents of her dossier. What if it revealed nothing but more trouble? She was reaching the limit of her endurance, she thought. Any human being could stand just so much.

After that, bang! Something would pop somewhere inside her, the head, maybe. Battle fatigue, they called it in the Army. Over-conscientiousness, in the civilian agencies. Then you landed in Walter Reed, or the Naval Hospital at Bethesda, or plain old St. Elizabeth's for the insane. In any event, you had plenty of predecessors—but for different reasons, of course. Thus far, the ideologically damned were only a few; but their ranks were growing.

Chandler swung the car around by the tiers of massive fountains north of the Capitol. The water spurted upward like small geysers, billowing and foaming, creating rainbows of spray and sunlight.

"So beautiful—so beautiful!" Faith said, "I could sit and watch them forever." Inwardly she added, *And not think . . . what a relief that would be!*

They parked, and walked a half-block to the flight of steps which led to the main entrance of the Senate Office Building. All along the way were little signs which read: "Reserved for Official Use"—"Reserved for Senators Only."

The steps seemed interminable. When they reached the top, Faith was breathless, and, by gentle pressure on Chandler's arm, indicated that she wanted to rest for a moment. Normally she would have run up this flight, without having been aware of the exertion. Now invisible weights dragged her legs, made her earthbound.

In the rotunda, with its circle of white marble columns, a guard looked at them suspiciously, but Chandler ignored him and they passed on. Faith shuddered. It was like a mausoleum, a sepulchre. She had the curious feeling that she had been executed, and this was afterward. Soon they would find a vault, or a crypt, and her name would be on it. Obediently she would climb into it, then say farewell to Dane Chandler forever.

She roused herself when Chandler said, "We're here." What weird, obsessional thoughts: she must put them from her!

Inside the high-ceilinged office with dark mahogany furniture, Chandler was introducing her to a bright-eyed young man with a wary look. "This is Bob Wilson, Senator Cahill's Secretary," he was saying, "—Mrs. Vance."

"How do you do," she said vaguely, with a sudden, crazy notion that in this old building one ought to curtsy.

"The Senator is all set to talk to you," Wilson was saying, "but an important military bill is up this afternoon, and the Senator felt he had to stay on the floor. He took your material with him, and asked that you call him outside. If there's any follow-through, let me know."

"All right, Bob, fine," Chandler said cheerily.

"Yes, thank you," Faith said with a mechanical inflexion. She noticed two girls typing. Efficient, she thought. What would they be doing in a tomb?

"One of the brightest lads on the Hill," Chandler was saying.

She supposed he meant Wilson. They were in the corridor again, she found, and Chandler was leading her by the arm.

"Yes, a bright lad," Chandler continued. "Plenty of people around here would like to get him, and maybe they will someday. They don't like the kinds of legislation he hatches— housing, health, anti-cartel, civil rights, and so on. Call him every name you can think of: socialist, communist, anarchist, paternalist, and a lot more. A lot more. Actually, he's the Senator's alter-ego, often his conscience, sometimes his soul. It's surprising how much history is written by people whose names you never heard of—people of ability, who scorn pork barrels and have a real sense of devotion to their country. But they're the ones who get denounced in the Senate and House for undermining the Government. This is a hell of a town if you ask me!"

"Yes," she said.

He seemed not to notice how taciturn she was, and put her in an elevator which was nothing but a big wire cage. She had a sudden fear that Chandler might go away and leave her in this cage. But he directed her to step out when the shriveled old man who was the operator said in a sulky voice, "Basement floor."

They walked a short distance to a point where a track came out of a tunnel. "Senate subway," Chandler said playfully in the tones of a sightseeing guide, as if she didn't know. She managed somehow to smile.

The air was dank and there were many pipes. The pipes reminded her of Melvin Thompson, and the failure of her White House mission. Everything she had tried had failed. Even with Chandler's guidance, she had failed. She was caught in the web.

The ridiculous little Senate subway car, which looked like a fugitive from a boardwalk, did not lighten her depression. It came whirring out of the tunnel, driven by a blubbery operator much too large for his seat. His wattles quivered when he brought the car to a stop. Two fluttery ladies in straw hats, with purple delegate ribbons angled across big bosoms, got off, aided by a portly gentleman who remarked, "Come, come, Madam Chairman."

The trip through the tunnel was another dream fragment. It could not, under any circumstances, have been real. She wondered what Dane Chandler was like as a 'teen-ager, taking his girl through a Tunnel of Love at a carnival, laughing and kidding and loving. She glanced down in surprise:

212

he was holding her hand. For the first time she felt a glimmer of reality, and of hope. Too quickly they arrived at the Capitol building, and he let go.

By elevator they reached the entrance to the Senate chamber. Chandler spoke to a guard, and the guard spoke to a page. The page disappeared. A dozen or more people milled about. Faith knew they were either lobbyists waiting to order and cajole a Senator, or constituents who wanted to buttonhole their man for a favor. None but the elect, the Senators themselves, and pages, were allowed on the Senate floor. Occasionally the great double doors opened for someone to pass through, and the sound of a high-pitched voice droned on and on, rising now and then to crescendo, falling off in a monotonous harangue.

Shortly the doors opened, and an impressively large man in a tan shantung suit stood before them. His flowing white hair was brushed carelessly back from his florid face. His eyes were the striking, important thing about him: they were both sardonic and kindly, and looked at you directly. Only after leaving his fascinating eyes did Faith notice that he wore a black string bow tie for contrast against his soft white shirt.

"Senator Cahill," Chandler said, stepping forward, "—I've brought Mrs. Vance."

The Senator looked her over, deliberately and thoroughly. "I'm glad to meet you, young lady," he remarked in a low-pitched voice which left the impression of great reserve power, "—I'm always glad to meet a real, live, Government Red. I've had the opportunity to meet so few in my time." Then he laughed, boisterously, as at a cosmic joke.

Faith blushed.

213

"You see!" said the Senator, patting her on the shoulder. "Now let's go put a cloakroom to good use for a change. I've got everything in my briefcase." He was speaking softly.

Faith was still embarrassed as they settled on green folding chairs at one corner of a long, ornately carved table. The Senator sat in the middle. Above them, in rococo gilt frames, hung huge paintings of the Battle of New Orleans and the Battle of Chapultepec, each partially obscured by time and smoke.

Senator Cahill slipped on a pair of fashionable heavy horn-rimmed glasses, and pawed through his briefcase. "Mmmm—let me see, I'm sure I've got it right here!"

Momentarily Faith wished that the dossier might disappear as miraculously as it had been obtained. Yet a termite-like curiosity began to gnaw within her. The curiosity gave way to a sense of intrigue, then a cumulative excitement. She was breathless again. She knitted her fingers in her lap and held them tightly. It was hard to believe that she had come to the Capitol to learn things about herself she did not know. That far above was the great dome, completed by Lincoln as a symbol of confidence in the Union, and topped by a colossal statue of Columbia. How could this Government, in its majesty, have time to bother with her? She felt almost awed by the attentions she had received.

Dane Chandler produced cigarettes and offered her one. She declined by a nod and a feeble effort at a smile. She was getting so jumpy she wondered if she could sit still.

"Well, well—here it is," the Senator said, pulling out a thick manila folder. "It's so fat I overlooked it. All on one little girl!"

At the sight of the dossier the nervous excitement within Faith became almost unbearable. Once more she was being smothered, as in a dream, and she longed to draw great, deep

214

breaths of clean pure air from some untainted source. What she longed for was the birdsong in the midst of battle. Intuitively she understood that she ached to return to the security of the vanished past, for in childhood and youth only the tangible has meaning.

Dane Chandler must have understood something of her ferment, for he gave her a smile of encouragement and reassurance.

"Now let me see," the Senator remarked again, propping his chin with his right hand, and thoughtfully tapping his nose with his forefinger. "Let me see. . . ." He ruffled the pages of the dossier. "I promised not to show this to anybody—but I *didn't* promise not to tell anybody about its contents. So if it's all right with you, young lady, and all right with you, Chandler, we'll leaf through, and I'll read a salient bit here and there. I wouldn't want to break my promise."

"Handle it any way you see fit, Senator," Chandler said.

"Of course!" Faith said, almost inaudibly.

"Mmm-m, thank you. Well, let me tell you that they've photostated practically every official document you've ever filled out, young lady—every job application, educational history, and everything else. And they've had a handwriting expert compare 'em, so they're satisfied the same person using the same name filled out all the forms. This is one reason your dossier's so thick. Also there are photostats of various and sundry petitions you have signed, with your name starred—here's one advocating municipal ownership of Washington trolleys and buses, another for staggering the hours of various Government agencies to avoid the traffic crush, another to reroute the wrong-way tracks around Dupont Circle, and another to lift the arms embargo against Loyalist Spain." The Senator paused. "Young lady, you ought

215

to be more careful what you sign." He looked at her with lifted eyebrows.

Suddenly the thread of fear, which had wound a tight cocoon of tension within her, snapped and floated off like gossamer. She laughed. "I'm afraid you're right, Senator Cahill. My activities are not only careless but reprehensible. I'll never sign another thing not first approved officially!"

The Senator laughed too, with a certain expression of satisfaction, as though he had been anxious to take the pressure off her before he proceeded to other matters.

"Now let's get down to business," he said. "This *is* business, we know." With the smile of satisfaction still playing around the sardonic eyes, he went on: "Your dossier, my dear young lady, begins in the summer of ten years ago."

"Oh, no!" Faith cried. "—I was only sixteen!"

"Oh, yes," the Senator said. "There are some people who consider young radicals the most dangerous—however, in this case, your precise identity is not known. Listen: *The Metropolitan Police reported that a car registered in the name of Hannah Prentiss Robles was driven in a parade organized in support of Republican Spain. It is assumed that subject was the driver, in view of her subsequent activities. . . .*"

"Mother's car! I *was* the driver!"

"Mmm-m-m—shall I enter it here? No? All right. The police have no legal right to make such records, you know. Well, the dossier proceeds in chronological order, so we'll take it that way, too. Listen: *Subject is known to have taken an active part in the Current Events Society at Bennington College, and to have had pronounced views. . . .*"

"What kind of views?" Chandler asked.

"Doesn't say. Just—views." He looked at Faith again with the upraised eyebrows, and tapped his finger against his

216

nose. "There's not a scintilla of evidence, one way or the other."

Amazed and incredulous, Faith shook her head. "I was a kind of a liberal, I guess," she said huskily. "It all seems such a long time ago. How can anyone remember all the things he said and thought in college?"

The Senator clucked. "Quite right: Now, on with the lesson. I hope all this is soaking in, young lady? I can't give you a photostatic copy—"

"Yes," said Faith, beset by conflicting bitter amusement and disbelief, "it's soaking in—deep."

"Good! Another item: *Subject's mother resigned from the Daughters of the American Revolution when said organization denied use of Constitution Hall to Marian Anderson, Negro singer. Subject is known to have urged Federal employees to attend subsequent concert given on steps of Lincoln Memorial. Sponsoring organization has been classified as subversive.*"

"It's true—about Mother and me, I mean. Mother was furious! Said it made her blood boil to think we'd lost the Civil War! Her grandfather had been killed in the Battle of the Wilderness, and she had a letter written— Oh, never mind! It's true, that's all!"

Senator Cahill put down the dossier. "I'm not cross-examining you, young lady. When the Attorney General doesn't like an organization, all he has to do is put it on his list. *You* don't have to say a word, if you don't want to. But on the other hand—possibly it wouldn't be a bad idea to formulate replies aloud. You may need to, someday." The lightness, the jesting, was gone from his voice. He wanted her to understand that the time for seriousness had come.

"Yes, sir," she said, her heart beginning to thump.

"*Subject is known to have associated with persons of*

217

*marked leftist New Deal sympathies; to belong to a union;
and to have made monetary contributions to organizations
not cleared by the Attorney General.*"

Faith thought of Mr. Cunningham, of Tommy Burkett,
of Abe Stone, of Medical Aid to Spain and the treasured
Goyas. "Oh, guilty!" she cried.

"Another premature anti-fascist, I'm afraid," sighed the
Senator. "With them it always goes hard. *On the basis of reports by reliable informants, subject was active in many
fields in behalf of Red Spain—*" Senator Cahill broke off, removed his spectacles and tapped them gently against the
table. "I'll tell you the rest. There is a long, detailed account-
ing of almost every meeting you ever went to, almost every
word you ever said. Even on picnics and parties in support
of the Loyalists. This is, clearly, the work of one or more of
what they call 'voluntary secret agents,' their euphemism
for stool-pigeons. They've had their eye on you for a long,
long time."

"One thing I'd like to know, Senator," Chandler said. "Is
there any reference in this dossier to an alleged bust of Karl
Marx in Mrs. Vance's home?"

"No—nothing like that. There is reference to her book-
buying habits, and to the publications she reads. But nothing about busts. One item, however, is certainly extraordinary: *the Spanish Embassy made inquiries about subject's
activities.*" He turned abruptly to Faith. "So you're known
in Franco Spain, girlie, and I'd advise you for reasons of
health not to take any trips there!"

The fear and confusion which had possessed her withered
under the fierce heat of her mounting anger. The utter indignity and indecency of it—American agents and Franco's
agents, snooping and spying, distorting and falsifying! But

it was not for herself that she felt the indignity and indecency—it was for her country. She thought of the love her
father held for this land, and she felt that this love had been
betrayed.

"My father," Faith said, with deep resonance, "—my father was once in the Spanish diplomatic corps. He hated
everything that fascism stands for. He hated it in Spain, and
I think he'd hate any part of it here!"

"Mmm-m—" the Senator said, plopping his glasses back
on his nose and flipping the pages of the dossier until he
found what he wanted. "That explains an item I almost overlooked—an item of some significance when found in a dossier. It says: *There is considerable doubt that subject is a
citizen of the United States. Further investigation pending.*"
He looked up toward Chandler and added gravely, "What's
your estimate of that?"

"I've taken it into account," Chandler said. "We're looking into the records."

For the first time, Faith thought she detected a note of
evasiveness in Dane's voice. Why should he be avoiding that
subject, she wondered. She could think of no reason, except
the possibility of new developments which might be alarming. And now, suddenly, she could not bring herself to ask.
She trusted him implicitly; he would tell her if and when she
needed to know. But there was one thing she did want to
know, at once and at whatever emotional cost.

"Senator," she said, and neither her voice nor her mind
quavered, "I wish you would tell me, please, the names of
my accusers?"

Senator Cahill frowned, closed his eyes, and rubbed his
forehead thoughtfully. "The stool-pigeons are protected," he
said with a twinge of anger; "their names are not included

in the dossier, and their reports are given by key numbers only. I knew that, so I asked for the name index as well—" He paused, opened his eyes, and looked directly at Faith. Gradually the florid cheeks became even more flushed as his anger deepened. He thrust out his chin.

"Well," he went on, "—to make a long story short, they refused. On the grounds of protecting their patriotic sources. Flatly refused—even me!"

# 10.

THE smouldering indignation within her glowed like live coals fanned by a bellows. When Evelyn and Maria, thinking to be funny, bade her "Good morning!" at four o'clock in the afternoon, she snapped, "Oh shut up!" She was taking it out on them, she knew, and instantly regretted her snappishness. But it seemed to her the dossier had been so unfair, she could bear nothing more from anyone.

She threw her purse in the drawer of her desk and got out a lipstick and mirror. She had the feeling she was smudged and smeared, battered looking. In the mirror, however, her features seemed little different than usual. Only her mouth was tighter, and a slight frown creased the ordinarily smooth stretch between the imperfect eyebrows.

Gradually it dawned upon her that Evelyn and Maria appeared unusually harassed. She put down the mirror. "What's the matter with you two?" she said.

Evelyn shrugged, and said in an undertone, "*He* got back

from New York this morning—we've had hell on wheels all day!"

She meant Mr. Cunningham. It was very unlike him to harry the staff, and especially unlike him after a field trip —when he usually returned relaxed and in good spirits. He believed that all Washington officials should be forced to make regular trips around the country, to keep in touch with the people and not forget they were public servants. Most were too damned possessive of their desks and titles, he often said. So a trip almost always made Duval Cunningham feel good.

"Something happened this morning—we don't know what," Maria said, half-whispering. "He was called upstairs for something—and maybe they put him on the carpet. Whatever it was, he came back sore as a boil. Made us retype every letter today, finds fault with everything. Even yelled at poor old Henry to get out of his office!"

Well, whatever it is, Faith thought, I've got to see him. I can't wait any longer—too much has already taken place.

She had a great deal of back work to take care of, and she made a pretense of getting busily at it. But her mind was not on her work, and she found that she had repeated one figure three times in the data she was copying. The figures blurred before her eyes, and she began to wonder if she ought to resign, as Mr. Cunningham had suggested.

She was hoping he would come out into the office and see that she had returned to work. Almost an hour had passed, and he had remained hidden—barricaded, she guessed— behind the big desk in the gloomy old office. She had the uneasy feeling that she was the cause of the mood which had fallen upon him.

Outside, the sky was clouding, just as it had the afternoon she waited to tell Mr. Cunningham about the subpena.

Another one of those storms, she thought, that compressed the breath in you. It would make Mr. Cunningham's office gloomier than ever.

His avoidance of her, after all the years they had worked together, had been very difficult to take. Possibly this rupture of relations, she thought, had been the worst thing about the whole business. It had shaken her belief in the essential kindness of people—and she recognized that without Abe Stone and Dane Chandler she might have suffered a lasting and bitter cynicism. Maybe she would yet. No, it was not fair to condemn all people because of the spiritual illness of a few. Even though she had suffered so outrageously at the hands of a Congressional committee, she could neither say nor feel that all Congressmen were either evil or confused. For every Daiken and Vincent there were Cahills. Oh, she wasn't licked, she told herself. Not yet. Not by a long shot!

The very absurdity of her dossier had added to its horror. But even a few hours' perspective had somehow lent her understanding, though the indignation was no less hot. Indignation and confused fear were different things. If only she could stop being afraid, stop *completely*—then she could use sensibly whatever strength she had.

Weighted by the burden of these thoughts, she did not at first hear Mr. Cunningham's buzzer. Then it penetrated, clearly, a long and a short—her signal. She was suddenly flustered. Then she summoned an outward calm and walked with measured steps into his office. She was aware, as she shut the door, that Evelyn and Maria were staring at her back.

"Yes, Mr. Cunningham?" she said.

He was pulling nervously on his pipe. His face was still chalky and lined, as the last time she had seen him—or perhaps it was the increasingly murky light of the old-fashioned office. The near crew-cut did not, for some reason, now promote his youthfulness, but betrayed his age.

"I buzzed," he said inanely.

He was putting off whatever it was he had to say. "How did you know I was here?" she asked.

"I overheard your thoughts," he said with a flash of the old celerity. "I—" He could not finish. Instead, he swung around in his chair and peered out the window. "It's going to storm."

"Yes," she said.

"Faith," he said in a hoarse voice, "I'm under instructions to send you at once to the Administrative Officer. I fought it out this morning—and I failed. You'd better go . . . right now. . . ."

She recoiled, more from his tone than his words. A visit to the Administrative Officer could mean anything. But it was evident this visit would be bad . . . bad. . . .

"I want you to come with me!" she cried, ashamed of the desperation she felt after the resolve of short moments before.

He shook his head. "It would serve no useful purpose."

The desperation passed. Looking at him coldly, she said, "Very well. I'll go now."

As she opened the door, he called after her, as he had that other time, "Faith—Faith, I'm sorry!"

This time she did not reply.

The corridor was empty, and her heels made a lonesome, hollow echo on the yard-square black and white marble tile. Many times she had marveled at how empty this building, one of the nerve centers of the world, could seem. There might not have been a living soul behind any of the shuttered doors she passed, for all the sound that came out. It was the close-of-day hush; all except a few top administrators were waiting for the time signal which would send them home.

Deliberately she wasn't thinking about anything. It was useless to think, now—useless to think, until she found out exactly what they wanted of her. She did not even dare consider the alternatives. There were too many to think of.

She chose to climb two flights of stairs rather than face the elevator operator. She had the feeling that everyone in the building knew about her, and speculated on her eventual fate. There was, she thought, something grisly in it—as though she had been thrown to the lions and the crowd was waiting to see her bones picked.

By the time she had reached the proper floor, she was out of breath and perspiring. Just outside the Administrative Officer's door, she stopped for a drink from a wall fountain. Though the water was lukewarm and tasted of chlorine, she gulped it.

River water, she thought; the nasty, filthy Potomac, that looked so beautiful under the stately bridges and crawled with bacteria! She realized that the palm of her hand which gripped the fountain handle was wet with cold sweat.

There was no help for it: she had to go in now, and face Bess Whipple.

Bess Whipple, the Administrative Officer, was known as the Holy Terror. She was the aggressive type of civil servant, having risen from a clerkship in her youth to a position with "extensive responsibility and wide latitude for exercise of authority"—as her green sheet quaintly put it. She saw to it that her underlings saw to it that time sheets were made up, leave slips filled in, towels delivered on fresh-towel day. She also controlled the mechanics of hiring and firing— though the final decisions were reached on a higher level.

She was known to have once dispensed with the services of a stenographer because the girl had the same name as a well-known radical Washington correspondent—though subsequent investigation proved the girl had never so much as heard of either correspondent or his publication, much less being a blood relation. Nevertheless, the girl stayed fired, and her case was one of the hushed-up scandals of the Department.

The residue of all these things was in Faith's mind as she stepped through the swinging shutters into the outer office.

The room was a large one, with about twenty clerks and stenographers seated at desks placed side by side in rows. They were putting their desks in order for the next day, and all active work had ceased. Almost to a girl, they glanced up when Faith entered. It was late for any official caller.

Faith was greeted by Miss Merrie Smith, Bess Whipple's assistant, whom Faith considered the most pathetic woman in Government. Now about sixty, she wore her streaky gray hair done up with rats and surrounded with a hairnet. The hairnet was always loose somewhere, and wisps escaped, so that Merrie Smith was forever tucking them in again. Each time this happened during a conversation, she forgot what she was talking about, and had to be reminded. To Miss Whipple she was like a faithful dog, cuffed and kicked for years but always loyal. The curious part was that this woman could smile, and often did. And moreover, she protected her girls on those days of wrath when Miss Whipple was out of sorts and spewed acid at anyone handy.

Now she seemed very tired. "Yes, Mrs. Vance?" she said wearily. "What do you want?"

"Miss Whipple, please," Faith said.

"Won't I do?" said Merrie Smith, managing a smile of sorts. "What is it? Maybe I can help?"

"I'm afraid not," Faith said. "I'm directed to report to Miss Whipple personally."

"Oh!" One hand went up nervously to tuck in the inevitable straying wisp of hair. "You say you want to see Miss Whipple?"

"Yes," Faith said.

Merrie Smith bowed to discipline. She pushed a button and spoke into the intercom. "Mrs. Vance is here," she said with timorous deference.

The reply rasped out of the intercom speaker. "Show her in!"

Bess Whipple was a large, dominating woman, mannishly tailored and carefully manicured and groomed. She was standing, and this accentuated her size. Her dark red hair was color-rinsed and carefully waved and set in the latest style. She was crisp, cold, and made a point of appearing highly professional and efficient. Beside her, Faith seemed small, almost frail, and very feminine.

"How *do* you do, Mrs. Vance?" Miss Whipple purred.

Faith summoned all her poise. Dealing with this woman always made her tremble inwardly, made her feel awkward and uncertain of herself. Now these feelings were doubled and tripled. "I understand you wanted to see me?"

"Yes—but you've been off the job so much of late, I was beginning to think I never would." She paused, and added like a prosecuting attorney, "Have you been turning in leave slips?"

"Certainly," Faith said, wondering if she had been called here to be grilled on so trivial a subject. Oh no, Miss Whipple would never waste her valuable time on an unimportant matter!

Miss Whipple, scanning the expression in Faith's eyes, tightened her lips and lifted her right eyebrow higher than her left. The gesture made her face seem like a painted mask. "You need not be seated, Mrs. Vance," she said rapidly. "I'm very busy. I merely wanted to notify you that your employment is terminated, with prejudice, effective the close of business today. And under the circumstances—of which you are well aware—I do not feel it proper to grant your accrued leave with pay. The official notice will be in your hands shortly."

The numbness spread by degrees over Faith's body. "Did you say—with *prejudice?*"

"Those were my instructions." She said it with satisfaction.

"You mean, I'm—I'm *blacklisted*, as disloyal, treasonable . . . ?"

The right eyebrow came down to a horizontal line with the left, but the purring satisfaction did not leave the voice. "That's a harsh way to phrase it, Mrs. Vance."

"But it's true—you know it's true!" She was trembling, now, all over, almost uncontrollably.

The cold thing that was Miss Whipple remained enormously distant, a glacier, an arctic zone where nothing could live. "After a fashion," her voice said, "—portions of your statement have some truth."

"I'm dismissed, with prejudice—*without a hearing?*" Incredulous, she advanced toward Miss Whipple's desk, until she touched its edge.

Automatically Miss Whipple retreated a step or two. "No hearing was specified in my instructions." Her tone indicated that she was tiring of the interview.

"Can I appeal?"

"No."

"No—?"

"You heard me: I said *no!*" Miss Whipple's voice was very sharp again.

227

Without warning, Faith struck the top of Miss Whipple's desk loudly with the flat of her hand, and cried, "But why? *Why* am I being fired with prejudice? *Why* can't I appeal for a hearing? *Why* are you so secretive? *Why* can't you give me a decent answer?" She was not afraid of Miss Whipple any more. She was not afraid of any of them. She would fight and fight and fight them until her final breath. She hated them at last.

Miss Whipple retreated another step. "Mrs. Vance," she remarked in a frigid tone, "—if you insist on becoming hysterical, I shall be forced to call a guard!"

Faith laughed. "You're a coward!" she said, and left the room.

# 11.

THE storm was at its height when Faith, drenched to the skin, ran up the steps of the Georgetown house. The front door, unaccountably, was locked, and she had to ring the bell. As she stood waiting, she shivered, despite the tropic warmth of the rain. Water ran down her body and dripped from her clothing, to form pools about her feet.

She had been unable to reach Chandler. He was not at his office and he was not at home. The first fighting reaction and near-bravado, induced by Miss Whipple, had worn off—and Faith had felt again the frantic urgency which pursued her after the Committee hearing. Unable to stop a cab, she had abandoned judgment and attempted to wedge herself into the first crowded bus that came along. Then she discovered she was on the wrong bus, had transferred, and finally had landed within a few blocks of her house. Oblivious of the rain, she had walked the remaining distance. Only when she stood at her front door did she realize that she was soaked.

She was not prepared for the shock of seeing Julia Vance, Thatcher's mother, open the door. There she was, hardly a wrinkle in the cameo-pale cheeks, fragile and white-haired, utterly unchanged since the time Faith had first met her. She was even wearing the same sheer black summer dress, trimmed with Valencienne lace, which Faith so well remembered.

Julia Vance spoke first. "Why Faith, dear," she said, "you'll catch your death of cold!"

For one paralyzed moment, Faith could not answer. Then she said, "The door—the front door was locked." This seemed to her both adequate explanation and greeting, so dissembled were her emotions.

"Why yes, dear," Julia said. "I never feel quite safe in the city unless the door is locked. Now you come inside this moment—you're standing there like a peddler on the steps of your own house!"

Faith shook herself and went inside. "My dress is ruined!" she moaned, though she knew it was cotton and not injured. She had to give vent to her feelings in some manner. The sight of Julia made her want to cry.

Delicately Julia held up one ivory cheek for Faith to kiss. When Faith had done so, resignation to duty in her eyes, Julia said, "You poor child—you must change at once, or you'll get pneumonia!"

"I didn't know you were coming, Julia," Faith said, in a tone of apology for filial dereliction. "Thatcher didn't tell me—"

"Oh no!" Julia said. "It was a surprise. Thatcher phoned me. Said you were so deeply involved in some sort of Governmental affair that you really hadn't time to look after Jeanie properly. He wanted me to help for a while, said you would be grateful. So of course I dropped everything and came at once! If Jeanie needs me, I said to myself, I'll sacrifice anything. So here I am!" She hovered close to Faith, and put one arm around her, as though helping an invalid.

With an abrupt movement, Faith recoiled as if stung by an unseen nettle.

"Why—what's the matter, dear?" Julia said in hurt surprise.

"Nothing, nothing!" Faith gasped. "I'm just upset by the storm, that's all. You know storms always affect me!"

"You always were so nervous," Julia said, smiling patiently as Faith turned toward the stairs.

In the bathroom Faith stripped and dropped her wet clothing in a heap on the floor. She was too weary to hang the dress and underthings on the shower rod. She rubbed herself with a rough towel until she was dry and her skin tingled. This was one of the sensory stimulations which always made her feel alive; but now there was no enjoyment in it. Still nude, she wandered back into the bedroom and sat disconsolately at her dressing table. She looked at herself. The golden buckwheat hair was wet and stringy, the dark eyes had darker shadows, the shoulders slumped, the breasts, she thought, drooped like an old woman's. What was this business of the pink paper doing to her? Destroying her outwardly as well as inwardly? She tried to brace her shoulders, but it was no use. She was too tired. All joy of flesh had gone

230

out of her. Before her stretched an eternal frigid lifetime, dreary and desolate. No love, no passion, no joy. Only in Jeanie was she left with hope.

From the playroom she could hear the murmur of Julia's voice and sudden peals of Jeanie's rapturous laughter. Julia would be telling Uncle Remus stories with all of Thatcher's charm. Perhaps, after all, this visit would be a good thing. A lonesome child needed the security of a grandparent. A lonesome child needed the security of a mother. . . .

But was there security in this family? Would there ever be, with all their latent and open conflicts? Slowly she began to dress.

The rain rattled against the windowpanes with staccato fury. Her thoughts turned, as they often did during a storm, to the Potomac—frothing now, dark and treacherous—and the special part it had played in her life. Shortly after she had saved Thatcher from the river, when the sailboat capsized, he had invited her to meet his mother for the first time.

He had said: "Mother wants to meet you, Ducky. She wants to see you in her own setting." And Faith had accepted with no misgivings.

Mrs. Vance's own setting was unforgettable. The house reposed on a bluff overlooking the Rappahannock River, rock-strewn at low tide and a broad blue mirror at high. Majestic oaks guarded the approaches, until the house itself was suddenly revealed in a wide, park-like clearing, with a horseshoe road curving in to the Georgian entrance door. Actually, the house was only of medium size, but its huge flanking chimneys and small white-painted lattice windows made its two stories assume mansion proportions. It was almost wholly covered with English ivy, but where the bricks showed through they were of the irregular, deep terra-cotta that characterized the hand-made bricks of the eighteenth century.

"Oh! it's beautiful!" Faith exclaimed. "When was it built?"

"The main house, about 1790," Thatcher said, pronouncing *haouse*, as always. They had motored down from Washington, and he slowed the car. "It's called Thornwood, and was built by one of the maternal ancestors of the Vances. Actually, it's one of the few old houses in Virginia still occupied by descendants of the original owners." He said this proudly, and added, "There's a rather fabulous boxwood garden which you can't see from here. The original box was brought over from England on the same ship that brought the Scottish masons to build the house. Inside, there are a lot of interesting knick-knacks."

"And your mother lives here all alone?"

"Except for the servants—all alone."

"Then," she said dreamily, "we have one thing in common, at least—our houses."

He looked at her with unexpected tenderness. "You have a great deal in common, darling!"

Once inside Thornwood, Faith was struck with the Sunday-afternoon quietude of the house, the shadowed-parlor atmosphere. Almost as though it had been prematurely arranged as a museum, it had something of the "polished-for-visitors" feeling of Arlington and Mount Vernon, Faith thought. But whereas everything in those great houses had been restored and seemed destined to last a thousand years, there was a pervasive dilapidation about Thornwood. Doors were no longer aplumb, floor boards had buckled, plaster had cracked, and wall paint was peeling. It cost a fortune in money or slaves to keep up a place like this; and now the Vances had neither. Probably the work was done by half or a third the original number of servants. As she caught a glimpse of the formal boxwood garden out a window, Faith saw that it, too, was languishing for proper care. It was ragged-ended, unpruned, and in places choked by vines. She felt a tightness in her throat. Evidence of decay had made her sad.

Julia Vance was waiting for them in the small sitting room. She had been occupied in some sort of fine needlework, and she dropped it when they entered. "Son!" she cried, as he took her in his arms.

After a moment she disengaged herself gently, and held out one hand in a gracious gesture to Faith. "So this is Miss —Robles?" she said. The fine spacing of her hesitation was almost indetectable, but it was there. The phrasing and intonation carried a genteel Virginia accent. She was slightly smaller than Faith, delicate-boned, consciously fragile. Her hair, soft and halo-like, was perfectly white, and her eyes, paler than Thatcher's, were cerulean blue. She was wearing a sheer black summer dress, trimmed about the neck with lace. With a quick, bird-flutter movement, she presented one cheek, cameo-pale and with hardly a wrinkle, for Faith to kiss. Faith kissed her, and she drew back.

"You see, dear," she said, "I feel as though I know you intimately. Thatcher has written me so much about you. And of course I've seen your photograph! You are very lovely to look at. And such an unusual combination—your hair, and those fathomless dark eyes! No wonder our Thatcher has been rhapsodic in his letters!"

*Our Thatcher,* she had said. Apparently already she was willing to share possession. A good omen. Thatcher's face was absolutely glowing—she had never seen him exactly like that. His mother's approval must mean a great deal to him . . . a very great deal indeed.

"It was so good of you to invite me, Mrs. Vance," she heard

233

herself saying. "Thatcher has told me all about Thornwood—and you. I think he carries a little bit of you around with him all the time."

Julia Vance raised her eyebrows and smiled. "A little bit, my dear? A very great deal, I trust . . . a very great deal!"

The words, Faith noted, were the same she had used in her thoughts.

So Faith was launched at Thornwood. In spite of Mrs. Vance's cordiality, she could not shake off an elusive discomfort. There was a decadence about the house which sent little shivers down her back. True that the long-stemmed pink roses in the silver bowls were perfect, almost exotic; but they were too perfect, like wax flowers—and not alive. And on the crystal chandeliers was a fine, almost imperceptible layer of dust—enough, somehow, to reduce their glister below the first magnitude. What had Thatcher meant, exactly, when he said she had so much in common with his mother? She was puzzled, unsure that she liked it, unsure that it was a good thing.

On the evening of the second day, after Thatcher had had an opportunity to be alone with his mother on several occasions, he asked Faith to marry him. She was not surprised, but she had not been expecting him to act in such prompt and obvious correlation with his mother's approval. She was both relieved and glad, however, because she intended to accept. She had thought it all out. For her, there were no longer any doubts or confusions; she was in love, and it never occurred to her that Thatcher's emotional state might not exactly match her own. As far as she was concerned, their future was faced with only one problem: the when and where of the wedding.

And that, as it turned out, was the point of the first real conflict. After tea with Julia, they had chosen a rustic arbor

234

covered with wisteria to escape from the late afternoon sun. The seat and some of the retaining posts had rotted, but the frame was sufficiently intact to shelter them—and the wisteria made a cozy, wonderfully secret hiding place from the outer world.

"What a delightful playhouse!" Faith said. "Like Christopher Robin's enchanted place. Did you come here often?"

"Not often," Thatcher said. "Rarely anyone to play with."

"But school—didn't you have friends from school, when you were big enough to go?"

"No," he said, "—mother tutored me until I was old enough to enter military school. Also, I had a German governess who taught me a number of things, like algebra and languages—except Latin. Mother taught me Latin. Mother was my constant companion."

"Oh!"

"What do you mean, oh?"

"Nothing," she said. "Please give me a cigarette!"

They smoked in silence for a time. When Thatcher finished his cigarette, he began to gnaw on his left thumbnail.

"Thatcher, *don't!*" she cried.

He flushed, and put his hand in his pocket. "Shall we set the date?" he said stiffly.

"Soon," she said, "—very soon."

"Mother thinks we ought to wait at least six months."

"So long?" she said in dismay. "I don't see the point of such a long wait. It seems ages."

"I was against it, too, but Mother—"

"Suppose we compromise on the end of October? Would that satisfy her?"

He sighed. "It might. And about the ceremony—"

"I don't care—a Justice of the Peace, or anything!" Her heart was beating at an astonishing rate.

"Mother thinks a church wedding, here—since your parents are dead. Besides, the rector is an old friend of the family's, and Mother has so many friends to invite."

By now, anger was gaining over self-control. "Honestly, Thatcher," she said, "I don't care two pins about a big wedding! But if your mother wants a church wedding, I'll go along, provided it's not a display. Just a few people—"

"Maybe she'll agree. I'll try to talk her into it. Incidentally, she's offered us Thornwood for the honeymoon—thinks it would be historically appropriate for me to bring my bride here. . . . We can go on later to New York, by boat from Norfolk."

Faith was unsure whether to cry or shout. She did neither, but her hands were trembling. "Listen, Thatcher, it's *my* wedding, not your mother's! And I'm marrying *you*, not Thornwood! Why can't we plan things the way *we* want them to be . . . ?"

"But just the same," he replied stubbornly, "I think Mother should have a say—"

As she watched the declining sun over the broad reaches of the Rappahannock, for the first time Faith questioned the wisdom of their marriage. Unaccountably, though Thatcher sat close to her and held her hand, she had felt isolated, alone. . . .

Now she sighed, fastened the black ribbon around her hair, and applied the last stroke of lipstick at her dressing mirror. She looked like herself again, and the revelations of her naked body were hidden. There were more immediate problems she had to deal with. And there was Dane Chandler to be told about the latest blow.

Dinner was an agony. It always was, with Julia present. Everything became rigidly polite and proper, and Thatcher treated his wife like Dresden china. He was Old South to a painful degree. But the chief object of his attention and concern was so obviously his mother.

After dinner, Julia said, "I'm worn to a frazzle by my journey. If you two doves don't mind, I'll go on up to my room."

"I'll help you, Mother," Thatcher said quickly.

"Such a thoughtful boy!" Mrs. Vance smiled.

Thatcher took her gently by the arm.

It was patent they wanted to be together, and for a long time Faith could hear the indistinguishable murmur of their conversation.

The storm was ending, giving place to a humid night with scudding clouds over a three-quarter moon. Alone, Faith stood at a window and watched the clouds, then turned restlessly to the piano. She was rusty and missed notes, for she had little time to practice; but gradually her fingers recaptured some of the sureness of other years. She found herself playing snatches of Debussy's *Iberia*, performed many times in this room for her mother and father. As memory reawakened, she slid into the second movement, *Les Parfums dans la nuit*, and heard in her mind the lonely song of the oboe and the vagrant bassoon and solo violin. Wonderful Spanish night, languorous and haunting, made for those who loved the earth—and for those who loved.

Exactly how long it was before Thatcher came downstairs, Faith was not aware. As he walked into the living room it was evident that his mood was severe.

"Will you please stop?" he said. "That noise will keep Mother awake."

She stopped with a crash of chords. "Thatcher," she said with repressed trembling, "—why did you bring Julia here without first consulting me?"

"Because," he said in a tone of deliberate provocation as

237

he poured himself a drink, "you're so damned busy with your politics you don't have time for Jeanie. She's got to have love and attention from somebody besides a nigger!"

"I'll have plenty of time from now on," Faith said with controlled violence, "—I was fired today. With *prejudice!*"

He set down the decanter. His hand shook slightly. "Good!" he said, with a malicious smile. "That cooks Cunningham's goose!"

"Good?" she echoed, incredulous.

He tossed off the drink. "I must admit I didn't expect them to do it with prejudice. But it hardly matters now, one way or the other."

"Hardly matters! How do you think I can get another job, public or private, with that stigma!"

Pouring a second drink, he said, "At any rate, it hardly matters to me."

"Very well," she said with chill calm, "—from now on you can make the living. All of it!"

"Oh!" he said, spreading his legs and rocking back and forth with the slow rhythm of a ship's deck, "that again. Kept man! I pull my oar!"

"You keep yourself in liquor—and that's quite an item, I'll admit!" All the repressed anger of many, many months was accumulating now, welling up, overflowing, spreading and eddying. She was aware dimly that both might drown in the depth of this anger . . . but she no longer cared.

He looked at her obliquely. "Well, while I'm busy drinking, how do you find Chandler on the side?"

Her face became very white, and the skin pulled taut over the cheekbones. "How can you baldly invent such a lie?" she cried. "Oh, Thatcher, how much you must hate me!"

"Hate you?" he said, his face contorting, "I've been sore at you for a long time, sore at you and your ways, sore at you and your bust of Marx!"

She turned from him and slowly her eyes focused on Mozart's head. . . . It seemed to waver, then came sharply into perspective. "Thatcher," she said, clipping the word, "I haven't told you exactly what I was accused of." She paused, and spelled out her next sentence painfully. "How-did-you-know?"

Momentarily he stared at her with an expression of dismay, then he shrugged with bravado. "All right, I'll let you have it! You've got it coming."

"What *are* you talking about?"

"Can't you guess? Can't you put two and two together like the supersmart girl you are? Come now! Did you ever hear of Jim Grayson?"

"Grayson?" she said.

"Sure! Grayson's an old buddy of mine—always hit port together in the Navy. Uncouth bastard, but great in his cups. Got to hand it to him there! Well, one night a while back—one night when you were 'busy,' Grayson caught up with me in a bar. . . ."

"Oh my God!" she moaned. She did not need to hear any more. She could picture the scene—Thatcher, angry, jealous, getting drunk. . . . The anger, stewing thicker, black as pitch, making him want to make her sorry for treating him so shabbily, wanting to get even, wanting to hurt hurt hurt. . . . And the malice and slyness in his eyes as he thought of her and looked at Jim Grayson. . . .

All the hostility came out in his voice now. "Sure I told Grayson! But I only told him—"

"No!" she cried, "no, Thatcher! I don't want to hear!"

But there was no stopping him. He was caught in the cataract of his own passion, in the savage joy of seeing her writhe. "I told him you were a two-bit Red—even had a bust of Marx on your piano!" He paused and laughed. " 'Some Committee you work for, Grayson,' I said. 'Some Committee—can't even root out a well-known Red like my good wife!' And from the way he smiled I knew your job was gone—right there, it was gone."

Thatcher paused and swirled the liquor in the glass. "All of a sudden I heard myself telling him all about you, and I was goddam glad then! But later I was sorry, Faith—I didn't really intend to get you in deep. I didn't know. . . ."

For the first time his recent behavior, his threats and contrition, began to make sense to Faith. He had acted in exact accord with his weakness. He hated her, but the fear of losing her had, for a long time, curbed and tempered the hatred. At last it had burst through all containment—and then he had become frightened at what he had done, and afraid for himself.

"You didn't know . . . !" she said with scorn. "You fool!"

His voice quavered. "Faith, I thought they'd fire you, and that would be the end of it. But when things got complicated, I tried to get Grayson to call off the dogs. I swear I did! But by then they'd dug up stuff on you even I didn't know!" His voice changed now, filled with self-pity. "For days I've been thinking: what am I getting out of this deal? It's *my* name that's being kicked around, my name that you've been smearing with your dirty Red activities! Subpenas, headlines, secret agents, tapped telephones, lawyers —where does it all end? And my name, tagged to a wife who never comes home. See why I got the jitters? Jesus—!"

She was rigid.

A malicious smile formed on his lips as he poured another

drink. She had never seen his eyes so blue, so cold, so brimming with sadism. He was enjoying his triumph to the utmost; it was clear that he felt he had become her master at last. With her old gesture of uncertainty and insecurity, she hitched up her right brassière strap. As she did so, a burst of mirthless laughter escaped from him.

"The Red sweater girl!" he said. He lit a cigarette and blew the smoke through his nostrils.

There was no question now that everything that had been between them was at an end, Faith thought. There was no longer either pity or excuses for his weakness and cruelty. There was no remnant whatever of the admiration, wonder and love she had once felt for him. He had burnt and shriveled everything in the brisk flame of his hatred. No emotion was left for her to return except hatred—and even now it was not Thatcher she hated so much as the illusion she had held and lost. She was filled with sorrow and regret, and for the Thatcher who stood before her—utter scorn.

In an explosion of loathing she got up from the piano stool, seized the bust once cherished as a present from Thatcher. She dashed it to the floor. It shattered with a crash.

"There!" she cried, "—*that* for your evidence!"

He started, then he said, "You can keep the pieces for a souvenir, Ducky. I'm clearing out, for good and all!"

"That delights me!" she said, and could not remember when she had felt such relief. It was as though a terrible constriction around her heart had been released.

"Don't crow too soon!" he said. "Why do you think I had Mother come up? I'll tell you why: to take Jeanie. No daughter of mine is going to grow up a Red! We're keeping the name *Vance* pure American, by God!" He paused, to watch the effect of his statement on her. As she dropped back

241

numbly on the piano stool, he delivered his final blow. "I've got an apartment all sewed up, furnished and everything. We'll move out tonight . . . so your radical friends can move in. I'll be taking Jeanie along, and you know you can't stop me. I'd hate for her to see me hurt you physically—understand?"

She turned her head because she could not bear to look at him. The release was all gone, and the pain which had taken its place inundated her wholly . . . her body, her mind, her heart. She might have known that he would exact his price. He would not give her freedom without destroying it in advance. In his own corrosive way he had loved Jeanie, but he was taking her now as an act of revenge. He was doing to his wife the one last thing in all the world he knew would crush her. Everything else he had done seemed as nothing compared to this. That he had been an informer, Faith knew, was an accident; but that he had planned for a long time to tear Jeanie away from her—this was the ghastly truth.

Stunned, she was unable to speak.

Misunderstanding her silence, Thatcher turned to her and said jauntily, "All right—I'm glad you understand. I'll gather up Mother and Jeanie now. And in the morning I'll come back for our things."

He started upstairs. On the first step, he halted. "I'd rather you didn't tell Jeanie goodby. It might upset her." He uttered a short laugh. "And incidentally—I suppose you know there isn't a judge in this country who would award custody of a child to a mother who is a Red . . . !"

She cried, "Thatcher, I warn you—!" Choking, she could not go on.

In that moment she longed to kill him. She did not look

at him again, but listened as his gloating footsteps receded on the stairs. She dropped her head into her hands, and the tawny hair slipped forward like a concealing veil.

Deep, quiet sobs racked her.

*Part Three*

# 1.

IN RESPONSE to her urgent summons, Dane Chandler came at once. She greeted him at the door, trembling. Over the telephone it had been impossible to say anything but "please come."

"Dane!" she said, holding desperately to the hand he offered, "—get me out of this house! I can't stay here—Thatcher's stolen Jeanie!"

Without asking questions, he said calmly, "We'll take a long ride."

Even in her misery she cared about her appearance in his eyes. "I must look like death," she murmured apologetically as she stepped into his car. "But what's happened—" She began to cry again, this time not sobbing, but releasing a stream of tears.

He waited quietly until she could control herself. He turned the car into one of the winding drives of Rock Creek Park, heading toward the Maryland countryside. All clouds had now vanished from the heavens, and the lopsided moon shone with complete serenity. The car's top was down, and the scented warm night air blew into her nostrils and pressed upon her damp lashes. The earth was refreshed by the rain, and the rock-strewn creek carried away the tumbling waters.

The road ahead was clear in the moonlight, and the headlights seemed unneeded. They passed lovers parked in cozy alcoves of trees, and picnic parties grouped around barbecue fires. In the tops of the trees and in the meadow lowlands the lightning bugs clustered like miniature nebulae.

She sighed deeply, the sigh of one whose wounds were bleeding. "Thatcher served on a mine-sweeper—" she said.

"Yes—?"

"—With Grayson," she finished.

Chandler understood at once. "I've thought all along that it could have been Thatcher."

"Why?"

"I wondered about him right from the beginning. You never mentioned him. I asked Abe about your husband. Everything you said—and didn't say—made it seem that he was not in love with you, that he resented you."

"It's my fault," she said. "I knew almost from the beginning that I'd married a child. But I couldn't admit it to myself. He kept building walls I could never look over. When Jeanie was born, I imagined—"

"And instead it got worse," Dane said softly.

"He used her as a weapon," Faith exclaimed.

She had another cry before she could tell him how this evening's crisis with Thatcher had come about. When she had finished, Dane Chandler gave a tremolo whistle.

"What do you want to do about it?" he asked.

She sat up with a fierce, convulsive movement. "He can't have Jeanie! I want a divorce!" she cried, "—and a suit to recover my child!" Then in weariness: "I'd forgotten to tell you I was fired today, with prejudice. I'll be broke until I can sell the house. Right now I won't even be able to meet the fees—" Curiously, she was almost glad to sell the house.

"Fees?" he said. "There are no fees. I take cases like yours for my own reasons. I thought you understood that. Unforeseen developments are the essence of a law practice; the relationship to the client doesn't change . . ."

248

There was an odd, choked inflexion in his voice which she did not fully understand. Ah—she thought; "the relationship to the client . . ."

He pulled off the road and stopped the car. "How about a walk?" he said abruptly. "I think best when I'm walking."

Her depression and sense of personal tragedy deepened as they walked. She realized she was reacting to some conflict which existed within him, a conflict in which she herself was inextricably bound. It struck her suddenly that she might have complicated his life far more than she knew. And possibly this involvement was serious, with implications she had not dreamed of. She was stricken with guilt and a desire for atonement. It was unthinkable that he should suffer on her account. She had no wish to damage his career or his life.

They were swinging along a gravel road between two firefly sprinkled fields. In one, cows reclined, and in the other, hay had been freshly cut. The odor was almost overpoweringly sweet.

She glanced obliquely at Chandler's face, and saw that he was unaware of the night's beauty. His emotions were concealed by the moonshadows, which hid the eyes and distorted the broad line of the upper lip. Even so, she could detect a tension unlike any she had seen in him, and a solemness beyond gravity. He was evidently in the throes of a decision which was proving not only painful, but costly. She could not fail to know that the decision concerned her.

On impulse, she exclaimed, "Wouldn't it be better if a new attorney took my case—?"

She did not look at him now; she did not want to see whatever change might come in his face—she would hate the relief and gratitude she might see there. Instead, she listened to the regular crunch of gravel under his feet, and waited.

"Better? For whom?" he answered slowly.

She caught her breath. "For you," she said. "After all—a civil liberties case is one thing; divorce and child-recovery suits are matters of time, publicity. . . ." She was astonished at the dispassionate logic she managed to get into her voice. Actually, she was making it sound as though she meant it.

The sound of crunching gravel stopped, as he paused and bent over to pick up a walking stick from the side of the road. Perhaps, she thought, he wants to be sure I don't see his face. He doesn't want to hurt me.

Still stooping, he said, "In my opinion—" and his voice carried an unusual vibrant timbre, "in my opinion, it would be better for your case to remain as is."

He straightened up, but there was a certain weariness in the movement she did not miss.

"Are you sure?" she asked.

"Absolutely positive!" he exclaimed, and clipped off the head of a weed with the walking stick.

He's too sure, she thought. If it hadn't been for Thatcher's action, he might have given up the case this very night. Maybe he had been preparing to.

At these thoughts, she felt a new desolation. Oh my God! she told herself, what will become of me? Aloud, she said, with quiet but firm insistence, "—I think we ought to talk about it. *I'm* not sure. . . ."

He glanced at her in real surprise. "You?" he said.

She nodded. She could not trust herself to make a sound.

They came upon a stone bridge arching a tiny brook which ran through a meadow, and by common consent stopped there. He spread a handkerchief to protect her dress, and she rebuked him with a casual, "Silly, it doesn't matter!"— the only tone she could manage at that moment.

The brook had all the fascination of flowing moonlight, and they watched it a little while in silence. Finally he spoke.

"Why are you unsure?" he said.

"You," she said, turning the tables on him.

He let the word and the way she had said it, gestate. Then he spoke in a low voice, supercharged with a personal element which was new to her. "I understand you very well, Faith—" He paused. "I'm going to call you Faith. I've found it irksome calling you You and Mrs. Vance."

"Yes," she remarked, as though urging him to go on.

"Your case—not the case of Mrs. Vance—is no longer one, but three. On case one, the search for your birth records must be completed; a brief must be anticipated if the Committee cites you for contempt—and they may yet; and we must force the Department to grant a hearing on your dismissal." He hesitated, and threw a stone into the water. "—And cases two and three have just begun. They will make you a celebrity in the yellow press. There's a special angle which plays into sensation-mongering hands—the sex life of an accused Red. You can imagine the headlines. . . ."

"And this hardly fits with the decorous reputation of a firm like Sterling, Hardy, Hutchinson and McKee?" she added softly.

"No, obviously, it does not," he said, with reluctance. "I might as well be truthful. The partners won't like it."

"Of course they won't! And that's what I said in the beginning—"

"Wait," he said. "I considered separating the cases. But—"

"And why not?"

"I may as well confess this, too. I didn't want any other lawyer horning in. I—"

"Oh!" she whispered.

"There is another factor, which I must tell you. I've been offered a partnership in the firm."

"Abe told me that was coming."

"How did he know?" Chandler said quickly.

"He guessed it. He said you were their fair-haired boy." She could feel him blushing.

"Well, it happened today. And they made something clear. With the greatest tact, of course. They said, 'As a partner, you'll be expected to devote your full time to the firm's business.' They want the partners to stick to corporation and administrative law. Private cases tend to disrupt harmony and confuse the firm's reputation in the public mind."

He hesitated, but continued, " 'You'll go along, we know,' they said. *Possibly it will seem advisable to disentangle yourself from whatever commitments you may have at the present time.*' That was the joker. I told them I'd have an answer soon. . . ."

"So if you go on with me, you lose the partnership!" Her voice was strained, almost breaking.

"Yes—that's about it." The words were interwoven with the tenuous thread of reluctance.

"Then the matter's settled!" She was gripping the stone tightly to control the swaying she felt in the bridge.

"Is it?"

"Certainly! I'll have no sacrifices for me! It's bad enough to have my own life in a mess, without being responsible for messing up somebody else's!" She was astonished at her own vehemence. Then she realized she meant what she was saying, that she did not want anything bad to happen to Dane Chandler, no matter how advantageous to herself. She felt she had to protect him, defend him against the insidious horror which someway had engulfed her—had come seeping

252

through the cracks in her life like some unseen radioactive poison.

"Suppose I overrule you?"

"Oh, you can't!" she cried. "I won't let you, I won't have it!" She shuddered. "This business can destroy what's inside you! Security! You don't know what it means until you haven't got it any more . . . !"

"Security?" he mused. "Security is a relative thing, at best. Depends, too, on what you mean. If you mean making a living, I could probably do that by hanging out my own shingle. Or I could take a spot I've been offered with a firm of civil liberties lawyers—something I've turned over in my head for a long time. Not as much money, not as much 'prestige.' "

"Oh Dane," she sobbed, "you'll be throwing away your reputation for nothing. . . ."

"Nothing? You think you're nothing to me?"

"What happens to me won't change the course of anything except my own life—and that's already wrecked!" She was shivering now, as if a cold wind had swept over the meadow and touched only her.

"Don't you see, Faith," he said, slipping his arm around her and, despite her unwillingness, drawing her close to him, "—don't you see that you're important to me, first, as a person; and then, because I've been fighting your case for years inside myself? Do you think I find many satisfactions in *my* life? Suppose I had lived in Germany in 1932, and your case had come along—and I had refused it. Do you understand what I'm talking about? The responsibility I feel—and would feel even if you were not you?"

She relaxed in his arms for a second, and he seized the opportunity to bend back her head and kiss her, tenderly at first.

Around them the night made an obbligato: bird calls, whirring cicadas, the rhythm of flowing water, cadenzas from crickets, and the reassuring bass of bullfrogs.

Shortly a car appeared down the road, approaching slowly, and its headlights picked them out. They were at first unconscious of its presence, but when the car rolled by, a dark sedan, Faith pulled away. It cruised on for a short distance, turned, and once more spotlighted them in passing.

"Dane!" Faith whispered, "police cars frighten me. I feel as if they were all after me. Do you think we're being followed?"

"Possibly," he said.

"Dane, oh Dane!" she cried. And the fear and the frustration came back to her.

# 2.

THE heat wave began on the day the Departmental hearing was scheduled. In the flat-roofed temporary buildings left from the first and second World Wars, the temperature built up like pressure cookers; and employees began to faint even in the great brick and stone structures. By eleven o'clock in the morning, all Federal workers not in air-conditioned buildings had been dismissed for the day. The city's transportation system was thrown into turmoil, and movie houses were packed with people seeking relief. Others took to the parks in droves.

Eleven o'clock was the hour set for the hearing, in the old

Departmental conference room—a room not air-conditioned and with windows half-blocked by heavy purple damask drapes. Nevertheless, the Review Board assembled precisely on the stroke of the hour, and, mopping their sweat-streaked faces, all five members, three men and two women, marched to their seats.

That they had assembled at all was a tribute to Dane Chandler's adroitness and perseverance. In the face of a flat denial of any review of Faith's dismissal, he had plead, threatened, and wangled until a review was granted. "If we can pin down the Department on the *reasons* they fired you, or if we can get them to remove the prejudice—it'll be a victory," he had said to Faith. "But don't hope for too much. Everything is stacked against you. Keep your fingers crossed."

She had kept her fingers crossed, but it seemed to her like hoping an earthquake wouldn't happen, after the tidal wave had already engulfed you. She was swimming and swimming, now, in an ocean of her own tears, kept afloat by the life-preserver of hope Chandler had tossed her. But she knew it was possible for her grasp to slip at any time—and Faith would be a goner, as Abe Stone had once said.

The building was already empty when she arrived, an enormous hollow shell devoid of life. It was as though some mysterious atomic malady had disintegrated all the usual inhabitants, and only ghosts of memories were left behind to haunt whatever observer chanced here. The emptiness depressed her. To have seen old Henry pushing his little supply cart along the corridor would have lent a reassuring human touch, and helped lift her sense of isolation.

She was ringing for the one elevator remaining on duty, when Dane appeared, in a snap-brim straw hat and fresh linen suit, and laden with a thick calfskin briefcase. Only he, of all the people she had seen that morning, seemed unaffected by the heat—perhaps, she guessed, because he wasn't thinking about it. Immediately she was refreshed by his air of cheer and assurance.

In the conference room, his superiority seemed all the more apparent when she compared him with the members of the Review Board. She looked at them almost as dispassionately as if she were not the one whose fate was to be decided. They were buzzing among themselves, preparatory to beginning the hearing, as though they were sharing with secret satisfaction some malfeasance she had committed. Some of them poured icewater from the silvered thermos flasks, others lighted cigarettes and dropped ashes into the oversize amber ashtrays. All dabbled at their faces now and then with handkerchiefs as they talked.

She knew them all, by sight or hearsay. Dane was speaking privately now with the chairman, Mr. Allison Rush, a Special Assistant to the Secretary, and whose jurisdiction included personnel. His resemblance to Herbert Hoover was striking—the round apple head, the thin neatly combed hair, the corpulent body. His name was of no small importance in Washington, since in private life he had been an influential member of a large New York investment banking house.

The names of the other members of the Review Board were not important, but their Government positions were. They were what was known as "strategically placed." One was the Chief of the Special Problems division. He was of medium size, dressed in dark brown tropicals, had a sallow brow and wore octagonal rimless glasses. His mouth was set in the mirthless line of a businessman about to consider a wage contract. The other was a Special Assistant to the Under Secretary. In appearance he gave the impression of being a ruddy-cheeked British civil servant, and was, in fact, a career man in the Department. It was well known that he had risen by virtue of his wife's wealth, social position, and connection with certain ecclesiastical dignitaries of the Jesuit Order. He wore gray flannel trousers, white shoes, and a pinstripe Palm Beach jacket. He had a dark, carefully clipped military mustache, and his hair, graying at the temples, was brushed back to conceal a baldspot on the top of his rather flat head. Faith fancied he was watching her appraisingly, as though he was conscious of her as an attractive young woman, but wished to express public disapproval in his eyes. He smoked, with calculated slowness, a cigarette in a gold holder.

It was the two women, on the left of the chairman, whom she most feared. One was in charge of Intercultural Arrangements; the other, Editor-in-Chief of documents. The first was known as supersweet; that is, she was always self-effacing, agreed with everyone, and wielded a stiletto behind people's backs. She was a small woman, a maiden lady, with a plain face and a sharp aquiline nose. Her pallor was accentuated by her use of bright lipstick on a thin mouth. The editor, a horsefaced woman with a mind for detail, wore pince-nez on a silver chain. She took them off and put them on frequently. She had never been known to misspell a word. Deeply religious, she had a strong sense of what she considered Right and Wrong, and often lectured her staff on their Duty. In argument, once she had made a point she was unyielding, and had never been known to change her mind. She, too, was unmarried. She scorned the use of paint and powder, as spoiling the natural beauty God had given His creatures. Nor did she smoke; indeed, she crusaded against this "nasty habit" by members of her staff.

This, then, plus the inevitable stenographer—a stenotypist, this time—made up the Review Board. Because they were informally seated around a conference table, they seemed less remote and more real than the Congressional Committee. But by that same token, and perhaps because she knew more about them, they seemed more terrifying to Faith. Could they, whose experiences and attitudes were so different from hers, *ever* believe that she had done nothing culpable at all? More important, she thought, did they wish to find her innocent—or was there in them, from the very start, a hidden need, a hidden craving, for the self-superiority which derives from the guilt and conviction of others? A heady wine indeed, the power to pass in judgment. Did they feel, in their secret hearts, she wondered, that official patriotism took precedence over justice?

The buzzing continued for a little while longer. Several of the Board members began making notes on large white pads. The badly ventilated room became more stultifying, and Faith could feel her undergarments clinging damply to her body. She tried to smile, but her lips seemed frozen. Her eyes, she knew, were big and dark and solemn. She thought that, with the ribbon in her hair, she must look a little like Alice in Wonderland. This *was* Wonderland, really. She felt as she had before the Committee; everything was dreamlike, bewildering. She remembered another fragment from her childhood:

*"What are they all doing?" Alice whispered to the Gryphon. "They can't have anything to put down yet . . ." "They're putting down their names," the Gryphon whispered in reply, "for fear they should forget them before the end of the trial." "Stupid things!" Alice began in a loud, indignant voice. . . ."*

The reverie was broken when Abe Stone, flushed and perspiring, slipped into a nearby chair. She glanced at him in

258

pleasure and nodded; he was scheduled to testify in her be-half. He returned her greeting with a wink of reassurance.

It was good, she thought, to have at least one extra friend here. The hearing was closed to the public (from fear of the public and some reporters, Chandler said), and only those with official invitations were permitted to enter. She was doubly surprised, therefore, when she saw Mr. Cunningham appear at the entrance. He came in without hesitation, and took a seat in the back of the room.

Why had he come? She wondered in alarm if the Board intended to use him to testify against her. Dane had said that the Board had given permission for only Abe Stone to testify. She noticed that Mr. Cunningham was smiling at her in an embarrassed way.

Indignant, she turned her head and refused to acknowl-edge him.


"It's time to begin," Mr. Rush, the chairman, said as he tapped gently against a thermos with his fountain pen.

The Special Assistant to the Under Secretary smoothed his mustache and coughed. "Ah—!" he said.

The Chief of Special Problems took off his rimless specta-cles and polished them.

The two women exchanged meaningful glances.

Mr. Rush took out his handkerchief and mopped his jowls. Obviously the heat was already telling on him. He had the attitude of a man who had a great deal to say, but had de-cided to cut it short.

"This Board, above all things," Mr. Rush said in pre-amble, "wishes to be absolutely fair. It has been the unfor-tunate and painful duty of this Board to hear a number of these cases, and I wish to assure the appellant and her coun-sel that we have come to each with open minds. However, we have consistently held to the rule that the welfare of the Department should take precedent over the welfare of the individual—and when a shadow of a doubt has existed in our minds, we have felt compelled to give the benefit of the doubt to the Department. . . ." He halted, and poured himself a glass of icewater. The glass dewed instantly, and as he drank, dripped onto his portly front.

"Now," he said, wiping his lips, "the discharge of Mrs. Faith Robles Vance was given the utmost consideration before the decision was made. But in the face of the evidence made available to the Department by various agencies of this Government, the decision was absolutely inescapable. Furthermore, in view of the evidence, it seemed essential to protect other branches of this Government from future proffers of Mrs. Vance's services—hence the decision to discharge with prejudice. We—the Department, I mean—felt it incumbent upon us to be absolutely sure. It was our duty to take no chances. This, the Department felt, was a reasonable approach to an unfortunate problem. Well, now I think I've said enough to make our position entirely clear. And I believe the appellant will understand our point of view absolutely. We are willing to hear what the appellant, and her counsel, have to say, and to consider it. That is the purpose of this Board. And we will be absolutely fair. . . ." Once more he was becoming overheated. His voice trailed off, as though he could not summon energy for further words.

"Mr. Chairman," said Dane Chandler, his tone easy, quiet and sure, "I should like, with your permission, to make a statement in behalf of Mrs. Vance."

"Proceed," said Allison Rush, holding his damp handkerchief in his left hand and doodling with the fountain pen in his right.

"Thank you, sir," Chandler went on. "Mrs. Vance was first

informed of her dismissal, with prejudice, verbally. Shortly thereafter she received the official severance papers from the Department, which stated merely that she had been discharged 'because of your unsuitability as revealed by investigation.' Immediately Mrs. Vance wrote to the Department and asked for the specific reasons she had been found unsuitable. To date that letter has not been answered." He dropped his voice for emphasis, and Rush stirred with unease and embarrassment.

"I hold, sir, that the Department has jeopardized the confidence of its employees, and of the American people, for that matter, by arbitrary action of this sort. Mrs. Vance has been an exemplary employee—her record speaks for itself, a record of 'Excellent' efficiency ratings year after year, and a steady rise both in classification and the responsibility entrusted to her. I make so bold as to demand that the Department produce the specific evidence against Mrs. Vance, and enumerate its specific charges. There are many cases in law which support the appellant's contention—Supreme Court decisions in *Ohio Bell Telephone Co. v. Public Utilities Commission, United States v. Baltimore,* and others. But since this is not a court, I shan't cite them in detail. I do want to quote, however, ex-Chief Justice Hughes, who wrote an opinion directly applicable in this case. . . ." Chandler paused a moment, to let his words sink in, and then continued, reading from a memorandum.

"Said the Chief Justice, in *Fred O. Morgan v. the U. S. A.: The right to a hearing embraces not only the right to present evidence but also a reasonable opportunity to know the claims of the opposing party and to meet them. The right to submit argument implies that opportunity; otherwise the right may be but a barren one.*" He paused again, and his tone became very firm. "Obviously, it is impossible to prepare

261

a defense when the charges against one are not known. Thus, without knowledge of evidence and charges, the actuality of defense does not exist. Do I make my meaning clear? I am contending that the procedure which led to Mrs. Vance's dismissal was unfair, and utterly lacked all the basic elements of due process. Hence the appellant has been denied, in fact, her Constitutional rights by an agency of the United States Government!"

There was silence in the room after Chandler finished speaking. The eyes of the other Board members turned toward the chairman, urging him to reply.

Mr. Rush made a nervous rat-a-tat with his fountain pen on the table while organizing his reply.

Faith believed she could detect a tension in the Board, now that argument had been joined, which implied defensiveness. They would not react that way, she thought, if they were sure of themselves. They were vulnerable, and they knew it, though they might never admit it until forced to. She scanned the faces carefully, and her impression was reconfirmed. She glanced, too, at Abe Stone. His expression was hard and set. Then, out of the corner of her eye, she noted Mr. Cunningham. He was smoking his pipe, and his forehead was wrinkled in a frown.

"I should like to state again the position of the Department," said Mr. Rush, "—since apparently I have not made myself clear. The Department itself conducted no detailed investigation of Mrs. Vance. That is not the function of the Department, and other agencies have been invested with that authority by the Congress. The Department found it necessary to make its decision with regard to Mrs. Vance's tenure on the basis of summary reports furnished by the investigating agencies. The request for the actual dossiers was denied, and the reports served as substitutes. From the reports, it was evident that Mrs. Vance was a bad security risk. We had to be absolutely safe, so Mrs. Vance was dismissed. Her associations were enough to condemn her—"

"From what you say, Mr. Chairman," Chandler picked up when Rush paused, "—the Department is doubly culpable. The Department doesn't actually *know* that Mrs. Vance's activities constituted grounds for discipline. It acted on summaries of evidence, which may or may not be supported and may or may not be true. How does the Department know that the reports are *not* based on information furnished by persons with personal grudges against Mrs. Vance? Character may be defamed by being called *un-American*—but there is no statutory definition of the term. The Department acted without admissible evidence, it acted without specifying charges, and it came to a decision based on guilt by association, on guilt by rumor! The Department should remand its action, reinstate Mrs. Vance with back pay, and remove all disabilities set up against her!"

A rustle of discomfort ran along the conference table, as the Board members moved restlessly in their chairs. As if by signal, they mopped their faces again. The Special Assistant to the Under Secretary fixed another cigarette in the gold holder and coughed.

Faith sighed. The same old story, she thought. Some incredible compulsion had gripped the highest levels of government, some malignant fear—fear of the democratic system, fear of the economy, fear of the people, fear of themselves. Surely there was nothing else to be afraid of—for they said, and they repeated, and apparently they believed that this was the most powerful nation on earth. Why, then, the fear? Why should an obscure and unimportant individual like Faith Vance, she asked herself, be caught in the morass of *their* fear? Good God! Were they all mad? Was a mass psychosis at work? Did the officials imagine she was some dangerous and ferocious creature destined to destroy them and their jobs? Such thoughts made her addled and half-hysterical. Her attention wandered; she could not follow the argument now going on between Dane and Allison Rush. From the sounds of voices she could tell that Rush was angry, and Dane was as firm as ever. . . .

"I move that the appellant's case be formally reopened by the Department," Dane was saying.

"Motion denied!" the chairman exclaimed. "The Board will, however, take the motion, along with all other motions, under advisement, for subsequent consideration. That is as far as we can go. Absolutely!"

"The appellant wishes to take the stand and answer point by point every charge brought against her," Dane said. "But how can she do so if the Department and the Board consistently refuse to permit her?" He raised his voice in the first bitterness he had allowed to show through. "Such tactics are nothing short of Hitlerian!"

"This hearing was not called for the Board to hear itself berated!" Rush said hotly. "The hearing itself is proof of the conscientiousness of the Department. Do all appellants expect automatically to be cleared? Nonsense! Absolute nonsense!"

Ennui settled over Faith, and again she lost track of the proceedings. Words! All useless, she thought. With the Board everything was cut and dried. She could see it in their faces. Why bother . . . why bother . . . ? In her mind she saw the image of the empty crib at home. That was why bother . . . she was fighting for everything she had lost . . . all the frightened mighty ones had to be told she would fight . . . even if defeated again and again. . . .

She forced herself to concentrate on the hearing. Abe Stone was standing up, talking to them, leaning forward on the big table so that the veins knotted in his powerful hands. She could see only the pitted back of his neck, but it was flushed a dark red, and she could imagine the degree of control he was exercising. What was he saying . . . ? Oh yes, he was talking about her, all right; about her, in duplicate, triplicate, octuplicate, and all the rest of the innumerable carbon copies of her throughout the Government.

"The Union of Federal Workers," Abe was saying, "cannot regard lightly such arbitrary disregard of the rights of one of its members. If the rights of one are threatened, the rights of all are threatened! This case sets a pattern, which, if followed, means that step by step a concealed reign of terror will be created within the Federal Government. All will be suspect! Then the sickness will spread to the States and the counties, the municipalities and the villages. What public servant will then be safe? None! Neither teacher nor street cleaner can work without the fear of secret accusations which may cost him his job and his reputation! Here and now is the time to stop this insanity! Here and now— that is the responsibility of this Board . . . !"

As he finished, the Board crackled with hostility like the static electrical discharge from an arched cat's back. It was obvious that whatever Abe said would be held against her. They resented and disapproved of the fact that she belonged to a union. They would damn her for that, if nothing more, she thought. Yes, she "associated" with Abe Stone. Guilt by association . . . strength by association. One way now, later another. Change, always change! The important thing to know: which direction is the current flowing?

She started. Someone was calling her name. It seemed to

come from very far away, and her head whirled. No—the question came from near at hand. Allison Rush was speaking to her.

"Mrs. Vance," he was saying with impatience, because she had not answered, "Mrs. Vance, there's one direct question we want to ask you. We assume you know the danger of making perjured statements to the Government. We want to know if you are an American citizen?"

"I am!" she said loudly. Much too loudly for the size of the room, she thought.

"Do you have proof of citizenship?"

Chandler interposed before she could reply. "May I answer that question for the appellant?" he said. When Rush nodded, he went on. "Mrs. Vance's birth records are not available. We have recently conducted a thorough search, and have discovered that the records were either lost, or destroyed by fire—we cannot be sure. Unfortunately, she has no living relatives who can attest place of her birth. There is every indication, however, that appellant is a citizen. The Department need have no concern on this point."

"The Department need have every concern on this point!" Rush snapped. "The Federal Government does not hire aliens! Furthermore, the penalties are severe for falsification of application forms. Makers of fraudulent statements are subject to fine and imprisonment, as you know very well, Mr. Chandler. Frankly, it occurs to me that the appellant should consider herself lucky to have been dismissed merely with prejudice, and not with prosecution! There are certain agencies of this Government charged with referring to a grand jury cases such as this! Appellant would do well to plead that her case be closed, and closed absolutely! Appellant is known to have worked in behalf of a foreign government, and it ill-behooves her to expect clemency of this Board. . . ."

Faith could not bear to listen to him any longer. "In other words," she cried, "you want me to slink away as if I were guilty of some crime! I'm not guilty of anything and I won't run away and pretend to be!" She had half-risen from her chair, and fell back exhausted.

A murmur of disapproval ran around the table. The two women shook their heads and the men scowled. A deep purple color spread over Rush's round face, then gradually receded. He mopped all over with his handkerchief.

"May I say something, Mr. Chairman?"

The voice was not Dane's, but so very familiar. Mr. Cunningham—she had forgotten him. Yes, it was Mr. Cunningham. He had gotten up and was coming forward from the back of the room.

"You have the Board's permission," Rush said grudgingly.

"Thank you," Mr. Cunningham said, taking the pipe out of his mouth and running one hand across his short-cropped hair. "Thank you very much. I think what I have to say is germane. As Mrs. Vance's superior over a period of many years, I do not see how her Americanism can be questioned. Whether she was born here is of no moment, of no importance whatever. She *is* an American. She has worked industriously and intelligently, up to the top limit of her ability, for her country. What more could anyone ask? If the criterion is love of the land where you live and work, she is an American!"

"Mr. Cunningham," Rush said, with a sardonic tightening of his lips, "—I want to ask *you* a question. As Mrs. Vance's superior, were you aware of her activities outside Government?"

Mr. Cunningham hesitated, and the recent chalky whiteness returned to his face. "I was aware—" he said at last.

267

"And, as her superior," Rush went on, "you did not remonstrate with her about these activities?"

"I did not." There was no hesitation now.

"And in fact you approved?"

"In fact I approved." His words were low, but without equivocation. "I definitely approved—and continue to approve!"

There was a sudden, perfect stillness, except for the frantic buzzing of a bluebottle fly which somehow had become trapped in the stifling room. But Faith could hear the swish of an imaginary axe as it fell, and see the head of Duval Cunningham as it rolled in the dust.

She glanced at Chandler, to be rewarded by the admiration for Cunningham she saw on his face. She would have smiled, but could not for the tears in her eyes.

# 3.

ABOUT ten days, all told, had passed since Thatcher's abrupt departure. After the tilt with the Review Board, which appeared as a flailing windmill and turned out to be a dragon instead, Faith came down with a case of nerves. When all her efforts to see Jeanie were repulsed, she went to pieces.

Each time she looked at the odds and ends of battered stuffed animals left behind in Jeanie's room, she was seized by fits of violent crying. The emptiness of the room haunted her by night, and through restless sleep she kept listening for the sounds Jeanie made when she was ill, or sleeping peacefully, or having dreams. All the gay times and all the nights of worry over thermometer-shattering fevers came back to Faith now, and she re-lived each with alternate pleasure and anguish.

And the house itself reproached her. It seemed impossible to live here any more. She had begun her married life here on the basis of happiness which had gone before; but the later layers of time and memory were crusty with tarnish—ugly and repulsive to behold in retrospect. The house no longer offered anything but pain. In consequence, Faith spent every possible hour away from home.

The house had seemed empty even when people came to commiserate and talked loudly to drive away the evil spirits they could see were deviling her. She had telephoned Mary Margaret in Baltimore, and good old Haswell had come right over to spend an indefinite period with her. After a day and a night, she had asked Haswell to go home—the strain of someone else's presence, and making conversation, was unendurable. Haswell could understand about politics, but not about the child.

And there were other visitors, as well as telephone calls from miscellaneous friends and acquaintances. Abe Stone, of course. Evelyn and Maria had called to say that they were sorry about what had happened at the office, and to wish her luck. The day after the Review Board hearing, Mr. Cunningham had dropped in with his wife for a moment, and spent the evening. Dane Chandler had joined them, and there had been much light but brave talk about Quiz Kids, Police Chaperones, and muckle-headed Congressmen.

In fact, Dane Chandler—aside from Donnie (Donnie had agreed to stay on for roomrent . . . indeed, had refused to leave), Dane Chandler was the one person who did not induce in her a state of raw agitation. Any loitering figure on the street, day or night, she suspected of being a secret agent. She jumped at every doorbell or telephone call. She mistrusted the groceryboy as prying for information; and when the corner druggist remarked casually, "Haven't seen Mr. Vance around lately, Mrs. Vance . . . is he sick?"— she snapped back with complete illogic and hostility, "None of your business!"

Even with Dane she was, on occasion, short-tempered. She knew how much time and effort he was spending in her behalf, but sometimes she wondered querulously whether he was doing all he could. Immediately after the Review Board hearing they came close to an open quarrel, on the subject of her birth records.

"Why didn't you tell me," she said, her throat tight and her voice strained, "—why didn't you tell me there was no hope of proving my citizenship?"

He looked at her calmly. "There is hope."

"—But the records. Have you tried the Embassy and everything?"

"Yes. Nothing was done about you officially through the Embassy. The assumption is that the attending physician took care of the matter."

"I told you there was no attending physician! The doctor didn't get there till hours after I was born!" Her tone carried a note of unreasonable accusation, as though Dane in some obscure way were responsible for these difficulties.

"Now Faith," he said, "the doctor would, in the normal course of events attend to the matter, unless he had expected your father to register you as a Spanish citizen. There might have been a mix-up on that score, and possibly no record was ever made at all. On the other hand, all the local records, covering the summer you were born, are missing. They may turn up—though so far I've hunted them over half the State of Maryland! You know this is just the sort of mix-up on which so many cases depend. It seems a ridiculous mole hill, but to the Government it's a mountain. So we have to pretend, seriously, that we believe it's a mountain, too! And sooner or later we'll find someone who can attest your birth!"

"Oh," she cried, "forgive me for seeming so fretful! But sometimes the strain of this business—"

"There's nothing to forgive," he said. "I understand a little of what you're going through. . . ."

After this conversation, the pendulum of her thoughts swung to the other extreme, and she began to worry that he was spending much too much time on her case, thus jeopardizing his position with the firm. She was reluctant to ask him what decision he had reached, if any, on leaving the firm. For her to pry at his taciturnity seemed too much like self-seeking, like urging an unwelcome decision on him for her benefit without regard to his own. She was sure that when he had come to a decision, he would tell her; but she so much wanted him to decide without making her case the pivot of the decision.

When she considered the matter dispassionately, she realized that a decision was not possible any more without her direct involvement—from his point of view, at least. Even if she were still bound hand and foot to Thatcher, the case would be an element in the way he decided to channel his future life. But it would have been easier to balance off prestige and wealth against his own philosophic ideals. Now, oh now, that he had felt the willingness of her body in his arms—

Torture for them both, she thought, but he ought to decide without *that* in his mind. Or maybe she was asking more than was humanly possible?

She saw him often, but they never approached the intimacy of that night on the little stone bridge. Something intangible stood between them, worried them, made them shy of each other. From her dreams, Faith knew (as she also knew consciously) how much she hungered for him. But in his actual presence, she was overcome by constraint.

Gradually she understood that the house, with its atmosphere of gloom, inhibited them both. But over and beyond the house, there was another and more subtle factor—Washington itself.

It was not the breathless intemperance of the heat, nor the possibility of more malicious gossip, which deterred her. It was, instead, the inescapable feeling of political pressure. It was the business of speaking in metaphors over the phone, of talking low in restaurants, of glancing over your shoulder at the makers of footsteps behind you.

Washington itself was a source of distortion, as if everything in it were a mirage, slightly out of focus and wavery. Inwardly, it produced a malaise of the soul.

She was caught in an invisible trap, she thought. If she was not wholly caught, neither could she wholly escape. All she knew was that her restlessness and frustration increased. She could not go on like this much longer.

On the fourth day of the heat wave, Dane, as if sensing her growing desperation, said to her: "Faith, you're going around in circles. Tonight we'll get out on the water."

She agreed with apathy, but once they were alone together, and away from the streets, her spirits began to change. They landed on a strip of sandy beach skirting Roosevelt Island, and together dragged their canoe well ashore. With luxurious slowness they ate a basket supper and drank beer.

"Delicious," she murmured. "The first food I've tasted in

weeks, to tell the truth. Cheese and salami sandwiches, and potato chips—a feast!"

Lying on the sand, their backs braced against a weather-beaten log, they watched the sunset. Through the haze of heat it was spectacularly brilliant, a fluid sweep of crimson and vermilion which was reflected on the river.

"I feel like Becky Thatcher escaped with Tom Sawyer," Faith said. The oppression so real an hour earlier now seemed evanescent.

When Chandler rolled over and kissed her, the grains of sand which clung to his palms as he caressed her felt scratchy and good.

"Faith, do I have to tell you I love you?"

She shook her head slowly.

They sat leaning against the log for almost half an hour. Neither spoke.

In the twilight they cast off, and paddled to the Watergate at the foot of the Lincoln Memorial. Already people were streaming onto the stone amphitheatre before the floating shell which housed the National Symphony orchestra. Above the steps, in perspective, they could see three of Washington's great structures illuminated in the early darkness of the east: the serene colonnaded temple to Lincoln; farther distant the glowing yellow shaft of the Washington Monument; and in the far distance at the end of the Mall, the symbolic Capitol dome. Viewing them now, Faith saw them as a tourist might—majestic and beautiful, without awareness of the political winds which swirled about them.

Gently Dane nosed the canoe against the stone break-water, and, clinging almost without effort to an iron ring, the craft rested outside the main currents of the river. Other canoes and motor launches drew alongside, the latter bearing red and green running lights which reflected on the dark water. On the barge, the musicians were not visible, but an auroral glow lighted the faces of the audience. Some of this indirect light found its way to Dane's face, and Faith lay covertly admiring the strength and candor and tenderness she saw there.

The orchestra played *Tales from the Vienna Woods,* Prokofieff's sweet and lilting *Concerto No. 2,* and Beethoven's *Pastoral Symphony.* Midway in the last movement of the *Pastoral,* Dane shoved off with his paddle until the current caught them, and they drifted downstream with the tide. Gradually the music became faint, until it was lost in the first stirrings of the night wind.

Neither spoke until the outline of the pier was silhouetted against the land lights. The land. The Washington land, she thought.

"Dane—" she said in a whisper, for with the land the convulsive fear had come back, "Dane—take me away from Washington, now—tonight!"

He shook his head, no. . . .

# 4.

SHE was a fool, she thought, to have new hope. In this business, it was better to expect the worst, and be pleased when the worst did not happen. Dane, as usual, had warned her against expecting anything definitive in her case. Nevertheless, she was incorrigible: she hoped.

Standing with Dane before the massive Government building, she looked upward and read aloud the words graven in stone:

### The Place of Justice Is a Hallowed Place

She slipped her hand into his and held on tightly. "Do they believe it, Dane?" she said in a troubled voice.

"Oh yes," he said, "they believe it. But sincerity of belief has nothing to do with context of belief. It's like Americanism —everybody's for it, but interpretations differ. *Justice* is an abstract word; I always like to tie it down by saying, *Justice —for whom? by whom?* When you do that, you discover that justice is related to time, place, class and social code. Oh, it's a fascinating subject! But right now we're concerned with the workings of justice, not the theory. What say we go in . . . ?"

Hesitant, she glanced into his eyes. They were serious and hard; but for her they softened, offering the mercurial smile and an exchange of personal intimacy which caused a rush of happiness within her.

"Let's go!" she said, and found that it was not necessary to muster courage, for courage came to her spontaneously with Dane.

In the murky sunlight the building cast ambiguous shadows, and the entrance, designed for giants, was an inky cyclop's cave flanked by open stainless steel doors. Faith had the feeling that once they passed inside, the doors would close automatically with a clang—to be sealed forever. In an effort to divest herself of this impression, she managed a feeble smile as they approached the uniformed guard. The guard did not return the smile.

As they waited for the elevator, Dane said, "Worried?"

He could have talked half an hour, and not said so much as he put into the tone of his voice. Now she smiled, and the smile was genuine and free. "Just happy," she said, "—being with you."

Actually, she had come to the point where her case was never—day or night—out of her mind. No matter how she controlled herself rationally, in the hours of sleep all her anxieties and fears were released—and she ran and ran from grotesques who threatened to capture her. Compared to the terrors of these dreams, she welcomed realities like today.

Recognizing the futility of further appeals and reviews, Dane, using the prestige of his firm's name, had arranged for an interview on the very highest level—the Attorney General. He was determined to find out, once and for all, just how far the Government was preparing to go in Faith's case. There were so many complicated factors, so many interlocking investigations and overlapping jurisdictions, that it seemed best to see the top authority concerned with any future prosecutions of his client. Once personal contact was established, he reasoned, and so informed Faith, it might be possible to snap some of the entangling bands of redtape which obscured the real situation. That he could get to the top at all, seemed miraculous to Faith—who was well aware of the difficulties placed in the way of such interviews. She was impressed and pleased; and her budding hope seemed not at all unfounded.

The air-conditioned outer offices were delectably refreshing compared to the street—the air itself was enough to make one feel crisp and optimistic. They walked in silence over the thick rug to the receptionist-secretary in the anteroom, and Dane announced their names and purpose with a certain note of deference.

The young woman, who was well-groomed and suave, consulted an appointment calendar. "Oh yes," she said impersonally, "I have your names. Will you wait a moment, please?"

She pushed a button and spoke into an intercom. "Mrs. Vance and Mr. Chandler, of Sterling, Hardy, Hutchinson and McKee, are here."

A woman's voice, fretful and metallic, replied, "Ask them to be seated. The Attorney General has not come in. There may be some delay." The intercom clicked off.

"There may be some delay," the receptionist-secretary repeated mechanically. "Will you please be seated?"

Dane nodded, and with a slight frown drew out a leather-upholstered chair for Faith. They lit cigarettes, and industriously began to study the portraits which hung on the walls.

The frown on Dane's forehead persisted.

By the time the pack of cigarettes was finished, Faith knew the faces by heart. Though the faces were all different—some with sideburns and chinwhiskers—there was a curious similarity of attitude and expression. She wondered vaguely if the prideful authority of the portraits was occasioned by the power of office. Only men with the simplicity of Lincoln, she thought, could reach the pinnacles of Government and remain untouched.

Thinking these thoughts, letting her mind ramble, she felt somnolent and surprisingly comfortable. She was content to postpone, if only for a little while, another crisis. One after another, each crisis had taken so much out of her emotionally, drained her dry. Occasionally she wondered where she had found the personal resources to meet them all. No human being could guess his own capacity for struggle until put to actual test—that was the answer, she was sure. Possibly most people could be far more tenacious than they ever dreamed. . . .

Her eyes and her thoughts came back to Dane. His face, she realized with a sudden shock, was gray-grim. Obviously the anger within him was reaching an explosive point. It was unlike him to become so exercised over a mere delay . . . how long, now?—why, going on forty minutes, she saw as she glanced at her wristwatch. He was making the church-steeple gesture with nervous intensity, unaware of what he was doing with his hands. It occurred to her that sometimes his hands were more revealing of his personality than all his words and actions. Sometimes the hands had a character of their own—hands that expressed the tactile love of physical labor, rather than the law. What was it in the War he had wanted to do . . . ? Oh yes, run a machine gun. A like anger was being expressed in the lean, strong fingers. There was in them now the desire to attack.

She laid one hand on his arm, as if to restrain him. He shook it off with impatience. "Something's wrong," he said to her in a low voice. "Nobody coming, nobody going—like vacation."

"Maybe they've forgotten us?" she murmured, almost wishfully.

He shook his head, and grimaced. "With all those card indexes and dossiers? Impossible!"

Abruptly the intercom speaker came to life with a blatant burst, startling them and waking the receptionist from the listless tabulation which engaged her. "Ask Mrs. Vance and Mr. Chandler to come in," said the voice, reverberating so loudly that the room picked up an echo. It was almost as if a miracle had happened, and they were being summoned by unseen trumpets On High.

Without volition they moved toward the paneled double doorway which concealed the inner office. As they approached, the doors slid apart as though operated by an elec-

278

tro-magnetic device. They saw in a moment, however, that the controlling force was a middle-aged Negro man, who stood respectfully aside as they passed, and closed the doors behind them.

Three secretaries sat quietly at highly polished walnut desks, surrounded by batteries of telephones—none of which were ringing. The first secretary, a gray-haired woman with an innocuous face, looked up.

"Will you go in, please?" she said.

"Thank you," Chandler said.

He took Faith's arm, to guide her toward a second set of paneled doors. As they crossed the carpet, it seemed to her the nap was thicker and more luxurious than in the outer office, and their progress therefore even more silent. Again the doors were opened and closed without sound. It was like the opening and closing of doors in a dream.

They stood in a vast room empty of any human being except themselves.

On one side of the room were great windows, richly draped; on the other, a row of green marble columns. At the end of the room was a very large and heavy desk and swivel chair, set before crossed silken flags, parade-size, with golden fringe and tassel, and gold eagles crowning the staffs. Nearby was a small conference table with thermos flask, and a leather couch and matching chairs, decorated with brass pins which shone in the sunlight.

Faith inhaled sharply, and shrank close to Chandler. "Where is he—?" she whispered.

Dane frowned. "We'll wait," he said, perplexed.

Awkwardly they started toward the sofa, but froze after the first step when a side door swung open. Two men came in.

The leader was fat and bald. His eyebrows were markedly black, and dominated his paunchy face. He smoked a short, badly chewed cigar. He was smiling, and his teeth were marked by tobacco stain. The man who followed was sharp-featured, thin-lipped, and predatory. His eyes were exceptionally bright, and made their appraisals with quick, darting glances. Instantly his look made Faith uncomfortable, prodded to life the depressing fear of being shadowed.

The fat one took the cigar out of his mouth and smiled even more placidly. "Mr. Chandler and client?" he said.

"Yes," Dane said with the stiffness of disapproval, "we have an appointment with—"

"Sure, I know," the fat one said, continuing to smile with the casual amiability of the professional politician. "But you see, there was a slight mistake. The Chief was under the impression, Mr. Chandler, that your *firm* was representing the client. Inasmuch as you're representing the client *personally*, it occurred to the Chief that you might state your problems just as effectively to me, as his Designated Assistant. He's a pretty busy man, you know." He paused, reinserted the cigar, and resumed the perpetual smile. "Now, if you'll just sit down, we'll hear what you have to say. My name is Coppini —Leon Coppini. . . ."

"And the other gentleman—?" Dane asked, his voice hard.

The fat one laughed. "Oh, he's just along for the ride, so to speak. Delegated by one of the Bureaus that might have an interest in these matters. Isn't authorized to discuss anything, of course—just to listen in. Now if you and your client will just sit down—"

"I see—" Dane said, pausing for a moment's thought.

Faith was conscious that her heart had begun a violent pounding. The very sight of these men had somehow blurred her vision, and they swam out of focus. She was trying to will them out of existence, she knew; but they remained, real and frightening—all the more so because of the joviality of one and the silence of the other. She could not talk to them. There was nothing she could say that they would understand. There was a gulf between them which language did not bridge, nor would logic have any meaning. It was evident from their faces that they respected solely authority and power. And Faith—had neither. With gratitude she heard what Dane was saying.

"Thank you gentlemen for troubling to come here. You may report, however, that I prefer not to discuss my client's case under these circumstances, but will reserve our arguments for the courts. So we'll not take your time. Good-day!"

The fat one stopped smiling. "It's no skin off my nose," he said, and shrugged.

Almost before Faith realized what had happened, they were back in the outer office, across the thick carpet, and into the anteroom. The receptionist stared at them as they retreated. The doors had opened and shut, opened and shut, opened and shut. . . .

In the corridor, Faith stopped, and collapsed weakly against a windowsill. Below, in the inner courtyard, a cool fountain gushed upward from a marble basin. A few employees lounged about, smoking cigarettes, for it was near the lunch hour.

"Look at them!" Faith cried. "How *can* they do what they do, be part of all this . . . !"

Dane took her by the shoulders and shook her roughly. "Faith!" he said, "—stand up!"

"It's no use!" she said, half-sobbing. "They've caught me on their flypaper, and they'll catch you too! I can't bear it any more . . . !"

# 5.

THEY lunched at the Occidental, but were oblivious to its bustle and the succulent odors from its kitchens. Indeed, they picked at their food so sparingly that their waiter became alarmed and asked if anything was the matter.

"Nothing's the matter with the food," Chandler replied, and the waiter went away evidently believing they were lovers who had quarreled.

"I've been thinking," Chandler said over coffee, "that the time has come for a serious talk with the civil liberties law firm I mentioned to you once—Goldman and McMurtry in New York. I want to lay your case before them, Faith, and maybe discuss my own future, too. . . ."

She looked up, questioning. "When?"

"Tomorrow."

For a moment she said nothing. She stirred her coffee aimlessly with a spoon, attempting to conceal the tremor in her hand. This was, she thought, an indirect confession from him of the serious state her affairs had reached, and raised again the whole question of his involvement. She shivered, and glanced pleadingly into his eyes.

"Don't leave me, Dane," she said, and the words were burdened with their several special meanings.

Smiling faintly, he reached across the table and took her hand. "I won't," he said. "You're coming, too."

She finished packing her bag, snapped the lock shut, and stood up. While she waited for the cab Donnie had called, she took a last look around. She was possessed by a welter of emotions she found difficult to analyze.

She noticed that Thatcher's portrait in military school uniform remained on the night-table. Curiously, in all these days, she had not seen it before. Had she imagined he took it with him? She would have expected him to. No, he left it as a taunt—something to remind her of the value of her loss.

With mixed sorrow and loathing, she slipped the photograph out of the frame and tore it into little bits. When the fragments were so small that no feature was recognizable, she threw them into a wastebasket.

This was a leavetaking of the past. There were echoes in the house—so many echoes. She could hear them now, some faint, some strong. Jeanie's laughter, the voices of her mother and her father, and her own voice questioning. Perhaps, like Thatcher, she had been overly preoccupied with the past. Perhaps she'd never really left home before, having loved too dearly some of the faintest echoes. But she was leaving now.

From the front of the house she heard a car honk. Donnie called, "Cab's here, Miz Vance."

She hurried downstairs, and Donnie appraised her with wide, understanding eyes.

"Goodby, honey," Donnie said. "You look jus' lovely!"

Faith was scheduled to take the *Congressional* at four o'clock, and a ticket for a private compartment awaited her at Union Station under an assumed name. Chandler, cognizant of the Mann Act and the danger of accompanying a woman across State lines for "immoral purposes," had preceded her on an earlier train. And in New York, separate room reservations had been made. "Oh, to hell with the Quiz Kids!" Faith had said when Dane insisted on these arrangements. But he had remained adamant: "We mustn't do anything to jeopardize the chance of recovering Jeanie," he said; "—we shouldn't flaunt our relationship in their faces."

With this conversation in mind, she turned to look out the rear window as the cab drove off. Half a block down the street a gunmetal sedan started simultaneously, and with the old inward constriction she waited.

The cab crossed the buffalo bridge on Q Street, swung around Dupont Circle with its memories, and headed lazily down Massachusetts Avenue. The sedan did the same, a discreet distance in the rear. She could plainly see the two men in the sedan, and they seemed to avoid looking at the cab.

She tapped her driver on the shoulder and said wildly, "Some men are following me! Go fast! See if you can shake them off!"

The driver glanced round at her with suspicion. "Listen lady, if you're in trouble with th' law, you sure better catch another cab!" He slowed and pulled up to the curb.

"Forget it," she said, managing a nervous laugh, "—it was only a joke, to hurry you up!"

He shook his head, and opened the door. "Out with you!"

She stood helplessly on the curb with her bag, trying to signal another taxi. The sedan had gone a short way ahead and stopped. How foolish to try to shake them off, she thought. They probably watched the house day and night, knew everything but her inmost thoughts. Oh Christ! She could not force back the tears which formed and blurred her vision. But somehow, as Dane had insisted, for Jeanie's sake she had to get away without Their knowing. . . .

A cruising taxi drew up in response to her signal. She

jumped in with the bag and slammed the door, realizing suddenly that she was sweltering.

"Where to, miss?" the cabby said.

She hesitated. "Some place cool," she said, playing for time to think. The sedan started again as the cab passed by.

"There ain't no such!" the driver said, laughing.

As she dabbled at her face with a handkerchief, she caught a glimpse of the Washington Monument through the trees. A plan came to her. It was a long shot, but she decided to try it.

"The Monument, please," she said.

"Oh you energetic sightseers—on a day like this!" the driver said, and laughed again.

It seemed forever before they reached the Mall, and circled up to the base of the massive stone obelisk. She was reminded of the dream which had so frightened her the night before the pink paper was served—and now the dream had come true in reality. She shuddered. She preferred to believe she was still dreaming; but it was not so. There was the sedan, gunmetal-gray, somberly insisting on its real presence.

They would think she was crazy, and perhaps she was; but those two would not follow her to the top of the Monument. They would wait comfortably at the base, listening to their radio, watching for her to come out and hail another cab.

Wilted and drooping from the heat, she lugged her suitcase to the shaft entrance—and, without a glance at the sedan, entered the cool darkness. Once inside, she waited to be sure they had not followed her, but she had guessed right. They did not come.

From a bored guard she learned the whereabouts of the ladies' room, and darted to it. Then, with rapid movements which permitted no fumbling, she unlatched the bag and

285

removed the black dress she had planned to wear in New York, and a scarf. Wholly possessed by her plan, she changed dresses with the same quick precision, threw away her chic straw bonnet, and knotted the scarf about her head peasant-fashion. When she had finished, she locked the suitcase and tossed it into a cleaning closet. No one had come in during the whole operation. She sauntered out and took the elevator as casually as any tourist.

When a sizeable crowd had gathered, the oversize cage creaked its way five hundred feet aloft, to the very peak, and discharged its cargo. Immediately Faith went to one of the slit-like windows and sought the gunmetal sedan below. It was still there, appearing now as nothing more than a toy, and no more dangerous. Then, with thudding heart, she began to watch for the means of her escape.

All Washington was spread below her, all the familiar columned buildings, the shady parks and avenues. She looked down at the circular Tidal Basin. To the right, the white marble neo-classic dome of the Jefferson Memorial rose up majestically above the cherry trees. Faith closed her eyes, remembering the scene in springtime, a cloud of billowing pinkness. Welcoming the cherryblossoms had become a sacred rite, and thousands of pilgrims flocked from every State to see the blooms. The beautiful blossoms, she thought, but sterile and bearing no fruit. And the larger-than-life bronze Jefferson stood looking out between the marble pillars at the cherryblossoms, brooding, and—Faith wondered—sorrowing that the trees were barren.

She opened her eyes, and changed the direction of her view. The Department, clinging to its weathered dignity, loomed near the White House, and she thought of Mr. Cunningham. He would not be there much longer. Among his kind, only the apostate could survive. She knew now that she would love him all the rest of her life. She shook away these thoughts, and glanced at her wristwatch. A quarter to four. She would miss the *Congressional*. What would Dane think when she failed to appear on time? Panic threatened to overcome her, and she debated whether to make a dash for it. Too late. Too late. She had to go through with what she had begun.

Dark clouds were gathering up the river beyond Great Falls, where the water foamed through stone canyons. So that was where the squalls formed, to sweep down over tidewater. It was interesting to watch the thunderheads boil. From up here it was easy to see how they seethed with violent winds. Good, she thought, good! A storm would make the escape easier!

An adolescent boy wearing green sun glasses elbowed in beside her at the narrow window.

"Gee!" he said when he saw the thunderheads, "—maybe lightning will strike us!"

She smiled at him sweetly. "I'll give you two dollars for your sun glasses," she said. "My eyes burn." She was afraid to offer more; he might become suspicious.

"You bet!" he said, "—it's a deal!"

She paid and adjusted the glasses on herself. She felt like kissing him.

At this moment she saw what she had been waiting for—a sightseeing bus, huffing its way up to the Monument. Shortly it parked, the door opened, and a crowd of people disgorged. Her heart pounded giddily as she watched.

Everything happened as she had wished. The tourists surged out of the elevator with the guide and overran the observation platforms. The guide began his spiel in a rapid nasal falsetto, accompanied by rising winds which threatened to drown his voice. Faith lost herself in the group which listened to the patter. An unnatural darkness was slowly closing over the heavens, thunder boomed, and some people fidgeted and showed uneasiness.

"Does this here thing sway?" asked a thin young woman with a South Carolina drawl.

"Okay, everybody!" the guide called, ignoring the question, "—we're clearin' out!"

They jammed into the elevator, Faith among them.

When they reached the base, they bolted for the exit, and, heads down into the wind, raced for the bus—Faith among them. A few raindrops slanted stingingly into their faces, and Faith held her head lower than the rest. She stumbled once in climbing aboard, and was frantically fearful that she had attracted attention. But no one noticed, and she found a seat on the side opposite the gray sedan. There she crouched, making herself small and insignificant under the head scarf and green glasses, hardly breathing until the bus was loaded and the driver spun the engine.

Then, slowly, the bus coughed off into the now pelting rain.

Faith slipped a handkerchief from her purse and wiped the sweat from her face. The sedan, so far as she could tell, was not following.

But she was still afraid. When the bus stalled in downtown traffic, she went forward and asked the driver to let her out. Grumbling, he did so.

Ignoring the rain, she dashed for a trolley and fought her way inside. She was pleased to stand, because her face was not visible to passing cars. She had done it! she thought in triumph.

Laboriously, and at last, the trolley crawled around the Columbus fountain and reached Union Station. With covert sidewise glances Faith hurried through the great arched waiting room with its warrior statuary, and on to the gates. Three minutes were left to make the five o'clock. Rushing far ahead to the coaches, she climbed into a car just as the last "Al-l-l aboa-a-ard" sounded. Almost collapsing, she found a seat and dropped into it.

She was wet from the rain and sweat, her dress streaked and rumpled, her hair straggled around her face. Oh my God, how wonderful I feel! she thought.

Smoothly the electric train gathered speed, began to outrace the storm. Rounding a curve, Faith glanced back at the city. The Klansman's peak of the Monument was obscured by ominous clouds, and the red aircraft-warning lights blinked of danger.

But now, flushed by the glory of her escape, she felt no fear.

# 6.

DANE was waiting for her in Penn Station. When she saw his face, she realized for the first time, fully, what she had come to mean in his life. The mature self-possession of his eyes was overlaid by a shattering anxiety, and there were furrows across the forehead and around the mouth.

He was standing at the top of the escalator, scanning everyone from the train. She glimpsed him almost at the bottom, and as she rode upward she watched. The anxious hope and disappointment she saw touched chords within her which she thought had lost all resonance. Suddenly the chords began to vibrate again, and then to sing.

"Dane—!" she cried, while still three steps from the top, whisking off the head scarf and green glasses.

He literally snatched her up and lifted her aside from the crowd, and for a moment held her tensely in his arms. Then he brushed her lips with a kiss, and stood back to look at her.

"My God, darling! What happened? I was scared stiff! I risked a phone tap, and called your house—Donnie said you'd gone. Then I got afraid they'd slapped a warrant on you!"

She was half-laughing and half-crying, but bursting with satisfaction. "They were trailing me—but I gave 'em the slip! Don't look at me—I'm a wreck. Had to throw away my bag, and here I am with no other clothes." Now she began to sniffle, as though looking pretty for Dane were far more important than eluding her pursuers.

He laughed at her and hugged her again. "Never mind, silly!" he said. "Tomorrow you can buy something to wear. Now tell me in detail what happened. Don't leave anything out. . . ."

While he led her toward the taxi stand, she began an animated account of her adventure. And as she talked, she reveled in a new buoyancy and sense of freedom. For the moment, at least, the Washington albatross no longer weighed about her neck.

When she had finished, he turned her head swiftly and kissed her again. There was admiration in his eyes. "How shall we celebrate your escape?" he asked.

"Go where people are having fun," she said. "Music—gay but not phony—and maybe some dancing. All right?"

"Perfect!"

"And food—" she added, somewhat ruefully.

On the way to the hotel he stopped the cab in front of a lighted pawnshop, and paid the driver.

"What's happening?" she asked in surprise.

"Gotta have luggage, not to attract attention when you check in," he said. "Don't want the house 'security force' to become interested in you. Register under your maiden name, as unobtrusively as possible. Everything according to Hoyle. We're in the same hotel, same floor, but different rooms. In court, suspicion means nothing, proof everything. If we registered together, and it became known, there would go your chance of recovering Jeanie—though not the divorce. Just being cautious, that's all."

"Oh!" she said in a weak voice, feeling abashed by guilt. She had, in her state of exhilaration, forgotten Jeanie. And Dane was thinking of Jeanie when— Oh, God, was she a callous mother? Or weren't there times when anyone might forget?

Chandler had selected a good English bag, covered with steamship stickers, and was asking her approval.

"Fine, oh fine!" she said, and the bland shopkeeper smiled with satisfaction at having made the sale.

"Even better with labels," Dane said jokingly when they were outside again. "Stickers make you an international traveler, instead of an overnight emigré from Washington."

She was almost ready to go down to the lobby to meet Dane, as they had agreed, when a knock sounded at the door. Startled, she shrank back, afraid to turn the lock. In a single instant all the dormant fears had been revived.

"Who's there?" she called, her voice quavering. "What do you want?"

"Bellboy, miss," came the reply, muffled through the door.

She heard the words with relief, then doubt entered her mind. What if it were a trick? Well, she couldn't stand here shaking forever, with her skin chilled by invisible icicles. She opened the door to peep: it was a bellboy, and the fear had been groundless. She opened the door the rest of the way, feeling ridiculous that she had been so frightened.

He brought in two florist's boxes, one large and one small. She tipped him, he smiled knowingly, and left.

The larger package contained a bunch of talisman roses, delicate-petaled and just opening to full beauty. The small package contained a band of camellias for her hair, to replace the hat she had left behind in the Monument. There was no card; none was needed. She touched the roses tenderly, then clasped them before her like a bridal bouquet and admired them in the full-length mirror. Dreamily she stood for several minutes, until, awakening suddenly to passing time, she dashed for the water pitcher and arranged the roses on the dresser.

Then she arranged the camellias in her hair. They transformed the black dress, kept it from looking mussed and too-long worn. I *am* pretty, she thought, and with the camellias I'm dressed for a party! She skipped happily out of the room.

New York was just what she needed. The impersonal comings and goings of the people in the vast lobby were reassuring. The Mayflower Hotel seemed small and intimate compared to this place. She even had difficulty, for a moment, finding Dane. The pleasure of meeting him was the climaxing satisfaction. Excitement permeated her now, to the fingertips.

"How do the camellias look?" she asked.

"You flatter them," he said.

"Thank you," she laughed.

The streets were nervously alive. The brick and stone canyons, the crowded streets, the restless agitation of the electric signs, all were in sharp contrast to Washington's broad tree-lined boulevards and the serene repose of its architecture.

"I haven't been here in so long," Faith said, "—I'd almost forgotten what it was like. I love New York!"

She had felt that way, too, on her honeymoon. But somehow Thatcher managed to turn their trip into nothing more than a glorified cocktail party. There had been cotillion rooms and postillion rooms, iridium rooms and persian rooms. And cocktail lounges ad infinitum. They had haunted the Plaza because that was the hotel Thatcher's mother had approved of. And they "did" Fifth Avenue, and the Museum of Modern Art, because it was the thing to do. All the while, Faith was longing to explore the docks and the side streets, drink cafe espresso on Bleecker Street, eat blini and rice pilaf, go dancing in Harlem. Once she broached her desires to Thatcher, and his astonishment was so genuine that she felt chagrined.

But tonight Dane sensed her mood. They headed for Greenwich Village, and had antipasto and chicken cacciatore in a wonderful hole-in-the-wall Italian restaurant. They talked trivia. Then they wandered the swarming streets, with the little art galleries and bookstores, and went to sit in the Square for a while. They smoked and watched pigeons and lovers and dogs on leashes and had nothing to say. It was a clear night, with a cool breeze from the sea.

"Oh dear—!" Faith sighed. Everything was too good to be true, she thought. She was too happy.

They went then to Café Society Downtown and drank champagne and danced and felt their pulses warm and throb to boogie-woogie which was passion translated into sound. It was the dancing which woke her fully to herself, and the feelings inside her when Dane held her tightly in his arms. She trembled at his holding her, and he was trembling too.

Back at their table, they sipped the champagne and listened to an ethereal blonde folksinger, who played a zither and half-whispered to a dreamy and floating tune:

> *"Down in the valley, valley so low,*
>   *Hang your head over, hear the wind blow.*
>   *Give my heart ease, love, give my heart ease;*
>   *Throw your arms round me, give my heart ease.*
>   *Write me a letter, send it by mail,*
>   *Send it in care of Washington Jail.*
>   *Writing this letter, containing three lines,*
>   *Answer my question, 'Will you be mine?'*
>   *Will you be mine, dear, will you be mine?*
>   *Answer my question, 'Will you be mine?' "*

When the singer had finished, Dane looked into Faith's eyes and said, "Shall we go—?"

She nodded.

The zither's notes were already a wisp of memory.

# 7.

SHE snapped out the light and stood naked by the window. The room was on the thirtieth floor. Greater illumination came from the stars than from the lighted streets below. The city was at peace, now. Only the grinding gears of an occasional taxi and sporadic hoots from East River tugs carried upward to this height. Looking at the darkened skyscrapers and the criss-cross shadows of the streets, she marveled at such quietude.

Dane seemed so long in coming. She had bathed and prepared herself for him, even going to the length of breaking off a rose for her hair. She was, she thought, emotionally ready to receive him. The evil spell of Washington seemed completely broken.

Her eyes had become adjusted to the suffused light in the room, and she glimpsed herself in the full-length mirror. Her heart spurted suddenly at her nakedness, so that she regretted the loss of the silk and lace negligee she had thrown away in the Monument. She felt so brash, standing there in a hotel room.

At this moment the awaited knock came at the door, and she was overcome by panic. She snatched the soft white chenille spread from the bed, draped it from one shoulder and wound it loosely about her breast and thighs in ancient Hellenic fashion. Somehow it fell together gracefully, and she was satisfied with her image as she moved toward the door.

At first she opened only a crack, to be sure that it was Dane.

"Hello," she breathed at sight of him, and stood trembling.

Without a word he slipped inside and kissed her lips with a kind of burning thirst.

Then he murmured, "You look like a Vestal Virgin."

The warmth of her skin betrayed her blush. "I am," she said.

It was like an exciting experience you had always known would happen, and understood in advance, but which, someway, had never quite come through from unconsciousness to awareness. It came through now in its full excitement—at last.

With a frantic haste she had never before seen in him, Dane released her and stripped off his clothes. And then, in a continuation of the same impatient movements, he unwound the Greek garment she had improvised.

Breathing hard, he scooped her up and carried her to the bed.

They slept and awoke, slept and awoke, as though to pack into a single night all of the past and all of the future. Toward dawn they awoke, and a mood to talk was upon them. He was kissing her from top to toe, beginning behind her ear and loosing delicious rivulets the length of her body.

Admiring his lean muscularity and broad shoulders, she whispered, "Thank goodness you aren't a Puritan!"

He paused, stroked her breasts, and smiled. "Did you think I would be a Puritan?"

"Not really—but sometimes it's hard for people to be free inside themselves."

"Hell, you're so lovely!"

She knew he meant her breasts particularly, and was relieved and glad. In nothing was he like Thatcher. There had been no reserve, no falseness. It was strange that the emotion of love could become so distilled, so almost unbearably intense. And yet she had never felt so placid, so serenely complete. She could think, too, without the terrible jangling fright which had seemed gradually to be destroying her.

"Dane . . . it's a long time since you've been in love?"

"Yes, it is."

"You didn't get married?"

"No." He cradled her with his left arm and gently caressed her with his right. "When I was at the Harvard Law School, I fell for a girl who was dark and trim and sleek like a raven. I thought it was the real thing: but her family disapproved of

296

me—I was too provincial, they thought. So with only a graceful sigh she gave me up. I figured I was better off unmarried than married to the wrong woman—and damned if Washington wasn't full of the wrong women."

The light was strong enough now to define the quixotic smile, and she could imagine the scattered shadows of freckles. The broad mouth was more tender than she had ever seen it. What bliss to feel her naked body against his, warm and alive, and to be held in this way.

"My mother and father are going to like you," he went on, after a while. "I visit them occasionally. My father was a hardware merchant, now retired, who absorbed the heady doctrines of the Populists in his youth and steadily became more conservative through the years. I mention this because he was the one who started me to thinking as I do—and because I came to the point where I quarreled with him pretty angrily. We've made up now, I think—but we never discuss such things when I go home. . . ."

"And your mother—?"

"She was the quiet kind. She grew up on a raw frontier farm in western Nebraska, and she knew how hard life could be. She never talked much, but she was always there when I needed her—and she used to sing wonderfully soothing lullabies. She could quote the Bible backward and forward—but her faith was, and still is, in the potential grandeur of man. She flew to Washington once, to visit me—and she flew, she said, because she wanted to get a quick bird's eye view of the changes in the earth since her early childhood. In one way I've been a big disappointment to her—she has always wanted me to marry."

Faith caressed him lightly, kissing his body as he had kissed hers. She savored the taste of his salty skin.

When she paused, resting, he ran his fingers through the

297

silken tawny hair, then playfully tweaked her nose. "I'm hoping," he said, "that when everything's straightened out, you'll come home with me as my wife . . . ?"

She did not answer.

In alarm, he said, "Won't you—?"

"Oh," she whispered, "I keep feeling I'm going to cry—but I don't dare cry, because if I started I couldn't stop . . . !"

Morning came so soon. The starlit night had given way to a damp mist, and the hotel room seemed to be floating in a cloud.

"Too bad that cloud isn't pink," Faith said ruefully. "It was a perfect night."

He gave her a brief peck for a kiss and rolled out of bed. "Perfect," he said. "Now we have things to do. Call room service and order breakfast—I'll duck into the shower when the waiter comes." He paused. "Breakfast for one—a nice big one."

She sighed. Without getting out of bed, she picked up the phone and called room service. "A double orange juice, ham and eggs, a pot of coffee, marmalade and sweet rolls."

"You must be hungry," Dane said.

"Yes, we are," she said, and blew him a kiss.

After the waiter had set up the table and disappeared, Dane came out of the bathroom. He had dressed in trousers and shirt, the shirt open at the neck. He needed a shave, still looked sleepy, and his hair was mussed. But, Faith thought, she looked sleepy too—and there had been time only to brush her hair and throw on a dash of lipstick.

"Let's drink out of the same coffee cup . . . a ceremonial," Dane said.

They did, with proper solemnity.

"Happy?" Dane said.

She nodded, and knew her eyes were sparkling. "Very!"

"I'm calling on Goldman and McMurtry first thing this morning," he said between bites of sweet roll. "Later I'll take you to see them."

Her eyes widened. "Have you made your own decision?"

"Not yet—"

"Aren't the partners pushing you?" It was the question she had wanted to ask for days.

"They gave me an extension of time," he answered. "They thought I'd snap up their offer—and when I didn't, they got worried."

"Dane," she said earnestly, "you must do the thing that will make you happiest. Once, such a connection would have frightened me. It doesn't now. In fact, I welcome it. I would like all the rest of our lives to be without sham. I know, now, after all I've been through, where my friends are—what side of the fence I'm on, if you want to put it that way." She recalled what she had thought and felt during that first interview in his office, and the veil of melancholy which had slipped over him. He had been a man afraid of something, and that something was himself. He was looking at her steadily, now, as if he could not form his decision without her.

"Dane—" she went on, "if you want to do this thing, and we have to live in a tenement for you to do it . . . I'm with you. Because I love you!"

He got up and kissed her gently on the right ear, and in mischief blew the soft little hairs so that they tickled. Then he became serious, and slipped his arm around her waist. "When I meet you for lunch," he said, "I'll tell you what I've decided."

He finished dressing, and when he was about to go, he caught her up and embraced her passionately. "Goodby, my wife," he said.

His voice was flat, but warm and tender as she would always remember it.

After he had gone, she dilly-dallied at dressing, luxuriating in her freedom from anxiety. Today was a perfect jewel, lustrous from the night's happiness. She could not, she would not, detract from it in any way.

She began to plan the clothes she needed; for Dane, even in the midst of business, she wanted to look beautiful. She prepared herself with minute care for her next meeting with him.

When at length she stepped out of the elevator and walked across the lobby, she was wholly preoccupied with her new happiness. In the street, the bustling life seemed wonderful to her.

The doorman whistled for a cab, and she waited under the awning, blissful and content. In that moment, two men, whom she had not noticed, appeared on either side of her. Each seized an arm. Their faces were expressionless.

"Just a minute, sister," breathed one of the men, "—you're coming with us."

She tried to cry out—but could not utter a sound.

# 8.

GULLS whirled and rode the air without apparent effort, following the launch as scavengers. The steady *chug-chug* of the engine was a hateful sound, as each revolution of the propeller bore her farther away from the peace and ecstatic happiness she had known in Dane's arms. The lengthening wake was a churning path she could not retread, nor did she know its terminal.

The two men had hustled her so quickly into a nearby sedan, and the waiting driver had pulled into traffic so quickly, that she had no time to experience any sensation except a simple naked fear. The flesh along her back and neck had tensed and prickled, in the danger-reaction inherited from ancestors of the dim and prehistoric past. She had a glimpse of the doorman's astounded face, then he was lost to view. It was then that panic swept her—for the impersonal, unknown doorman was her last link with a secure world.

Suddenly she awoke to what was happening. "Let me out!" she screamed, and began to scratch and bite at her captors.

Each bent an arm behind her, and held her tight. She quivered and lay still.

"Be good, or you get handcuffs," said one of the men.

"Where's your warrant to arrest me?" she answered.

He gave a laugh of amused superiority. "You're not arrested, sister. You're just in custody." He laughed again.

"See?" He flashed a badge at her, but she could not make it out.

"Where are you taking me?" She tried to sound calm, but she was shaking inwardly and her heart felt swollen and on the verge of bursting.

"You'll see—in due time."

She clamped her lips and decided not to talk any more. Why should she give them the satisfaction of baiting her? It was strange that their faces made no impression on her whatever. They were just two average middle-class faces, well fed and rather soft, freshly shaven and with a faint odor of a cheap after-shave solution. Though one was dark and the other light, both wore brown summer-weight felt hats—of cheap quality, and stained with hair oil around the bands.

Never in her life had she known such a feeling of helplessness as the car hurtled along. On the streets she saw hurrying people in raincoats, thousands and thousands of people, and she could not call out to them. The car was headed downtown, and as they passed through the financial district she thought that Dane was there, somewhere near, unaware of what was happening to her. The thought made her writhe.

They drove out onto a wharf and stopped alongside a sizeable motor launch. It rode uneasily in dull water, surrounded by oil slicks and bits of floating trash. A mingled odor of garbage, salt, and oil arose from under the pier and assaulted Faith's nostrils, offending her.

A man, in oilskins which glistened from the spray and sporadic rain, came out of the cabin. "So soon?" he said, and laughed. "You musta put salt on her tail!"

The two escorts grinned.

"Wouldn't we like to!" one said.

"Hop in sister," said the other. "Your crystal ball says you're gonna travel!"

Silent, Faith did as she was told.

Now, in the harbor, the skyline shrank and blurred through the mist and spray as the launch took the heavy waves. Huddled on a bench in the cabin, she watched through a porthole which smudged from time to time. Her world, she thought, had contracted to that small sphere. She was sick.

Staring fixedly out the porthole, she clutched her hands in her lap and inwardly struggled with the apathy which threatened to overcome her. She remembered Dane's question, during that first interview, about the mouse and the lurking cats. Well, she was the mouse, and the cats had caught her, and what now could she do? Unexpectedly resentment flared at Dane: maybe this wouldn't have happened, the cats wouldn't have caught her, if she'd stayed in Washington! No—that was unfair. It was she who had first urged him, that night in the canoe, to take her away. She *had* to get away from that place, and he had merely understood and acted on what she wanted. Unfair to blame him! But at least he needn't have left her alone—that was why they caught her, she was alone. Any fool would know they wouldn't have dared touch her with a man by her side. Unfair! Unfair! He couldn't stay with her always . . . sooner or later, at an unguarded moment, the cats would leap! Oh no, even Dane could not save her; she could be saved only by a force more powerful than Dane, a force . . . oh, but how would all the hurrying people in raincoats know or care?

The launch rolled and tossed, and she wished bitterly that it might sink. Sink? Then Thatcher would have his full triumph at last. She could guess now that he had borne an implacable resentment toward her for having been saved by a girl that time in the river. She had saved his life but hurt his pride. Perhaps he had even thought of the marriage as a

303

reward for heroism—yes, that would fit with his romantic conception of life. Why had she been so naive and ignorant then? She marveled at herself. Or did the process of growth always involve pain . . . ?

This harbor, and that sparkling October morning of their honeymoon. The coastal steamer from Norfolk, and Mr. and Mrs. Thatcher Vance leaning against a stanchion like a Count and Countess freshly arrived from Europe! The bronze-green Statue of Liberty forming out of the blue haze, the Manhattan skyscrapers gradually thrusting upward out of the water. Then the blasé disguise was thrown off, by Faith, at least, and like any excited newcomer—an immigrant, almost—the game of see-the-sights was begun: Ellis Island, Governor's Island, Brooklyn Bridge. . . .

She closed her eyes, and the lashes quivered. She knew that the veins in her neck were swelling from the intensity of her fear. There was a contraction in the pit of her stomach, a sharp pain. Dizziness stage by stage was overwhelming her. She opened her eyes again in an effort to fight off the sickness.

"Where are you taking me?" she cried to the agent who sat directly across from her.

"You'll find out," he said. Then he looked at her closely. "You're turning kinda green. Wanna stick of gum?"

"No," she said.

She watched his jaws with horrified fascination. Once before, gum, and jaws, moving in that insensible rhythm. How well she remembered! The first Nazi she had ever seen, in full SS uniform. She had turned from a side street into Massachusetts Avenue, and there, directly in front of her, walked a plump young man in full regalia, dagger, swastika and all. His jowls stuck out from the chinband of his stormtrooper cap, and as he walked he kept slapping the calf of his right boot with a short whip . . . in rhythm to his jaws as he chewed gum. She had lost all sense of time and place until the SS man strode briskly through the entrance gates to an imposing mansion. How strange he looked on a Washington street, she thought, how strange and utterly un-American!

Now the man in the brown felt hat leaned forward and scowled. "Whatcha glaring at me for, sister? You going nuts?"

"Where are you taking me?" she said again, in a monotone.

He got up and steadied himself against the roll of the launch. When his feet were firm, he wiped the condensation off the porthole and peered out. In a moment he turned toward Faith.

"There," he said, "—you can see for yourself."

She crossed the cabin to the porthole and searched through the mist outside in the direction he had indicated. Finally there loomed a weatherbeaten pier, a ferry slip, and a cluster of dreary slate-red buildings, set back on barren land. The mist closed, and the scene vanished.

"What is it?" she asked in an anguished whisper.

The man shrugged, and said: "It's Ellis Island."

# 9.

To ALL questions, she gave a single answer: "Without counsel, I have nothing to say!" The green-uniformed little man who smoked innumerable cigarettes put down his pen with a gesture of exasperation. She continued to look at him solemnly. She seemed to be trying to see everything in a fourth dimension—through to the core. Why are you here? she seemed to be silently asking the little man—as if his questions to her were entirely unintelligible.

"Take her away," the Inspector said in disgust.

They removed her, and the little man seemed no more real than a dream fragment.

She had been escorted through many entrances and exits, long corridors and short hallways, small foyers and great waiting-rooms. Emptiness pervaded everything. She had glimpsed a few people grouped in what seemed to be huge pens, all men, or women and children waiting on long wooden benches. Some of the women wore shawls, as in generations before. There were uniformed guards all about. And sometimes she caught the peculiar herd odor of massed humanity mingled with disinfectant. She wondered without fright if they would put her in a pen. She was not frightened because, as in severe physical shock from a blow, numbness preceded pain.

Besides, she told herself, it was all a dream.

They put her in a cell with walls of clean white tile. At first she thought they had made a mistake and locked her in a bathroom. But there was a metal bunk, with the coverlet neatly tucked in, and a small barred window. She felt the tile: it was cool and damp to the touch.

It was raining—sometimes in sheets and torrents, sometimes disguised as a wraith-like mist. The walls and gables of nearby buildings were bleak, and beyond, indistinctly, she could make out the high mesh fence topped with barbed wire. She could hear the sea. There were hoots and whistles of boats in the harbor, and the mournful clang of a channel buoy.

Still, she did not cry. She sat on the edge of the bunk with her head in her hands. This was not a dream. It was real. How long, she thought, would Dane take to find her? How long . . . how long . . . how long?

That was the refrain.

The day passed. They brought food, but she could not eat. The night came, and she slept fitfully. The bellbuoys tolled through her dreams and the whistles jibed at her. Dawn was only a gradual seepage of light through the mist.

She sat up, thinking of one short dawn before. By closing her eyes she could relax again on Dane's shoulder, feel his hand on her bare thigh.

In the city, milkmen would be delivering milk, waitresses going to work, newsstands displaying the morning editions. Shortly children would pour into the streets, their faces scrubbed and their hair neatly combed to begin the day. In Washington, the trolleys would be starting from the barns, and the multitudes of Government workers would soon converge on the Bureaus and the Agencies. Somewhere clerks, in lassitude from the heat, would casually extract from files the dossiers which bore her name. Everything that had happened to her here (how well she knew!) had been conceived in Washington; and everything that happened in the future would depend on Washington. Escape? It had been impossible. There was no city, no town, no hamlet where the fingers of the bureaucracy did not reach. For them the Nation was only a suburb clustered about an authoritative center, and New York only a place-name. The Potomac River flowed outside this iron-barred window, the Potomac River with its sewage. . . .

She combed her hair and applied lipstick. She had never seen her face so pale, nor her eyes so mute.

For breakfast, she managed to drink some coffee and eat some bread. When the guard came to take the plates, she asked, "Have there been inquiries for me?"

"Don't know nothin'," he grunted.

The paralysis returned. She sat down heavily.

All day the gray light filtered through the narrow window. Toward late afternoon, breaks began to appear in the clouds and occasionally sunlight shafted into the cell. She did not, however, move from the bunk. It was as though she sat suspended in a trance, with only her mind active and alive.

The sound of footsteps echoed in the outer corridor, and she stirred. What next? she thought.

Though she had been waiting so many hours, she was not prepared to see Chandler walk in when the guard unlocked the door. Nor was she prepared for his expression. He had the face of a man who had experienced agony.

"Dane!" she cried, and flung herself at him.

Tears burst from her eyes, and she stood back to look at him. "Oh!" she cried, and the paralysis was ended.

The guard closed the door and stood outside.

As he wiped her eyes with his handkerchief, she said, "I thought you'd never come! I was afraid you'd never find me."

"Find you?" he said. He laughed with grating irony. He slipped an arm around her waist and walked them both backward and forward the length of the cell as though one person were pacing. He continued to talk in a hard staccato voice. "I got to the restaurant and discovered you weren't there. I waited a half hour—a half century! Then I called the hotel and found you weren't there, had left no message, hadn't checked out."

She could say nothing. She tightened her arm about him.

"I combed New York. First I tried the hospitals, then the

police. Nobody knew a thing about you. I could only conclude that you'd been detained. I couldn't take legal action until I knew where you were. I didn't dream they'd have the gall to spirit you here and hold you incommunicado . . . !"

She clasped him tighter. "How did you find me?" she whispered.

He paused and looked down at her. Before he could speak she said, "Washington—through Washington, of course!" Her lips twisted in a wry smile.

"Yes, if I'd waited for an official announcement . . . It was Senator Cahill who located you. He raised cain. They had to tell him. You should have heard the long-distance line sizzle when he phoned me the news."

In an effort to cheer her, Dane thrust forward his lower lip, wagged his head in imitation of the Senator: "By God, Chandler, this is where we put our foot down. This nonsense has got to stop. Hauling off a charming girl like that, snatching her off the street in broad daylight! By God, Chandler, the United States Senate is going to hear about this!"

"Can he stop them?" she asked.

Dane sobered. "No. Not without a majority of the Senate behind him."

She shook her head in weariness, and sighed.

"Once I'd discovered where you were," he went on, "I tried to send a message. Finally in desperation I called Melvin Thompson at the White House, direct, in your name. I told him . . . well, you can imagine what I told him. He acted. And here I am."

"Oh," she said, "—things are as bad as that."

The blood drained from her face. "Tell me, Dane. Tell me the complete truth. I don't want anything covered up or softened. I want to know exactly where I stand." She felt amazed at herself, amazed not that her voice and words could be so

309

firm, but that inwardly she was prepared for no equivocation.

"Let's sit down," he said, leading her to the bunk. "We have a lot to talk about."

She sat beside him and entwined an arm in his as if she could not bear to lose the touch of his presence.

"First I want to know how long they can keep me here."

Almost imperceptibly the set of his jaw changed. Fleeting shadows of sorrow, fear, and anger crossed his eyes. "It depends—" he said grimly, "depends on many things."

Her expression reflected his gravity. "Go on."

"I've tried already to get you out on bail, under a writ of habeas corpus, but . . ."

"But?"

"It was denied. The judge held that the right to admit an alien to bail rests solely in the hands of the Attorney General of the United States."

"So I'm an alien, an alien without rights! Without . . . a country!"

He spoke softly. "That's what they say. So we must persuade the judge to change his mind, or persuade the Attorney General—one or the other. You see?"

"Oh, Dane," she choked. "They can keep me here as long as they like . . . !"

He turned his head and looked at the blank white tile wall. "Yes, they can," he said with reluctance. "But they won't. They'll find it inadvisable. If your bail is blocked by the court, Melvin Thompson has promised to have you freed. More than this he will not do. Like all the others he's afraid for his skin . . . the Frankenstein has begun to devour the masters. So the fight henceforth will be up to us —to you—and me."

The dark iris widened in her brilliant eyes. "Dane," she said softly, "I cannot bear to have you risk so much for me. Your future . . . !"

His eyes came back to her and regarded her with tenderness. "That?" he said, and the cheer in his voice was unassumed. "The decision has been made. And not by me, but by the most important case I've ever handled—and all the other cases it symbolizes."

"Oh, Dane, how I love you!" she said. She kissed him, then let her head nestle against his shoulder.

"You see," he went on, his voice flat and impersonal, "this case is like a Shakespearean play. It's a case within a case within a case. Not only was the defendant seized on the street as an alien and locked up incommunicado, not only was habeas corpus denied—but there's a fearful and fascinating tangle as to what crimes shall be charged against the defendant. Picture the situation for yourself: it has leaked out that a Congressional Committee has voted in secret, at long last, to cite the defendant for contempt. And it has been discovered that the Executive Branch will ask a grand jury for indictment on charges of fraud and perjury. And between the Branches and within the Bureaus and Agencies there is a bitter feud as to where the glory lies for having discovered and apprehended the criminal. I don't say *alleged* criminal, for they assume her guilt. So now the rivalry begins for the glory of her conviction. And tomorrow morning the papers will carry her story, with all the different Committees and Agencies and Bureaus claiming credit. The defendant will become a celebrity, and it will appear in the press that only in the nick of time has the Government been saved from subversion. . . ." He paused for breath.

She knew why he had taken this tone, and she loved him for it—but she no longer needed to have the tragedy of her situation diluted. "What are the penalties for all these—these crimes?"

He sighed. "We can add them up later, if you like. But the total is more money in fines than we both have, and more years in prison than we can possibly spare."

She got up from the bunk and began to walk restlessly around the room, rubbing her forehead and eyes with her right hand. At length she cried, "Do they have the power to do this?"

"They have the power," he said, "and they exercise it. But don't think we'll sit supine! We won't! Public opinion, that's the key. People will be with you. They've forgotten the people. Senator Cahill is aroused . . . Abe Stone is organizing a national labor committee . . . civil liberties groups will make an issue of the case . . . and there's court after court to fight it through."

"And how long will all this take?" Her voice quavered.

He shook his head. "Long enough to win! But you must prepare for that."

"Dane," she said, leaning weakly against the white tile wall, "—one thing I don't understand: why did they bring me *here*, to this Island?"

He hesitated. "Their intent was to deport you."

"Deport—?" She spoke as though the word were meaningless. "To—Franco Spain? Can they?" Now the words were wrung out in anguish.

He drew a deep breath, and made the old familiar church-and-steeple gesture. "They can. They can deport you instead of preferring all the other charges against you. Or they can wait, try to convict you, sentence you, and afterwards deport you. They think they have a winning hand, any way they play it. Sweet, isn't it? But we'll fight this along with the rest.

You'll be fighting for your country, as well as for yourself. This island is a kind of no-man's-land."

She walked slowly to the barred window and stood looking out at the low-hanging rainclouds, an expression of unreality on her face. From somewhere she heard the wail of a small child, and the cry grated on her heart. Years—her defense might take years, the years of Jeanie's growing up. She longed with a burning hunger to see and hold Jeanie in her arms once again, to ask her not to forget her mother. What to say? Remember me? Remember that I love you, Jeanie? I'm Mother—

"Your thoughts?" Dane said with surprising huskiness.

"My child—" she said simply, "—and what will become of her if they send me off to Spain."

His face was grim and hard. "You have not gone."

Through a break in the clouds and a curious refraction of rays from the sunset, the Statue of Liberty appeared momentarily in the harbor, bathed in a russet light.

As she peered at this apparition, a sudden excitement welled up into Faith's throat—and then the excitement died. She spoke in tones bearing more of sorrow than of irony, and her words might have been meant for Dane, or for persons invisible outside.

"Have you ever noticed," she said, "—that Liberty's back is toward this Island?"

From the door came the clink of keys, and the guard's voice mumbling, "Time's up, you people. Time's up—!"